Work of Art

By Sinclair Lewis

NATAL PUBLISHING LLC
ARS LONGA, VITA BREVIS

1

The flat roof of the American House, the most spacious and important hotel in Black Thread Centre, Connecticut, was lined with sheets of red-painted tin, each embossed with 'Phoenix, the Tin of Kings'. Though it was only 6.02, this July morning in 1897, the roof was scorching. The tin was like a flat-iron, and the tar along the brick coping, which had bubbled all yesterday afternoon, was stinging to the fingers.

Far below, in Putnam Street, a whole three stories down from the red tin roof, Tad Smith, the constable, said to Mr. Barstow, the furniture-dealer, 'Well, sir, going to be another scorcher, like yesterday.'

Mr. Barstow thought it over. 'Don't know but what you're right. Regular scorcher.'

'Yessir, a scorcher,' ruminated Tad, and went his ways--never again, perhaps, to appear in history.

But on the red tin roof above these burghers, a young poet was dancing; child of the skies, rejoicing in youth and morning and his new-found power of song. He was alone, except for Lancelot, the hotel dog, and unashamed he saluted the sun-god who was his brother. Whistling 'There'll be a Hot Time in the Old Town To-night', he strode up and down, his hands swinging as though he were leading a military band, his feet making little intricate patterns, his whole body lurching, his head bobbing from one side to the other in the exhilaration of youth and his own genius. Lancelot barked in appreciation--the first, this, of the applause the Master was some day to know.

The young poet was named, not very romantically, Ora Weagle, but he had read a good deal of Swinburne, Longfellow, Tennyson, and Kipling. He was fifteen years old, and already he perceived that he belonged to a world greater than Black Thread Centre. In fact, he despised Black Thread, and in particular all manner of things associated with the American House, as owned by his father, old Tom Weagle.

The recollection of the fabulous poem he had written last evening turned Ora's faun-like effervescence to awe, and (while Lancelot looked disappointed and settled down to scratching and slumber), he began to croon, then to murmur, then to shout--Ora, the young Keats, rejoicing in his masterpiece, aloft between Phoenix Roofing and the sky:

'Cold are thine eyes and the flanks of the hands of thee,
Cold as crushed snow on Connecticut hills,
But lo! I will break and dissever the bands of thee,
Till with blown flame thee the power of me fills!
See, I am proud, I am potent and terrible,
Dust of the highway I tread in my scorn!
Thou unto me art a field that is arable,
In sun-soaring splendour thy soul shall be born!'

'Gee, I don't know where I get it!' he whispered. The booming glory exalted him, and he paraded again, tossing his arms and chanting:

'Proud, I am proud,
I am
    Potent and terrible,
     Potent and terrible,

Listen! I'm proud
  And
    Potent and terrible,
     Terrible, terrible proud!'

And the sun-god showered him with rays which clothed him in double glory as they were reflected from the red tin roof.

The whistle of the 6.07 train from the Berkshires reduced Ora from cloud-treader, bright with morning fire, to kindling-splitter for the American House. Though he still murmured 'Potent and terrible', he was drawn to look over the coping at the actualities of provincial life. Up from the station of the New York, New Haven, and Hartford walked a typical, an unavoidable, a cosmic travelling salesman, carrying his two grips. Below Ora, abysmal depths below, his brother, Myron Weagle, was watering the sidewalk with a despicable battered green can. Ora watched this tedious daily comedy with amused eyes. His generosity toward Myron was as much a part of his poet's sovereignty as fire and potency and terribleness.

Poor Myron! Myron had, Ora meditated, no imagination, no passion, no ambition, no consciousness of beauty, no desire to be creative or to do anything but keep busy with the trivial daily jobs that seemed to satisfy him. Though Myron was theoretically two years older--seventeen--Ora felt himself a generation older and more worldly. Even physically you could see the difference: Ora, so slim, quick, dark, with fine hair black like black glass; Myron, then tall and lumbering, with big red hands and an absurd natural pompadour of rope-coloured hair. Often Ora had thought that he himself was like a cat--sinuous, swift, independent; while Myron was the perfect dog, and no greyhound or Scottie, but a farm dog--clumsy, contemptibly good-natured, loyal to any insignificant master.

'Well, the poor devil,' thought Ora, 'he'll probably be happier in his hick way than I will. I'm going to New York! I'm going to make me some perfect Work of Art! Golly, I bet I suffer like all get out, like in *Sentimental Tommy* and *David Copperfield,* while he sticks here and scratches himself in the sun--like you, Lancelot!'

Ora watched his dull big brother clumping down the street to welcome the travelling salesman and take his bags.

'Like a servant!' Ora sighed.

'Come on, Lancelot, we gotta go down and get a little breakfast,' he commanded. But before Ora left the coping, he looked distastefully over Black Thread Centre, and found nothing there. From the roof of the American house, towering as it did a whole story above any other building in town, he could view the microcosm of the village.

(There were people, reflected Ora, to whom Black Thread Centre and East Black Thread made up the Hub of the universe, from which you measured distances to Rome and Shanghai and Tierra del Fuego; people to whom a train or a circus or a religion was important as it did or did not touch Black Thread. Ora marvelled at their provinciality. For him--oh, New York, London, Paris, Berlin, Monte Carlo!)

He regarded with disfavour the red-brick village; Cal Bigus's store-- clocks, watches, jewellery, bicycles--beside the hotel. Barstow's furniture emporium, undertaking in all its branches, across the street. The frame station of the N.Y., N.H., and Hartford with its greasy platform. The village square and the grey cast-iron statue of a Civil War soldier. He could, it is true, see the light-flecked Housatonic river across the tracks, and on the other side of town, a hill thick with elm and maple and spruce.

'But even so, just sort of ordinary country. Nothing historical. No castles. Aah! Come on, you, Lancelot!' said Ora.

He thumbed his nose at the stolid Myron, carrying the travelling-man's bags, and skipped to the trap-door, singing, 'Potent and terrible'. He paused to muse, 'Nothing romantic. Not a doggone thing! What a name for a town! Black Thread Centre!'

The Reverend Thaddeus Prout, of Beulah, Connecticut, had Sunday after Sunday, through 1637, warned his complacent people that they must guard the hill-gap to the north and east against the Indians. 'I preach unto you eternal mercy and I also preach unto you eternal vigilance,' roared the old pastor in the high pulpit of the church. 'I preach to you the incessant practice of prayer . . . and the incessant practice of musketry, as I learned it in His Majesty's Own Right and Royal Worcestershires. I tell you that this hill-gap is a black threat . . . a black threat . . . a black threat to our peace and well-being!'

He said it so often that his parishioners began jestingly to call the settlement north and east of them (a settlement of one log tavern and store, and four cabins) 'the Black Threat'. They jested too warmly and too soon. When the Indians did tiptoe through the gap and circle Beulah, the settlers fought with axe and rifle, led by the Reverend Thaddeus, with a sabre-belt round his broadcloth and his white beard smeared with blood, but the goodly village was almost wiped out. Thereafter, the settlement beyond them was called 'Black Threat' with more anxious reverence.

It was a young government surveyor who put the name down as 'Black Thread' in 1810, considering, in his Harvard manner, the probabilities of spellings and the idiocy of myths.

Of all this Ora had never heard--nor anyone else, perhaps, in Black Thread Centre in 1897.

Followed by a subdued Lancelot, the subdued kin of the sun-god crept down the ladder from the roof into the hotel, into narrow hallways carpeted with straw matting worn in channels like foot-paths, into the enveloping smell of cheap pink soap and cabbage and sweaty clothes and old cotton sheets. The American House had thirty-four bedrooms; twenty-nine singles and five doubles. It was, the Weagles considered, a vigorously modern hotel; it had gas instead of kerosene lamps; and in the office was a telephone, in a long dark box like an up-ended coffin.

Each of the single rooms--Ora could see them as he passed open doors--contained one wooden bed, the varnish a little cracked, one straight chair, one strip of carpet beside the bed, lace curtains, very dingy, a gas light in so crafty a position on the wall that it neither illuminated the mirror nor enabled the guest to read in bed, one wash-stand with pitcher and bowl, painted with lilacs or a snow scene, a slop jar standing on a strip of linoleum not very successfully imitating marble, with white oilcloth tacked on the wall behind it, one cake of streaky soap, one thin towel, and a concentration of the prevailing smell.

But the double rooms were more elaborate. They added an extra towel, an extra straight chair, a table, and usually a calendar on the wall.

The mattresses on the beds were lumpy and sagging in the middle. The sheets were coarse, scratchy cotton--though, with Edna Weagle, Mrs. Tom Weagle, as housekeeper, they were immaculate and free of the bedbug. Edna spoke often and bitterly of bedbugs and pursued them daily. The blankets were of cotton and the comforters filled with cotton batting. They were very heavy and not warm. On winter nights, experienced travelling salesmen laid their overcoats on top them.

Though he was so used to the hotel, his home these years, that he rarely saw it, to-day Ora was so heightened by poetic triumph that for ten seconds he did stop to look into No. 20.

'What a hole!' he sighed. 'Sometime I'll have a room with a great big leather chair and a bed with silk sheets! Maybe black!'

He was too Black Thread Centre, too 1897, to admit that he was considering how voluptuous his slimness, the fine whiteness of his body, would seem against black silk sheets.

In the hall he met Flossy Gitts, the second maid. Now Ora was fifteen and Flossy was twenty, but she was generous and without prejudice: she had ringlets and what was then known as a bust; she dallied happily with any male from the age of ten to one hundred, though she preferred a ripe travelling-man of thirty-five, who wore a Masonic ring and was willing to hire a livery stable rig to give a girl a good time.

'Say, lissen, Ora, Myron is sore as a boil you ain't cleaned the basement and the sample-rooms!' said Flossy.

'The hell with him!' said Ora.

'Yeh, but what he'll do to you!'

'Aw, give us a kiss!'

'You behave yourself now! Oh! Why, Ora Weagle, you oughta be ashamed yourself, acting like that!'

'I am potent and terrible!'

'Gee, I bet you swallowed the dictionary--all them words! Lissen, Ora, I'll help you clean the basement, soon's I do No. 23 and 15.'

'All right, sweetie!'

Ora swaggered down to the 'office'. He did swagger. For all his conquests among the village girls of his own age, this was his first triumph as a gigolo, a young gallant cajoling an older woman.

The walls of the office were lined with cane rockers alternating with brass spittoons. The desk was of grained pine. Back of it hung the room-keys, attached to chunks of wood so that they might not be carried off, and on it were a pen stuck in a potato, and a register swung on a brass swivel.

The register was always open, of course, for hotel-men of that period knew nothing else so certainly as that, if the register was ever closed, you would get no more business that day.

There was no one in the office.

Ora was relieved not to see Myron. Perhaps, after carrying the travelling-man's grips to his room, he had hustled out for early-morning shopping--old Tom was supposed to do all the buying, but he often slept late, almost till seven, and Myron was simpleton enough to be willing to run out for an extra pound of bacon in case of a breakfast rush. Ora felt free again. He slipped through the dining-room and billiard-room to the bar. If Jock McCreedy, the regular bartender, was on, he would be able to coax a tiny glass of beer before breakfast. But when Ora opened the door into that haven, with its cool smell of beer, magnificent mahogany bar, delicate pyramids of glassware, and that greatest painting Ora had ever seen--a nude lady lying among cushions scarlet and saffron and emerald-- he hesitated, for it was Myron who stood behind the bar, with an ebony slicer removing the excess foam from a glass of beer for the first morning customer.

'Hey, you, come here!' thundered Myron.

'What's eating you?' whimpered the sun-god's heir.

He edged in, irritably facing Myron's sergeant-major eye. Seen close, Myron's tow-coloured exuberance of hair was stiff, as though his scalp had some extra vitality. His strong skin was of the Norse snow-fed pallor that no sun ever tanned, no adolescence ever blotched. Myron had, Ora sometimes admitted, a certain broad-shouldered power and health in him- -if he could only have Ora's imagination, instead of being a mere human broom standing up-ended!

'Ora! You haven't swept the balconies for two days! You didn't have any kindling, when I started the range this morning, and the wood-box about half full! And the basement--here's a travelling-man just come in this morning; wants a sample-room right away, and both of 'em dirty!'

Feeling safe, across the bar, Ora jeered, 'What're you going to do about it?'

Through the air flew a tiger.

Myron had stepped on a beer keg and vaulted the bar. He was shaking Ora like a kitten. 'I'll whale the everlasting daylights out of you, that's what I'll do! I'm sick and tired of your loafing! The only person around this hotel that never does any work! Do you clean the sample-rooms and so on and so forth right now, or do I lick you?'

'All right! All right! Gosh! Gee whiz! You don't have to act like a hyena!'

'With you, I do! Now git! I'll let you have breakfast first, and then . . .'

Ora, already at the door, popped his small head in to retort, 'You'll let me have breakfast! It ain't yours to let! I guess it belongs to Pa and Ma!'

But he retreated with speed. He knew these 'lickings' by Myron: rare but extraordinarily painful and lasting.

Alice Aggerty, the bulky colleague of Flossy Gitts, was serving breakfast. Standing between two travelling-men she was chanting: 'Omeal, choicaveggs, baconam, steakchops, sausage, wheacakes.' Ora himself breakfasted poetically on oatmeal, pork chop with an egg, wheat cakes, bacon, coffee, and just a nibble or two of johnny-cake, and toast smeared with plum jam. The coffee was weak, with grounds floating on it. The butter was artificially coloured and, as it had come out of a tub preserved with salt, there were salt crystals apparent on the brilliantly yellow pat. With the chop, which had been fried in lard, there were last night's potatoes, warmed up. If Ora's delicacy and vision were offended by this coarse plenty, there were no signs of it as he wolfed it down.

He ate at the family table, behind the two long ones for the public. The dining-room had green wall-paper with yellow roses, bare floor and, for splendour, an enormous black walnut buffet adorned with silver cruet stands and fruit-and-nut bowls of imitation cut-glass--thriftily empty save at Sunday noon. Beside the double door, on a small table with a decorous white linen cover, was a large bowl of toothpicks.

The cloths of the long tables were clean, but that of the Weagle family table was somewhat geographic, with its islands of egg yolk, catsup, gravy, and butter.

While Ora was breakfasting, his father joined him.

Tom Weagle had a corded brown neck which his watery beard did not quite conceal. He wore steel-rimmed spectacles, crookedly, and behind them his expression was wistful and rather vague. His nose was red. Though he seemed frail, he had the leathery hands of a farmer.

'Morning,' said old Tom.

'Morning,' said Ora.

'Did you sweep the basement, like you was told?'

'Sure.'

'Well . . .'

That seemed to cover the subject. Tom, after ordering oatmeal, steak, fried eggs, and a double order of wheats--all of which would vanish without evident effect into his meagre corporation--was silent. He was long-winded enough with travelling-men, in the narration of anecdotes about old days on the farm, the wickedness of guests who did not pay, servants who did not work, and the wonders of his one trip to New York, but with his family he saw no gain in wasting wit.

They chewed opposite each other, Tom looking vague, Ora looking sleepy. But Ora was meditating like a quiescent volcano.

That big brute, Myron. . . . Didn't know any way of trying to deal with a slick brain like his brother's except by threatening to lick him! . . . And such stinking melodrama--vaulting the bar, like that big, fat, ridic'lous hero in the melodrama that played here under canvas last week, 'Barry O'Leary's Own Company in *Bonnets o' Dundee'*. Myron wouldn't even know the meaning of the word melodrama! Huh! Yuh! Sure! No brains, no education! Could Myron make a line like 'Till with blown flame thee the power of me fills'?

He could *not!*

Ora felt better, much better.

He was damped a little by the spectacle of a fat, moist forefinger beckoning from the door to the kitchen (the white paint of the door was worn in a blotch halfway up by the hips of urgent waitresses pushing out with trays of dirty dishes). It was the finger of a lady who had the honour of being not only cook of the American House but also mother of Ora Weagle--Edna Weagle, who combined the seemly plumpness of a cook with the worried intensity of the wife of a drunkard. Ora slowly forsook blown flame and potency and terror; he scooped up the last sweetness of syrup and crumbs of wheat cake with a spoon, while Alice Aggerty, the waitress, scowled at him. To think of that darn' boy using up a whole spoon, and it would have to be washed now, for just one mouthful!

Ora sauntered gracefully into the heat and the smell of frying grease in the kitchen.

'What do you want, Ma?' he complained.

'Your Pa has got to drive over to Beulah this morning, about some chickens, and we're short of lard, and I want you should go to Aldgate's sometime this morning and get a pail of it.'

'Gosh, I gotta do everything around this hotel--clean the basement and sweep the balconies and fill the wood-box and everything!'

'Yes, it's too bad about you!' Edna Weagle scoffed, and wiped her hands on the not very clean apron round the plumpness of her gingham-covered middle. 'I've only been working since five! You get that lard, or I'll have Myron . . .'

'Myron! Myron! Myron! Ain't I ever going to hear anything all my life but Myron! Me highest stand in the whole Soph'more Class, and him way down near the foot in the Senior!'

'Yes, baby, I know. Yes. I guess that's right. Maybe you ain't suited to this kind of work, like Myron is. I do believe and hope that some day you'll be a dentist or a lawyer or even a preacher! There.' She stroked his hair-- which Ora hated, because she smelled of soft yellow soap and doughnut fat. 'You just go ahead reading and studying and all. But you won't forget my lard, will you!'

'No, sure not!'

Recognized for the pundit he was, Ora swaggered upstairs, to find the fair, fond Flossy Gitts and to persuade her to help him sweep the inevitable basement. She grumbled a little at having to leave a bed half made, but she came, and the sample-rooms and the furnace-room were cleaned and made beautiful. It was a satisfactory division of labour: Ora talked and Flossy worked. She swept, dusted, and nailed down a loose board on one of the long tables which, set across trestles in the sample-room, would presently bloom in un-Black-Thread-like splendours of the Orient; with silk Scotch plaid blouses, Eleganto brand leather belts in two colours, dainty Dot veils, gauntlet gloves; in fact, with all the choicest wares of M. & I. Vollschutz's Ladies Wear Company of New York, Cincinnati, and Kansas City, for the inspection of the ardent merchants of Black Thread Centre--this modern Oriental market, where the vendors did not squat about fires of camels' dung, but in check suits, smoking cigars, standing upright with the freedom and efficiency of 1897 in America, chose beauty with an eye to profit.

'You've done it pretty good, Flossy. Come 'ere and kiss me!' said Ora. 'Bye! See you later!'

He left her--somewhat perplexed, as later many ladies were to be, as to whether she had done too much or too little--and galloping up the stairs he swung through the alley behind the American House to Putnam Street, slinkingly followed by Lancelot. He had a moment's shudder at the greasy garbage in the alley, the debris of hotels and the whole frowziness of communal living, but he forgot it in the clean hot sun of the street, and Lancelot, again convinced that he was the dog of a sun-god and not the dog of an hotel, chased an imaginary cat and after it barked 'Potent and terrible'.

It must be stated that Lancelot was so named only by Ora. To the rest of the hotel personnel he was 'Spot' or merely, 'Get out of that'.

Not once, all day, did Ora remember the lard for his mother.

After all! There was a story, once much read, about Mary and Martha. And it was Ora's vacation time, it was summer, and beyond Black Thread Centre, up on Elm Hill, there were things more worth the inquiry of a young poet than lard and the state of a sample-room for the travelling representative of M. & I. Vollschutz.

2

Up to the little groves and hollows, to the peace and freedom of Elm Hill, pounded a young poet and his dog. But they stopped a moment at the garden of the man who had taught Ora that much existed in this world besides the lilies and Sunday-morning languors, the roses and strictly respectable raptures of Connecticut. This was the Reverend Waldo Ivy, the Episcopal pastor. Despite his name, Mr. Ivy was round, red, and breathless. He loved liturgy, tradition, cleanliness, and poetry. Black Thread thought him 'queer'. In ten years in this church he had found precisely one soul who understood his gospel, that beauty is truth, truth beauty, and that was Ora Weagle.

He loved to be called, and never save by one was called, 'Padre'. Again that one was Ora. Ora had probably got it from Kipling.

He had taught Ora everything he knew--provided Ora did know anything.

In High School, in which he was to be a Junior, this coming Fall, Ora had learned that the ways and finalities of literature are thus: In the far past--ever so long ago, even before the American Revolution--there were good writers. Quite good. There was a gentleman named Caesar, who went to England and Americanized the natives. There was Cicero, who objected to a man named Cataline, and so killed all gangsterdom for ever. There was Virgil, who was somehow very beautiful. And--though these were actually read only in swell schools like Andover--there were Greeks, like Homer and Sophocles and Aeschylus, who were pretty important. Then the history of literature skipped a long while--two hundred or maybe two thousand years--and you came to Jane Austen, Dickens, Thackeray, Scott, Tennyson, Longfellow, Whittier, Walt Whitman, and Poe. These authors were all dead. In fact the Age of Literature was dead, like the Age of Chivalry, though there were some pretty good hack writers living now-- William Dean Howells and Mark Twain and a Frenchman named Anatole France. But the Reverend Waldo Ivy had told Ora that literature was only beginning; that the world's struggle for beauty and justice had never been so glorious as now. The boy's eyes lightened, his breathing grew rapid, as Mr. Ivy testified to his gospel. And in that little Episcopal study, smelling of the leather bindings of old Greek books and the buckram of new novels, Mr. Ivy at last trusted one disciple, and read to him:

Till the slow sea rise and the sheer cliff crumble,
  Till terrace and meadow the deep gulfs drink,
Till the strength of the waves of the high tides humble
  The fields that lessen, the rocks that shrink,
Here now in his triumphs where all things falter,
  Stretched out on the spoils that his own hand spread,
As a god self-slain on his own strange altar,
                    Death lies dead.

It was such a little study, Mr. Ivy's, just behind the church; a plaster room, looking on a garden seven feet square, with a cement walk which he called his ambulatory. There were stiff crocuses and timid pansies in the garden. On the walls of the study were pictures of S. Paulo Fouri le Muri, of Thoreau and Emerson. The priest, after he had read Swinburne, looked at Ora diffidently and said:

'There is a greater poetry than all of this. It's from the Bible. I wonder if you know it. You see, my dear boy, the Fathers of my Church knew, so long ago, all that afflicts us now. Would you like to hear it?'

'Sure!' said Ora.

'This is perhaps the greatest poetry that has ever been written. Listen, my son:

"Or ever the silver cord be loosed, or the golden bowl be broken, or the pitcher be broken at the fountain, or the wheel broken at the cistern.

"Then shall the dust return to the earth as it was: and the spirit shall return unto God who gave it.

"Vanity of vanities, saith the preacher; all is vanity."'

Mr. Ivy looked up, over the eyeglasses that creased his red face.

The boy was weeping.

'I didn't know,' he sobbed, 'that the Bible was poetry! I thought it was nothing but religion!'

But that had been two years ago.

This July morning, when Ora condescendingly nodded to Mr. Ivy, over the fence, he was not awed. For he himself was a poet now, with no need for reverence for the old stiffs that were his rivals.

'Ora,' said Mr. Ivy, 'do you know the Wordsworth sonnet that begins, "The world is too much with us--late and soon"?'

'Sure. It's swell. Well, gotta be hustling on,' said Ora.

He did not know the sonnet, but then--it was morning, and vacation, and he lurched on, followed by a lurching Lancelot.

As it was called 'Elm Hill', naturally it was covered mostly with spruce and pine. There was a secret hollow which, Ora felt, no one save himself had ever discovered. He lay in its hot, resinous sweetness, while Lancelot panted and coughed and scratched beside him. He dreamed--the formless, visual dreams of a young poet: Castles. Girls milk-white. In Xanadu did Kubla Khan a stately pleasure-dome decree. Sleek greyhounds with silver bells. God through unending aeons drowsing on his throne of sharp-cut granite. Swords slender as pain. California and sunlight intolerable upon yellow poppies. Wings of the albatross. Wild white horses galloping through the desert, beneath an orange mesa. An archbishop chanting mass, in vestments stiff with gold. A starving explorer staggering into a Tibetan village. An English cottage among roses. An air-ship--only there could never be any air-ships, of course!--flashing through the empyrean at sixty miles an hour. . . . Empyrean! What a lovely word! Myron wouldn't know a word like 'empyrean'!

I saw Osirian Egypt kneel adown before the vine-wreath crown. Yea, with red sin the faces of them shine; but in all these there was no sin like mine. In the highlands, in the country places, where the old plain men have rosy faces, and the young fair maidens quiet eyes. The Courts where Tamshyd gloried and drank deep. A woman wailing for her demon lover. Set forth in something, something mail, to search in all lands for the Holy Grail. Delectable. Faerie. Clad in white samite, mystic, wonderful. Glamour. Casting down their golden crowns around the glassy sea. The owl for all his feathers was acold. Lances, lances dipped in light.

'Oh, dear God, if I could only *do* it!' whimpered Ora.

Like most healthy young animals, Ora was perpetually hungry. Yet rather than go back to the horrors of the American House, to his mother nagging, his father nagging, Myron nagging, and Alice Aggerty or Flossy Gitts intoning, 'Oysstew, creamtomato, steak, chop, Irish stew, roaspork, vegables,' he lunched on a corn pone which he had thoughtfully stolen from the kitchen while talking to his mother.

'What nahm de ploom will I use?' he inquired of Lancelot. 'Golly! A writer can't be called Ora Weagle!'

Thunder cracked, lightning vaulted, and inexplicably out of the unknown came his nahm de ploom, Marcel Lenoir!

'Jiminy, what a peach!' murmured Ora. 'I just don't know how I do it! *Marcel Lenoir!* What a beaut! Hey, you, Lancelot! Hear that! Marcel Lenoir!'

Thus, in a fragrant piney hollow, was born a poet-hero: Marcel Lenoir.

Pete Breyette, who was the reportorial staff of the *Black Thread Centre Star and Tidings* had just finished an important story,

Mrs. Trumbull Lambkin last Thursday entertained the Epworth League. Coffee, doughnuts, and ice-cream were served, the Reverend Swan gave a brief prayer, and a good time was reported by all.

Pete leaned back, pocketing his pencil, and sighed with contentment. He looked down at the yellow copy-paper. There it was, complete literature, the crude fact immortalized. But he sprang up, all pride in his style oozing away, for through the wide window of the one-story *Star and Tidings* building Ora Weagle was staring. Now Pete was a man of eighteen, and Ora but fifteen, yet Pete knew that, seasoned journalist though he was, competent to cover the G.A.R. parade or even the County Fair, Ora had a genius beyond him. He beckoned, and Ora came in, murmuring, 'Marcel Lenoir!'

'Huh?'

'Marcel Lenoir. My pen-name. Like it?'

'Gee--yes--that's swell. Something *like* a name. Lissen, Ora, what d'you plan to do?'

'Whaddha I plan to do? Whaddha you mean?'

'About your literary career.'

'Oh! Well, I'll tell you.' Ora sat down, tilted his chair, and put his heels on the desk like Pete at his best. He accepted a Sweet Caporal cigarette and smoked it in the manliest fashion, coughing only a little. 'I'll tell you. It's like this. First, I'm going to be a reporter. Of course you got to be a reporter before you can become an author--any reporter will tell you that. I guess I'll be on the *New York Sun,* but I won't be ready to accept a position there for two-three years; think I ought to have a little more schooling first. Then I'll wander--anywhere outside this doggone ole town! I think maybe I'll accompany an exploring party to Africa or like that. Then I'll get a job as secretary to some big author--say like Mark Twain. I guess he'd be pretty glad to have a secretary that was a literary fellow himself! And educated. Then I'll be ready to write. First I'll do poetry. But what I want to head for is big novels. I expect I'll be the Dickens of America. Golly! With a big house and a swell pair of trotters and six-seven suits of clothes! That's how I plan it. Course I may change my mind. I might go out and own a big ranch in the West for a while, instead of Africa. But time enough t' decide that later.'

'You certainly got ambition, Ora. I shouldn't wonder if you might do all that.'

'Why, certainly I will! Whaddha you think!'

'Well, why don't you get out of this hick town now?'

'Oh, it's my hayseed brother. He makes me stick here in school, when I already know a whale of a lot more than the teachers, only they can look at the book while you're reciting and catch you on dates. God, Pete, you don't know what I suffer from Myron, the big bully! He hasn't got brains enough to hate working in an hotel! Hotel-keeping! What a business! Havin' to be nice to drunk guests! Smell of cooking! Making beds all morning! What a job! And he doesn't even beef about it. Myron's got no imagination, no pride, no sense of beauty, you might say. He just naturally couldn't never understand how a real artist feels, never!'

3

Myron Weagle was seven years old when his father sold their rocky and isolated farm north of Beulah and moved to Black Thread Centre, with a notion of having ease and fortune in this metropolis of 1600 people. The father, Tom Weagle, was complacently certain that he could succeed as livery-stable keeper, grocer, undertaker, electric and herbal healer, or in any other of a dozen arts, but he chose keepin' hotel because his good wife, Edna, was a renowned cook. Her doughnuts and lemon meringue pie were without rivals in Beulah County, and at the Laurel Grove Congregational church-suppers, her scalloped potatoes and devil's-food cake roused even more exclamations than Mrs. Lyman Barstow's potato salad and sweet-pickle relish. She was also, Tom considered, a great hand at keeping bedrooms clean, though she was rather sluttish about her own neck and nails and hair, and her aprons were always smeared.

They did not, at first, enter the glories of keeping the American House, with its thirty-four bedrooms. They began in an eight-bedroom boarding-house, in the old Tatam Mansion, and within a month, Mother Weagle's troubles had started. Tom had always had a nose for apple-jack and now, with nothing much to do and twenty-four choreless hours a day to do it in, he had the leisure, along with money from the farm, to soak diligently. He had always resented the seclusion of the farm he had inherited from his father and had placidly let run down; he had resented having so few neighbours to whom he could boast of his ability to make a million dollars. Now, Tom sat in the back of Earle Peter's grocery, guzzling apple-jack, or with unshaven cronies and a jug of white mule, he rowed down to the Island, to fish, and crawled home in the evening with his jaw hanging and trembling.

Mother Weagle whisked him out of sight of the boarders and, after trying to do her duty in the way of scolding him--but she never could really scold anyone--she let him sleep it off. When they first took the boarding-house, Tom found plenty of little busynesses--nailing up shelves, laying a cement walk, which immediately cracked. But as he gradually found himself free for urbanity and apple-jack, he did nothing whatever, save carve at table when, if ever, he was sober.

And Myron became, before he was ten, the Man of the House.

Mother Weagle liked Myron and Ora equally; Tom preferred Ora who, even at the age of five, when they first came to Black Thread, regarded his father as an exciting character. When he was seven, Ora would sit in the flat unpainted punt which Tom had moored in the shadow of willows that leaned over to lap the water, and gape and bounce while Tom held his long bamboo fishing-rod over the side, took occasional pulls at the jug (leaning it on his shoulder and deftly tilting it up), and told endless stories--some of them almost true: How he had killed the last bear found in the state of Connecticut. How, as a young man, he had gone clear out to Michigan and seen Indians who, it seemed, always said, 'Ugh, me heap big Injun'. How, as a boy of thirteen at the end of the Civil War, he had seen the last Connecticut troops march out, and they were all six feet tall and very valiant, and most of the officers ran about six-foot-six and carried swords four feet long. And he would sing:

'Oh, bury me not on the lone pe-rar-ie,
Where the wyuld coooooooyotes will howl over me
Where the rattlesnakes hiss, and the wyund blows free,
Oh, bury me not on the lone pe-rar-ie!'

Ora leaned forward, transported from boarding-house kitchens and greasy school desks to a realm of soldiers and cow-punchers and lone mountains. And as much as his father he resented it when they returned to the monkey-like scolding of Mother Weagle and the scowls of Myron. They both suspected, as they sneaked in to their late supper of hash and coffee, that while they had been gone, gallantly trying to help the struggling household by catching fish, Myron had dined on the fat of the land--the thickest steaks, the hottest clam chowder, and three helpings of butter.

Before he was eleven, Myron had been trained in housework--'just like a doggone girl', Ora snivelled, when he had been particularly slapped. Myron wiped dishes, he sometimes washed them; the big lummox could shine a water-glass better than his mother, and his large hands were firm in handling a fruit-dish. He swept, he made beds, he fried or boiled the eggs, he could cook a chop. He learned from his mother's anxious whisperings to cajole an irritated guest by listening rapturously to any complaint and bubbling, 'I'll get Ma to fix it up right away quick'. He even learned, watching his mother, a little about cuts of meat, and how to tell a ripe melon or a sound pear.

But he learned more from a certain boarder than from his mother.

The star boarder was Miss Absolom, the elegant New York lady who taught in the high school. In the dining-room, Myron watched Miss Absolom, while he helped Minnie, the hired girl, wait at table. Feeling that, as a farm boy, he ought to learn table-manners, he spied on all the ten boarders. He noted that Horace Tiger, of the New York Dry Goods Store, had a strikingly refined way of drinking coffee: when he raised his cup his little finger stuck out as though it detached itself from the coarseness of mere guzzling. Miss Abbott, the milliner, picked her teeth behind an ample napkin held up before her face. It was evident to a waiter, standing behind her, that she did a great deal of struggling and gouging, but he was edified by her modesty. And contrariwise he was certain that, though they had always done it on the farm, it was not nice in old Mr. and Mrs. Glenn to blow loudly on their soup and, drinking coffee, to leave the spoon in the cup and anchor it with a clutching thumb.

But Miss Absolom never seemed to have any manners, good or bad. He never could remember just what she had done. On the infrequent occasions when she did use a toothpick, she just used it, without orgies of delicacy. She did not make much of laying her knife and fork across her plate when she was finished; the others were very clattering and exacting about it, but somehow her knife and fork were there.

'Gosh, she's so *easy* about things!' meditated Myron, as he polished the heavy plated cruet-stand with its bottles of catsup, vinegar, pepper sauce, and Worcestershire. 'I wonder if that's how you ought to do--so's people don't notice how swell your manners are?' It was a profound and disturbing theory. Not get any credit for being refined? What was the use, then? Well, he'd have to do it. He'd rather be like Miss Absolom, thin, dark, resolute, straight-backed, than like the plump and puffing Horace Tiger.

He was taking a cup of tea to Miss Absolom on an evening when she had what was then known as a 'headache' and had not come down to supper.

'Come in; talk to me,' she demanded.

According to the tradition of exotic New York ladies marooned in small towns in 1891, the room should have been voluptuous with Turkish hangings, a samovar, and Chinese lanterns--such lanterns as glorified a strawberry festival on a Black Thread lawn. Actually, there were none of these Oriental splendours. But the pine table was covered a foot deep with books; beside it was a chintz-covered chair; and covering the bed was a Chinese rug. (That was funny, Myron always thought--a rug on a bed! But it did look kind of nice; made the white iron bedstead seem kind of less ornery.) Otherwise the room was of the same clean, bare, plaster-and-matting simplicity as the rest of the house.

Miss Absolom was in the deep chair. 'Sit down!' She waved to the bed, and he teetered there, embarrassed.

For a boy in the sixth grade to talk privily with a teacher way up in the high school was for a private to be chummy with a major-general. But at the age of eleven he was, after four years of being right-hand man in a boarding-house, uncannily acquainted with human beings and their loves, their secret whisky bottles, their dirty tricks in the matter of weekly bills, generosities to one another regarding hot-water bottles and store candy. He was, in fact, as sharply aware of human ways as any normal boy of eleven would be if he were not squelched by the jealous demand of parents and teachers that they be allowed to do all the talking and deciding. Yet for all this premature knowledge, he was embarrassed when he met Miss Absolom not as a boarder, to be bedded, boarded and billed, but as a social acquaintance.

'Sit down, Myron. Like keeping a boarding-house?'

'Oh, I guess I like it all right. I guess so. Gee, I bet sometimes *you* don't like it much in a little place like this, after New York!'

'Not so bad. Escape from too much Hebraic Bach and Hebraic Kaffeeklatsch and Hebraic cousinry.'

'Hunh?'

'I mean . . . don't mind it. I'm just trying to be funny. And gallant, or something nasty like that. It doesn't mean anything. Myron! What are you going to do with yourself? You work hard, I've noticed. What's your ambition?'

'I dunno. I guess maybe a doctor.'

'Why?'

'I dunno. I guess it would be kind of interesting, taking care of people . . . I mean . . . learnin' all about them.'

'You want to get away from here?'

'Oh, I guess so. I never thought about it much.'

'Well, my child, whether you go or stay, you must learn to make a little better effect. I mean, be more careful about how you dress. I don't mean like Horace Tiger, with his silly white vests and his hair that smells like a barber-shop. . . . You'll be a big, impressive man, some day. You may as well take advantage of it by dressing well. Let me see your nails.'

He exhibited them, shyly. They were, within reason, clean, but they had been hacked short with his mother's larger shears.

'Don't you think mine look a little neater?' demanded Miss Absolom. Her almond-shaped nails were probably nothing extraordinary but to Myron they seemed exquisite, sleek as polished agate. 'You can get a nailfile for ten cents at the drug-store. File 'em, my child, file 'em. Now let me do your tie. You've just jerked it together.'

She patiently unknotted and re-did his slightly frayed blue bow, patting the ends. He leaned over, faint with her warm feminine scent. 'Now look in the mirror.' He marvelled at the cockiness of his tie. It had, now, a waist and symmetrical ends.

'I'll sure work on it!' he said fervently. 'Ora always can tie his good, and him only nine! But he won't work.'

'And listen, young man. I've been observing you. You bully Ora, to make him work. I don't blame you. He's a lazy little hound. But a solemn young man like you, earnest about all good works, must watch himself in a thing even more fundamentally spiritual than nail-filing. You must wrestle with the Lord and try, a little, to keep from being a prig. Tall, clean, earnest young gentlemen have a tendency that way . . . as do intellectual Jew girls!'

'Gee!'

'A prig is a person who . . . well, you see . . . of course when it comes to defining. . . . Well, a prig is a person who thinks he's marvellous, and lets everybody see it. He's . . . oh, he's like a man in a wagon who keeps jeering at all the people on foot, "Look at me! I'm riding!" Even when you're riding, and Ora is snaking along in the moral dust, don't feel too proud. The horse may run away!'

'I . . . guess . . . maybe . . . I . . . see . . . how . . . you . . . mean!'

It seemed to Miss Absolom obvious that he did not. But he did.

It is one of life's ironies that the suggestion of a passer-by--a man met on a train, the unknown author of an editorial, an actor repeating a pure and pompous sentiment in a melodrama--may be weightier than years of boring advice by parents. Myron, when he became a man and would normally have been too absorbed in affairs to think about clothes, years after he had forgotten Miss Absolom's name, remembered her rebuke of his carelessness and uneasily, unwillingly, was forced to dress the part of a successful urbanite, which, in despite of Carlyle, had an excellent effect on his self-respect and power to command men. He came to believe that Miss Absolom and he had talked many times, many hours. They had not. She was a goddess in his private mythology, with the indestructible sway of a goddess, immortal because she had never existed.

Whether she also cured him of potential priggishness cannot be said. Probably, like other 'successes', Myron was priggish. Nor is it certain that the enjoyment of priggishness is not one of the most innocent and wholesome of pleasures, as seen in the careers of most bishops, editors, sergeants major, instructors in athletics, and Socialist authors.

The next day Myron took twenty-five cents out of the two dollars and sixty-five that were his savings and bought a red tie, which he wore to Sunday School. It was violently red, and Myron considered it very choice. Also, he had filed his nails to the quick. They hurt considerably. But Miss Absolom did not even notice him. He whimpered, but he was the more determined to impress her; to impress all the shrewd, cynical Miss Absoloms in the world, and make them recognize him as one of them.

On Saturday evenings, Mother Weagle's guests in the boarding-house always had a party, with a climax of welsh rabbit or scrambled eggs or ice-cream, in the small, square parlour with its worn red carpet and lavishly nickled Garland stove. There was a forlorn palm in one corner, and among the seats were the last of the horsehair sofas, a patent rocker upholstered in Brussels carpet, and an interesting chair made by cutting a segment out of a barrel and gilding the remains.

Occasionally Miss Absolom played things she called 'Mozart' and 'Mendelssohn', names which Myron had never heard, but Horace Tiger was the chief entertainer. He could play on a saw, and did. He sang 'Oh my name is Samuel Hall, damn your eyes', only he was refined enough to render it 'darn your eyes', and 'Daisy, Daisy give me your answer true; you'll look sweet upon the seat of a bicycle built for two', and, invariably:

'There is a boarding house
Not far away,
Where they have ham and eggs
    Three times a day.

'Oh how the boarders yell
When they hear that dinner-bell,
See how they run like--thunder,
    Three times a day.'

All the boarders laughed like anything when Horace hesitated and winked at them, and put in 'thunder' instead of the naughty word. So did Myron--after looking at Miss Absolom, to see if she smiled, which she always did. But Mother Weagle invariably fretted (fifty-two Saturday evenings a year), 'Now I don't think that's real nice! I'm sure you don't get ham and eggs three times a day here!'

And Horace did imitations: a negro preacher, very realistic, beginning a sermon with 'Ah absquatulates to guess,' which made every one feel very happy and superior to the lower races; and a Maine farmer whose remarks pleasantly started off, 'Well, by heckalorum, Cy!'

Miss Absolom always encouraged Horace, extensively; she sat with her chin in her thin dark hand, twinkling her eyes at him and murmuring, 'Bravissimo'. It did not occur to Myron till months after his session with her in the matter of nails that she was too encouraging to Horace. He was embarrassed after that by Horace's smirking parade, and with the inarticulate brooding of a boy of twelve he fretted that he must protect himself; not give people a chance to ridicule him.

He thought thus none the less when the child prodigy, Ora, was persuaded to speak that elevating piece, 'The Wreck of the Hesperus'. Myron gloated that his brother was a natural-born wonder, recited just like a regular actor, and him only ten! But he did kinda wish, he sighed, that Ora wouldn't wave his arms and pat his stomach in moments of eloquence, as though he had an ache.

Myron learned much from the Saturday evening parties. He learned that people have to be 'amused'; that they would do almost anything, listen to almost anything, rather than sit alone and read, and as for sitting alone and meditating, that could be tolerated only by the dullest-eyed clods or the calmest-eyed sages. He did not, as yet, formulate this for himself, any more than the fisher-boy formulates the tricks of steering through surf, but he began to perceive that if he ever had to care for a number of people, he must keep the childish brutes 'amused'. Bread and circuses, sleigh-rides and church-suppers, radios and talkies, opera and the horse-show--in any era, in any caste, anything to keep from beginning to doubt your complacent superiority by being alone.

With a hoarse secrecy rare to her, for generally she bawled and chuckled her thoughts all over the kitchen, while she stirred biscuit dough or whisked the whites of eggs, Mother Weagle summoned Myron to the room she shared with her husband. Tom was away for the afternoon, theoretically hunting quail. She had, after a quarrel in which she had threatened to leave him, taken control of all their money, and she let Tom have only a dollar a week, but on that he managed mysteriously to get drunk with frequency and ardour.

Myron suspected that his father stole food from the kitchen and sold it.

Myron was a month short of thirteen, now, five feet seven and skinny, but with a sign of big bones to make broad shoulders. He did not smile much. His hands were rough from incessant housework. To his mother, at least, he was always affectionate.

They sat on the edge of her bed; she fluttered with large-bosomed sighing, while he watched her anxiously. Her room was dusty, the bed was unmade, with a swirl of bedclothes from Tom's nightly threshing when he came out of the stupor of alcohol. On the floor was the last week's laundry, half open, a clean sheet dragging in the dirt. It was the only room in the house besides his own and Ora's that was unkempt: Mother Weagle had no time for herself or her own resting-place.

'Myron, you're awful young to talk to you about it, but I ain't got anybody else. You know how your Pa is. Well, I been thinking all this past year, and I got kind of a notion he wouldn't act up this way if he had something more to do. Ain't hardly anything for him to do round here.'

'I could let him help me make beds and saw the wood, if he wanted to,' said Myron, not trying to be funny.

'Well, I guess he wouldn't care for that. He'd like to be at the desk, showing off. The fellow that's running the American House is going West. It's for rent, furniture and all. I been kind of saving, and I could manage the rent for two years. Then your Pa could be in the front office, and maybe he'd straighten up. What do you think?'

'That would be something elegant!'

Within Myron's eyes was a vision of the splendour of the American House: the long spaces of the lobby, where forty people could sit, in contrast to the chubby little parlour of their boarding-house; the gilded radiators; the brilliant tall brass cuspidors; the enormous dining-room, with real printed menus, at least for Sunday dinner; the unending rows of bedrooms, with no less than four bath-rooms; and the building itself, three towering stories of brick, and an entrance that had always fascinated him--not just a door flush with a wall, but right on the corner, cut diagonally across. And the people! He was used to the boarding-house residents; most of them elderly local couples who had given up the woes of housekeeping. They were as familiar and uninspiring to Myron as a wart. But entering the American House, staring out through its splendid plate-glass window on Main Street, were valorous birds of passage: travelling-men in sporty pink vests, Ascot ties, and collars almost cutting their lower jaws; the star of the Original Drury Lane Touring Company, with his astrachan-lined overcoat and hair like a horse's tail.

'Gee, Ma, it would be slick! Peachy! But you'd have to work so hard.'

'Oh, I'd have more help. You'd help me, wouldn't you, wouldn't you? Wouldn't you help me?'

They clung together. He was never, all his life, to be so close to any other human being as to Mother Weagle.

'We'll make a dandy hotel!' he crowed.

'Yes, maybe we will,' she meditated, roused a little out of the melancholy which drugs all of us when we contemplate actually doing any of the things we have always wanted to do, such as getting married, or dying, or wearing spats, or keeping an hotel.

It seemed risky to give Tom Weagle charge of a hotel which included a bar-room. But Mother Weagle in a blind, rustic way understood people--the first requisite of hotel-keeping, as it is of law, medicine, or any other learned profession. Tom went on sneaking in little whiskies, but he tried to live up to the spectacle of himself as manager of a real hotel, one who met the glossiest travelling-man as an equal and had the power to make him comfortable or shunt him off to the meanest room on the third floor. He went so far as to keep his coat on in the office, except on the hottest days. He impressively rang the bell for Myron, or Uncle Jasper--the venerable negro ·who was porter, 'bus driver, saloon cleaner--to 'carry up the gennulman's valise and hustle with it'. His proudest task was to carve the cooked meats, on a table at the end of the dining-room instead of in the kitchen, as normally, during meals. Tom was congenitally a master carver, and carving, though the layman guest rarely appreciates it, is one of the most occult priest-crafts of hotel-keeping. He loved the staccato clash of carving knife on steel sharpener, the grandeur of the knife's horn handle and Roman blade, the war-like flash as he flourished it high, and his surgeon's skill in piercing a wing-joint at the first precise stroke. Helping him, admiring and learning, Myron perceived that in at least this one mystery, his father was a savant.

Tom even tried to keep the books, and made so few errors that Myron could usually correct them.

Myron's position in the hotel, outside of school hours, was definite and simple: he did everything that no one else wanted to do. He wiped dishes and scrubbed floors; he swept halls and steps and the office; he cooked the breakfast eggs before galloping off to school; he roused irate travelling-men for the 4.14 freight to Waterbury; he occasionally tended bar. He learned in his very bones the insignificant, unromantic, all-important details of hotel-keeping.

He learned to broil chickens and steaks instead of frying them into a semblance of boot-soles; he learned that there are soups outside of oyster stew, cream of tomato, vegetable, and chicken, and potatoes other than

German fried, French fried, baked, and mashed; he learned and proved, over his mother's horrified protest, that what she called the 'nasty-looking' feet of chickens should not be thrown away but skinned and used to make soup stock. He even learned, at the bar, under the tutelage of the professional bartender, Jock McCreedy, to mix such sacred, old-fashioned, and now forgotten drinks as the timber doodle, sherry cobbler, golden fizz, spread-eagle punch, fish-house punch, pousse-café, balaklava nectar, white tiger's milk, rumfustian, and alligator's ear; the very names a feast of poesy, and the beverages themselves a foretaste for honest drinking men of nectar in the innermost saloon bar of Paradise.

For Myron showed uncommon talent, the first ever he had shown in his industrious life: he bought a cook-book. That was not extraordinary; people do buy cook-books, particularly brides. Between 1896 and 1931, 'The Boston Cooking School Cook Book' had sold a million and a half copies, making the author, Miss Fannie Merritt Farmer, one of the only five important American authors, along with Charles Sheldon, of *In His Steps,* Harriet Beecher Stowe, Arthur Brisbane, and Laura Jean Libbey. But thereafter his mild talent beat up into indisputable genius, for he actually read the cook-book, through and through.

And he built a linen-chute down the stair-well from the third floor to the basement, while old Tom (he was only forty-three, now, in 1894, when Myron was fourteen, but he was born old and it is believed that he became gently drunk on his mother's milk) sat on the stairs and helped by holding the nails and giving bad advice and quarrelling mildly at Myron for not doing better in school, since aside from seven or eight hours' work a day in the hotel, and perhaps seven wasted in sleeping, Myron was able to give all the rest of his time to attending high school and long, sweet, inspiring hours of study.

4

Not the triumph of entering college, nor even the triumph of a broker receiving his LL.D. degree from Muskingum College as a recognition of piety and generosity, is so satisfying an academic victory as emerging into high-school Sophomoredom. Sophomores are admitted now to be men and women, and they are still certain, on misinformation and belief derived from their parents, that it is worth while to become adults and have the privileges of shaving and bearing babies and tending the furnace and belching after meals. It is now that the boys are expected to smoke, though perhaps secretly, and the girls to have fellers and silk stockings.

Though most of his energy and his ideas were absorbed by the American House, now that he was fifteen and a Sophomore, Myron found high school diverting. The physical background was fairly bad. Not yet had New England towns discovered that the young can be educated only in a milieu of tapestry brick, Vita glass, $100,000 swimming pools, gymnasia with professional instructors, and marble-lined model kitchens. The Black Thread Centre High School was a slate-grey wooden shack with small, dirty windows and no ventilation. The floors were worn into channels around the knots in the boards, and the only decorations were portraits of the good grey poets. The students' desks were cramped, and the teachers still kept apples and punitive rulers on their desks instead of graphs of daily variation in individual suggestibility.

After daily enforced intimacy with old, worn travelling-men--thirty and upwards--Myron liked the association with causelessly giggling youth. As to the studies that year, except for plane geometry and German, he did not think so much of them. Caesar was dull--Latin in general was dull. What the dickens did the ablative absolute, or gerundives, or the fact that the accusative was used with ad, ante, apud, circum, contra, inter, per, and trans have to do with daily life in Black Thread, or in New York or California either? Nor did he much care whether Hamlet was crazy, or what was the date of Charles Martel--what was Myron Weagle to Charles Martel and what was Charles to Myron? He rather liked droning in the music-hour, and trying to sketch pots and petunias in the drawing-lesson. And German, now that *was* something! With it he could talk to the little colony of Heinies up the river at Dutch Bend, and have a lot of fun pretending to speak it with his friends. 'Be gehts it Ihr, meiner Frund?' they bellowed at one another and, in more serious hours of confessed ambition, squatting on the river bluff, they planned that some day they would go up the Rhine, observing castles and Fräuleins, and they sang softly:

'Ik weiss nick wot soll it bedeiten
Dass ik so traurick bin.'

Particularly, plane geometry was fun. Myron liked the neatness and precision of it, sleek triangles and deft segments of circles and provable facts about the degrees of angles--not all the fuzzy obscurity of Caesar's opinions about the Gauls. Anyway, he had to get through the year, because next year he would be allowed to take up this new course in book-keeping, and that would be useful, whether he should become a lawyer, an hotel-man, a railroad-man, or keep store. But beyond all, his reason for excitement at the beginning of Sophomore year was that he had fallen in love with his handsome classmate, Miss Julia Lambkin.

Julia Lambkin practically belonged to the aristocracy of Black Thread Centre. Her father, Trumbull Lambkin, was not only the leading druggist in town, which made him almost the same as a doctor, but also a director in the Housatonic Savings Bank, a member of the library board, and a vestryman in the Episcopal Church, and the Lambkins had lived in Black Thread for three long, tradition-crusted generations. Julia was a tall wench, with a high laugh, a high colour, and a richness of chestnut hair, which she had put up before any of the other girls in her class. She danced much, and entertained--entertained whole bevies of young people at summer-evening parties on her porch, with almost unlimited raspberry vinegar and lemonade and banana layer cake. She was one of the eleven members of the exclusive Pequot Cycling Club, which scorched with a soft whirring of wheels on cool evenings, all of them humming 'Sweet Marie' and looking down their noses at the common people and she was the only girl in town so luxurious as to own a Columbia bicycle!

With such charms in a classroom seat only three from his, it was not extraordinary that Myron (along with seven or eight other young gentlemen) should have fallen volcanically in love with Julia. Though he did not feel that he belonged to her set, they went to many of the same parties. In the '90's, small-town Connecticut was still sufficiently democratic for that. He waltzed with her, and he waltzed well, but he was lumbering and ridiculous when he tried to caper through the figures of the square dances--grand right 'n' lef, sashay all--and Julia snapped at him, 'Oh, don't be such a galoot!' It was dreadful, he admitted, to be a galoot.

All day long, in school, he sneaked glances at her over his geometry, while she bridled and would not look back. The other Sophomores watched them and giggled, and one little snip of a girl, with the daring of small contemptible females (this girl has become a woman and a mother since and has done no good; she plays contract by night and by day, and goes to a handsome chiropractor) passed along a row of seats such notes as 'Myron is crazy about Julie,' which everyone read and sniggered over. Evenings, whenever he could get away from the hotel and his home-work for a quarter of an hour, Myron plodded by Julia's house, poring upon it with hang-jawed and sad-eyed longing. The Lambkin mansion was in all of Black Thread surpassed only by the homes of the Boston Store owner, and of Mr. Dingle, the banker. It was of rather faded red brick, with dark-green shutters and a mansard roof. The porch was not, as was usual, exposed in front, but at the side, where it had a choice, mysterious secrecy. Myron gaped at the more fashionable and skittish of his classmates--some of the richer boys in white duck pants--lolling on the steps of this porch, and conversationally screeching at Julia.

He did not dare join them. He felt too big and awkward and graceless; he felt *déclassé.* But his heart swelled to take in every aspect of Lambkinism--the Lambkin residence, the fine new Lambkin surrey with its fringed whipcord top, Mr. Trumbull Lambkin with his grim leanness and grey side-whiskers and smell of camphor and formaldehyde. Myron looked with a brother-in-law's affection upon Julia's sister, Effie May, aged four. She was a dear little golden-haired tot, and had all the attributes of a hyena. 'Gosh, Effie May certainly is one cute lil trick!' glowed Myron. He took into his devotion the Lambkin dog, Fred, a foul animal who was collie in front and Newfoundland behind and mean all over, and given to nipping night-roaming lovers who slowed up at Julia's residence. He even fawned upon Julia's brother, Herbert, a cold-eyed, even-eyed young gentleman a year older than Myron, who responded to an effusive 'Good morning,' with a frosty nod, and who, when it was amiably inquired of him, 'Going to work in your dad's store this summer?' snapped, 'Certainly not; I'm pursuing my studies for Yale and for a career of architecture.'

Herbert really talked that way, and for the time being, Myron endured it. He walked past the Lambkin house and walked past it and walked past it and agonized over the chatterers on the porch, and his heart was lonely--lonely still when he got back to the hotel and his father (who, this past hour, had done nothing more important than pick his teeth and scratch) scolded him for not having taken a travelling-man's trunks down to the sample-room. He was lonely even when he took the late trick at the bar, and the room was filled with the flat rattle of poker chips and the clank of glasses touched in toasts of 'Lookin' at yuh' and guffaws over the new one about Napoleon and the dead fish.

He had fallen in love on the first day of Sophomore year, when his submerged passion had been revealed to him by the fact that, with her hair put up for the first time and her fine chin held high, Julia was the image of the Gibson Girl, who was the Venus and Helen of Troy of the time. Yes! He saw it now--saw his own heart. She was the real Gibson Girl, and to be worshipped beyond all other mortals. Since he was blossoming into the perilous age of fifteen, he longed for her with a sickening, defenceless ache. He was entirely vague as to what he wanted to do to her. He never dared think consciously of anything beyond sitting beside her on the steps of the porch, and perhaps shaking hands at parting, but that ambition kept him awake in his airless and cob-webbed room in the American House, as he pictured her: dear face, her large bright hands, her droll mouth, even the stuff of her beautiful percale blouse with its fashionable puffed sleeves.

Not till after a month of his passion and martyrdom, not till an October evening, did he catch her alone on the porch. For all his awe of her, he was not too timid a wren and, though he had to force his courage, he stalked up the path and firmly squatted on the top step, below her rocking chair.

'Hello,' he said.

'Hello.'

'Kind of cool.'

'Yes, it is kind of cool.'

'You all alone to-night?'

'Yes,' she admitted, 'I'm all alone. Nobody loves me, I guess.'

'Gee, I do, all right.' He was pleased by the feat of having got just the right lightness and stylishness into his tone.

'Oh yes, you do!' sardonically. 'You never come around.'

'Well, I got my work in the hotel, Jule. Have to help out.'

'Well, you could get off sometimes.'

'Well, it's awful' hard to get off.'

'Sure, you could get off lots of times.'

'Well, I can't get off much of the time.'

'Well, if you wanted to, you'd get off.'

'Would you like it if I got off and came over?'

She tossed her head--not quite the thing for a big, handsome Gibson Girl--and sniffed, 'It don't make me no neverminds, smarty. I guess you don't want to come, or you'd get off more.'

'Well, I'll try to get off more.'

'Well, if you manage to get off more, then maybe I'll believe you want to.'

'Well, I'll get off more--you see if I don't! Say, Jule, couldn't you go buggy-riding with me, some Sunday afternoon? We get half-rates from the stable, at the hotel.'

'Uh-huh, Mr. Smarty! So that's why you're so willing and all to actually go and take me driving--because you can get a rig cheap!'

'Oh, gee, Jule, I didn't mean . . .'

'Well, that's what you said; just prezactly what you said--you get half-rates, so maybe you might be willing to condescend to allow me to go driving!'

'I did not! I didn't mean it that way at all, and you know doggone well I didn't! If you want to go, all right, but if you don't, cut out the high and mighty! How about it?'

Rather weakly, Julia peeped, 'Oh, I'd like it, but Pa and Ma wouldn't stand for it.'

'Why *not?*'

'They wouldn't mind it if you came here, right under their eyes, but they wouldn't let me go riding with you.'

'Why the heck not?'

'Oh, I hate to say it but--they don't exactly approve of you, I guess.'

'Why not?'

'Pa's an awful old crank about some things, I guess, and your Dad is a saloon-keeper.'

'He is not! Just because there's a bar in the hotel . . .'

Thus far he had been bold and fluent, but he did not know how to finish, because he realized, appalled, that actually his father did belong to the class, pariahs in choice Connecticut villages, of saloon-keepers. He finished in confusion: 'He is not a saloon-keeper! He's an hotel-keeper!'

'Well, but I guess Pa doesn't think so much-a-much of hotel-keeping, either. He thinks waiting on a lot of people and feeding 'em and making their beds is kind of common.'

'Let me tell you, Julia Lambkin, my dad never made a bed in his life! He's the proprietor and manager! He just hands out keys and keeps the books and all like that!'

'Well, *you* make beds sometimes, and once you washed out a pair of socks for a travelling-man--your brother Ora told us!'

'The dirty little snitch! I'll poke his face in! And anyway, what's the diff? Don't your father have to wait on people, behind the counter, and make up prescriptions for their bellyaches?'

'I've never heard such disgusting language in all my life! No decent boy would *dream* of using a word like bel . . . like what you said, in the presence of a lady! And I'll have you to know, Mr. Smarty Weagle, that a druggist doesn't wash socks or sweep floors; he's a professional man, that people come to consult him in serious sickness and want his advice and let me tell you right here and now, Mr. Smarty, that old Doc Winter, and I heard him myself, with my own ears, and he said that my dad was a better doctor than nine-tenths of the people that *call* themselves "doctors", and if you think for one minute that I propose to sit here and let you insult my Papa, you're very badly mistaken.'

She dashed into the house. She was so subtle that, after starting to slam the door in a nice, normal, furious way, she closed it with rebuking quietness. Myron sat collapsed, like a half-empty hot-water bottle. He rose with pain and removed himself with anguish.

But this time he kicked Fred, the dog, and enjoyed it.

All the way home, amid tornadoes and dust-storms of humiliation, he vowed, 'When I get to be a big doctor or lawyer, or maybe own a great big hotel or something, she'll be sorry! I'll show 'em!'

He thought of ways of aggrandizement, as he sat on a fallen willow trunk in a secret corner near the bridge. He would never wear a celluloid collar again, but always linen, as on Sunday, no matter how much his father complained of the cost. He would learn German perfectly, and astonish Julia Lambkin by discoursing with the teacher (which would, as a matter of fact, have been considerably beyond the teacher's powers). He would somehow, maybe by picking and selling huge quantities of blueberries, get a horse and a second-hand buggy of his own and drive scornfully past her house, and when Herbert or she wanted a ride, he would answer curtly, 'Sorry, but I have an engagement.'

His plans for himself flowed into plans for the hotel. If it were a statelier establishment, Mr. Lambkin might be impressed. Of course Myron would get rid of the bar-room. (Of course he wouldn't, he admitted, even in his temporary insanity.) He'd persuade his mother to put in a 'ladies' parlour. Recently, on a Saturday, he had driven with his father to Torrington, and there, in the renowned Eagle Hotel, which had seventy rooms, he had seen a parlour all red plush and gilt. 'Add a lot of class to our place,' he meditated, almost forgetting Julia.

He did actually get his parents to install the parlour of his dream. His mother hesitated: it would cost so much, and take the space of one of their bedrooms. But Myron insisted that only at rush seasons, when the travelling-men were in the thick of spring or fall orders, were all their bedrooms occupied, and with a parlour they could cater to the schoolteachers and other lone females who had been their mainstay as 'steadies' at the boarding-house but who hesitated about living at an hotel in which the only lounges were a bar-room and an office infested with spittoons and men with hats cocked over their eyebrows.

The parlour was assembled--Myron Weagle's first triumph as a creative hotel-keeper, as he was some time to be called (to his slight but active nausea) at Rotary Club luncheons and Chamber of Commerce dinners.

The new parlour of the American House was an artistic triumph. Mother Weagle and Myron went by train clear to Hartford, to the second-hand shops there, for the furnishings. It had a golden ingrain carpet--at first Myron did not like it so well as the hot crimson of the carpet in their boarding-house parlour, but after a time he considered it more delicate, and likely to knock the eye out of even an aristocrat like Julia Lambkin. The wall-paper was of poison green, with yellow blotches like headless fish. The furniture was ample: four easy chairs upholstered in worn brown velvet, with doilies of imitation crochet pinned on back and arms, three straight chairs, four china cuspidors, and a folding desk incorporating a bookcase in which were six novels left behind by guests and a directory of Beulah County ten years old. There were impressive lace curtains, and plush side curtains with ball fringes. But the two glories of the new parlour were the enormous vase covered with stamps pasted on and glazed over, a vase to be filled with pussy willows and gilded cat-tails, and the rare centre table, which had interesting bandy legs and a real marble top only partly concealed by the embroidered cover. It was, altogether, the handsomest room Myron had ever seen, aside from the Lambkin parlour, and for several days after Mother Weagle and he had completed the arrangement of the furniture (how breathlessly they tried the effect of the exotic stamp-vase on this side and on that!), he slipped upstairs to peep in and sigh with ecstasy. And when he caught Ora reading *Swiss Family Robinson* in the parlour, humped up in one velvet chair with his feet on another, Myron yanked him out by the ear.

Yet at the sight of Julia going to church the next Sunday, in a new blue frock with ruffles which swept grandly through the dust and a superb large new hat on which unnatural violets and forget-me-nots bloomed upon a tufted bank of green velvet, all the splendour of the parlour seemed trivial, and his ambition of the last few days to become an hotel-man, to go on to even greater achievements than the parlour, became vulgar in his eyes. He longed to have a new blue-serge suit and a new Derby hat, and to follow Julia into church.

(None of the Weagles went to church. Hotel-keeping, especially when Sunday-noon dinner is the gala meal of the week, is not conducive to attending public worship. Tom Weagle sometimes grumbled, 'Well, you can say what you want to about Religion, but lemme tell you it never did nobody no harm to be religious, and it's the only thing that'll keep a lot of these yahoos and toughs and iggoramuses in order.' Mrs. Weagle observed, 'I says to him, let me tell you, I says, I guess a book like the Bible, that has lasted four thousand years like it has, and nobody has been able to contradict it, it must be inspired by the Lord, and there's no argument about it, I says.' But probably none of the Weagles gave five minutes thought a year to theology or ecclesiology, except for Ora, who occasionally stirred up a lot of interesting family irritation by announcing that he was going to become a Catholic, an Episcopalian, a Buddhist, or a Seventh Day Adventist.)

When pride in the new parlour slipped from him, when Julia in her gardened hat, entering the Litchfield County Gothic portal of the Congregational Church, seemed to him like an embodied light that dazzled him and left him dizzy and ridiculous, Myron wistfully gave up his plans to become a great hotel-man, and sought for a profession more worthy the traditions of Trumbull Lambkin, that distinguished seller of patent medicines and bath-sponges. Within a fortnight Myron was finally and irrevocably determined to become a doctor, a lawyer, a West Pointer, an explorer, a banker, a tobacco planter with a thousand lordly acres in the Connecticut River valley, the captain of a liner, and a professor of Greek--which language he chose as being the most unfamiliar of all known tongues. Just in between, and not quite so seriously, he considered becoming a tramp or a starved trapper in the Northern woods, and breaking Julia's cold and brittle heart by letting her know that she had ruined his life.

The game of 'what'll we do after school' was familiar enough in high school, but none of the other boys went at it with such earnestness, such brisk and practical drawing up of detailed plans, such excited sending off for university catalogues, as did Myron. He discussed it with Ora who, though he was but thirteen, was fuller of words and bookish misinformation than any boy Myron knew. Ora often exasperated him; Ora sulked and wailed; he never conceivably did any of the light work assigned to him in the hotel, and he was always late for meals. But now Myron turned to him, as to an oracle much travelled in the realms of gold.

'You ought to be a business man,' condescended Ora. 'You can stand sitting at a desk doing figgers. You didn't even mind arithmetic. Gosh, it drives me crazy! But then, I'm never going to be a business man. Maybe a nauthor.'

From earliest historical times Ora had desired to be a nauthor. Unlike Myron, he had never been tempted by law or banking, though where he first got a nauthorial ambition no one has an idea, for he had never met one of those exotic night-flying creatures.

Myron half agreed, though he blunderingly indicated that he was less interested in making money than in administering institutions--hotels, hospitals, law-courts. Maybe there were business men, and successful ones, who were not money-grubbers but creators, he suggested. The new notion inspired him, and for the next fortnight he was, in council with Ora, a bicycle-manufacturer, the president of a rifle-factory in New Haven making guns so cheaply that any farm boy could afford one, and head of all the brass industries in Connecticut. Never had he been so intimate with Ora as now, when he overlooked disagreeable facts like unfilled wood-boxes and submitted his unromantic destiny to Ora's poetic vision. He even let Ora quote *Hiawatha* to him, at length.

But their brotherly comradeship ended in tragedy.

Myron, returning from school, came round a corner to find Ora, encircled by cheers and jeers, in a desperate fight with Herbert Lambkin, who was three years older than Ora and twenty pounds heavier. Ora's nose was bleeding all over his fashionable Eton collar and his hair was mingled with his fluent tears, but he was not doing so badly. He was butting Herbert in the belly, kicking his shins, and scratching his neck, and though the older champion occasionally got in a stout cuff on Ora's ear, he was giving way, and the gang were yowling plaudits to the young warrior-bard.

Myron gave a bark of rage and threw himself in as though he were diving. He seized Herbert's collar, he socked Herbert upon the salient Lambkin nose, he kicked him, ran him up an alley, and came back beaming to his dear little brother. As they went off, Ora was sobbing, and when Myron chirped, 'There, there--you done simply grand!' dear little brother howled, 'Damn you, damn you, damn you, you went and spoiled everything, like you always do!'

'Huh?'

'I was scared of Bert. Then I went and made myself unscared, and I jumped on him when he grabbed my hat. And then I wasn't scared any more. I was sore. I wasn't scared. And I was licking him. And you butted in and kept me from licking him and spoiled it all, and you'll get all the credit, damn you! That's what you always do!'

For weeks Ora would not be confidential, and Myron had by his lone self to puzzle out whether he was, to-day, a predestined doctor or sea-captain or revolver-manufacturer.

Then to the American House came the inspired priest of commerce, Mr. J. Hector Warlock, and made everything clear.

5

Of all the drummers working out of Bridgeport in 1895, none was handsomer, more affable, or more affluent than Mr. J. Hector Warlock, travelling representative, as he called it, of the Spurgis & Pownall Hardware, Stove, and Kitchen Equipment Corporation. He was thirty-four years old. His hair was very black, very wavy, and very thick, like the more popular manly Christian evangelists of the day, and no evangelist could troll out a hymn with a soapier bass. (Not that Mr. Warlock was likely to be heard actually singing hymns in the House of the Lord on a Sabbath morning; he was much more likely to be sleeping off a late Saturday-night poker game.) His famous and frequent smile was enlivened by two gold teeth, and on his soft, white, swollen fingers he wore a Masonic ring, and a ring in the guise of a golden snake, with rubies for eyes; while his large watch-chain bore a tasty emblem in the way of a golden miniature kitchen range.

He was tall enough and broad enough by nature, but made to appear the taller and broader by his correct garments for 1895; the Derby hat, the thick dark suit with shoulders enormously padded, the stiff-bosomed shirt- -though its solemnity was lightened by sprigs of tiny violets in the pattern- -and the large bow tie. To this he brightly added the fanciest of fancy vests, and he owned not just one, like local sports, but half a dozen: yellow with red polka dots, blue with white stripes, tan with scarlet sumac berries. He also wore the most stylish pointed toothpick shoes ever seen in Black Thread.

His was a face that barbers loved. That broad, pale yet healthy, meaty yet jolly expanse of visage received more attention than the cheeks of a duchess. He always took what he called 'the whole works' at a barber's: shave, hair-cut, singe, shampoo, facial massage, violet water, talcum powder, and delicately lilac flavoured tonic for his dense hair.

He was impressive, yet he was not overpowering, so hearty and insistent was his good-fellowship. He called all trainmen, bellhops, bartenders, and waiters 'Cap'n,' and when they saw him coming they chuckled, 'Hello, Mr. Warlock! You with us again?' His customers, the greater hardware-men of Southern New England, he addressed as 'Boss', with a nice mixture of friendliness and deference, and they liked him, they gave him epic orders, they had him at their homes for Sunday noon dinner, which is the accolade of a travelling-man.

At the American House, Black Thread Centre, the staff lamented that J. Hector came so seldom--only four times a year. Mother Weagle would, without visible cue, suddenly burst into a communal silence with a giggling, 'The very idea--that Mr. Warlock--chucking an old hen like me under the chin and telling me I was the best cook in Connecticut! Fresh!'

Albert Dumbolton, *vulgo,* 'Dummy', who as a grocery salesman (out of Torrington) got around once every ten days, was of nothing so proud as of friendship with J. Hector, and he frequently informed the entire bar-room, 'Say, I've been on the road twenty-six years now, and I want to tell you that I've never met a finer drummer, or a better man of any kind, than J. Hector Warlock. Say, he's got a heart of gold, that fellow has! Pays his bills, stands back of his friends, tells a good story, treats you like you was the Queen of England no matter *who* you are! And say, that fellow, when he's playing poker he can keep his trap shut like he was deaf *and* dumb, and then next morning he'll go into a hardware store and talk the hind leg right off a donkey. Why, he can sell anything! He could sell fleece-lined overshoes in Hell! And successful, say, I'll bet Heck Warlock makes his forty-five or forty-eight hundred dollars every year--more money than any man in *this* stuck-up town! And educated, why say, often on a train, when there ain't anybody he knows to talk to, he'll read clear through a book!'

It was this warrior-hero-prophet who came to Black Thread just as Myron, aged fifteen, was trying to determine his spiritual destiny--which, in the United States of America, meant his future job.

Myron was on the desk when the 7.36 p.m. from the South came in. There was presently a crepitation of 'Hello--hello--back again?' outside. Myron wandered to the plate-glass window giving on Main Street, and saw none other than J. Hector Warlock rolling up the street, seeming to fill it, his left thumb in the arm-hole of his vest, his right hand waving to the admiring citizenry. He was trailed by a boy pushing his suit-case in a wheel-barrow. It was not for J. Hector to tote his own bag, like an ordinary drummer; still less would it be his way to sleep in his shirt in the hotel and wait for his bag to be brought, along with his sample-trunks, by the drayman in the morning.

He hurled open the door, roaring at Myron, 'Hello, Cap'n, here's the baby elephant back again! How's tricks? Chased your dad out and took charge of the hotel have you? Well, how about a handsome suit with private elevator and a solid gold bed?'

He patted Myron's shoulder. Myron beamed. Myron exulted. J. Hector treated him as though he were grown-up, really were the manager . . . This was one of the moments, in hotel-keeping.

He galloped behind the desk, smartly swung the register about on its brass standard, held out the pen, then hastily changed it for another, with a better nib. While he wrote, with a flourish and two little marks, like quotation marks, under the dashing signature, J. Hector asked genially, 'Who's in town? How's chances for a little bout of skill?'

'Al Dumbolton is here.'

'Fine! Where's a boy?'

'I guess he's up in his room, writing out his orders. He was down here at the desk, but the fellows got to kidding him--they put a fire-cracker under his chair--and he got sore and went up. But I guess he'll be down in the bar, pretty quick.'

(Poor Al! He looked like a rumpled red-satin sofa cushion. The fellows did 'get to kidding him' with frequency.)

'He will! He will! Right down in the well-known bar! Trust Dummy. But say, Cap'n. Listen. I got an idea. You go up and knock and tell him the sheriff is here looking for him. I know doggone good and well he's been sniffing after that cute little wife of the night watchman at the mill, and he's kind of scared about it. Speak to him real serious. I'll be right behind you.'

It was not easy for Myron, as it would have been for Ora, to enact nervous excitement, but he would try anything for J. Hector Warlock. He knocked, and when Mr. Dumbolton came, in shirt sleeves and slipperless grey woollen socks, Myron croaked, 'Say, Al, gee, the sheriff is downstairs and he wants to see you! Looks awful mysterious, and like he was sore about something. I told him I thought you was out. You could sneak down the back way through the kitchen.'

Mr. Dumbolton gaped. His frightened voice sounded like steam from a locomotive. 'D-did he say why he wanted to see me?'

'No, but he sure did insist.'

'Oh, God, I might of known! What a fool I--Myron! I'll skip out the back way. Catch late freight at the crossing. You hold my valise. Tell the damn sheriff you can't find me. Make out like you're looking for me. Keep him busy! I'll make it quick!'

J. Hector Warlock, in a voice convincingly changed from his natural humorous basso-profundo, growled, 'You will not! You won't make it at all, Dumbolton!'

While the victim shrank from a big red sofa-cushion into a very little red sofa-cushion, J. Hector pushed past Myron and stood grinning down at Mr. Dumbolton, who stared and wriggled, then groaned, 'Well, I'm a sock-eyed son of a gun! I might of known! I thought you wasn't coming for a week! If I'd of known you was within fifty miles, I'd of known it was you, you old potato-face! I'll get you for this!'

The two men pounded each other's backs, most affectionately and painfully.

'How about a little devotion to the Goddess of Fortune, this evening? How about making the aces gallop?' suggested J. Hector. 'No, Myron; wait a minute.'

'Sounds elegant to me,' said Dumbolton.

'Then look, Myron. Who's in the house that's good for an innocent, friendly little test of skill . . . with dynamite in the gloves?'

'Mr. Wood Harris is here from Hartford--boots and shoes?'

'Fine. Yes. I've played with him. Ask him to come up to my room in half an hour. By the way, you've given me the double room with the private bath as usual, I hope, Cap'n.'

'Why!' Hurt and a little indignant. 'Sure! Of *course,* Mr. Warlock! Number 4.'

Thirty years hence, Myron would remember, as it was indeed his business to remember, that J. Hector Warlock had been pleased to play cards with Mr. Woodland F. Harris; that he had the room with private bath; and that he--most extraordinary and inexplicable thing about this great man--actually preferred tea to coffee for breakfast.

Only there was no room with private bath in the American House, Black Thread. The bath was really one of the four public tubs, a 'down-the-hall-bath' as it was called. But it did have an entrance not only from the hall but from Double Room 4, and some six or eight times a year it was demanded as a private bath, it was called a private bath, and thereby, magically, as in theology, it became a private bath.

Mr. Warlock was proceeding, 'Get hold of Harris, boy. Then chase out or send that fresh brat of a brother of yours out and see if you can get hold of Cal Bigus and Ed Stuart and that livery-stable keeper, what's his name? for a game this evening. And shoot a bottle of Old Taylor and plenty of glasses and ice water up to the room. Here. Don't waste this. Invest it in New York Central Preferred.'

He handed Myron a whole quarter. The largest tip Myron had ever received was fifty cents; that was from a man who had stayed two weeks and who as he had developed symptoms of delirium tremens, persecution mania, arthritis, acid stomach, and nympholepsy, had required some attention. His normal tip was ten cents--no, his normal tip, for dragging a leaden bag upstairs and bringing a pitcher of ice water, was nothing; ten cents was a New Yorker's tip.

'Oh, gee, thanks! I'll send Ora--my brother. I'll be right back up with your valise.'

He was not going to miss the chance of as much time as possible with his idol, J. Hector, who had, to Myron, all the subtlety of Miss Absolom, and considerably more point. He bullied his father into leaving a game of casino in the bar and coming in to take the desk. He bribed Ora to search for Cal and Ed and the livery-stable man; bribed him with fifteen cents out of the quarter. . . . Perhaps Ora was right in saying that Myron was born to business, not the arts, for even in this moment of excitement at J. Hector's golden coming and of strain in getting the alienated Ora to do anything whatever, Myron did not fail to make his righteous, capitalistic profit of ten cents.

He summoned Mr. Woodland F. Harris from the bar, and tugged J. Hector's mighty suitcase up to Room 4. As long as he could without feeling intrusive, he hung about watching J. Hector unpack, getting a foretaste of the luxuries in the Great World to which he hoped some day to belong.

J. Hector had such accessories to living as Myron had hitherto seen only on the bureau of Miss Absolom, and J. Hector's were richer, more male. From his bag, while Myron stood at the door and goggled, J. Hector produced not one but two hair brushes, thick, heavy, without handles. 'Military brushes!' throbbed Myron. He had read of them in advertisements in the New York papers.

And shoes with dinguses in them, like pale-yellow wooden feet, to keep them unwrinkled. And a bottle with a rubber bulb and a sprayer-thing on it. This last J. Hector squeezed in Myron's direction, and Myron was conscious of a rarer, stranger scent than ever he had known. And these newfangled pyjamas, instead of a white night-shirt neatly edged at the neck with red binding such as Albert Dumbolton and Tom Weagle--and Myron and Ora Weagle--naturally wore. And not one or two but no less than six several neckties. And a whole box of fifty cigars, with red and gold bands. And--aside from the Old Taylor that Myron had brought up--a bottle of whisky curiously named 'John Haig'.

And even a book.

The book J. Hector tossed to Myron. 'Read much, Cap'n? Good thing to do. Broadens your mind and gives you a vocabulary, so you can get the customers dizzy and unload the orders on 'em, and even be able to make a speech at church suppers.'

Myron regarded the volume with awe. It was bound in paper, with a striking picture of a gentleman with moustache kissing a high-haired young lady in the presence of moonlight and a church tower, and it was entitled 'The Perils of Passion: or The Struggles of Sally St. Cyr: a Story of Humble Hearts and Proud Blood o' the Cumberlands'.

His unpacking done, J. Hector, brave with cigar smoke, thumbs in his arm-holes, lolled in a straight chair which seemed transformed into a velvet fauteuil. (Myron knew the word 'fauteuil' from the catalogues he had studied when they were furnishing the hotel parlour.) Myron did not ever, like the blandly intrusive Ora, assume that his presence was always wanted; but J. Hector seemed glad of his company till the poker game should begin, and Myron stood beaming, shyly dragging his foot, while J. Hector discoursed on Bridgeport, New York ('lot bigger burg than Bridgeport, but you take my word for it, boy, not half as live a town'), the wonders of the new Spurgis & Pownall kitchen range and the quixotic amount of nickle Mr. Pownall had caused to be spread upon it.

To any American village in 1895, except for the half-dozen old and wealthy families who were familiars of New York or Boston or Chicago or Europe, the travelling-man was the one missionary from the Great World, and the young people listened to him with reverence. He was the Marquis back from Paris; he was Erasmus and Casanova; he was the Phoenician galley-captain returned from Ostia; he was the radio and the Harvard graduate and the Book of Etiquette.

J. Hector gossiped of cocktails at the Waldorf bar, of planked blue-fish in Fulton Market, of champagne at Martin's, of the gigantic liners *Campania* and *Lucania,* each 13,000 tons, big as cathedrals, sailing from New York to Liverpool, and of an intimate friend of J. Hector's who had actually sailed on one of them and spent no less than eight weeks abroad, becoming authoritatively acquainted with England, Scotland, France, Holland, Belgium, Germany, Austro-Hungary, Italy, Switzerland, and Spain.

Myron looked rapturous and dragged his foot harder than ever. 'Golly!' he said.

The gamblers arrived, each affectionately greeting J. Hector as a horse-thief, a son-of-a-gun, and a card-sharper. While J. Hector pump-handled them and called them hicks, bank-robbers, and cradle-snatchers, Myron bustled blissfully. He brought glasses and ice-water, the ice clinking against the side of the white earthenware pitcher as he tramped down the hall; he neatly opened the bottle of Old Taylor; he snatched an extra table from a vacant room and brought it in, balancing one end of the table against his stomach, panting and staggering with it.

The five available players, J. Hector, Dummy Dumbolton, Woodland F. Harris, Cal Bigus, the jeweller, and Ed Stuart, the station agent, stripped off their coats, took off their stiff cuffs, and opened their vests, with a slight snifter of rye between operations, and sat down at the two joined tables with a firmness which indicated that they were here for business, and not to be taken lightly. J. Hector started by turning his chair about, facing the back, instead of waiting till he had to change his luck. This innovation astonished and impressed the local sports, and Myron was ever to remember it as a professional sort of thing to do. But the sports, and Myron, were yet more thrilled when J. Hector, tossing an unopened pack of cards on the table, stated unboastfully, 'Well, boys, to-night we don't play with any fifty-two slabs of butter. That's a fifty-cent pack, right from lil old Bridgeport!'

Myron had not known that you *could* pay more than fifteen cents for a pack of cards. When they were opened, he edged over to look at the backs. They did not have red and white scrolls, like all the cards he had ever seen, but real pictures, art pictures--a crescent moon against which reclined a lovely young woman who was, Myron thought, pretty much undressed.

He could find no further excuse for staying. But he came back, half a dozen times, to renew the ice water, unasked, and once, very urgently asked, to bring two more bottles of Old Taylor. Ordinarily he was in bed by ten-thirty, up at five-thirty, but to-night he stayed with the greatness and adventure of the game, and he saw moments of the titanic struggle.

He came in at midnight, with ice water, and found J. Hector and Ed Stuart watching each other with expressions of determined expressionlessness. The other three had dropped out and were looking on with something like awe. 'Nice lil pot,' Dummy Dumbolton whispered to Myron; '*only* sixty-five dollars!'

'Sixty--five--dollars!' groaned Myron.

Ed Stuart was no mere victim to J. Hector. He was himself rather on the Homeric side, and it was told of him in the streets and lands and secret places of Black Thread that he had once sat in for thirty-six hours on a poker game at Beulah. And he was what Black Thread esteemed, 'pretty darn well-to-do'; he was not only station agent but he also had an interest in the bicycle shop, and owned and rented out a quarter section six miles north of town. Yet his voice was sharpening a little now, while J. Hector's was bland as mayonnaise.

'Raise you two white ones,' snapped Ed, unbuttoning his collar.

'And two!' crooned J. Hector.

Myron, having that invisibility which is sometimes the humiliation and sometimes the protection of waiters, was able to see their hands. Ed Stuart held a full house, while J. Hector sat lovingly over the four of spades, the seven of diamonds, the eight of diamonds, the jack of hearts, and the queen of clubs, a combination approximating the absolute zero.

Ed stared at his hand again; he forgot the esteemed virtue of looking completely dumb; he glanced anxiously at J. Hector as he hesitated, 'Well, up it two little ones.'

'And fifteen cold bucks more!' chuckled J. Hector joyously.

'Oh hell, take it!' wailed Ed, and as J. Hector coyly laid down his cats and dogs, one by reluctant one, all of the players howled and did homage to J. Hector Warlock.

At one o'clock they had stripped to their undershirts (two red flannel, two balbriggan, and the elegant soft silk and wool of J. Hector). At two, they were speaking with furry and wanton tongues, and J. Hector bribed Myron (he need not have) to go down and break the law and sneak them another Old Taylor. At three, J. Hector had dropped from a lead of seventy-four dollars to fifty cents, but he did not, like Ed Stuart, look put upon; he looked red-eyed, and his profuse hair was in his eyes, but he was good-natured. He alone seemed to regard this as a game, something having a distant but traceable relationship to pleasure. He rumbled at Myron, 'Good Godfrey, boy, you ought to be in bed! We keeping you up? You go to bed now!'

'Oh, gee, I don't mind. I want to see the game.'

'All right, Cap'n, you're the boss. No wise drummer ever butts in on the Mine Host of a caravansery. Never knows when he may need. . . .'

'Hey, are you playing poker, Heck, or giving a Ly-*ce*-yum lecture?' snarled Ed Stuart.

'. . . may need the manager to explain to folks about the hairpins in the bed. But if you're going to stay up, Myron, how about frying us a couple of eggs--or hippopotamus's ears, or whatever's handy?'

'Bet I will, Mr. Warlock!'

When Myron swayed in with an enormous tray with ten fried eggs, bacon, toast, coffee, and the crabapple jelly his mother always put up, J. Hector broke all the liturgical rules by rising in the middle of a hand, clapping Myron's shoulder, and observing, 'Well by the great jumping Jehosophat! You're the best night clerk *I* ever saw, Myron! George Boldt better watch his step; you'll be running the Waldorf, 'long in about five years! Well, what's the damage?'

'Oh, I don't know how to charge you. Usually it's a quarter when a guest gets a lunch if he's going to catch the late freight or the 6.07 to Bridgeport.'

'Well then, by golly, we'll call this two bucks--that's forty apiece for the grub--and here's fifty cents for you, Myron.'

'Oh, I can't . . .'

'The hell you can't! Here.' He roughly thrust two dollars and a half into Myron's pocket, turned him around, shot him out of the door, and jovially commanded, 'Now you go to bed, or I'll know the reason why, and if I hear you snoring or fighting with the bedbugs, I'll be up there and know the reason why! You git! Bless you, son; you took fine care of us!'

Myron stood outside the door and worshipped, 'That's the swellest fellow I ever knew!' He sleepily contrasted J. Hector with the bleak and whiskery respectability of Trumbull Lambkin, with the snippy superiority of Julia and Herbert Lambkin, with the dreary industry of Mr. Barstow, the furniture dealer across the street, with the feeble irritability of his father, with the contempt of Ora, even with the disconcerting secret smile of Miss Absolom.

'He's just grand!' said Myron.

That was at half past three. At a quarter to five, when Mr. Dummy Dumbolton tacked wanly down the hall from the grandeur of Double Room 4 to his own exiguous apartment, he found Myron sleeping in a sway-backed chair beside his door. Dummy peered owlishly at this phenomenon. It was all a part of the great unreality which had befogged the world, this last half hour. Myron awoke, sharply, awoke all awake, begging, 'Did he win, Mr. Dumbolton, did he win?'

'Di' whru win--win what?' gurgled Dummy.

'Mr. Warlock? Did he win?'

'Yesh--couple--guesh couple, couple dollars. G'night. . . . Oh my God!'

It was too late for Myron to go to bed; that would only make him feel the worse when he got up. He would be on duty in three-quarters of an hour. He wavered down to the kitchen, let the water run till it was icy, soaked his head, and not too uncheerfully began to sweep. He knew that the three local gladiators would have ganged up on J. Hector, and that if J. Hector had won anything at all, he had done well. Myron had, he felt, triumphed that night along with his idol.

By six, he was whistling, awake and lively, which was as it should be, for the ability to stay up brightly all day and all night and all day again is, probably more than any technical trick or profound learning, the secret of hotel-men, physicians, sea-captains, aviators, bootleggers, and bridegrooms.

When Myron came home from high school at noon, J. Hector was in a leather-upholstered rocker in the office, looking red-eyed but cheerful.

'Morning, Cap'n. Get any sleep?' called J. Hector.

'Oh, sure, plenty!'

'Well, can't say as I did. I sort of realized it this morning, when I tried to sell Brother Hickman a line of refrigerators at his store, and caught myself informing him that they would run on coal, wood, or old rags, and were unexcelled for broiling, roasting, and baking. Well . . . Say, that was an elegant spread you gave us, last night. Did I pay you for it?'

'Yes, sir. Say, uh, say, Mr. Warlock . . .' Myron ventured to sit down beside J. Hector, and to confide, 'Say, do you think hotel-keeping is a good business? Or do you think that a fellow, if he's got any ambition, had ought to get out and become a banker or a manufacturer or a doctor or something?'

'Look here, son! Somebody been ribbing you about hotel-keeping not being a dignified and highfalutin line of business? You tell 'em to go soak their head! Dignified--why say, fellow was telling me, he was a college professor or something, I met him on a train, and he showed me where in the Olden Days surgeons were barbers, too, and folks didn't think much of them. They about ranked with the third assistant hired girl. But now, good Lord, when a surgeon agrees to cut you up, you'd think he was the King of France! Hotel-keeping--well, up till now it hasn't been so good because the hotels--taverns they used to call 'em, and inns, and so on--and they weren't so good. But that's all changing. I tell you, way I figure it, some day there's going to be even bigger and sweller hotels than the Waldorf, and then, as the hotels get better, the hotel-men are going to be more important. Lots of swagger folks will get sick of housekeeping and go live in hotels. It will be one of the most important lines of business in the country, with some of the biggest folks in it.

'And as for the usefulness of hotels, well say, it takes a travelling-man to appreciate an hotel--come in all tired and wet and sick of day coaches and cinders, and get a good hot cup o' coffee like Mother Weagle makes, and a good clean bed like here--though you *might* have some of the mattresses made of straight-grained pine, next time, and not all this knotty stuff. But I'm just joking. Nothing you could do more important--*or* interesting--meet all kinds of people, and see 'em with their shirts off, you might say; see the Senator soused and the up-state banker meeting a peacherino. And you belong to the hotel; you've got the start. Nobody, hardly ever, learned hotel-keeping right down to the ground unless he was born under the kitchen sink and did his teething on a file of overdue bills! Go to it, boy! You'll have to learn a lot. You'll have to get into a lot bigger hotels than this--say, like in Bridgeport--biggest city of its size in the U.S.A.! You'll have to learn accounting and purchasing; not just run out and pick up a beefsteak, like you do here, but deal with big supply houses for maybe a thousand knives and forks, a hundred turkeys, five kegs of oysters--how to bargain and how to stand in with 'em. You'll have to learn *manners*--learn to be poker-faced with guys that would take advantage of you. Now, of course, you're only a kid, but even so, you're too doggone open-hearted; I can tell right away when you're pleased or kind of hurt. You'll have to know all about china and silver and glass and linen and brocade and the best woods for flooring and furniture. A hotel-manager has to be a combination of a house-frau, a chef, a bar-room bouncer, a doctor for emergencies, a wet nurse, a lawyer that knows more about the rights and wrongs of guests and how far he dast go in holding the baggage of skippers than Old Man Supreme P. Court himself, an upholsterer, a walking directory that knows right offhand, without looking it up, just where the Hardshell Baptist Church is and what time the marriage license bureau opens and what time the local starts for Hick Junction. He's got to be a certified public accountant, a professor of languages, a quick-action laundryman, a plumber, a heating-engineer, a carpenter, a swell speech-maker, an authority on the importance of every tinhorn State Senator or one-night-stand lecturer that blows in and expects to have the red carpet already hauled out for him, a fly-cop that can tell from looking at a girl's ears whether she's sure-enough married to the guy or not, a moneylender--only he doesn't get any interest or have any security. He's got to dress better 'n a Twenty-third Street actor, even if he's only got a thin dime in his pocket. He's got to be able just from hearing a cow's moo to tell whether she'll make good steaks. He's got to know more about wine and cigars than the fellows that make 'em--they can fool around and try experiments, but he's got to sell 'em. And all the time he's got to be a diplomat that would make Thomas F. Bayard look like John L. Sullivan on a spree. He's got to set a table like a Vanderbilt and yet watch the pennies like a Jew pedlar. If you can do all this, you'll have a good time. Go to it, Cap'n. Well, I think I'll go in and feed.'

Not again, for more than an occasional hour, did Myron aspire to anything save becoming a hotel-keeper--a great hotel-keeper of the fabulous coming post-Waldorf days.

6

To Myron, his brother Ora was a greater mystery than Miss Absolom or the Pleiades. He could not understand why Ora had no apparent satisfaction out of doing, neatly and on time, his small tasks about the hotel; how Ora could enjoy reading Scott and Dickens and Thackeray and Tennyson for hour on hour. Golly, didn't the kid ever get tired of all those fairy stories and lies about a bunch of knights and so on? And where did Ora get all these curious ideas?

Ora would confide, 'Some day I'm going to Venice. . . .'

'That's in Italy, ain't it?'

'Hell no! It's in Finland! I'm going to Venice and I'm going to have a gon*do*la of my own, and ride around in it, and have a bunch of wha'-juh-call-'ems to sing Ytalian songs to me. By moonlight. Every night for years.'

'Gosh, I wouldn't think that would be much fun, Ora. Not after the first couple a nights. I'd rather get some time off from the hotel and go up to Maine, duck-hunting.'

'You would! And I'm going to know a lot of princes and dukes and all like that. And the Riveera. Gambling at Monte Carlo!'

With venerably shaking head Myron fretted, 'Never thought much of gambling. Good way to waste your money.'

'Well, your darned old Hector Warlock--with his fancy toothache vests that look like catsup spilled on a tablecloth--he gambles!'

'That's different. Just a little cards, with friends. And you say anything against Mr. Warlock and I'll slap your face off!'

'You would! That's about the only way you *can* argue. Warlock! I'm going places he never even heard about, with all his gassing about Fifth Avenue and Boston and the Parker House! I'm going to have a chalette right up on top of the Alps, and sleep all day and sit up all night and look at the stars. . . . Did you ever think, Myron: the stars are flowers in the fields of heaven?'

Myron looked at him suspiciously. Was Ora trying to kid him? But his brother was entirely serious. Myron did not jeer; he never jeered at Ora, however often he longed to assault him. 'No, I never thought about 'em that way. Sounds like Reverend Ivy.'

As the pretty thought had indeed come to him from the lips of the Reverend Waldo Ivy, Ora answered furiously, 'It does not! He never had as good an idea as that in his life! I got lots of ideas. Wait 'll I get time to compose books and poems out of 'em! You'll see! I'll make so much money

I'll have a yacht, and go off cruising to--oh, to Cambodia and Nantucket and the Vale of Avalon and all over.'

'Well, I hope you do. Say, kid, how about filling that wood-box now?'

Myron worried, 'He's certainly got elegant ideas. I guess he has a real superior mind. That poem he wrote--what was it?--

'Through distant seas I long to sail
To quest everywhere for the Holy Grail'

something like that, anyway; it certainly was quite an unusual poem. Only, why can't he do first things first, like Mr. Warlock always says? All fine and dandy to dream about Europe and the Alps and all them, but meanwhile he's here at the American House, and why not do the jobs he's got to do--and he has got to; I'll see he does 'em! Then get ready to go all them places when the time comes. I don't understand a fellow that just hasn't got a pride in doing well whatever he's got to do. . . . Oh, well, prob'ly I'm just an old stick. Prob'ly I'm like Ora says: No imagination. Just about as bad as that old stiff-neck, Trumbull Lambkin. . . . I wonder what kind of hotels they got up on the Alps? Must be big ones, with a view all over. Wonder if they have many private baths?'

In all the Black Thread High School there was no boy more popular than Myron Weagle. Yet he had no friends. For in boyhood, friendships are strictly based on leisure hours. Friends are the companions of your evening games of pom-pom-pullaway and prisoner's base, of Saturday afternoon hikes through the woods, of lolling at the swimming hole. They need have, these friends of boyhood, no two thoughts in common with you, nor any similarity of taste; met after a lapse of twenty years, they may be stranger than any chance acquaintance of yesterday in the Pullman car. They are comrades at arms, not intimates. And thus, having no leisure in boyhood, Myron could have no friends.

It never came to the jolly Tom Weagle or to the affectionate Mother Weagle that they kept Myron so busy, every second when he was not in school or in bed, that he had no authentic boyhood whatever. They treated him handsomely, they felt. Didn't he have, with hotel fare instead of the normal boy's restricted home table, more than enough to eat? Didn't he have a new suit of clothes every single year? And whenever they asked him just to do some very tiny little extra task (which they did approximately fifty times a day), didn't they put it politely, with 'If you can get around to it and it isn't too much trouble'? And didn't he usually seem willing to do it?

Thus they would have argued if ever, by a miracle, Tom and Edna Weagle could have achieved the profundity of thinking in any way whatever about their method of rearing Myron. . . . They thought enough about rearing Ora, though. Ora saw to that, by constantly and heroically complaining over whatever he was asked to do, and energetically not doing it.

As he had no fast friends, so Myron had none of the contact with Nature which often compensates a village boy for provincial dullness and nastiness, for nowhere to go in the evening save the same promenade down main street to the same drug-store for the same choc'late or strawb'ry ice-cream soda, for the invariable family conversation at supper table, with dad's same mean little joke about the boy's laziness and huge appetite, for the same tight crankiness of teachers who are teaching only because they have not been able to get married.

With most village children, this is usually balanced by a consciousness of flowers, groves, birds, little valleys in summer haze, but Myron never had time for hours of inspired loafing on hillsides, and without these hours of letting the sound and colour of the world soak in there can be no knowledge of Nature. But if he did not have a lover's intimacy with Nature, he did love scenery. The two are not at all the same thing.

The authentic city-man, to whom all properly planned Nature is of cement evenly marked out in squares, may for half an hour be able to admire the alienage of a Vermont valley with woods sloping up to a stalwart peak, even though he may not be sure whether the trees are date-palms or monkey-puzzles, and whether the hazy mountain is built of reinforced concrete or merely green-painted brick. Ora could tell a vesper sparrow from a thrush much farther off than Myron, yet when Myron stood on the roof of the American House, he found exciting and refreshing the view of angling river and demure hills which completely bored the sun-god who desired to enthrone his solar divinity in a private gon*do*la.

Nor had he sports.

Over that, the high school wept. The baseball captain insisted that Myron was a natural pitcher. The football captain protested that Myron's chest and shoulders and a certain quickness of attack, as beheld in fights behind the schoolhouse, marked him as a tackle or half-back. Didn't he have any pride in his school? Wasn't he going to Do Anything for Good Old Black Thread? Was he so lazy and so unpatriotic that he would sit back and let Beulah H.S. lick Black Thread again this year?

Myron could not, he felt, explain that he was unable to get away from the hotel. That would be a criticism of his father and mother. He hedged and smiled and covered up, and with a poker face, as taught by J. Hector Warlock, he concealed his longing to be out on ringing autumn afternoons, practising with the team.

'I'll sure try to make it, but I'm kind of behind on that doggone Latin,' he lied amiably.

He was sixteen now. For a whole year, under J. Hector's spell, he had been a professional hotel-man, and he knew the loyalty of the guild.

If Myron lacked intimacy with arbutuses and squirrels, he had an intimacy with the much wandering, hard-headed hotel employees for which other boys envied him. Wise Uncle Jasper, the darky porter, cackled of the 1850's when, still a slave, he had swept the bar of the pavilion devoted to high-minded drinking at the Rockbridge Alum Springs, in Virginia, where the 'young gemmun' were exalted by the brandy crusta, the Louisiana sugar house punch, gin and tansy, and port wine negus. He told of driving General Grant when he had had a victoria at the stand of the Eutaw House in Baltimore, and Myron gloated. Some day *he* would have a hotel to which titans like General Grant would come, and he would know them!

'I trust this suite is to your Excellency's liking, General. Pray inform me, General, if there is any service which I can--may--may have the pleasure of rendering you, and it is my humble hope that your stay with us may be most agreeable, General. What, your signed portrait? Why, sir, that is a most thoughtful and highly appreciated favour, General. My very grandchildren will prize it.'

From Mrs. Hobby, the oldest of the waitress-chambermaids--she was a reduced lady, considerably reduced, and she liked being called the 'housekeeper'--Myron learned about repairing torn towels on the sewing machine, running across the tear over and over. Even from Imogene Heck, the frowsy and grease-scented wench who washed dishes and prepared the vegetables for Mother Weagle to cook, Myron learned kitchen tricks: cleaning copper with rock salt and vinegar, cleaning foggy water bottles with diced raw potatoes and boiling rancid oil with a potato to sweeten it. But it was Jock McCreedy, the bartender, who had most to teach Myron, and whose amiability made up to him for the loss of sun and wind and running laughter, for living most of his out-of-school hours in the queer, damp caverns of an inn.

No character in pre-Prohibition America, or in the few good 'American bars' in Europe since then, was quite so friendly with such a variety of people as the competent bartender. His court was the only authentic democracy America has ever known. The confidant of travelling princes and admirals, of thirsty authors and scientists, of apprentice drummers and of anxious insurance salesmen who wanted to know the rich men in town, of tired surgeons and swivel-eyed newspapermen, of crooks and yeggs and pan-handlers, of pompous merchants and mufti-cloaked clergymen from distant towns, the bartender was privileged, or gloomily fated, to know them better than did their own brothers, as the magic of alcohol opened their wicked hearts and made them say what they really thought to the one confessor near at hand. He listened to their dirty stories. It was a slow day when he didn't hear the Latest One at least seven times over. And he cured their morning shakiness. He heard out their troubles with their wives, and gave sage advice--the advice was never taken, but it did comfort afflicted husbands to find someone who was willing to listen to their troubles without sneaking away. He lent them money and sometimes got it back. He knew the best churches, the best fishing-tackle shops, and the best prostitutes in town. Better even than a veteran hotel clerk he could divine from the set of a stranger's lapels whether he would pay his bills, beat his wife, cheat at poker, and appreciate real French cognac.

No one, not even a gigolo or a popular pastor, was required to practise the art of universal conversation so masterfully as a high-ranking bartender. If he could not discuss the mechanics of hydro-electric plants, the probabilities of the English being the lost tribes of Israel, the value of sewing-machine oil in cases of ear-ache among juveniles aged 3-7, the styles of Bulwer Lytton or of this new author, Richard Harding Davis, the amount that should be paid for a blue suit with extra pants, the comparative values of pointers and setters in quail-hunting, the record of Maud S., and the merits of Predestination as a dogma, then was he lost and disgraced, and no mastery of mixing a Blue Blazer would excuse his lack of intellectual supremacy.

And it was a lord among bartenders who trained Myron in the social graces as he crept from sixteen to seventeen and eighteen and to graduation from high school.

The scene was agreeable, especially on an August afternoon when outside the pavement was aching with heat. The cool bar-room, smelling of beer, of acrid whisky, of water sprinkled on sawdust; the pyramids of glasses and the nude which Ora admired; companionable men playing casino, humming 'Down Went McGinty'; and Jock McCreedy and Myron, in superbly clean and starched white jackets, ready for the late-afternoon rush.

As a stranger came in, Jock muttered, 'Watch him--get the money--don't like his eyes.' But when it was a familiar dead-beat, Jock did not leave him to Myron's youthful sentiment but tackled the monster himself, crooning sweetly as any mother over a cradle, 'Lil drink, Pete? First, how about something on account, old man? Tom Weagle told me this morning that he'd just about fire me if I didn't collect from you. We got to pay the rent. How about five dollars?' And when one of the village potentates, a strong church and temperance man who never drank anything but liquor, came hastily in and muttered, 'Little hooch--got a bad cold', Jock served him with the manner of an acolyte before the altar.

They were great days! Myron began to feel that he knew his job--kitchen and linen-room and bedrooms, front office and dining-room and bar. He felt the virility of competence. He was ready for his graduate school and learned degrees in the science of hotel-keeping.

The moment he finished school, he announced to the family that he was going to Torrington, to seek a job in the magnificent Eagle Hotel, with its seventy rooms and, since it was near the depot, its awe-inspiring restaurant business from railroad passengers.

His mother wept, with her old apron over her eyes. How could she carry on without him? He would probably not have gone, never in many years have left Black Thread, had not old Tom Weagle masterfully rushed in with, 'Sure! That's always the way! After all the years I've brought you up and done for you, now you try to sneak away just when you're getting so you might be a little bit of use to your mother and me! I've boarded you and fed you and taught you manners and given you fifty cents a week spending money, just to throw away, and by God, this is the thanks I get for it! No, you shut up, mother. Time for me to take a hand and tell this thankless young serpent's tooth just what kind of a--what kind of a serpent's tooth he is, by God!'

Myron walked the fifteen miles to Torrington, carrying his suitcase. The first five miles he wept over the image of his mother. The second five miles he was exuberant with adventure and freedom. It was the first time since they had left the farm, when he was seven years old, that he had had time to go off and be his own man on his own road. The last five miles he was much too hand-sore to think about anything else whatever--even the fact that he was going to be welcomed with cheers by the Eagle Hotel, and immediately become a hotel manager, famed country-wide.

He slept in a haystack a mile from Torrington.

He could only gape, his heart cold, next morning, when Mr. Coram, manager of the Eagle, a slim, professorial man with eye-glasses, told him that there was no place for him. He nearly starved, though not once did he consider going back to Black Thread, during the ten days before he got a temporary summer job as bell-boy in that most disreputable resort hotel, the Fandango Inn, at Buttermilk Springs.

7

He shared, with the other three bell-boys at the Fandango Inn, a small room slashed by the slope of the roof almost into a pentahedron. The only ventilation was from windows two feet high, down on the floor, under the roof-slope. This carpetless, paperless room was frequented by bedbugs, and the beds were hard canvas cots without sheets, and nothing can be harder, after six hours' sleep (which was about what Myron got, nightly) than tight-stretched canvas. It was rather like a prison cell, but probably not so interesting. Myron had been more comfortable in the littered 'single room' he had shared with Ora at the American House; he had even been more comfortable on rush nights, when travelling-men were sleeping on billiard tables, on dining-room tables, and on cots set out in the hall, and Ora and he had bunked on blankets in the airy kitchen.

His uniform was another distress; it was very tight, it had such crampingly tight trousers, and there was a confounded row of little brass buttons to do up and keep done up. In it he felt like a grind-organ monkey, though when he presented this thought to his fellow bell-boys, they assured him that he didn't look so--he merely looked like a gorilla.

And he was badly paid and worse tipped.

But it was the toughness, the boisterousness, the shadiness of the guests at the Fandango that most worried the innocence of Myron, fresh from his mother's housewifely inn-keeping. Bad eggs had come to the American House; Myron and Jock McCreedy had dragged a homicidal drunk to bed and locked him in; but for the most part the travelling-salesmen and farmers and widows and itinerant oculists who had been their guests were glad to get wearily to bed at ten.

The guests of the Fandango had all the vices of Monte Carlo, done in oilcloth instead of in velvet. They were the 'cheap skates', the 'tinhorn sports', the 'two-bit spendthrifts' whom in secret confidences hotel-men bewail along with taxes, leaky coffee percolators, devils who cut new towels while wiping razor blades, ash-tray stealers, skippers, passers of rubber checks, loose carpet edges in dark halls, and the other major tragedies of their profession. The Fandango guests left Torrington and Hartford and Waterbury and New Britain as humble clerks or shop-keepers; they arrived at the hotel as two-weeks gentlemen, as millionaires who by God were used to Service by God and were going to by God have it or know the reason why; and they simply threw away money--on everything but laundry and tips.

The goodwife who for years had sat down contentedly at home to a supper of creamed chipped beef, johnny cake, cocoa, and apple sauce now expanded her proud, jet-glittering bosom in hauteur as she viewed a menu with bisque of lobster, brook trout, sweetbreads, roast duck, curaçoa sherbet, glace panacheé, and thirty other items, and wailed, 'Is *this* all they got for supper?'

How they ate! How they drank! And how, and how badly, they sang of a moonlit evening, like hound-dogs howling down the moon. Half an hour before meal-times, even though for the men-folks it meant leaving the delights of the bar-room thirty minutes early, the whole corps of guests planted their rocking-chairs as near as they could get to the dining-room entrance, and the second the double doors were slid open by the stately negro head waiter, they made a cavalry charge, while the head waiter, visibly paling, leaped away to save his life.

Fat men ate and re-ordered and ate three helpings of steak, two helpings of salmon, three kinds of pie. Fat men ate and drank and panted, and all day long, between meals, delicately rested their tender and uneasy bellies against the bar rail, while they tried the interesting effect of lacing rum punch with gin and maraschino. Lean men stalked ladies along the immense porch and crept into rockers beside them and cleared their throats and began, 'Hm. Nice day. Been here long, Madame?'

Almost every night, Myron and the other bell-boys and the porters had to remove some lean man from the bedroom of a more or less indignant lady, while the lean man explained alcoholically that he had mistaken this for his own room, and that the Fandango had gone to hell and he would be leaving in the morning. And lean men and fat men and indescribable between-men played poker all night long, noisily, quarrelsomely, not with the deft, swift quiet of J. Hector Warlock.

The Fandango Inn had unusual facilities for sport--for 1898. There were four croquet grounds and a tennis court. There were saddle-horses and, not very far away, through not very much of a thicket, a small lake where one could swim if one liked that sort of thing. It was rumoured that in North Buttermilk, only a few miles distant, one could even play this new-fangled game, golf. But none of the Fandango's guests over the age of eighteen wasted their hours in sport. They ate. They drank. They rocked. They dozed, and waked to eat again. They made the resplendent night loud with the smack of wide dripping kisses, and before they went to bed, they had light snacks of ham, tongue, corned beef, and fish salad at the bar.

The manager of the Fandango, a smooth-spoken person with oily black hair, who never glanced at you when he talked, rubbed his hands and looked content, and when there was a perfect devil of a shindy in some bedroom after midnight, over a euchre game or an affair of gallantry, this manager walked the other way and said softly to the bellboys, 'Mind your own business. What you don't hear won't ever make you deaf!'

And once, when the manager was behind the desk and a lady and gentleman, with no baggage other than a bottle of bourbon in a paper bag, registered 'President McKinley and grandmother,' he simpered and gave them a room. He left it to the bell-boys and porters to hush illuminated guests when other rooms complained too much; if they didn't quiet the rioters, he threatened to fire the boys; if they did quiet them, and the rioters themselves complained, he fined the boys a day's salary, and beamed, and went into the bar and had a drink on the money thus saved.

But that summer Myron learned, or so he believed, how to handle any sort of objectionable guest short of a maniac with a meat-axe.

The bell-boys had one way of revenge for underpayment and over-work. Drinks of rye served in a bedroom, as frequently they were, over card-games, cost twenty cents a drink; and a dollar bottle of rye furnished from ten to twelve drinks--and late at night, fifteen. The oldest bellboy invented an interesting device of buying a new bottle at the bar and paying for it, on pretence that it was for a guest, then hiding it in an empty room and from it serving the separate drinks in the bedrooms, at a profit of one to two dollars. He generously gave the idea to his colleagues; two of them adopted it, with cheers, but Myron balked.

'It's grafting,' he complained.

'Sure it is. Don't they graft on us? The way they pay us--telling us when we signed on what a whale of a lot of tips we'd get, and then about one lone dime a day from these cheap pikers! And the room and grub we get! Anything we can hold out on this joint belongs to us,' explained the senior bell-boy, who got fifty cents a week extra, and the title of Captain free.

'I know--I know--but it's bad practice. If we don't like it here, we ought to get out.'

'F' Christ's sake, Weagle, do *you* like it here?'

'Well, you can learn a lot.'

'The hell with that! I've done my learning. Say, I went clear through eighth grade and had prett' near a whole year in high school! I've done my learning! So you won't come in with us! Getting religious on us, are you? Our little Y.M.C.A. secretary! Our cute Sunday-school teacher!'

The senior bell-boy meant by 'religious' something like 'moral', Myron decided. Naturally, at eighteen, there is no accusation so grievous as that of morality and general priggishness. Myron didn't want to be anything like that. He didn't want to be moral. He spoke very evilly of morality to the senior bell-boy. He asserted that he was a practising hellion; probably about the worst young fellow that the senior bell-boy had ever met. He hinted that he drank like a cart-horse and was a menace to all women. But he could not graft on the job.

Even to himself he could not explain it. The word 'loyalty' was not yet in his vocabulary--which was, perhaps, just as well, for within a couple of decades 'loyalty' was to be altogether too much in the vocabularies of all luncheon-club inspiration-merchants. It was just . . .

'Oh, thunder!' he writhed, trying to get it straight. 'I'd of been sore if I'd caught Jock McCreedy knocking down even ten cents on us at the American House. Even if he did think we gave him a raw deal--which I bet Pa did, sometimes! I guess I'm a fool not to do the Romans like the Romans do. But I'll be everlastingly doggone hornswoggled if I'll get ahead by dirty little grafts, even if I never do get to the top. . . . But I will!'

When he returned to Torrington, in September, Myron again stalked into the Eagle Hotel and asked the manager for a job.

Mr. Coram demanded, 'Aren't you the young chap that was here early this summer?'

'Yes, sir.'

'Do you propose to keep on coming around here bothering me till I do give you a job?'

'Yes, sir.'

'What can you do around an hotel?'

'Everything, sir.'

'No. Oh, no. There's only one man in any hotel that can do everything, front office or back of the house, and that's the manager. At least, that's the theory. And unfortunately, son, the manager's job here seems to be taken. So I'm afraid there's nothing for you. Besides. Why don't you start some easy career, while you're young, instead of taking up hotel-keeping, which means having to stand for all the meanest cranks just when they're away from home and at their meanest? You seem a wide-awake young fellow. Take up something comparatively easy--say deep-sea diving or Arctic exploration. Sorry there's not a thing for you. *Good morning!*'

'Yes, sir.'

Myron lived luxuriously on his summer's savings, $18.65, with lovely long hours of sleep, for the two and a half weeks before he found the job of assistant night cook at the Bijou Lunch-Wagon--Never Closes, in Torrington.

Being eighteen, he found working all night at the lunch-wagon exciting. He felt like a man grown, to stay up through the forbidden hours. There was mystery in the shadowed alleys, the still street lamps, the huddled hurrying figures of strangers by night, and dawn was freshest and most grateful when it came after a trance not of snoozing but of back-break over a low gas-range, in the fumes of frying. His customers had a leisure unknown in the busy day, and they were odd people, phantoms of the night--the two town policemen, the Eagle Hotel 'bus-driver who had been a sailor, stray hoboes with a precious dime, and furtive travellers.

He learned nothing much here save to be cheery when his eyes were gummed with smoke and sleepiness, and the craft of lightning cookery-- cracking open an egg and frying it in, apparently, ten seconds after the order had been given.

There was much drawling gossip at the Bijou. One night in January the Eagle 'bus-driver confided that the meat-cook at the Eagle was 'getting through', because he had a better job in Hartford.

That morning, at nine, after an hour and a half of sleep, Myron was in the office of Mr. Coram.

'Oh, Lord, I suppose I'll have to give you the job to get rid of you. But can you do it?'

'Yes, sir. Been cooking at the Bijou Lunch-Wagon since September.'

'That's not roasting and boiling. Lunch-wagon! Huh! Short orders! Ham and eggs! Hamburger steak! Fried spuds on the side and make it snappy! Lunch-wagon! This is an *hotel,* young man.' Mr. Coram spoke proudly. He was forty-two years old, and he had worked in hotels for thirty-one.

'Done lots of roasting and boiling and so on, sir. American House, Black Thread. Mother's cook there. Helped her on everything.'

'Well, all right, I suppose I'll have to try you, so you'll get it out of your system and have the sense to go back home. I'll start you at thirty a month, and board and laundry. You'll have to hire your own room. When can you come?'

'Week from to-morrow, sir--week's notice at the lunch-wagon.'

'All right. Be here at 6.45 in the morning. By the way: of course you have your own white jackets and aprons and cap and light overalls? And your own knives and cleavers?'

'Certainly, sir.'

That was the only lie of our young moralist, and it was no longer a lie when he reported for work. He had spent every penny he had saved, along with five dollars borrowed from his mother, for his kit.

All the first morning he was in a panic. They'd find him out--he was merely a brat who knew nothing about cooking. He was quiveringly polite and anxious when he met the head cook (rarely called 'chef' except by himself), who was a dried codfish from New Hampshire, named Clint Hosea.

By noon he perceived that though the Eagle Hotel kitchen was twice as large as that of the American House, and served three or four times as many people, the food was of about the same dreariness, and no more than Mother Weagle did Clint Hosea ever do anything so revolutionary as to study a cook-book. Neither of them had tried any new dish these ten years. By night Myron was confident, and rejoicing in the fact that, though he was not exactly over them, the kitchen maid who peeled vegetables and cleaned floors, the proud lady dishwasher, and the waitresses all received less wages than he.

For two years, Myron worked for the Eagle Hotel, and several times Mr. Coram gave him a two-for cigar, and once a slight rise in wages.

He had learned the carving of cooked meat from his father. His difficulty was cutting up the raw material, for he was butcher as well as meat-cook. But he had the originality to study the diagrams for dissecting unfortunate beasts, as given in any cook-book, and evenings he gave voluntary help at a butcher shop with whose proprietor he had been friendly at the Bijou Lunch.

EAGLE HOTEL
TORRINGTON, CONN.

DINNER

SOUP

Oyster Stew   Cream of Tomato with Sippets

-o-

FISH

Fried Pike with Chow Chow

-o-

BOILED

Mutton   Corn Beef and Cabbage

-o-

ROAST

Prime Ribs of Beef   Fowl

-o-

ENTREES

Pot Roast   Pork Chop   Beefsteak with Sauce Tartar
Banana Fritters with Wine Sauce
Fried Cornmeal Mush with Maple Syrup

-o-

VEGETABLES

Peas in Milk   Baked Beans with Brown Bread
Succotash
Plain Potatoes   Mashed Potatoes   Scalloped Potatoes

-o-

DESSERT

Mince Pie   Apple Pie   Rice Pudding   Apple Sauce
Stewed Apricots   Canned Peaches
White Bread   Graham Bread   Corn Muffins
Parker House Rolls
Tea   Coffee   Milk

-o-

HOURS FOR MEALS

Breakfast 6.30 to 9   Dinner 12.30 to 2.30
Supper 5.30 to 7.30

Dishes ordered not on this Bill will be charged extra

March 12, 1899

Neither the Weagles, Clint Hosea, nor any of the three bell-boys with whom Myron had worked at the Fandango Inn knew that there were such things in the world as hotel periodicals. Mr. Coram subscribed to the weekly *Hotel Era,* but he rarely read any of it save the gossip that Jack Barley, 'the well-known and ever-popular chief clerk of the Memphis-Corona, has accepted a corresponding position in that ever-popular establishment, the Tartley, of Chicago, and his many friends and well-wishers all over the south are wishing him every success in his new position and predicting for him an ever enlarging career as a Boniface', and that 'M. Wilson Stewkey, Mine Host of the Hoamfrumhoam Villa, in bustling and beautiful Jax, Fla., is planning an extensive three-weeks' tour of the West Indies with his missus. Bum voyadj, as the Frogs say, Bill.' (This was almost a generation before hotel trade-journals became less jolly and along with personals featured such articles as a treatise on 'The Norm in Kilowatt Production in Independent Hotel Plants', which could be readily understood by any manager with authoritative knowledge of graphs, differential calculus, thermo-dynamics, and electrical engineering.)

Myron saw the *Era* in Mr. Coram's office, and he was excited. That was a fine idea! A publication all about hotel-keeping, from which he could become acquainted with managers and chefs and stewards all over the country, from which he could learn about new recipes and kitchen-ranges and material for sheets, about silver-polishing machines and bottle-openers and linoleum for floors. He subscribed for the *Hotel Era* with the money he had been saving for new shoes--a bold and doubtful piece of adventure, since kitchen work is even harder on the feet than store-clerking or being a colonel of infantry or any like proletarian occupation.

In the *Era* he found an advertisement of a book called *The Steward's Handbook and Dictionary,* by Jessup Whitehead, and rather doubtfully he sent for it. The book had first been published in 1887; in 1899, when Myron discovered it, it was still an authority, and well into a twentieth century that was to be anaemic with 'scientific diets' the handbook carried rich savours from a time when citizens, not yet being much afflicted by time-saving machinery, considered time not as something just to be fanatically saved, but to be devoted to eating, hymn-singing, and laughter. Beside it, the contemporary manuals of the 1930's on the preparation of canned clam juice and sandwiches of cream cheese and walnuts look pallid and vomitable.

So Myron found his Book of Words.

Whitehead was to him what an anthology of Shelley, Milton, Chaucer, Byron, Swinburne, and the lyrics of Lewis Carroll would have been to a young poet who, reared in the sticks, had never seen any verse save Longfellow and Bryant. Opening it, Myron felt like some watcher of the skies when a new planet swims into his ken, like a scientist with his first microscope, a youthful capitalist with his first dollar. Whitehead revealed to him all the succulences of eating, the perfections of service, the elegancies of table-decoration which he had, without ever seeing them, vaguely known must exist.

Not for himself did Myron Weagle desire these juicy dishes, these tables fantastic with glass and silver. All his life, though he was, as a scientist, curious to taste new dishes, for his own daily fare he preferred toast and cold chicken and a glass of milk, eaten on a corner of a kitchen table, in a surrounding of busy cookery. But he had the instinct to provide them for other people. Why he should have had that instinct, why he should want to provide too-rich food for too-rich people, is as much a mystery as why other, more verbal poets, should actually desire to provide rich and smoking sonnets for unknown readers.

For many months Myron read Whitehead every evening in his narrow, straw-matted furnished room, and every luxurious half hour of loafing between crises of bending over reeking broilers and stew-pans. He saw and seized the world not only of Waldorfs and Tremonts and St. Charleses, but of hotels in London and Paris and Berlin as well. He was as fascinated by it as any newly rich guest first staying in a Grand International Royal Hotel, with the difference that Myron, unlike the parvenu, knew that gorgeous tables are not entirely evolved in the brains of affable super-gents in morning clothes, equipped with gardenias, in the panelled Front Office, but by sweaty cooks in overalls, an agitated steward in shirt-sleeves, and a panting crew of helpers in that hidden, humble, greasy, all-important mass of dens, the Back of the House.

The handbook quoted the menu of an Italian dinner given to Sr. Salvini. What more swagger language could there be, yearned Myron, than 'Animelle di Vitello alla Minuta con Tartuffi' or 'Ravioli al Brodo' or 'Zabbaglione'? He had no notion what they meant, but weren't they simply lovely words?

Later, when he learned from the handbook's dictionary of dishes that they were only veal and paste and beaten eggs and wine, he was yet not disappointed. Mighty nice things, he reflected, you could do with eggs and paste and veal; grand noble dishes to rejoice the stomach of mankind and make a hotel famous.

There were other literary novelties in the steward's handbook. The menu of a dinner given by an association of travelling-men in New York was 'written in imitation of a railroad ticket, with coupon attachments, to be read from bottom to top', and it displayed with each course quotations from the choicest poets. With the chicken and terrapin there was somewhat cryptically quoted, 'This lapwing runs away with the shell on her head', and with the liqueurs, 'Spirits, which by mine art I have from their confines call'd to enact my present fancies'.

A Pink Dinner, in Washington, had fairy lamps with pink shades, cheese sticks tied with pink ribbons, and 'menus printed on broad pink satin ribbon, fringed at either end, and bearing at the top the name of the guest for whom it was intended'.

This thirty-dollar-a-month meat-cook, aged nineteen, was exhilarated by reading about 'a tropical dinner given by a wealthy man, which cost $175.00 a cover, exclusive of wine and music. The table was arranged around a miniature lake, in which palms, lilies and ferns appeared to be growing, while tropical trees rose from the banks amid miniature parterres of flowers. Small electric lights, with varicoloured globes, were arranged about the lake, and by a unique arrangement electricity was introduced under the water of the lake and caused to dance about in imitation of varicoloured fish. A beautiful palm-leaf fan was placed on the table before each guest, and on these the plates rested.'

'Golly, it would be nice to have a chance to fix a spread like that, without having to worry about the amount of butter you used,' thought Myron.

If he felt envy or any irritation at this superb example of Conspicuous Waste, he did not know it.

Still more enticing to the folly of the young poet were the decorated dishes at the renowned reception given by the first ducal Mrs. Vanderbilt: '. . . a game pie of pheasants resting on a flat surface of wax, the entire piece upheld with deer's antlers. Underneath were two rabbits playing cards, while to the side of the players was a bridge, under which gleamed a lake of water with goldfish swimming about. One of the most artistic pieces was a two-foot salmon, resting in a wax boat, while on the back of the fish sat a cupid; the boat was supported by a Neptune at each end, seated in sea shells and driving sea horses before them. A fine piece was a flying Mercury poised upon a ham, finely ornamented with a delicate tracing of truffles.'

'Gosh almighty!' breathed Myron.

And menus presenting ortolans!

He was not quite sure what sort of a bird an ortolan was, but it sounded far-off and romantic. When he read in the dictionary of the handbook a quotation from some casual European chef to the effect that 'ortolans should not be killed with violence, like other birds, as this might crush and bruise the delicate flesh--to avoid which the usual mode is to plunge the head of the ortolan into a glass of brandy', then he felt sick.

It came to him, as he sat tilted back against the bed in a hard straight chair in his little bedroom, that all the animals and birds he cooked had to be slaughtered, bloodily, messily, cruelly; that the veal which some red-faced, grunting guest slobbered over came from a soft-eyed calf that had come frisking up to the butcher and had its head instantly crushed with a sledge hammer.

He forgot it, then, as the medical student forgets the dissecting-room with its cold hacked corpses, as all young and ambitious men forget--for else they could not endure living--the perpetual horror and cruelty of the world.

Myron had read in his handbook for many weeks before he dared to criticize it . . . the young poet had long read his Milton before it came to him to wonder whether there may not be some thumpingly dull passages in *Paradise Lost*. In his Book of Words Myron found the menu of an annual game dinner given by Mr. John B. Drake, once the dean of Chicago hotel-men, to the dignitaries of the city.

There were one hundred and fourteen items, including (for this must have been given back in the '80's, when such frenzied novelties still existed) ham of black bear, leg of mountain sheep, buffalo tongue, saddle of antelope, opossum, woodchuck, wild turkey, killdeer, plover, Wilson snipe, sandhill crane, Gadwall and canvas-back and red-bill Merganser ducks, American widgeon, red-necked grebe, Dunlin sandpiper, red-winged starling, and scores of equally fantastic prey. For the first three or four readings, he was awed. The poet was privileged to peep through glass at a volume of sonnets, printed in gold on blue-dyed vellum and bound in scarlet silk--and suddenly his common sense flashed out and he wanted it bound in morocco and printed in honest black on decent white!

'This darn bill of fare is a darn sight too darn long!' he protested, feeling reckless. 'Too darn much is bad as not enough. Take a fellow, say he has ten dishes out of all this; still he'll see all these others that he didn't get, and be sore, and feel he just hasn't had anything. When I own an hotel, I'm going to keep the bill of fare small and everything awful good!'

With a pencil he cut fifty-two items out of the hundred and fourteen.

'And still it's too big,' he sighed. 'But anyway, I've saved some money for Mr. Drake and not hurt his party! Hope he remembers it on my steward's salary! . . . I wonder what the deuce American widgeon is? I wonder if I'll ever taste it? I'm going to taste an awful lot of curious new things, in a lot of curious new places, before I get through!'

The appendix to Whitehead's handbook was a section entitled 'How to Fold Napkins, with Many Handsome Styles and Diagrams Which Show How It is Done'. At that period, the great restaurants and hotel dining-rooms were prouder of nothing than of tortuously twisted napkins, stiff and white and tall, in files on the long tables, and in this appendix were revealed the secrets of the greatest conjurors in napkin-folding. There was the 'chestnut pocket', making four pockets to be stuffed with nuts; the 'mitre' with its centre and horns; the 'double horn of plenty', whose folds were to be filled with flowers, the 'bridal serviette', which looked like a model of a four-story decagonal building, and such spirited modelling in stiff linen as 'the heraldic rose and star', 'the fleur-de-lis', and 'the colonne de triomphe'.

They seemed, after the simple cocked hats which decorated the American House and the Eagle Hotel, like the masterpieces of a napkinate Michael Angelo. Myron gaped at the sketches of their frosty beauty. And here was something he could do with his fingers, forthwith.

It was difficult to start cooking Filet Mignapour aux Truffes et aux Champignons with the resources of the Eagle Hotel kitchen, but napkins were napkins, and filching half a dozen of the Sunday Dinner best ones from the pantry, Myron began trying to erect a 'Hamburg drum'. It is quite simple, if you know how. 'Fold the serviette in half lengthways. Turn down the corners, fold it in half across the centre, inwards, from A to B, keeping the corners inside. Fold it again from C to D, let down the point E, turn down the corners F and G to make a triangle. . . .'

Perfectly straightforward and simple. Yet Myron sweated over it for quarter-hours, till his chair was surrounded by piles of crumpled napkins and the head waiter came in to stare, bellow, and complain, 'What in hell are you doing with my clean napkins, you damn pot-walloper?'

After that, Myron tried it at home, with stiff paper as a substitute for linen . . . a tall, rangy young man, with rope-coloured hair, sitting in a stale furnished room with his small chair drawn up to the bed, patiently folding paper for hours, solemnly, with the tip of his tongue in the corner of his mouth. In a fortnight he could do even such intricate jewel-work as 'the Victoria Regia', 'Mercury's cap', 'the swan', and 'the lorgnettes', and felt himself prepared to meet any dining-room crisis.

For did not Whitehead himself say, 'Hotel napkin folding--an art worth more than foreign languages. There is nothing a waiter can do, if a stranger in a strange place, that will so quickly give him introductions and acquaintances as to take a dozen sheets of stiff white paper and with them execute the finer patterns shown in this book and set them up for display. They attract attention at once and prove better than a letter of introduction for a young man seeking employment, and fortunately, this useful art is far easier to learn than a foreign language.'

Myron saw himself studying the innkeeper's art all over the world, able to get instant and agreeable employment in Egypt, China, Finland, or Wales by setting up for display his sculptures in linen or stiff white paper. He'd do it. And by and by . . .

Suppose, he reflected, he were a waiter in Claridge's in London, and the head waiter dashed into the pantry just before a banquet to Royalty, clapping his hands to his brow and moaning, 'Who amongst you, my waiters, can fold an "Imperial crown"?'

The other waiters would flinch and stand dumb, while Myron Weagle, from distant America, would step forward and say modestly, 'I can, sir.' And next day he would be made a captain of waiters, on his way to becoming steward.

Myron was getting into exalted society. He read in the handbook that the Earl Cadogan (hm! that was a slicker name for a lord than any he had encountered in the few novels he had read) had given a dinner at Chelsea House to forty-eight, including the Kings of Denmark, Greece, and Belgium, the Crown Princes of Sweden, Austria, and Portugal, the Prince and Princess of Wales.

In waking dreams Myron saw that feast. What would kings be like in private life? Did they wear dress suits, or uniforms plastered all over with gold lace and medals? The King of Greece, now; Myron was sure he had a half-moon of black moustache, the Crown Prince of Portugal had black whiskers.

The waiters were leaning over them, reverentially murmuring, 'Sure, Your Majesty, I'll hustle in another side order of peas right away'. And perhaps Claridge's had lent that clever captain of waiters, Myron Weagle, the American, to the Earl Cadogan for his dinner, and Weagle was standing quietly but authoritatively back by the big--buffet, would it be? and was Chelsea House a private home or a London hotel?--but anyway: he stood back there quietly, but his eagle eye never missed a single miscue of the waiters, and afterwards, when they were smoking fifty-cent cigars and drinking big goblets of brandy, one of the kings said to Earl Cadogan (that *was* his title and not his first name, wasn't it?)--he said, 'Earl, I want to congratulate you on that dandy head waiter you had here to-night. He knows service like I know my throne. Never missed a trick. Don't suppose I could get him for my palace, do you? I'd make him a Sir, and give him a swell house of his own.'

And during the dinner a princess had whispered to her neighbour, 'Who *is* that tall, handsome man with the blond hair standing back there by the sideboard? Isn't he one of the guests? Why don't he sit down with us?'

Myron studied the dinner which (according to Whitehead) he had caused to be served for the Earl Cadogan. It included Whitebait, Cotelettes d'Agneau Duchesse, Chaudfroid de Cailles aux Truffes, Poulardes aux Pruneaux, Filets Piqués froids Sauce Cumberland, Ortolans sur Canapes, Bavaroise à la Montreuil, Soufflés de Fraises, Croustades aux Fromages.

It was not a mere list of things to guzzle. It was the Catalogue of Ships. It was the recitative of names that were fourteen sweet symphonies. It was, to Myron Weagle, poetry with Sauce Cumberland.

'Not much like cornbeef and cabbage and fried pork chop and apple sauce,' he sighed, and, 'I wonder if they had any of the chow resting in wax boats with cupids on it?' and then, violently, 'American widgeon me eye!'

Along with the wax cupid nonsense and menus on pink ribbon, he stored away solid notions from Whitehead, Ranhofer of Delmonico's, Monselet, Brillat-Savarin, and from hotel magazines. These he clipped and rustled and sputtered over with the air of an earnest beaver. He knew at least the names and ingredients of a thousand dishes.

But it had, like all other poetic frenzies, the disadvantage of alarming more prosaic souls. When he prepared an experimental dish of mutton cutlets and brought it proudly to Clint Hosea, boasting, 'Taste this. I think it would be swell to serve. It's with Sauce Béarnaise! I made it!' the sardonic Yankee cook piped, 'It's with what?'

'Sauce Béarnaise.'

'And will you tell me what the hell Sauce Bernice may be?'

'Oh, there's white wine vinegar, and young onions--couldn't get shallots--and beef extract and egg yolks and herbs. . . .'

'Take it away. Taste it, hell! Want to poison me?'

'Well, could I make it with some Sauce Duchesse then, and just try it once and see if the guests like it?'

'You could not! We don't want any Bernice sauce or any Dutch sauce or any other kind of crazy Dago sauce! You put some decent brown gravy on it, like any other cook ought to, and get out of this and don't bother me. You know what I think? What's the matter with you? *You been reading books!'*

8

During his first year at the Eagle Hotel, Myron slowly built up his plan of preparing himself for managership. He would try out every job in the establishment, and be intimate with every member of the staff. It was not too easy. There are more castes in an hotel than in India, and no Gandhi to starve himself. The Front Office looked down on the Back of the House as scullions, and the Back of the House observed frequently and publicly that the young men in the Front Office wore ragged underclothes beneath their natty gents' suitings.

Myron saw to it that when he met one of the bell-boys or the majestic clerks, at a soda-fountain or a pool-room or anywhere in the looser and more adventurous atmosphere outside the hotel, he should be polite but friendly. He feigned respect for their Front Office opinions of guests and of psychology in general which, after years in the American House and the Fandango Inn, he certainly did not feel. He was even attentive to the Eagle night-clerk, a notorious crab who, the Back of the House believed and stated, would never have been able to hold his job unless he 'had something on' Mr. Coram.

The night-clerk was one of the jacks in office, common in the hotel-world before 1915 but demoted to the poor-house in the days of competition since then, who were proud of 'never taking nothing from no "fresh" guests'. They have been replaced by the 'Greeter', who chants thirty times a day the first Beatitude of American hotel-keeping: 'Blessed is the Guest, for he is always right'. None of the Greeters, of course, are such idiots as to believe it.

The Eagle night-clerk boasted, as he sat in one of the tall thrones along the wall of the pool-room, that whenever any 'damn tightwad crank of a guest that's trying to let on what an important gazebo he is' complained about anything whatever--missing baggage or sour coffee, an unmade bed or a room without soap or the fact that he had not been called at seven, as promised--he 'just looked the guy straight in the face and told him, "Well, I'll tell you, brother. Of course you're used to chumming around with the Astors and Vanderbilts and having a vallay to look after you, but this is just a rube hotel for common folks like me, and I guess you'll have to put up with our hick ways till you can get back to your suite at the Hoffman House!" Say! Maybe those fourflushers don't look cheap when they meet a real *man* behind the desk, and he's got the nerve and the savvy to show 'em up!'

To him Myron listened with peculiar attention. He was more useful to Myron than Whitehead's handbook; he so perfectly explained what not to do.

It was not a large Front Office: Mr. Coram, who was chief clerk as well as manager, two other day-clerks, of whom one was also book-keeper and cashier and attendant on the cigar-counter, the night-clerk, a porter who cleaned the floors, two bell-boys, and three bartenders. But Myron studied them, found as many exciting and curious quirks in their ways of meeting guests and kitchen-hands as though they were an entire regiment. He was Jane Austen in a tavern.

Clint Hosea, the cook, particularly scorned the Front Office, including Mr. Coram. They were, he said, a bunch of cheap dudes whose mothers were all washerwomen or members of even less honoured professions. He composed dreadful scandals about them, cackling, as he shoved a dish of baking apples into the oven, that the 'grouch of a night-clerk had been thrown out of a bedroom at midnight, turned right out, bang! on his ear, by the little grass-widow up in 57'; that it was he, Mr. Hosea, and not Mr. Coram, who made up the bills of fare every day; that Myron was sucking around that gang of softies because he hoped to be invited to Mr. Coram's suite and steal his whisky; and that, as a consequence of his social climbing, Myron didn't know corn-beef from roast duckling.

But Myron persisted.

By coming to the kitchen at five-thirty in the morning--though he had a thirteen-hour trick of his own, from 6.45 a.m. to 7.45 p.m., with an hour's loaf in mid-afternoon--he was able by helping the baker-pastry-cook to learn bread, rolls, and cakes, even vast ornamental cakes in the elegant forms of ships and castles.

He cultivated the supercilious head waiter, who daily informed the world that he had worked in no less a city than Pittsburgh. He learned from the head waiter and from the older waitresses all the subtle and ancient technique of waiting: the setting of a table, from which side to serve, the proprieties of dress jackets and aprons, remembering six orders at once, polishing silverware, washing salt-cellars, moulding butter and all the other details of 'side work', tactfully keeping cranks out of the seats preferred by regular boarders, with what dishes to serve mustard, how to open champagne, and, more weighty, how to open boiled eggs, and, profoundest of all, how to smile so flatteringly upon mean customers that they would leave a respectable tip. (Such is the low custom of waiters, showing them to be as menial as physicians flattering their patients, lawyers flattering their clients, authors flattering editors, announcers flattering the vast radio audience, merchants flattering the good taste of their customers, college-presidents flattering the board of regents, senators flattering everybody--all of them making certain of their tips.)

Initiated into this wisdom, Myron tried to get taken on as temporary waiter for evening banquets. It was difficult. Everyone, even the alert Mr. Coram, was astonished by such eccentricity, and Clint Hosea, that baked-bean philosopher, heir to Emerson and Jonathan Edwards, remarked, 'What I always say is, a cook is a cook and a waiter is a waiter, and there ain't no two ways about it!'

But in an emergency or two, at a wedding reception and at the dinner of the Northern Connecticut Izaak Walton and Annual Re-stocking Association, Myron was permitted to try his hand. The head waiter was exasperated to discover that Myron had already bought a waiter's uniform for himself, and that there was nothing else for which he could rebuke this presumptuous scullion who had come out of the smoke into the refined airs of the dining-room.

After his two years at the Eagle, Myron went--with an agreeable farewell to Mr. Coram, who sighed, 'I wish we could afford to keep you here, son'--as meat-cook to New Haven, to the Connecticut Inn, which was almost a really good hotel, with a hundred rooms and occasional interesting food and guests who shaved daily. There were men waiters, and lunch instead of dinner was served at noon, which seemed to Myron very urban and fashionable.

After a year and three-quarters in New Haven, he had risen to the colonelcy of second-cook, and sometimes he was permitted to go to the open markets and help the steward buy meats and fowl and vegetables. But he went mad again, and informed the steward and the head waiter that, like a prototype of Colonel Lawrence of Arabia, he wanted to chuck his commission and re-enlist, as a regular waiter.

He was twenty-two, no longer a boy and a butt in the steamy back caverns of the hotel, but esteemed as an excellent cook who, with no jeers now from the chef, did conjuring tricks not only with his early loves, Béarnaise and Duchesse sauces, but with half a hundred--Bordelaise, Cumberland, Poivrade, Admiral, Sainte-Menehould, Raifort, Espagnole, Cardinal, Nantaise, Niçoise, romantic names which he crooned to himself--mispronouncing them badly--as he sifted and stirred. The bustling steward admired, 'I wonder where an upstate boy like that ever learned so many flavours!' It never came to the steward that all of Myron's magic, like precocious success in many other occupations, consisted in looking up the recipes in a book and having the remarkable energy to try them out.

They besought him, now, not to give up his career, not to 'monkey with the buzz-saw'. The steward remarked, 'Way I figure it, a cook is a cook and a waiter is a waiter and no sense trying to be both, and that's all there is to it.'

Myron insisted, and became a waiter, newest and least in his watch, making, with wages and tips, one-quarter his salary as second-cook. So he stopped smoking cigars, took to cigarettes, and was content as he learned every strategy of table-waiting.

When he had sufficiently mastered it so that he did not have to worry over broken dishes and unchilled celery, he began, through articles in hotel magazines and by snooping about the Inn between hours, to study the storekeeper's systems of keeping track of the receipt and issuance of hotel supplies, the housekeeper's inventory of linen and soap and curtains, the office's record of bills payable, the hundred ways in which the checker and cashier can keep the waiters from socializing the money paid by guests, and the three or four ways of keeping the checker and cashier from doing the socializing themselves.

Was he too weary after working all day and studying all evening?

Is any poet weary or dolorous when he sits up till dawn over a newly come parcel of books?

9

When Myron first went to the Connecticut Inn, New Haven, he remembered Herbert Lambkin of Black Thread Centre, now a Senior in Yale College. It seemed a thoughtful sort of thing to go visit with him. Wasn't Herbert the brother of Julia--with whom, Myron recalled in an amused, mature way, he had had some kind of boyish flirtation--the brother also of that golden-haired and most tot-like tot, little Effie May? Hadn't they played catch together, and jovially pretended, in the halcyon days, to be fighting? Why certainly! He'd give good old Bert a treat by calling on him!

He found Mr. Herbert Lambkin living in no extraordinary luxury in the old dormitory called 'South Middle'. He clattered up the hollowed wooden steps and knocked briskly.

'Come . . . in', sighed a thin and discouraged voice.

Myron threw the door open on a rather dirty room with a cot bed, a broken-backed revolving chair before a desk heaped with black-smeared textbooks and copies of that racy periodical of the day, *The Standard,* a bureau which looked irredeemably second-hand--as though it had been second-hand even when it was new. The only luxury was a window-seat cushion upholstered in gaudy imitation-Oriental cretonne portraying Burmese temples, Egyptian camels, Sinhalese elephants, Tangier dancing girls, and Florida palms.

In the midst of the mess stood a young man whom Myron barely recognized as Herbert Lambkin, so tall and weedy and unhealthily pale had he become, and so thickly spectacled. He wore decayed trousers and a sweater.

'Oh!' Herbert whined; and 'Oh, you're Weagle, aren't you? How are you?' But Herbert did not sound as though he really cared how Myron was.

'Yes, sure--Myron Weagle! Long time since I've seen you.'

'Oh. Yes. Wel--have a chair! Have two chairs!' This was advanced collegiate humour, in 1901, and possibly in 1931. 'What are you doing in New Haven, Weagle?'

'I'm working here. Got a job in the Connecticut Inn.'

'Oh. What doing?'

'In the kitchen--I'm meat-cook.'

'In the kitchen!' Herbert's giggle was at once high-pitched and harsh. He looked as though he were still being jocular as he observed, 'I rather thought I smelled grease, when you came in!'

'You did *not!* I've got on a new suit of clothes and had a real barber-shop bath!'

'Oh well, my dear fellow, why be ashamed of it? Nice wholesome scent, kitchen grease. No doubt it's much more fragrant than the odour of printer's ink and the midnight lamp, such as afflicts a poor scholar like myself! And your mother was a cook, too. Interesting example of heredity!'

Myron was too angry to talk, even to grunt affirmative interest, while with heavy airiness Herbert discoursed on the pleasures of being a Son of Old Eli, on his success in getting third prize in the Matthew Twitchell Competition in Greek Prosody, on his remarkably close friendship with Stub Van Vrump, the scion of no less a family than the prehistoric Van Vrumps of Washington Square, and on the probability that he, Herbert, would study law and with no considerable delay become United States Senator from Connecticut.

His confidences were interrupted by the arrival of two of his friends, apparently class-mates. Myron, from a certain experience as junior hotel-keeper, sized them up as being amiable, less boastful than Herbert, rather poor, and of the most minor ability.

It had always been reputed throughout Connecticut that all 'Yale men' were young gods, with athletic prowess and awe-inspiring wealth. Myron now perceived that they were extraordinarily like human beings.

The newcomers were agreeable enough to him in their greetings, but non-committal, waiting to see what manner of non-collegiate heathen he might prove to be. While he wore his clothes better than any of them, and was vastly easier in manner, he occasionally said 'He don't', and that puzzled them. Herbert was patently alarmed lest they learnt that this fellow who dared call him 'Bert' was a pot-keeler. He turned his back on Myron, and with shrill false excitement drew his class-mates into a discussion of one 'Bill' and his chances of 'making' the football team. Myron, in growing fury, sat apart on the window-seat, bumping the base of it with irritably swinging foot, not understanding a word of what they said. He looked out the window, aware of the peace and dignity of the campus, with the famous Fence in the shadow of the elms, and hated the arrogance of that unearned peace. He endured his humiliation for five minutes, then popped up, considered punching Herbert's long nose, dismissed it, said curtly, 'Must be running along', and marched out with no handshaking.

If he did not hear Herbert's sneering laugh behind him, he imagined it.

Not for two years then, not till Ora came down from Black Thread to see him, did Myron ever step on the Yale campus again, and though he saw Herbert in the Connecticut Grill and on the street, he did not speak to him.

Yet if this Yankee Jude was obscure enough, he could not be awed into remaining so. And he was not bitter, as his father would have been. He was too good an hotel-man. He had had too much experience with hot and testy boss cooks on the one hand, and cold and testy guests on the other, to be shaken by any good, normal, human beastliness. He merely grunted, 'I'll show the Lambkins, some day!'

Though sometimes, after having been imprisoned in the kitchen for all of a blue April day, he did hate the young gentlemen of Yale as he saw them sauntering, singing, free, passing the 'mucker', the townie, without a glance.

Myron had turned from second-cook to waiter when Ora, now twenty, came down from Black Thread Centre, to view Yale, New Haven, and his brother, in the order named.

Not for a year had Myron been able to get leave and visit his family, and in the meantime he had convinced himself that he had not only admiration but noble affection for his younger brother, with his astonishing culture, his fancy and observation, and his ambition to climb beyond the tavern--all the qualities, in fact, Myron sighed, that he himself was too stupid and fussy ever to have.

Ora, commendably graduating from high school at seventeen, a year younger than Myron, had remained in Black Thread, cynically amusing himself with jobs which Myron considered unworthy of him, while doing what Tom Weagle described fondly as 'further pursuing his studies'. He had clerked in the American House, he had reported for the Black Thread *Star and Tidings* at a dollar and a half a column, he had been agent for a Hartford laundry company, for lightning rods, for Little Giant Sporting Tackle, and for Dr. Sibelius's World-Renowned Soaps, Facial Creams, and Flavouring Extracts. To the local banker, he had sold the first horseless carriage known in Black Thread, and he had had accepted by the *Christian Advocate* two poems entitled 'Baby's Bedtime Blessing' and 'The Woods Were God's First Temple'. Mother Weagle, astonished that her Ora had all this while been concealing such religious sentiments, began again to hope that he would turn out a preacher. She thought the poems were just lovely.

Ora thought they were tripe, and he so expressed himself to the editor of the *Star and Tidings,* with the intimation that he had merely written them to sell, and that his own real poetry would deal exclusively with vampire women of dusky sunken eyes, strange sins, all articles that were scarlet-coloured, and the isles of Greece. Anyway, he explained to the Black Thread editor, he had received three-fifty apiece for the poems and they had taken him only half an hour each. Therefore he could, if he worked a ten-hour shift, make seventy dollars a day; conservatively, over twenty thousand dollars a year! Could do it right now!

He was indignant when the editor sniffed, and he took these financial tidings home to his mother.

Whatever he did, Ora went on living at the American House. Theoretically, he paid board, but on any given Saturday he found that just this particular week he was a little short of money.

He went to New Haven to investigate entering Yale. He felt a little overripe for it, at twenty, but somehow he must gather a much larger stock of beautiful words, so that he could write for *The Century* and get much more than three-fifty a poem--perhaps ten or twelve, which would make fifty thousand a year.

He wore the latest thing in Black Thread pool-room clothes; a red-striped grey-green suit with lapels sticking out like the ears of a jackass, with pockets slashed diagonally, and the flaps decorated with large pearl buttons.

Myron was uncomfortable when he saw that garment conspicuously walking through the dingy hauteur of the old New Haven station. 'I wonder if I could get him into a nice quiet grey suit, without any thingamabobs on it,' he fretted. 'But better not try. Ora's so sort of fine and sensitive, he might have his feelings hurt.' And he welcomed his young brother with shouts of 'Well, well, well, well!'

He had taken an afternoon and evening off from the hotel. He conducted Ora through the metropolitan hustle of Church and Chapel Streets; showed him the wonders of the world from East Rock--where, on a bright day, you can look clear across to the alien, magic shore of Long Island--and finally, uneasily invading the preserves of the gentry, dragged him rapidly through the Yale Campus, pattering off, 'Durfee Hall--dormitory; South Middle--dormitory--ver' old; Dwight Hall--Y.M.C.A.; Osborn Hall--rec'ta-tions--let's get out of this now and have a nice ice cream soda.'

He escorted Ora to a real theatre that evening (it was the third time that Myron himself, with all his metropolitan experience, had ever been so extravagant and time-wasting) and they saw a splendid play called 'Midnight Villa', in which a Duke, who had a kind heart but lamentable habits as regards gambling, told his haughty family to go to hell, and married the lady secretary, instead of the thoroughly nasty Lady Montjoie. His Grace also shot a burglar, won a motor race at forty-five miles an hour (he did this off stage, but he came staggering on in a duster and goggles in the most convincing way), and saved the lady secretary's father from bankruptcy by presenting the old gentleman with his winnings at the Monte Carlo Casino that evening, which amounted to no less than a million francs. And at the end it proved that the father was really a Hungarian prince, characteristically in hard luck, and his daughter, therefore, a princess.

'Golly!' sighed Ora, as they ate Bird's Nest Soup and New York Chop Suey, at a Chinese restaurant, after the play. 'I'm going to Monte Carlo some day. Golly! That was an exciting play! Dandy acting! I'm going to write a play! A real highbrow Ibsen play . . . I wonder how much you get for a successful play on Broadway?'

In the room which Myron had taken for Ora on the same floor with his own in the rooming-house, Myron tried to make it clear, for communication at home, that though he was but a tyro waiter, he was doing well, really learning his trade.

'. . . and I can run a crew of waiters, I think. I honestly believe I could do it right now, if I had to. It looks to me, unless I make another switch, say to the Front Office, that I'll be head waiter in some smaller hotel in another couple years, and then a steward in another three or four.'

'Oh, yuuuuuh, sure, I guess so,' yawned Ora. 'Just climbing like a dear lil chipmunk, aren't we! Learned how to cook fried rootalulas and then how to hustle the hash! Sure, you'll go right on crawling up. You'll be manager and chief cook and bottlewasher of some great big cockroach warehouse someday. Regular Horatio Alger story: "From Bell-Hop to Boss." Don't mind me. I'm just kidding. You've done swell--I guess. Well, I think I'll turn in now.'

When they had explored the Yale Campus, Ora had insisted that they call on Herbert Lambkin who, after a year in Yale Law School, had decided that his talents were better suited to professing a subject called 'English Literature', which dealt with embalming and the revivification of mummies. He was staying on to acquire the priestly title of 'M.A.'

Myron had hesitated, 'Oh, we won't have time to-day. Maybe later.'

The second day, Ora insisted again, and Myron blurted, 'No, I won't. Bert hasn't been very nice to me. Thinks he's too good for a waiter! Maybe he is, but I don't care so much for his showing it!'

'All right. Hell with him,' said Ora.

Myron had to return to work that second day, and Ora was left to wander by himself. When Myron took a tray of free lunch from the kitchen into the bar-room at five, he found Ora and Herbert Lambkin together, at the bar. They ignored him. As Myron left, they glanced at him and giggled. The back of his neck was rigid with wrath, but--oh, thunder, Ora was still a kid! He was the only brother Myron had. Ora didn't mean so bad; he was just heedless. He must keep his temper and try--after all these years of failure at it--to be really friends with the kid and to appreciate his wonderful ability at word-slinging and imagination and all like that.

He did not mention Herbert when Ora came to the rooming-house, at nine-thirty, to pack for the Black Thread train.

'I had a dandy day,' glowed Ora. 'Oh, I ran into Bert Lambkin--by accident. I agree with you about him. He's a cheap snob. Say, I got a raft of Yale catalogues and stuff to-day. Maybe I'll try to get into Yale next fall. How'd it be to have a real Yale Man in the family, ole man? Say, My, could you let me have twenty-five dollars till I get home? I'm kind of low just now. I'll shoot it right back to you.'

When Myron next heard of him, Ora was a reporter on a Waterbury newspaper. Of his entering Yale, Myron heard as much as of his returning the twenty-five dollars.

It irritated Myron occasionally, occasionally it made him gloomy, to be that unheeded and automatic machine, a waiter, among the Yale students who frequented the Connecticut Grill where he often served in the evening and late afternoon, when the dining-room was closed. He liked being attentive to old, timid people, who were grateful for his help. He could even endure those pests the hotel children, the children of the 'permanents', with their golden ringlets, shrill voices, monstrous orders for sweets, and their assumption that everyone on the staff was not only a personal servant but filled with joy at being called on to entertain them--to bring them extra cakes, to let them ride in the elevator, to wash off doors the pencil marks they so playfully scrawled there. These he could endure, and the average middle-aged guest, travelling-man or other, was an amiable and friendly customer. But to be irrevocably a stranger among young men his own age, of not markedly better manners and of rather less curiosity about the mysteries which are supposed to be hidden in books, was to be an exile from the self-confidence of youth. They were most of them polite enough to him, these young gentlemen in tweeds and ties of shot silk who crooned 'Bingo' and 'Delta Kappa Upsilon' in corners, and talked actively of journeys to Europe, of polo, of week-ends at Northampton, or, at humblest, of sailing on the Sound, but after a hundred meetings, after he had even guided them out of the door and boosted them into cabs when they had had too much crème de menthe or pousse café, they still did not remember him. He could only meditate, 'Well, probably I'm better off than if I were a mechanic in Winchester's and never had a chance to meet any new kinds of folks and learn there are different ways of living', and again, with a growl like a hurt animal's, he would resolve, 'I'll show 'em all!'

'Some day, when I'm manager of a whale of a big hotel and these boys are teaching school or clerking in a bank and forget they ever were swell Yale Men, it's going to be funny to watch 'em coming to me, trying to get friendly and hoping His Nibs, the Manager, will be so kind and let 'em have a cut rate. No idea they ever saw me before. It'll be funny then . . . Maybe it will.'

The lonely and love-starved women living in the hotel were the greatest trial, and transport, of a stalwart young waiter. It has increasingly been the contention of novelists and psychologists that practically all of a man's emotion and secret thought are devoted to 'sex'. Probably this dogma is as false as the Victorian dogma that no respectable male ever thought of such matters, and invariably, when he happened to notice an unclad lady in his bedroom, did so only with dismayed surprise. It is to be observed that the citizens diligently given to amorousness are often anaemic and sedentary and adorned with lop-sided eyeglasses, while the deep-chested human gorillas, whether bond-salesmen, economists, or pugilists, are often known to flee chastely home to their wives on the 5.57, and to spend more Sunday afternoons on golf and gin and balance-sheets than in dancing with the wives of neighbours. If this be heresy to the psychoanalysts, yet we have the authority of the Bolsheviks and the Baptists, who for once agree, in contending that a lusty male will be less devoted to lechery than to his work.

Myron Weagle was a vigorous young man, and certainly he had applied most of his thought to work, not dalliance. At twenty-three he was still a virgin. Yet he had trembled at the revelation of girls' ankles and throats on picnics, and in his yearning over Julia Lambkin he had, without admitting it to himself, longed for much more intimacy than just a kiss.

He was first seduced, quite unromantically, by a meagre widow who went about the country 'demonstrating', advertising the virtues of Humming Bird Cake Flour by exhibitions of cookery in grocery shops, and who between campaigns lived at the Connecticut Inn . . . This was five years after Ora, at the age of sixteen, had made his first laboratory experiments with a German farm girl, the laboratory being a disused quarry.

Myron was sometimes drafted from the dining-room as a floor-waiter. He had taken a tray of breakfast to the demonstrating widow in Room 64. She was sitting up in bed. She was not enticing. Her face was like crumpled paper, but she had rouged extensively and put on a cap of lace and blue ribbons and, over her scant nightgown, a bed-jacket of knitted pink silk. She was at least forty.

'Shall I put the tray on the table, Madame?' murmured the perfect waiter.

'Oh no-no--that's not so cosy, do you think, Myron? Oh nowy no! Ithn't tho thweet, thitting up at dweat big tables, for a small, little girl like me, do you think? Put it down beside me, boy.' She was crooning. She made the 'boy' sound like 'dear'.

While Myron was setting the tray on the bed, and wondering where the devil she had got hold of his Christian name, she seized his hand and bubbled, 'My gracious me! What big strong hands! And such lovely strong shoulders. You ought to be in Yale, playing football, instead of waiting on silly nobodies like silly little me.'

He was alarmed. He wanted to escape. But she retained his hand as she went on: 'Don't be in such a hurry. I get so lonely, Myron--out on the road all week, and then just this lonely room to come back to instead of a real, cosy home, and not hardly knowing anybody and all. Sit down on the edge of the bed for just a sec' and talk to a fellow, can't you?'

He sat, as gingerly as though he was occupying an armchair in company with a pussy cat.

'Don't you get lonely, too, Myron, after hours?'

'I don't know. I guess I don't think much about it. I read quite a lot. It don't seem so lonely . . .'

'It *doesn't*. Not "it don't". I'm going to give you some lessons in grammar and vocabulary, Myron. I used to be a school-teacher, but they paid so badly. I'll lend you a grammar and some exercise books and make you work hard and speak like President Hadley. Would you like that?'

'Gee, I'd love it!' He was grateful; he was no longer shy.

'I'll look through my trunks and dig out the books to-day. Could you drop in about nine o'clock this evening . . .'

'Why . . . uh . . .'

'Just to get the books, I mean.'

'Sure, I'd be glad to.'

'Then give me a little good-morning kiss, and run along, you funny, timid child!'

He leaned toward her lips, uninterestedly, mechanically, but that was no mechanical kiss from a kind teacher. Her mouth was like hot cream; it was not a sensationless organ like the chill lips of the school-girls he had kissed in playing 'Post office' at parties, but an entity with a tense, skilled life of its own. He forgot that she was wrinkled. He shook with astonishment and bewildered emotion, and he did not draw back till she had pushed him away with a wiry hand on his chest, laughing, 'Now run along! You see, you're all safe with the Wild Widdy! Just a friendly good-morning kiss. Nine to-night, then. Don't let anybody see you come in. They might misunderstand.'

He stood outside in the hall, shaking as though he had a chill. All day, while he bustled with platters and droned, 'Yes, sir, beans on the side, sir', he was mooning over the Wild Widow. He pictured her as generous and merry and beautiful. When he came stumbling in at nine, she was in a dressing-gown of lace and peach-coloured satin. Silently they clasped each other; quite silently, without explanation in anything so worn and frazzled as words, they swayed together toward the bed. Not all the youth of Julia Lambkin had seemed so fresh to him as the flesh of the widow's arm about his neck.

The Wild Widow was altogether, in every way, good for Myron. She was kind, wise, and grateful. He was conscious of a lessening in the physical tension which had kept him awake nights worrying about cloudy nothings, in the spiritual tension which had been making him too grave, too diligent, too near the priggishness against which Miss Absolom had warned him in the Black Thread boarding-house.

She did teach him many things about proprieties of speech. He was supposed to have studied courses labelled 'English Grammar' and 'English Literature' in school, but since in the American pre-college educational system--of that day as of this--it was not necessary for a tall, amiable youth to learn any rigid facts or stern laws, but merely to smile on the amateur lady teachers and look interested, Myron knew rather less now of the rules of English speech than of those pertaining to French. Syntax had been a meaningless treadmill in airless class-rooms. Now it was a sharp need for his career, for association with the men whom he pleasantly hoped to oust in the hotel business. The only thing for which he really much envied the Yale students upon whom he waited was that even when they gabbled the slang of the moment, they still seemed to be talking more gracefully than

Mr. Coram of the Eagle Hotel, or the fussy little manager of the Connecticut Inn.

With the Wild Widow he read *King Lear* aloud, and patches of Charles Lamb, Addison, De Quincey, and the rather highfalutin editorials then regarded as suitable to the great newspapers of New York.

When, without warning, she suddenly married a mysterious Captain somebody from Montclair, New Jersey, and moved to that town to live, Myron was shocked. He moped for weeks. He pictured the Wild Widow as a Helen of Troy, but wiser and more tender. But in three months he became interested in a pretty chambermaid, and there were a stock-company actress and yet others after her, without any complications, or any particular significance, for it is very doubtful whether he was ever so interested in any woman after the widow as in a proper Sauce Béarnaise.

10

The manager of the Connecticut Inn was also the proprietor. He was a high-powered ant. He was a moral fellow who drank nothing but hot rum and who talked of closing up the bar, though he never went so far as to do it. He was named Wheelwright, and was known to the travelling-salesmen as 'Deacon' Wheelwright. He was not deliberately cruel, but he was a fusser, a nagger, a discusser, a reminder; he had regular habits and did not see why other people's regularities should not jibe with his own. And he hated to pay salaries.

The nearer he was to people, the more he was irritated by their loose ways, so that while he was on reasonably good terms with the cooks and waiters in the Back of the House, he was always rushing in the manner of an agitated hen at the clerks immediately under his eye, and the labour turnover in the Front Office was prodigious. So Myron had his chance at clerking.

The third night-clerk in six months was gone, and when Deacon Wheelwright came nosing into the pantry, Myron tackled him with a bland, 'If you haven't got a new night-clerk yet, Mr. Wheelwright, I wish you'd let me sit in on the job till you get one. I've had experience--American House in Black Thread--father owns it. I could serve dinner here and still manage the night-desk.'

'Well, I'll think about it, young man, I'll think about it, I'll think about it.'

He called Myron in before dinner and, after questioning him briefly about his ancestry, education, religion, politics (none of which four Myron chanced to possess), and habits as regards alcohol, pilfering, women, cocaine, ballad-singing, and bathing, he doubtfully let him try the job as night-clerk. For a week then, Myron was on from five in the afternoon till eight the next morning, and later, when other clerks called the Deacon a 'mean ole hound' and slammed their clothes into small trunks and went their ways, Myron had further opportunity of learning the profound science of saying 'Good morning' civilly and choosing from among fifty rooms, all alike, which one to 'give' to the newly-arrived guest.

He began now, as night-clerk, to study accounting, and to dip into house-decoration and architecture. In the afternoon he sometimes climbed down to the basement, had the engineer demonstrate to him the balky ways of dynamos and boilers, and he read the manuals in the engineer's greasy, cheerful office, smelling always of a corn-cob pipe and somehow like a ship's hold.

While he sat studying late at night, the only sounds were the street-cars on Church Street, the march of a policeman. After the clatter of kitchen and dining-room, the stillness was like a plunge into sweet waters. He strode now and then to the water-cooler, a zinc barrel enclosed in staves of varnished dark-brown wood, the nickled handle of the tap worn through to the brass where many thumbs had pressed. He washed out the thick water glass and dried it. He looked proudly at desk, register, neat pigeon-holes for mail and room-keys, lines of chairs--a great hotel, and *his*. He was in supreme charge, from eight in the evening--or at least from midnight, when the proprietor had gone to bed--till eight in the morning. In case of fire, burglary, a guest's illness, a quarrel in a room, *he* was the boss!--it was *his* hotel!

After eight months of this, when Deacon Wheelwright was having unusual trouble in getting a new permanent night-clerk and Myron had sat in for a fortnight, Myron braced him curtly with, 'Why not put me on regularly instead of just temporarily? I think I can do it all right now'.

Deacon Wheelwright's pale eyes flickered, and he complained, 'But you ain't a clerk! You're a waiter. And didn't you use to be a cook?'

'Why, yes, but I think . . .'

'No, no, no, no! An hotel's like any other business. It's got to be run on regular, established principles and according to Hoyle, or it just goes to pieces, and there's no better rule of business than that a fellow has got to stick to the line he's trained to, if he's going to get results. That's why a lot of these fellows that take on an employee just because he seems like a bright fellow, without due and proper attention to how well trained he is, don't--well, you don't ever see 'em running a big hotel like I am! You prob'ly never thought about it this way, but if you get right down to brass tacks, a waiter is a waiter and a clerk is a clerk, and you can't get beyond it!'

'But I have had some training . . .'

'No, no, no, no! And that's one thing I don't like about you: you always want to argue and discuss and chew the rag about things, instead of coming right to the point, with no long-winded gassing about it!'

'But, sir, I *have* been on the night-desk--six weeks during this past eight months, and I don't think I've fallen . . .'

'No, no, no, I tell you! That's entirely different! That's just being on *temporary*!'

So within three weeks Myron had gone to the Old Eli Hotel, New Haven, as regular night-clerk. When he quit, Deacon Wheelwright sent for him and said that he was a fool, that he was a hasty and ill-regulated young fool, and that, if he just had the sense and the gumption to wait, the Deacon might take him on as a permanent clerk almost any time--in a year or so.

The Old Eli was a smaller establishment than the Connecticut Inn, and considerably less respectable, though the pay of employees was somewhat better. Myron was uncomfortable there. He was not too rigidly moral, for a native of Northern Connecticut; he liked his infrequent highball and he had come to regard his little friend, the stock-company actress, as a very sweet and reasonable young woman. But that did not mean that he vastly enjoyed working in a brothel.

The Yale students who never dared enter the pious plush and walnut lobby of the Connecticut Inn with fly-by-night females knew that at the Old Eli Hotel they could, as they gratefully said, 'get away with anything'. On Myron's first night there, when he refused to give a room to a celebrated football star and a flimsy little female in mussed crèpe de chine, both drunk and minus baggage, the manager came in on the controversy and hesitated, 'Don't do to be too strict, Weagle, when the gentleman's an old friend of the house', and 'It's all right, Mr. Blank. Boy! Show the gentleman and lady up to the Governor's Suite and see there's plenty of ice water and towels.'

The manager was a good-natured person, like so many who are engaged in catering to what is arbitrarily known as 'the vices'. He said nothing to Myron afterward save, 'Don't do to be too strict in this business, long as people mind their own affairs. Besides, these Yale guys are real gents--not like a lot of roughnecks. Give 'em anything they want, if they don't get noisy. See how it is?'

Myron saw, and did not especially like it.

And there were theatrical parties, late and extraordinarily noisy; magnificent training in fact for a night-clerk who had to keep the party-givers happy while soothing the embittered guests who were trying to sleep next door, and who telephoned down every fifteen minutes. (The Old Eli advertised that it was a 'high-class, de luxe, family and transient establishment', and that it had been the first hotel in New Haven to install electric lights or separate room telephones.)

The Old Eli was a favourite resort of the lesser and more sporting sort of actors. At this time, late in 1903, the touring troupes were still numerous, and their custom was important to hotel-keepers. The troupers had not yet been killed off by the automobile, the movies, the radio. There were hundreds of companies constantly out on the road, and even in Black Thread Centre, the young Myron had encountered actresses who cooked sausages with garlic on chafing dishes in their bedrooms, did their washing and ironing in the public bathrooms, let their long-haired, drooling dogs sleep on bed pillows in a corner, and chose 3 a.m. as the appropriate hour at which to tell a husband that if he was caught flirting with that nasty little female blackface comedian just once more, there would be trouble and lots of it.

The stage, like tavern-keeping, poetry, and pugilism, has become respectable, and thereby lost most of its colour and joy. Its practitioners wear spats and collect first editions. (No philosopher has yet explained why the precise opposite to this has occurred in the lesser professions of banking and publishing. In 1890, all bankers and publishers were middle-aged or ancient, invariably had whiskers and broadcloth coats and dignity, and took exercise only in squeezing interest and royalties. In 1933 all of them--except for the really trifling percentage of bankers who are in jail--are youthful, frivolous, given to driving fast motors, and, in checked stockings and maniacal sweaters, to playing golf. And consequently no one takes either actors, tavern-keepers, poets, pugilists, or bankers and publishers at all seriously to-day.)

But in 1903 the touring actors still retained a joyous and gipsy irregularity. To the Old Eli Hotel came the stars of burlesque, minor actors in 'straight drama', players of vaudeville, and old comedians from melodramas. Before midnight, they sent down for cheese crackers, Worcestershire, ham, ale, and whisky, and they received local admirers till four in the morning. Sometimes lone laymen came down from actresses' rooms considerably later than that, looking sheepish and wondering whether it was the swell, metropolitan thing to give the attentive night-clerk five dollars.

The theatrical shindies Myron did not mind; he was guilty, even, of joining them for five minutes at a time on dull nights. But he disliked the fact that any obviously unacquainted male and female could come in and register for a room. It made him feel like a procurer.

Early in 1904, when he was not quite twenty-four years old and had been at the Old Eli for only four months, he began to look for another job. That year the Louisiana Purchase Exposition was to be held in St. Louis.

To get out of this house of easy favours, to go West, to see the world, to learn quite new ways in hotel-keeping--and incidentally in living--that would be an adventure of the highest. In his weekly *Hotel Era* Myron found an advertisement of the Elphinstone Hotel and Restaurant Company of New York for 'all classes empl. St. Louis world fair hotel, open April 15th to abt. Oct. 1st, send foto and ref. first letter'.

He sent foto and ref. first letter. He signed the letter 'Myron S. Weagle'. The 'S' in his name stood for nothing whatever. He had put it in three years before because, obviously, a successful man can't go about naked, with no middle initial.

He was engaged by the Elphinstone Company as night-clerk at the Pierre Ronsard, adjoining Forest Park, St. Louis.

He pictured it as a chateau with heraldic shields chiselled in the stone of immemorial walls.

11

Between New Haven and St. Louis, after a week in Black Thread with his mother, Myron made a pilgrimage to the hotels and restaurants of New York, nor was any palmer ever more refreshed by actually seeing the shrines of which all his life he had heard in reverent gossip. Stepping in awe through their corridors, humbly peeping at the morning-coated high priests and acolytes in brass buttons and monkey caps, he viewed the Waldorf-Astoria, the Hoffman House, the Holland House, the Fifth Avenue, the Murray Hill, the Savoy, Fraunces Tavern, the ancient Brevoort, Delmonico's, Sherry's, Mouquin's, Martin's, and Jack's, that chapel for night-hawk journalists and actors and politicians. . . . The poet, incredulously seeing the actual floors trod once by the masters at Dove Cottage and Stratford and Weimar; the poet standing stilled in the English Cemetery in Rome before the grave of one whose name was writ in water.

Myron did not lodge at any of the cathedral hotels; he stayed at the Grand Union, for a dollar a night, and once in the lobby he saw its famous manager, Simeon Ford, the wit, and stood staring, foolish with admiration.

He wanted to, and did not quite dare, introduce himself to clerks and head waiters as an hotel-man. They would laugh at such a country cousin. But he did--and thereby used up most of his savings beyond a reserve for fare and Pullman to St. Louis--dine at the Waldorf and Delmonico's, and actually behold and (rather less important) taste the Pompano à la Potentini, the Pancakes with Orange-Flower Water, the Mousseline Waleski, the Cuissot de Chevreuil à la Francatelli which he had known, these years, only in a theoretical and literary way, and for the first time he had champagne and a half-bottle of Moselle.

He was amiable but demanding with the waiters. There is nothing a waiter so vastly enjoys as being a guest while on vacation, and lording it over the menials. He is like a surgeon with a chance to operate on his personal dentist; he is as intolerable as an author reviewing the lesser opera of his rivals.

If Myron had gone to New York a practical hotel-man who found his work interesting, he came out of it a fanatic who found it a holy cause. To give Chaudfroid de Bécassines--snipe in a bright brown-jellied gravy--to dreary and disillusioned men who considered their offices tiresome and their wives infuriating and their sons sapheaded--that was a sacred office. Myron did not, it is to be feared, reflect on the economic value of giving these fat and wealth-oozing guzzlers the good Chaudfroid or anything else whatever. He did not know yet, if indeed he was ever thoroughly to know, that there was a class struggle, a proletarian class, economic determinism, or the theory of conspicuous waste. To say this is not to praise Myron for his typical poet's absorption in his art; it is to indicate a lack in his many patches of knowledge.

So, softly whistling, he took train for St. Louis and the Great West.

He had never in his life made a greater journey than the seventy-two miles from New Haven to New York. He had never till now, at twenty-four, been in a dining-car or a Pullman, nor had he ever seen an observation car, with its glass sides and arm-chairs and platform like a back porch. He was fascinated by every trick of decoration or service; he was privileged to see them with the fresh excitement of an untravelled boy, yet with the trained observation of an expert in making wayfarers comfortable.

His poet's mind noted not new adjectives nor flower-names handy for rhyming, but berth-lights for reading in bed, the deftness of the porter, tucking in sheets so that they were anchored against the worst restlessness of insomniacs, the inlaid mahogany and rosewood of this period before the coming of steel cars, and the magic of the immense menu served from the tiny condensed kitchens. He was not so wary of the dining-car steward as of the baronial head waiters of New York, and he spent an entire afternoon examining the ice box, the gas stove, the miniature sink of the travelling kitchen, and in gossiping fraternally with the steward and the coloured waiters and cooks.

He had never before met Southern darkies. They delighted him, and all afternoon he exchanged with his colleagues the most scandalous anecdotes about cranky guests--the ones who wanted corn muffins made in five minutes, the ones who let their coffee stand and then complained because it was not hot, the peculiarly pestiferous ones who tried to walk out, absent-mindedly humming, without paying their bills.

He was more interested in such technicalities than in the new scenery, though out of that scenery he got enough thrill to stock a whole tourful of school-teachers. He was just more silent about it.

He gloated on the farms of Ohio and Indiana and Illinois, fields of a hundred acres that would soon be brilliant with young corn and wheat, fields gigantic to the New Englander to whom a stretch of twenty acres had been large.

He could not believe what the Pullman conductor said: that in Kansas and Nebraska there were fields ten times as great as 'these dinky little Illinois patches'.

For almost the first time since his conversion to a life of hotel service by J. Hector Warlock, he wanted to get out of steamy kitchens and dark corridors into the green sunny world. 'Be fine to live here and ride a horse all over--in this fresh air--for miles--completely free--no confounded city streets to stop you--no grouchy guests to have to cater to,' he meditated; but immediately thereafter, 'Terrible little frame hotels in these villages. Dirty. Shanties. Wonder how a chain of really good ones would make out--simple food but well-cooked?'

So he came, ruddy with adventure, to the Mississippi River and across it to St. Louis and the memory of pioneer wagon trains.

When he was met at the station by Mr. Alexander Monlux, the manager of the Pierre Ronsard, Myron perceived that Monlux did not regard him as a back-stairs apprentice but as a Trained Eastern Hotel-man.

Mr. Monlux had come from Iowa; he had never been East of Chicago, and he believed that any innkeeper or college-degree or red-wheeled buggy imported from New England must be better than any innkeeper or degree or vehicle from the middle west. He was not over thirty-two. He tried to keep up the dignity suitable to his very first position as manager, but it creaked a little. With Myron he was like the president of any American university meeting any English author-lecturer.

Myron let himself be received with éclat. 'This is a dandy fellow. Him and I--he and I are going to get along splendidly,' he decided, as they rode to the Pierre Ronsard in the luxury of a real automobile taxicab. (In both New Haven and New York he had ridden only on street-cars and the elevated.)

Within a week they were calling each other 'Alec' and 'Myron'.

Until three years ago, Monlux had been clerk in a Des Moines hotel. He was sleek, slender, eager, fond of bar-room melodies and of keeping the neatest account-books in the West, and he had a small black moustache. He had a girl named Isdrella, in the state university, and he had showed her picture to Myron before that evening. Even more proudly he showed Myron a clipping from the *Hotel Era*--his first recognition by the Press as a national celebrity: 'Alec Monlux, assistant manager of the Swilleby, Des Moines, goes as manager to the Ronsard at the Big Fair. Alec has a real grip among Knights of the Grip.'

But if Alec Monlux was promising, the Hotel Pierre Ronsard was appalling.

It had been built only for the Exposition. It was expected to last six months, but the contractors had been too optimistic. It had bedrooms for six hundred and fifty sightseers from the prairies, and all the floors rocked gently whenever a fifty-pound child trod upon them. It was built of secondhand boards, painted crimson and yellow, and had a turret roofed with bright green tin in imitation of tiles.

'Regular barn, eh?' said Monlux.

The two young experts grinned.

More barn-like yet was the immense lobby, two hundred feet long, with its miles of cane-seated rockers and dainty, innumerable flowered spittoons. Later in the spring and summer, when the cheerful, perspiratory tourists flooded in, the lobby floor would be littered with tracked mud, cigar stubs, rumpled newspapers, and chewing-gum wrappers, wearily dealt with by insufficient bell-boys. The desk, made of second-rate pine daubed with red and yellow paint, was large and busy, with its four day-clerks and assistant manager, and the cigar and candy stand was still vaster, all prettified with tinsel and paper roses. It was later to do a famous business in cheap candy, cheap cigars, picture postcards, and such memorable Souvenirs of the Exposition as spoons, ash-trays, glass paper-weights, and statuettes of jolly darkies holding banners inscribed, 'Ah's been to St. Lou, boss.' And in stacks was the song of the day:

Meet me at St. Louis, Louis,
Meet me at the fair.

The lobby was lined with canary yellow wallboard in panels with strips of red pine, and hung with imitations of medieval French banners printed on bunting. There was even a tin suit of armour from a theatrical costumier's in one corner. The ceiling was covered with fireproofed burlap dyed a wild sunset red.

Wallboard, but of a more modest grey, sheathed all the bedrooms, and a sneeze in the farthest room on the fourth floor could be heard in the basement. The hotel was not quite finished when Myron arrived; the carpenters were still desperately nailing floor boards on the long porch, and panting expressmen still carrying up the stairs the lop-sided second-hand furniture which the Elphinstone Hotel and Restaurant Company had bought at auction. It was new as March. Yet within a month the stairways (there were no elevators) would begin to sag and squeak, the walls to open in widening cracks between panels of wallboard.

But it was World's Fair time, holiday time, and the farmer guests had to pay only a dollar and a half or two dollars for their rooms, and along the corridors there were real city baths, gay with tin imitation tile. All of them, guests and 'help' felt that it was a sort of gala, like camping out, and there was little complaint even when the vat cracked and there was no soup, or when the announced sweetbreads for Sunday dinner proved to be pork chops. Every evening the dining-room was cleared for a dance, with a real five-piece negro orchestra. The lobby was full of running, yelping children, and Myron did not mind . . . since he did not go on duty until after the children had been put to bed. It was full, too, of hearty rustic laughter, and of the contented gossip of new acquaintances--of couples who had found that 'the man at the next table to ours in the dining-room is the cousin of a great friend of a neighbour of our son-in-law in Keokuk!'

Myron breathed better than ever he had in the Connecticut Inn. And he learned; he was again learning; he was learning 'Service'.

The higher professors of the Science of Hotel-Keeping were, in 1904, already pronouncing the thesis that a hotel clerk should be what was sweetly named a 'Greeter'; that he should bestow on every guest not only food and lodging, but a metaphysical blessing called 'Service'; that he should be at once the Little Brother and the Kind Uncle of every one who registered--call them by name (so that, for example, a Mr. Worthingby Bones would be irritated eighteen or twenty times a day by being affectionately hailed as 'Mr. Worthington'), advise them about theatres, get their letters especially mailed, look up their girls, and ask them tenderly about the Folks, illnesses, weather, and business conditions Back Home.

Myron, as a clerk, was never so gifted as his rivals at oozing unfelt cordiality. It was always to cramp him as an aspirant, it would possibly be fatal, that though he liked people, especially children and the weary old, though he was patient with cranks, was swift to fulfil and slow to forget orders, yet he never could kiss the feet of customers, if indeed 'feet' is the accurate technical word in the Science of Service.

But he was unconscious of his lack, in the present bustle. With all the cheerfulness of this gipsy fair, there was tremendous work for the employees. Myron was on alone at night, except for two bell-boys and a porter who also acted as doorman, when he happened to think about it. The hastily installed plumbing, apparently stuck together with flour paste and suspended along the walls with cotton thread, was always going out of order. Sometimes Myron could get an engineer from the basement to stop a toilet flowing or to get it to flow at all, but mostly he, with a bell-boy if one was left on the bench, had to trot up and try to adjust it himself, after shouting to the porter, who was much too dull to entrust with anything so delicate and morose as plumbing, 'If anybody comes in to register, tell 'em to sit down and wait--understand me, Tyrone--to *sit down*--oh my God!'

'This won't do at all', Myron thought guiltily, a week after the hotel was actually open to guests. 'I'm an ignorant pup. I don't know anything about plumbing.'

Thereafter, getting up an hour earlier in the afternoon than he wanted to, he tagged after the regular hotel plumber; watched him, questioned him, learned to handle his tools; and he solemnly sent for another of his perpetual manuals, one on Plumbing in All Its Branches by a Master Plumber: with a Complete Appendix on the Mathematical Calculation of Adequate Radiation for Those Who Combine Steam-fitting with Plumbing. Within a month he knew rather more about such spicy points as stopped sinks and gaskets on faucets and the correct temperature of soldering irons than the hotel plumber himself, and he amused himself late at night, by making a plan of a proper plumbing installation for the Pierre Ronsard--if it were only an hotel instead of an overgrown tar shanty.

A month later he had climbed to successes even beyond plumbing. He had been able to keep, in the eyes of Alec Monlux, his position as a superior Easterner. Monlux had introduced him to the rest of the staff impressively, and on off evenings he went with Monlux to beer gardens, to drink the good St. Louis beer, and sometimes to pick up a couple of girl stenographers. Together they visited the Fair, to admire the Grand Basin and the Pike--and, still more, the Inside Inn, built by E. M. Statler and, temporary though it was, the largest hotel ever known in the world, with 2,257 rooms. . . . They were much edified, also, to discover among the other hotels the 'Christian Endeavour' and the 'Epworth'. It was 1904, and God and William Jennings Bryan were still alive and popular.

Myron's intimacy with the manager, and the general opinion of the staff that he was a sealed adept in night-clerking, gave him such self-confidence as he had not known before. He forgot tending bar at the American House, and bell-hopping at the Fandango Inn, as though they were comic incidents in the life of someone else--a man he had known once but lost from sight.

So hastily organized was the whole Pierre Ronsard staff that there was an open road for careerists. Presently Myron was helping the chief accountant on quiet evenings, and when the assistant accountant quit in an agony of snarled books, Myron found himself assistant accountant, working daytimes, with an increased salary and with, for the first time, a private office of his own.

It was not much of an office. It was an eleven-by-eleven wall-boarded coop, roaring with the sound of adding-machines and typewriters in the general office outside, furnished only with a desk, files, and two chairs, and looking out on a coal pile and an ice-cutting machine. But to Myron it was a throne-room.

He stayed late each evening to finish his accounts, and during the day he frequently dashed out to help the clerks. He was checking in a hot, irritable mob one afternoon, with Alec Monlux also behind the desk, when Alec whimpered, 'Oh, my Heaven! There's the Old Man himself! I thought he was in New York! Didn't think he'd ever come out here!'

'Huh?' said Myron.

'The Old Man! Mark Elphinstone! The pug-dog coming toward us! President of the Company--they own nine hotels, besides this ole barn! . . . Why, Mr. Elphinstone! Didn't have an inkling you were coming! Well, sir, mighty proud to see you! Why didn't you tip us off, so I could 've met you at the train and had a suite ready. We've got two of them here, you know!'

Mr. Mark Elphinstone's name remains in the history of the American hotel-world from 1900 to 1933 as ranking almost with those of Ellsworth M. Statler, John McEntee Bowman, Lucius Boomer--cardinals, deans, Pulitzer Prize Winners of hotel-keeping. He was not lordly of frame; he was short, squat, with cropped sandy hair, and freckles on neck and wrist, but he stood squarely, like a man who expected to control everything in sight, he gave his orders in brief barks, and Myron was later to see him in his New York office, posing with stubby fingers thrust between his vest buttons, directly under a portrait of Napoleon.

He was barking now:

'Suite? Here? Never stay at hotels like this, Monlux. Dreadful. Got suite at the Planters. Never seen this place before. Dreadful. You boys done well. Made some money for us. I'll just poke around. Want to see you and assistant manager and clerks. Book-keepers. Cashiers. Steward. Housekeeper. Head waiter. Chef. Captain of bell-boys. After I've snooped around. Borrow your office. Give 'em each five minutes. But you get fifteen. Have 'em ready to come in, right on the second. Start with you at three. Then the others, right on the dot. So. Three. Prompt. Prob'ly leave for New York morrow morning. So. Prompt!'

'First really top-notch hotel boss I ever met. Gives you a kick. Gee, he's a dynamo,' sighed Myron to Alec Monlux.

'He's that, all right,' said Monlux. 'He's the biggest of 'em all. The company owns some pretty rank hotels, like this, and I believe our Florida one, Tippecanoe Lodge, is lousy, but of course our New York hotel, the Westward Ho, is a top-notch house, and we've got good places in Buffalo and Hartford and Worcester and Akron and Scranton, and we own that chain of armchair lunches through New Jersey and Pennsylvania--the Pan Dandy Lunches. Elphinstone himself! It must be grand to be a really *significant* man like that!'

When Myron, in his turn, was admitted to Monlux's private office for his audience with the Napoleon of Innkeepers, Mark Elphinstone was standing by the desk, his left hand resting on it with the arched fingers outspread like the roots of a banian tree, the right hand ready for oratorical gestures. A still-faced intense private secretary, who played arc-light to Elphinstone's dynamo, was sitting at the desk, calling New York (and later Worcester and Trenton) on the long-distance telephone. Neither Myron nor Alec Monlux ever knew just how the secretary had come. He had not been seen entering the hotel. He was just there. He would be. He had eye-glasses and tight lips and a low voice that you always understood.

Waving his free hand, Elphinstone commanded Myron, 'Sit down. No, I'll stand. Well young man' (Myron shivered), 'you seem to be a night-clerk, a day-clerk, a book-keeper--or accountant, as they like to call their grubby trade now--a plumber, a waiter, and a cook. Apparently work all the time. What's the trouble? What you trying to hide? What vice you covering up? Not normal, working all the time. I do. I'm not normal, either. Eaten up with fool ambition. What *is* this vice you're trying to forget? Booze? Drugs? Women? Women, eh! Fine big fellow like you?'

'No, sir.'

'Well, then, gambling? Ah ha, yes, little gambling, eh? Fun to watch the hosses run, eh, or sit back with a full house and watch a flush trying to bluff you, eh? Yes, good fun!'

'Never play cards, sir, not more than twice a year, or solitaire when I'm on nights and get sleepy.'

'Then what the devil are you hiding? What's the matter with you? Working all the time! Idea!'

'Guess it's just the same as with you, sir. Ambition. I want to get ahead. Like to learn all about hotel-keeping.'

'You never will! You learn how to run a five-hundred room hotel, and they put up a thousand-room monstrosity on you and some thirty-year-old snip shows you you're old-fashioned and out of the game--and he shows you *right,* by God! Next to love, nothing that loses its rank so quick as a "leading hotel". So it's ambition, eh? I *knew* it--I knew you had some vice, and you've picked the worst of the whole damn bunch! I can see you walking over my neck, one of these days. Well. . . . You dress fairly well.

Neat grey. I'd get just a tiny bit darker shade of blue in the necktie, with that suit. What you going to do, this fall, when this dump closes?'

'I don't know yet, sir.'

'Had many offers? Other companies?'

'None, sir.'

'Hm. Truthful *and* ambitious. Oh well, I'm getting ripe. Time to be picked off the tree by you young Marshal Neys. Want to go to Florida, Tippecanoe Lodge, 'tween St. Augustine and Daytona, coming season, as assistant manager? Vile place. Nice country, but vile hotel. Not much better'n this. Assistant manager. Fifteen a week more'n your present salary here, whatever that may be, if any. Want it?'

'Yes, sir, I . . .'

'Done. Report there, November fifteen. Manager's name Fred Barrow. Report to him. No need to bother me. No need at all. Needn't bother me. Just report to Barrow. Hobbs!' (to the intense secretary). 'Make a note of this--make a note of it. Weagle here hired assistant manager Tippecanoe. Check on his wages here. Fifteen more a week. Send him a letter confirming this when we get to New York. And inform Barrow. Make a note of it. So. Good morning, young man.'

Myron walked out, ten feet tall. He had gone into the office a captain; he came out a full colonel, having skipped the major's and lieutenant-colonel's ranks of day-clerk and chief day-clerk. He was, most magic title, a real assistant manager! His attitude toward Mark Elphinstone combined his feelings toward his mother, J. Hector Warlock, Miss Absolom, Julia Lambkin, Mr. Coram of the Eagle Hotel, Alec Monlux, and Brother Ora-- that is, his feeling for Ora on the off days when Ora was agreeable.

The staff of the Pierre Ronsard became slightly hysterical during the last month of the season, when that already aged shanty was quietly falling down. The stairway to the fourth floor gave way, and they shut off the floor. Half the bathrooms were out of order. A thick fog was enough to make the roof leak. The paper roses on the candy and souvenir stand felt, as the stories say, the chill breath of autumn. The long porch sagged so that it made an admirable slope down which yelping children scooted on thunderous roller-skates. The head waiter left, and it was too late to hire a new one: his place was sometimes taken by the steward, sometimes by Myron, sometimes by Alec Monlux, to the considerable disorganization and sniggering of the waiters' crew. With these tokens of human mortality about them, it was impossible for the staff to pursue man's final purpose of chasing dollars with anything like solemnity. Monlux climbed down from his dignity--no vast descent, in any case--and the staff and the guests chattered, laughed, danced, played practical jokes; the captain of bell-boys was confidential with even the youngest of his privates, the porters openly admitted it when they had been so inept as to get only a ten-cent tip instead of a quarter for bringing down a heavy trunk, the haughty French chef confessed that he had never been nearer to Paris than Quebec, the earnestly hemming steward put a burr down the neck of the hotel doctor--who was twenty-five and very professional and serious--and the prophet and poet of inn-keeping, Myron Weagle, discovered with some astonishment that his art could be gay as well as prayerful.

Mark Elphinstone's query into his secret vices had worried him. Behind a certain mockery he had felt authentic criticism of his Y.M.C.A.ish sobriety and industry. It keyed far back to Ora's frequent complaints about his unimaginative bossiness, Miss Absolom's warning about priggishness, and the disgust of the senior bell-boy at the Fandango when he had refused to rob the inn of its whisky profits. He worried. Was he a prig? He must do something about it. So, on his next off evening after Elphinstone's visit, he had gone out, not with Alec Monlux but with the kittenish reservation-clerk, and with earnest determination had become thoroughly boiled on cocktails and Bourbon, and had gone to her home with a lady of 'uncertain reputation', which means that her reputation was extremely certain. He felt horrible, all next day.

'Hell, I guess I just can't be a sport, any more than I can be an imaginative, poetical cuss like Ora,' he groaned, amid the fumes that filled his head and the world. 'I guess I'll just have to go on being a grind.'

There is no sadder, less sympathetic character than a young man who is so inhibited that he cannot enjoy going to the dogs and thus become dramatic. But so it was, though it is still related in hotel circles that on the day the Pierre Ronsard closed for ever, amid cracking two-by-fours and falling plaster, Myron danced a hornpipe through the lobby, accompanied by the housekeeper, a venerable and Presbyterian lady, and afterward kissed her soundly and induced her to drink a gin rickey, and to tie a sign 'Just married' on the suitcase of Alec Monlux, who was off to an hotel in Kansas City. What is not common knowledge is that next day, with the house-wreckers already at work on the roof of the Pierre Ronsard, Myron returned to it and, sitting on a very little box in front of a very big box, finished up the final report for the Elphinstone central office of the chief accountant, who had gone home the day before, and that he showed his inescapable unromanticism by whistling over the forms and looking altogether more cheerful than when he had danced through the lobby with ledger leaves in his hair.

Just before the Pierre Ronsard closed, Myron had received a note from Ora, and with it a copy of that popular wood-pulp magazine the *Yankee Doodle,* containing Ora's first considerable work of fiction, a long short story, or perhaps it was a short long story, entitled 'Navajo Moon'. It dealt with the wanton adventures of Heck O'Gorra who was, it seemed, a homicidal but benevolent and witty cow-puncher resident upon a ranch in or near Arizona. Though heroic, Heck was a man of doubtful habits, felt Myron. He was given to drinking, playing red dog, knocking out the teeth of officers of the Law, and on all occasions using such foul language as 'Why, you beetle-headed, flap-eared cur', which Ora had got out of Shakespeare, 'You contemptible scoundrel', apparently a dreadful objurgation, West of the Mississippi, and 'Why, you unfortunate accident, I'll pound your polyglot--I'll make your ears and chin-whiskers change places--I'll drive your medulla oblongata right through your saddle-horn, you hornswoggling, barn-burning orphan-robber you!' But never were the pages of the *Yankee Doodle* stained with such horrifying words as Hell or Damn or Bastard. The writers spelled it 'H--l', so that none of the travelling-men, mechanics, trainmen, and osteopaths who read it could guess what the naughty word was, and be thus led on down the path to H--l.

'Navajo Moon' was jammed with Local Colour; with words like riata and arroyo and mesa and Judas tree and greaser and manzanita and chuck-wagon, and with the liveliest description of heat-shimmering mountains and jolly times around the banjo in the bunk-house. There was also a real Western gal, Heck O'Gorra's gal, who wore a short, fringed doeskin skirt, embroidered with dyed porcupine quills, and a silver-mounted ·44 six-gun. She was all-fired Western. She was a breath from the boundless sage. She was also a breath from the Arizona glaciers, and she considered Easterners lousy--though, in 1904, and in *Yankee Doodle,* Ora had not used so obscene a word as 'lousy', but translated it as 'stuck-up tenderfeet that don't know a prairie dog from a by jiminy stem-winder'.

Myron wondered. It seemed to him a considerable feat, for he knew Ora had never been west of Poughkeepsie. He did wish, though, that Ora, with his high-class, refined education--always reading poetry, and cultured British novelists like Mrs. Humphry Ward--would adopt more elegant themes, like Harvard men on the Riviera, or Yale men encountering human magnolia blossoms upon Southern plantations. His congratulatory letter to Ora he ended with, 'Some time you must see more of the hotels. Some of the old-timers among the hotel-men could give you a lot of material about quaint characters among guests, etc., that would sure make a best-seller.'

Not till he had read 'Navajo Moon' a second time did Myron realize that it was uncomfortably flippant about morals, and that the character of the raw young tavern-keeper was probably intended for a portrait of himself.

He decided then not to go home for his vacation, between October 10th, when the Pierre Ronsard would close, and November 15th, when he was due at Tippecanoe Lodge.

He was eager to see his mother, but the picture of his father's frowziness, Ora's jeering, the chilliness of Julia and Herbert and Trumbull Lambkin, was forbidding. It is only in fiction that busy young men far from home spend much time in longing to view the dear, bright, vacant faces of childhood friends and every loved spot that their infancy knew.

But next spring he would have his mother come to New York, for her first journey there, and show her the town. (Later, he actually did it!)

His free month he spent in another pilgrimage to famous hotels, zigzagging north and south, to Toledo, Detroit, Columbus, Cleveland, Pittsburgh, Richmond. Now that he was a real assistant manager and less humble, he came to know many hotel-men; Middlewesterners and Southerners, gayer and friendlier than the sound but over-cautious managers of New England, and readier to experiment with every innovation, from room-telephones to ten-story towers for towns of fifty thousand. He was eager as he crossed the prairies and came to the booming towns and bustling inns. Many old and famous hotels he saw, too. Alas, that most of the famous establishments which then seemed to him indestructible monuments were to be torn down before 1930, or, far worse, be degraded into lodging-houses, like a portly proud old gentleman in filthy linen! The competition of future forty-story titans was as unimaginable to the Myron of 1904, who pleasantly believed that he had seen the 'utmost in modern hotel construction', as is to the hotel-man of 1933 the sort of hotels that will rule in 1962--whether they shall be of 150 stories and 10,000 rooms or, in a smashed civilization, be again squat and filthy inns.

He attained to artistic ecstasy at the old Galt House in Louisville, the Burnet House of Cincinnati, and in Chicago, the much-hymned Palmer House, Sherman House, Briggs House, Bismarck, and Chicago Beach. At the Grand Pacific in Chicago he remembered criticizing the famous game dinners of John B. Drake, which had actually been served right here where he was now standing--he, a much wandering boy from obscure Connecticut hills! In Pittsburgh he searched for the Monongahela, which had been built in 1841, and in 1857 housed the first Republican National Convention. It seemed to him prehistoric; he gaped at it. 1841! True enough, there were a few houses in Black Thread Centre built before 1790, but they were not hotels. Age, like virtue, is comparative; the antiquarian who is all of a bother over an arrowhead which must date back to 1400 is likely to be indifferent to a hillside rock which has been there for uncertain millions of years. The old farmhouses at Black Thread meant to Myron only changeless farmers in patched trousers, while the Monongahela gave him lively, satisfying pictures of ladies in crinolines and a Mine Host (Myron called him that, being a reader of hotel magazines) in vast, curving beaver, and blue tail-coat with shining brass buttons; he saw Civil War generals ride up to the stoop, and heard the long, broken ululation at the news of Lincoln's murder.

He doubled back for an hour of worship at Newcomb's Tavern, in Dayton, built in 1796, though since it had never been what he regarded as a Modern Hotel, his interest was only nepotic and amiable.

In Philadelphia he saw the Continental, Lafayette, and Girard House; in Baltimore, the Eutaw House, built in 1835, even more venerable than the Monongahela. But just that year, in February of 1904, the Baltimore fire had destroyed those distinguished haunts where great men had eaten great oysters, the Carrolton, Howard, and Maltby, and Myron trotted reverently out to mourn on their remains. He would have hung a rue-draped harp upon them if it had been very feasible, and if he had thought of it.

Washington was his veritable Mecca. He had little time, or so he decided, for the Capitol, the White House, the Washington Monument, Mount Vernon, and it did not greatly interest him that just while he was in Washington, Roosevelt I defeated Mr. Parker for the presidency. But he had plenty of time for studious poring upon the Willard, Shoreham, Ebbitt, Riggs, Raleigh, the Arlington, where Mark Hanna had throned it during all his regency, and the National, built in 1827, where Henry Clay and J. Wilkes Booth had lived.

So, filled with pride, proud as a collector coming back from Europe with a Rembrandt, Myron went his ways to Florida.

Where the ordinary traveller would have seen in all these hotels, new and brisk or sunken with memories, only the distance from the railway station, the price-per-day, the extra cost of a private bath, the quality of the coffee, and the nimbleness of bell-boys, Myron looked through their walls and saw the founders risking their fortunes and that of their friends in building what would inevitably be called 'Howard's Folly' or 'Leland's Folly'. He saw distinguished chefs, homesick for Paris, struggling with sullen Yankee helpers to create the one really reasonable art, that of enticing cookery. He saw ratty little 'bus-boys growing up into bland *maîtres d'hôtel.* He saw guests glad of a refuge, committing suicide in despair, blessing the hospitality or cursing the bills, planning to pay with a false cheque, planning to become much better acquainted with the pretty lady across the hall, waiting--always guests nervously waiting in hotel rooms--for customers, for brides, for mistresses, for the police, for death.

He decided, meditating as he sat, chin in hand, on the train, that no church or capitol or university or fort or hospital has so known the heart and blood-circulation of history as a great hotel, where all the people, famous and petty--but especially the famous, since they must travel most--have rested and made plots, forgotten their masks in the exhilaration of wine, whispered in darkened chambers and roared at banquets in the admiring presence of all the press and dignitaries, and publicly thrice thrust aside crowns that had never been offered them.

He was ferociously proud of his profession as he learned, first-hand, the history of hotel-keeping . . . along with such perhaps not less significant matters as his new discoveries about the most compact form of towel-racks, the commercial value of free shoe-rags, the best position for bedside lights, and the excellence of planked Lake Superior whitefish, fried onion tops, Philadelphia scrapple, pepper pot, and beaten biscuits.

And, on many several trains, he became a very pretty authority on Pullman laundry-methods, repair of upholstery, and food-supply, and received from a conductor with five service-stripes the extraordinary compliment: 'Well, you're only an hotel-man, brother, and, of course, you don't have to bottle-feed a lot of greenhorn passengers night and day, like we do, but I swear, I believe you'd make a fair Pullman conductor!'

So he came to busy Jacksonville, to contemplative St. Augustine, down the coast to the sandy, unpainted village of Tippecanoe, and three miles in a crumbling barouche, with a crumbling darky driver, to Tippecanoe Lodge.

12

The wide grounds of Tippecanoe Lodge lay beside an estuary leading from Pontevedra Inlet, which was separated from open sea only by the long sand-bank of Pontevedra Island, with its hard bathing-beach. As they drove along the inlet, Myron was disappointed by the thickets of anonymous grey-green shrubbery. Was this the tropic-coloured Florida? It looked like ragged undergrowth on cut-over timber-land. But as they passed through the somewhat lopsided wooden ornamental gateway into the Tippecanoe grounds, he stiffened with admiration. The grounds were a little wild, but they were radiant, they were scented with orange trees, lemons, coco-nut palms, hairy-trunked palmettoes, live oaks cloaked with Spanish moss, cypresses through which glistened a swamp alive with bird-wings. He had never before seen palms outside a park. And here the geranium that in his Connecticut had behaved as a modest pussy-cat sort of plant towered up like a bush wanton with crimson.

'Tropics!' whispered the Northerner.

On the distant beach, across Pontevedra Island, he could hear the long rollers.

But as they drove among the gardens and lawns immediately surrounding the Lodge, he was shocked. On one side was a row of tar shanties apparently belonging to the negro 'help' of the Lodge, and in front of the shanties, directly upon a driveway supposedly kept chaste for the fashionable eyes and noses of the guests, quite pantaletteless negro babies tumbled in the weeds, wild roosters chased ragged-tailed hens, scabby wash-tubs rested on palmetto trunks, and old men sat in listed rockers smoking corncob pipes.

It cannot be said that after twenty years of training in neatness, Myron liked his picturesqueness quite so close at hand. He preferred it in China, or in books.

Nearer to the Lodge, the grounds were slightly more trim, but over them was an air, an odour, of slackness and decay. The two supposedly gravelled tennis-courts were grassy, a shining-leaved magnolia was full of dead and broken branches, the rose-beds needed weeding, and newspapers soggy with yesterday's rain were left on random benches that needed painting.

The Lodge itself was astounding. It was built of cypress logs, with a vast porch in front and balconies above it at the second and third stories, and supporting them all, high reared, were pillars of peeled cypress, reaching from porch to cornice of carved timber.

The porch was scattered with sweaters, tennis rackets, dog-eared books, cigarette butts. A negro girl, who presumably was supposed to be cleaning, stood at the rail, resting her two hands on the broom and gazing off hazily at the live oaks.

Myron had not been met at the station by the manager, as he had been at St. Louis. He moved hesitatingly into the large lobby, with its unsheathed rafters of cypress and rustic chairs of Carolina pine with the bark left on. The desk was a broad slab cut from a single pine log, stained and polished. The lobby was dimmed by the wide porch roof outside, and at first Myron thought no one was about. Certainly no one was behind the desk to receive him--a major crime in a country hotel just after train-arrival time. He did at last make out a couple of aged and raddled dames knitting and chewing gum--it may have been tobacco--at the far end of the lobby. But all life seemed to centre in a room to their left. Coming from it he could hear singing, earnest but not very sober, and a web of voices.

Irritably, he stalked there, and through an arched open door into a magnificent bar-room panelled with waxed pine. Four darky barmen in handsome white jackets were very busy, and before the bar, drinking mint juleps or straight Bourbon, were at least thirty Southern gentlemen. (Many of them, though, had been born in New York, or in Poland, and had become native Southern by learning to sing 'Dixie Land' and by spending portions of two winters in Florida.) Eight of the gentlemen, with their heads back, their glasses slightly wavering in their hands, were singing 'In the Gloaming'. Seven were gathered about a gentleman who was telling stories which produced cackling laughter. Three were violently discussing the Russo-Japanese War, using the phrases 'brave little fighters', and 'lazy damn Moujiks' rather often. The others before the bar were attentive to their drinking. In one of a series of alcoves along the side of the bar-room, five men, less liquefied, were snappishly playing cards.

Myron stood frowning. From the group about the local Boccaccio a round ruddy man detached himself; a man round and red as a child's rubber ball, and you felt that he would be as flabby to the touch.

'Anything I can do for you, brother?' said he.

'I'd like to find the chief day-clerk. Can you tell me where he is?'

'Well, to tell the truth, he's kind of passed out. We've been kind of having a party to-day. Jerry Lietrich--you know, the New York stock-broker--fellow that's telling the tall yarns--he just got in from the Big Burg to-day, and we been kind of holding a celebration--every year when Jerry hits town--great egg--comes every year.' The human rubber ball hiccupped mildly. 'But maybe I can do something for you. I'm Fred Barrow, the manager.'

'Oh! Oh! Well. . . . Pleasure meet you, Mr. Barrow. I'm Weagle. I believe I'm to be assistant manager this season. Mr. Elphinstone . . .'

Mr. Barrow whooped with a voice unbelievably basso in so soft a little man, 'Gentle-men! Gentle-men! Lend me your ears! Here's the new assistant m.g.r. I told you was coming! We'll all have a drink on him! Real, sure-'nough New York hotel shark! Lemme make you all 'quainted with Brother Weagle. Tim! Set 'em up all around--on Dr. Weagle here! Come on, boy! Come on in! The water's fine--as a chaser!'

When he had escaped from Fred Barrow and the too-congratulatory bar-flies and had begun to unpack, in his little suite (his first hotel suite!) Myron was angry. 'It's all very well for Barrow to raise the devil. He has his position, as manager. I've got to make mine. And everybody will think this crazy-house is my fault. Damn funny position when a subordinate, like me, has to coax his boss to be allowed to stay sober and go to work,' he fretted. 'Well, maybe it'll just be to-day.'

But every day thereafter was another 'celebration'--for the coming of another habitué of the Tippecanoe, like Jerry Lietrich, or for his leaving, or for his just staying on, while the food became greasy, the bell-boys disappeared half the day, the elevator was stuck between floors--how everybody in the bar-room did laugh at that, and at the memory of fat Boylston Leclay climbing up from the elevator by step-ladder. The socks and handkerchiefs and small change of guests disappeared, the floors became dirty, and the employees, all of them coloured save the front office staff, became daily more impertinent and full of idle laughter, for which Myron did not blame them. Fred Barrow and Jerry Lietrich were the masters of ceremony on these daily drunks, and the affable Barrow apparently did not mind the two day-clerks and the night-clerk and the dissipated and aged male stenographer imitating him. His only complaint, in fact, was against Myron for being so stand-offish as to want to quit after two drinks.

So Myron undertook rather more jobs than at the Pierre Ronsard; he was, at different times, manager, assistant manager, night-clerk, all the day-clerks, accountant, cashier, auditor, and sometimes bell-boy; with two fingers he typed answers to inquiries about reservations; he went out to the kitchen to complain to the chef about a menu consisting largely of fried potatoes and corn pone--and little good it did him, for the chef and all the other help were united in a clique which adored the kind Mr. Barrow who laughed with them and gave them drinks and did not expect them to do anything so exhausting as to work. Immediately they hated Myron as a snooper and a spoil-sport and a crank and a hypocritical Puritan.

He was so alone! There was not one person, employee or guest, in whom he could confide, with whom he could take counsel, as to what he ought to do.

He could not, at first, believe it was possible that an hotel, not too cheap or convenient, should go on with such filth, such sour food, such slack service, but as the season grew higher and they came to mid-December, every one of the 110 rooms was filled, and the door to the terrace outside the bar-room stood open night and day, to accommodate the extra drinkers, while the unused tennis courts grew weedier, the riding horses stood uncurried in the paddock, and the boat which was supposed to take bathers across to Pontevedra Island and the beach lay at the pier half-filled with slimy water, while the negro boatman slumbered on the pierhead. Compared with Tippecanoe, the Fandango Inn, where Myron had been a bell-boy, was a Y.M.C.A. camp with basket-ball and light, cheerful hymns.

Myron found the double answer. Not only did the guests, women as well as men, come to this secluded and shadowy place for a thoroughly good drunk away from the rebuking eyes of wives and partners, or of husbands and children, but they had the pleasure of rarely paying. Fred Barrow regarded them as his dear friends. He let their bills run on week after week, to Myron's protesting horror as he sat evenings, in the quiet lobby outside the howling bar-room, glowering over the carelessly kept books . . . the poet, condemned to read doggerel in which 'man' rhymes with 'lamb'.

But he was not meek about it. He had laughed in gipsy days at the Pierre Ronsard, when he had had to repair toilets at three in the morning, or take the place of the head waiter. He did not laugh now. He considered quitting, he was increasingly tart with Fred Barrow, and he put in a good many hours--wearily sitting on the edge of his bed when he had awakened at five, after having gone to bed at twelve-thirty, smoking a dawn cigarette and feeling shipwrecked--in fervently hating the Napoleonic Mr. Mark Elphinstone for having lured him to this Bedlam.

He might have left but for the guest whom he most despised, the anecdotal Mr. Jared Lietrich. Mr. Lietrich had been coming to Tippecanoe Lodge for years. He had some vague association with stocks and bonds in

New York; he wore many various clothes and drank champagne and actually paid his bills. For this Myron might have loved him. But it was Mr. Lietrich who was always the first in the morning to take Fred Barrow away from his office with a rollicking, 'The top of the mornin' to ye, Fred. How do you feel, the morning's morn? Me, I feel like hell and raise you one! How about a little of the hair of the dog--just one, cross my heart, and then you can go back to your dull and sordid toil, and old Uncle Jerry will go out and hoist his self on a hoss.' And at three, then, Lietrich and Barrow would still be at the bar, too dubious of stomach to have taken noon-dinner or anything whatever except eight or ten drinks.

Yet it was Lietrich who stopped at the desk when Myron was alone, stamping the letters the bell-boy should have stamped that afternoon, and grunted, 'Evening!'

'Good evening,' snarled Myron. *('How I'd like to poke him one. Maybe I will. Good way to wind up here--a decent fight. I'd feel better then!')*

'Come in and have a little drink, Weagle?'

'Thanks, no!'

'Well, you're right. Look here, son; get me. You're right to stay off the big booze, and we're wrong. Probably we just do it because we're bored. You're not. You like work and having things shipshape. You're lucky, son! Wish I did! And--I've never heard you spill a word about him, but I know just how you feel about poor old Fred Barrow, the damn rum-hound! He's a prince, and I'm mighty fond of him, but I admit he must be a pest as a responsible boss. But give him credit. He made this place. Before he came here--and that was before Elphinstone took it over, and Fred along with it--it was just a big boarding-house. He made the grounds, the sports--oh, there used to be plenty!--and he enlarged the house by maybe forty rooms, and built the swell bar-room. In those days, he never took a drink except to be sociable. He was a corker at writing letters and getting high class, top-notch swells to come here. Then the booze got him. I know--bad. Don't be too hard, son. Don't think because you happen to have the kind of natural-born make-up so you don't care for getting stinko and singing "Nelly was a Lady" and generally making a fool of yourself, that folks not so lucky are all bad. Stick around, son. Don't quit. Try to cover poor old Fred as long as you can. He's kind of scared of you! Knows you despise him. He's got a heart of gold--honest fact--honest to God. He'd just love you, if you didn't freeze him. Well, you can't help that. Don't blame you. But cover the poor old coot as long as you can. See how good you can make the place without him.'

After an hour's meditation, Myron vowed, 'I will!'

He sought out Fred Barrow in the bar-room and demanded 'I must have just a word with you! In your office.'

'Sure, my boy! Have a hundred. But have a lil drink first?'

'Not to-night, but thanks awfully.'

Barrow was cheered at hearing a kind word from his subordinate, and trotted out so meekly that Myron was touched and snapped at himself, inwardly, 'Just as Miss Absolom said! A prig! All right then, hell, I am! And I'm not going to see this hotel become a pigsty. I am an hotel-man!'

In the private office, he said, 'Mr. Barrow, I was going to quit.'

'Don't do that, son! You're the only executive I've got that isn't cock-eyed all the time! Even if . . .' No more than Myron was Fred Barrow preternaturally meek. He stopped, glared, and wound up with an emphatic, 'Even if you are a long-faced, blue-nosed, water-guzzling, hypocritical baboon!'

'I may be all that, but it's scarcely the point. I can keep this place going, if you let me. The way the accounts are now, we won't last till spring. . . .'

'Well, we've gotten through a good many years!'

'You won't this time. I've dug out the books. Seventeen per cent more unpaid accounts than a year ago.'

'Honestly?'

'Very! I could do something. But I must have authority from you, and your complete backing, to hire and fire anybody I want to, and to dun your friends for payment. Do you care to let me do that, or would you rather I quit--this evening!'

Barrow looked thirsty. Dreadful, having to stay away from a drink for ten minutes like this! Mouth full of cotton! And if Myron went, there would be many evenings even worse, when he would have to be in the lobby. But--seventeen per cent behind last year?

Barrow wailed, 'All right! Hire and fire who you want to--except me! And make the damn dogs pay up. I mean, you take charge for a week or so. I haven't been feeling well. You probably think I've been hoisting too many. Not at all. Not t'all. Scarcely drink anything. But I haven't been feeling good. Be all right in couple days. You just take the bridge till then. Well . . . Got to skip into bar, just a minute. Something Jerry Lietrich wants to talk over with me.'

That same evening Myron walked out to the porch behind the kitchen, found the chef happily smoking there in weariness and majesty, and discharged him.

The chef called out Fred Barrow from the bar-room and made complaint. Barrow threw a glass at him, by way of indicating that they were no longer chums. The chef minded this violence much less than Myron's cold brevity, but he did get the idea that he had really been fired.

Next morning, Myron telephoned to a Jacksonville employment agency for a negro cook, who should not be a Floridian, with possible relationship to the present Tippecanoe staff, but a West Indian. The new cook came at five in the afternoon, after a breakfast and noon-dinner, prepared by a worried second cook, which were worse than the chef's only in that the second cook had tried to cook fancy, instead of giving them the good, plain, homelike, watery hash and soda-reeking biscuits for which his native gifts were better suited. Myron himself met the new chef, a sleek, agreeable-looking quadroon with a Jamaica accent, which is to Oxonian what Oxonian is to the tongue of South Bend, and addressed him: 'Featherstonaugh--that the name?--I'm making some changes at the hotel. I don't want you to be too intimate with the other help. They're good boys, but they've gotten a bit into habits of shiftlessness. You come to me for advice, not to them.'

'Certainly, sir, I shall be delighted to,' said Mr. Featherstonaugh.

That evening, at ten, when he had run up to his apartment for a clean handkerchief, Myron heard Mr. Featherstonaugh discoursing to the rest of the kitchen staff, 'And this chappie, this Weagle said to me, "Me boy, don't be too pally with your fellow-slaves. They're slackers. You are graciously permitted to be intimate with me, but never with them, no ne'er, me boy!" My word, I thought he was the owner, at least, and not a clerk! So I'm to beware of you lads and lassies, what?'

'He-yah, he-yah, he-yah!' cackled the others.

Myron, still and very lonely at his dark window above, sighed as the brisk Myron of the Connecticut Inn could never have sighed, and went grimly down to lie in wait for Mr. J. Surtayne Staub, the jovial Wilmington patent-medicine manufacturer who owed the Tippecanoe for three weeks' board and room, and 294 drinks of rye.

He got something done. The discharging of the old chef, even though he was supplanted by an oilier and subtler conspirator, had slightly disquieted the staff, and Myron was able to have the lobby and corridors more nearly cleaned, the tennis courts weeded--on behalf of the two young men who, out of some hundred and fifty drunks, occasionally played tennis--and unscorched chicken added to the menu. He collected a few overdue bills, but only a few, for over each indignant victim Fred Barrow pleaded, 'Look here, Myron, ole boy, don't push Smith too hard--he's sure t'pay--fine fellow--just waiting for a cheque.'

The monthly financial report, to be sent to the New York headquarters of the Elphinstone Company before January 1st, 1905, would show thirty-seven per cent of bills, payable weekly, unpaid for from two to six weeks, Myron estimated. He so informed Fred Barrow, who gasped, 'As bad as that? My God, I'll have to get busy and collect. You don't know how to handle these bums, my boy. Takes old Uncle Fred to get the money out of these guys with paralysis of the pocket-book!'

For a day Barrow was busy cajoling his chums into deigning to pay part of their bills. Then he forgot it.

While the sunnier souls, enjoying the Florida sunshine, the luck of being able to find a drinking-companion at any hour from eight a.m. to three next morning, and the lack of money-grubbing cashiers, had a glorious Christmas Eve, ending with a dance round the Christmas tree at five on the blessed morn, Myron was sick over the chicken-yard messiness of the place and the feeling that he was a failure.

The monthly report--including expenses, receipts, inventory of supplies on hand, and estimated future repairs and replacements--should have been mailed by December 28th, and on that day it had not even been started. When Myron scolded the book-keeper, he answered, 'Mr. Barrow told me to hold it up a few days till he collects some more cash, so's it'll look better.'

On January 2nd, headquarters telegraphed, 'Monthly report not received stop send at once.'

Myron fussed up to Barrow with the message.

'I *will* get busy to-day--right away! We can just do a little fancy back-dating on the collections, date 'em December, and the report will look all right,' bubbled Barrow, from behind a strong Bourbon breath. 'I'll turn to and help the damn book-keeper, and we'll get the reports off to-morrow morning. I'll work at the report all night, if necessary.'

But it was at no financial report that Mr. Barrow worked all that night.

Myron went early to his room, angry, depressed, hopeless. 'I'll give him a week's notice, to-morrow. I feel *dirty* here. Aah!'

Just then Tansy Quill came in, to turn down the bed.

Now Tansy Quill was the one girl, or indeed female of any generation, whom Myron had noticed at Tippecanoe. As at the Connecticut Inn, with the Wild Widow, the conveniently unattached Myron had received hints from lady guests that they would be glad to see him in their rooms, what time their husbands were devoting themselves to serious drinking down in the bar. He had been too worried, too gaunt of mind, to consider their thoughtful offers. But Tansy had, in the few words between them, become his one sure friend at Tippecanoe Lodge.

And Tansy Quill was a chambermaid and an octoroon.

Her skin was the colour of a tawny chrysanthemum; her Caucasian features were fine but not too sharp; her laughter was easy but never meaningless. She was intelligent and bookish. She had probably read more, and more discriminatingly, than anyone else under the roof of Tippecanoe Lodge, except for Jerry Lietrich. And hers was the common tragedy of the superior negro, in that the poor whites and the poor blacks equally feared her superiority. Even more savagely than the thick-headed white roustabout, the black peon yelled after her, 'Yeh, uppity high yaller--sleepin' wif all de hotel clerks!'

Resented by the blacks as too white, and by the whites as too black. Resented by the illiterate as too sophisticated and resented by the sophisticated as exposing their provincial sophistication. Laden with all the complexities of twentieth-century America heaped upon the dark burden lugged up from old Africa's abyss.

Tansy had been grateful to Myron for treating her as neither black nor white, as neither intellectual nor chambermaid, but simply as a colleague whose work he found competent. She would have hated it if he had lavished on her that excessive attention with which Bohemian and radical white circles, trying to put the negro brother at his ease, make him more uncomfortable than would any insolence. Myron's most extensive greeting had been, 'Good evening, Tansy', but with it had gone an authentic smile--smile curiously weary, just now, for a man of only a little over twenty-four.

She peered at him to-night, as she bustled over the top sheet and patted the pillows.

'Tired, Mr. Weagle?'

'Yes, horribly.'

'The bar-room's noisy to-night--hear 'em way up here.'

'God, yes!'

'Mr. Weagle! It's not my place--and I suppose none of the other girls and men would agree with me--and I hope I'm not being impertinent--but I do know how you've worked to make a decent place out of this dump.' She was anxiously clasping her hands, tapering and coloured like old ivory, in front of her. 'Please don't get discouraged and leave us! It would be terrible, without you. The gentlemen would--oh, I reckon they'd bother me again. Oh, I'm afraid I'm forward! I'm sorry! Good night!'

She fled.

In amazement he blurted to himself, 'Why, she's lovely! Lovely! I could fall in love with her.' He imagined stroking Tansy's hand; he gloated that he did have one ally; and that night, for the first time in a fortnight, he really slept.

The next day the Elphinstone headquarters telegraphed: 'Insist on report at once,' and Fred Barrow, looking sallow, plodded about the bar collecting bills. But the labour, and the disgrace of seeming not to trust his dear friends, was too much for him, and he was dead drunk at five o'clock.

Two days later, a telegram not from the head office but from Mark Elphinstone himself: 'What's idea send report or will be plain and fancy slaughter.'

Barrow commanded the book-keeper, 'All right. We'll have to shoot in the figures just the way they stand now,' and to Myron he explained, 'It'll be all right. We'll pull through. Old Mark and me have been friendly for years. He appreciates all I've done for him, and I reckon he must've cottoned to you, or he'd never have sent you to an old, established place like this from a crazy shack like your St. Louis hotel. Sure. Let's have a drink. Don't you worry, my boy. Besides! I'll get busy right away--this morning. Work night and day, if necessary, and the February 1st report will look swell. I feel better now. I'm going right out and make those damn lazy gardeners clean up the grounds.'

He departed for the gardens--by way of the bar-room.

Three mornings later, when Fred Barrow was again, or still, in the bar-room, and Myron, grown reckless despite the soft encouragement of Tansy Quill, was refusing to let one of Barrow's best drinking-mates take his baggage before he had paid his bill, Mark Elphinstone trotted into the lobby.

13

Mark Elphinstone shook his head at Myron, commanding silence, and slipped out through the dining-room, into the kitchen. He reappeared in ten minutes and went upstairs. He popped into the lobby again, and charged on the bar-room. When he came out, Fred Barrow was following him, wailing, while Elphinstone yapped, '. . . I know, very useful then. I'll give you a pension of fifteen dollars a week. More than deserve. Now get out. Go up and pack. Expect you out of here by this evening.'

The recalcitrant guest, at the sight of Elphinstone's entrance, had paid his bill and tiptoed upstairs. Elphinstone leaned on his pudgy hands, flat on the counter, and gazed across at Myron.

'You're the new manager-in-chief. Try to keep from losing any more money this season. Prob'ly all you can do.'

'Why, I . . . I have the authority to hire and fire and make guests pay. . . .'

'You're the manager, I said! You're the manager! That's up to you! You're running things. You're the boss. You're the boss! I'll raise you. Don't know what you're getting. Don't know at all. Have it looked up at head office. Write you. Good morning. Got 'nautomobile waiting. Catch train at St. Augustine. Good morning.'

Before noon, Myron had telephoned to the employment agency in Jacksonville for a new skeleton staff of chef, second cook, working steward, storekeeper, head bartender, housekeeper, bell captain, and head waiter, all coloured; and two clerks and a book-keeper, white. He specified that none of them should ever have worked within twenty miles of Tippecanoe or have any relatives there, that they should be on the train by eight next morning, and that they should be confidentially informed that the new Tippecanoe manager was a regular damnyankee slave-driver and they would better not take the job if they expected to loaf.

Before evening supper, Fred Barrow had sadly gone off to catch the evening train south, and with him had gone Jared Lietrich and half a dozen other lights of the bar-room. They said good-bye to Myron coldly. He felt guilty. And before supper he sent to every employee in the hotel an order which he himself had typed and mimeographed, that whether they were then supposed to be off-duty or not, all of them should meet him in the dining-room at nine-thirty, under penalty of discharge. The order included the bartender. The bar-room would be closed for the rest of this day; the front door of the lobby be closed and locked, and guests could use the little side door. On the front door he hung up a sign which he himself had painfully lettered, 'Hotel under new management and being reorganized. No new guests received till January 11'.

All afternoon he was besieged by thirsty guests, horrified at the drying up of their well-loved oasis. He solemnly gave each of them a free drink and a blessing. Few of them came back to bother him.

At nine-thirty he was facing the entire staff, in the dining-room, which had the cool, lifeless smell of second-rate hotel dining-rooms everywhere; of slightly rotted woodwork, and old flour paste behind the wall-paper, and lemon pie and cold tomato soup and butter, and the yellow pasteboard of menus.

'Sit down, ladies and gentlemen--no, not back there, come up to these tables nearest me.'

The white office-staff anxiously took the table nearest Myron; the tables behind were edged with dark faces that looked shy but cheerful. Myron held up his hand, deliberately histrionic, till the rustle of whispering had stopped, and he spoke sharply and loud. He saw Tansy Quill's kind face among the chambermaids, but he put the thought of her from him as he made oration:

'Gentlemen and ladies, all of you know, probably better than I do, that this hotel has been going very badly--bad service, bad food, bad collection, and too much drinking. Something severe must be done. I am the new manager, the head boss, understand me? My orders go, and no one else's, understand? And I'm starting by firing you, all of you, every single person! You're all fired!'

A universal gasp trembled in air, like a sudden breeze rising on a still afternoon. Myron was conscious of Tansy's pitiful face, of the fury of the sleek Jamaican chef, of the horror of the coloured head bartender who, just that morning, had been a revered authority on mint juleps and the confidant of white Wall Street financiers.

'When I've finished, I'll be in my private office--formerly Mr. Barrow's--till midnight. I'll be glad to see any of you, and some of you I may hire back, provided you understand there's a complete new deal! I do not, however, include the following; none of them will be rehired under any circumstances: chef, second, steward, storekeeper, head bartender, housekeeper, bell captain, head waiter, or any of the office help. I don't want to see any of you again--ever!--except that you can come to me and get your money tomorrow morning. That's all. Those that want to talk to me can form in line in front of my office, right away. Good evening!'

The polished chef, who had been such a cultural success that in his few weeks here he had already been elected president of the Drama and Fraternal Insurance League of the village of Tippecanoe, rose to ask suavely, 'Boss, am I permitted to say one word?'

'Yes--just about one!'

'Has it occurred to you that with no cook and a few other lacks, the guests are not going to enjoy this place particularly--are excessively likely to leave?'

'It has, praise the Lord, brother. You're all dismissed!'

He faced them for an uncomfortable minute, and inside he was thoroughly frightened. There were whispers; there were angry faces. He wished that he had summoned a couple of deputy sheriffs, and then he was glad that he had not done anything so silly. He perceived, coldly watching his own hot inner fear, that he was bluffing; that he was depending on his position of authority, like a policeman outstaring a mob who, accustomed to be ruled by symbols and formulae, see before them only the blue uniform and brass buttons and not the scared young rookie inside the brass and blue.

Their eyes shifted from his, and he walked out through them.

When he reached the lobby, he realized that the back of his neck was iron-stiff with anxiety.

Most of the staff, save the leaders whom he had discharged without right of appeal, came humbly enough into his office before midnight, begging for their jobs and assuring him that he always had been the apple of their eyes and their notion of a little white father. He rehired perhaps four out of six. He had a moment of relief from troubled responsibility when Tansy Quill hesitated in.

'Would you . . .' she began.

'You're the one person I wanted to be sure to keep, Tansy--only you're raised to assistant housekeeper. I'm sorry I had to include you when I fired everybody. Otherwise I'd have spoiled the show, you understood. Good girl! Of course I want you.'

He patted her hot hand--the only time he ever touched her, except for shaking hands at parting, when Tippecanoe Lodge closed, the coming April.

Otherwise, his one-man court martial was fairly horrible to him, with the necessity of discharging poor men who needed the job. He wanted to weaken, to retain everybody. But he was part of a machine, as helpless as they, and if he kept on anyone who had been too thoroughly trained in the methods of Fred Barrow, they would all be fired, himself along with them, and possibly Elphinstone would close the place entirely. So he brusquely halted the pleading of timidly smiling man after man, the while he was sickeningly aware that it meant debt and hunger for a family.

Near midnight, when he had almost completed his ordeal--and theirs-- a guest shouldered through the line of applicants and, bulking over Myron's desk, demanded, 'Have you had enough of your damn-fool, silly melodrama, Weagle? When are you going to open the bar? I'd suggest right now, if a mere *guest* has any influence in this crazy hole!'

'It will be open at noon to-morrow, provided this place is a little sobered up by then, Mr. Fanton.'

'And I also hear that you've fired every flunkey in the place. What are we to eat? Florida air?'

'Breakfast will be rather slim, but there will be a complete staff again before dinner. By the way, while you're spreading rumours about my madness, Mr. Fanton, just let the guests know that to-morrow morning I shall lock the room of everybody who owes for more than ten days, and their baggage will be held till they pay. Your own bill, if I remember, has now run for three weeks!'

'By God, I have never in my life . . .'

'"Heard such impertinence from a counter-jumping glorified hotel-clerk"! I know. You wait. You haven't even heard the beginning! And don't tell me that everybody will pay up and leave. That's too good to be true! Good night, Mr. Fanton. I'll have your bill put under your door in the morning.'

It was so done. But Myron did not 'have it put'. There was no bell-boy left to put it. Myron himself made out a new (perhaps the third) copy of Mr. Fanton's bill, and slipped it under the door before he went to bed, at three.

It took a certain amount of resolution for him not to lock his door, that night.

Of course nothing happened.

By the following evening he had an inefficient but astoundingly willing staff at work; he had collected every overdue bill, except four belonging to guests who considered the amount of their debt greater than the value of their sequestered baggage and who blithely walked over to Tippecanoe village to catch a train. Out of the hundred and fifty-two happy guests who had been with them the morning before, Myron had lost sixty-five.

He had expected to lose more. But those who remained seemed slowly to decide that, though Myron meanly expected them to pay for what they had, and though the grave new head bartender did not encourage them to melody and to confidences about sexual experimentation, still, they could get down as many highballs as ever, and on the whole it was agreeable to have better food, cleaner floors, and service that actually bustled up and served.

And Myron, his staff working, was utilizing everything he had painfully learned about cost-accounting and auditing at St. Louis and in his furnished room at New Haven on evenings after work. He slapped his face with cold water to keep sufficiently awake to give attention to dancing figures along dizzy lines. He was checking the books of the former steward, chef, and storekeeper. He was discovering how many hundreds a month they had stolen from the hotel in purchasing materials and selling left-overs. He was devising new systems so that weak mortal flesh would not have a chance to be so careless again. And when the kitchen reports came to his desk, daily, he actually read them, unlike Fred Barrow, who had demanded reports but had felt that to go so far as to look at them would be carrying accuracy to a point of pedantry.

Myron's balance-sheet for January twenty-seventh to February twenty-seventh, scrupulously mailed to the New York office on February twenty-eighth, showed only a slight loss in operation, and the number of guests had increased from the eighty-seven who had been left two days after he had taken charge to one hundred and twenty-three. He had retained the address of every prosperous-looking guest whom he had known at the Pierre Ronsard, along with the addresses of most of the 'better-class'--i.e., richer--guests whom he had met in New Haven. To all of these he had written about the glories of swimming at Pontevedra Island beach and playing tennis among the palms what time the north was paralysed with snow. He had written also to his new acquaintances in the hotels he had explored on his way south. These letters he dictated to a young stenographer whose salary he was paying from his own pocket till he should be able to judge of the wisdom of his experiment.

Myron was certainly one of the first hotel managers in America to write personal letters, curiously frank and not too hand-rubbingly cordial, to possible guests. Perhaps he was the very first.

The chary world gives credit to Homer and Hippocrates and Gutenberg and the Wright Brothers and Edison and Ivy Lee, inventor of government by propaganda, but no one remembers the originators of really important details of life--the discoverers of fire and coffee and the wheel, the inventors of the pocket handkerchief and cigarettes, the innovators who first discovered that man can sleep from midnight till eight instead of from six to two, or the creators, like Myron, of the first enticing and flattering sales-letters.

His report sent out March twenty-eighth--next to the last for the year, as the Lodge closed on April fifteenth--showed a small profit, the first in a year and a half; it would provide about two per cent on the investment, which was about twelve per cent more than Fred Barrow had been able to earn in the two years since he had taken to the amusing hobby of collecting jags.

But before that end-of-March report went to New York Ora Weagle had descended upon Tippecanoe Lodge.

Ora walked in as casually as though he had seen Myron yesterday, not a year and a quarter before. Myron, arranging a picnic for half a dozen guests, gaped over their heads at his brother. Ora was shabby, not much shaved, and his hair saw-edged in front of his ears. He swayed as though he were half-drunk even now, at nine in the morning and just off the train. But he waved at Myron most airily, he shouted, 'No hurry, kid', and slouched over to a chair, in which he promptly went to sleep.

When Myron woke him, Ora peered up blearily, shivered into wakefulness, and croaked, 'Oh, Oh, hello, Myron. How about some breakfast? Haven't had anything to eat for two days. *And* a drink!'

'You haven't lacked *that* for two days!' complained Myron, sniffing.

'Oh no; I don't want to be a fanatic--carry things too far! Well, hello! Touching picture of reunion of two loving brothers! I got sick of New York--remember I wrote you from there? Damn cold and sleety. Thought I'd come to see this celebrated land of romance, if you can put me up awhile? Could you--conveniently?'

Ora had ended his speech with less hint of jeering than usual, and Myron roused to cry affectionately, 'Why, sure! I'll give you the best room in the house! Tickled to death you could come down here. Seen so blame little of you, recent years. Like a bath? Then I'll have some breakfast sent right up to you, or you can come down, as you prefer. We have some beautiful sun-ripened oranges--don't get 'em like that up in your lousy frozen north!'

'And the drink?'

'Well--if you want one.'

With a bath, a large breakfast--of which Ora was able to endure only orange and coffee and one finger of toast--a private bottle of Scotch, a jar of dusky roses, and a large dim room with a balcony from which he could look across hammock-land to Pontevedra Inlet, Ora felt reorganized, and when Myron came up to the room, he sniggered, 'Well, I suppose the Big Boss, the manager here, will bawl you out, you poor white-collar office slave, for sticking your insignificant brother in the bridal suite! Huh! Hack-writing may not pay so much, but it certainly leaves me independent of grouchy bosses!'

'I'm the boss myself.'

'Huh?'

'I'm manager here now, manager-in-chief.'

'The hell you are! Manager.' Ora reeked with contemptuous laughter. 'Well, I told you so, long ago--in New Haven, I guess it was. I told you you were a regular Horatio Alger Rags-to-Riches hero. Sure, the real climber! Industrious. Cautious. Never taking a chance--or taking a drink with a man who wouldn't be useful to you! Typical American fiction-hero; the edifying young moucher! Kiss the boss's hand and keep sober and write a nice Spencerian hand, and you'll be able to marry the Old Man's daughter and grow a fat belly and be a complete success, while the poor, lazy, irreverent sap of a poet is a failure in the gutter.' Ora had a drink--another drink. He was rolling it on his tongue and thinking up a new dunciad when Myron plunged.

'I get the idea, Ora. Let's admit I'm a dull plodder, and you're a winged genius . . .'

'My God, Myron Weagle, you've been trying to hatch a vocabulary! You're lucky, you night-clerks that can sit up and have a chance to read while I'm trying to pound out Wild West stories! You'll talk like a regular little gent, if you keep on!'

'Will you shut up?' Ora stared at this new, unapologetic brother. 'It's quite true that you have imagination or ingenuity or whatever it is, and I haven't much. But I'm good and sick and tired of your sneering, Ora. I am what I am--and then some! I'm glad you're here, and I thought your story in *Yankee Doodle* was a swell yarn, as I wrote you, but I haven't done so badly and I know it and I don't want any more would-be funny lip--or any more of your getting drunk in the morning like this--at ten o'clock, and you a boy of only--let's see, you're only twenty-three. Think of it! I'll try to give you a good time here, but I don't want any more of your being cute. Savvy?'

'Oh yes--yes--sure--I was just trying to be funny. Really, I'm awfully obliged to you. Ora, my son, your skit is a frost. Go choke yourself,' said Ora with a demure smile which suddenly changed him from a haggard wastrel into a charming boy.

They went fishing together, next day.

Ora was a more talented fisherman than Myron. He had been trained by Tom Weagle, with a book of verses underneath the boughs of Housatonic willows, and jug of applejack.

The day after that Ora saw Tansy Quill.

She was bustling down a corridor, fresh in a new linen uniform, inspecting rooms. The pile of towels on her arm did not seem menial, for they were of the shining new linen which Myron had purchased to replace the wormy old towels provided by Fred Barrow.

'Lord, what a picture! Swell-looking dinge. Who is she?' Ora demanded of Myron.

'Assistant housekeeper--Miss Quill, Miss Tansy Quill.'

'Introduce me!'

'I will not! You keep away from Tansy!'

But that night Myron saw his brother ambling through the grounds with Tansy, and heard from him, from a distance, wailing '. . . yes, a hard-working poet, just an impractical poet . . .' and '. . . agree with you; old Myron, the finest, keenest mind I've ever . . .'

Worry about Ora's intentions toward Tansy quenched half Myron's pleasure in receiving from Mark Elphinstone, early in April, the letter for which he had prayed:

'Dear Weagle: When you close up the Tippecanoe, come see me in New York. I'll have something for you to do, don't know just what yet, depends on our talk, come see me as soon as you arrive.'

He tried to get Ora to go north with him, but Ora announced, 'No, I think I'll stay here a while--maybe till June. I've found a cabin on the Island that I can rent for ten dollars a month. Swell place to write. I have an idea for a long story about the big swamp here--it's full of atmosphere--thousands of square miles of gloomy cypresses and wild orange trees, and secret waterways and moccasins and panthers and a hidden refuge for niggers escaped from the chain-gang, and their Queen--a marvellous coloured wench. By golly, I'll give the world the first real psychology of the negro in love and in trouble! To say nothing of the grand atmosphere. And of course right here is the place to get all the dope!'

'But there isn't any thousands of miles of swamp here! The biggest one within fifteen miles is about four acres. And I doubt if there's a panther within two hundred miles. And you don't know a thing about the psychology of negroes.'

'Oh hell, that just goes to show you don't understand! If you've got a trained eye for observation, you can see all you want in four acres--or half an acre. And Tansy Quill has promised to help me with the psychology. She's quite a bright girl, for a chambermaid. Now don't go scowling. You've got a dirty mind! Typical Puritan, you are--always seeing wrong where there isn't any! Tansy and I are just friends. Oh, say, could you possibly let me have a hundred dollars to see me through till I finish my big story? Send it back the minute I get my cheque. You know how I am: I always pay my debts.'

14

When Myron left for New York and Ora had moved to his little cracker cottage, with its scant table, bed, and two chairs, the theory was that Tansy was merely coming in to cook for him. She was an orphan, living with an indifferent uncle who let her drift as she would, and one night of relaxed indolence, it was too much trouble to go home, and she rested content beside him on the corn-husk bed, and was glad in the morning when he (for he did have that genius) was neither ashamed nor irritable.

She worshipped him, then, and Myron in him.

And he was happy in her, till he felt that he had explored her soul and come out on the other side, through the jungle to a shore facing new lands which he must enter. No staid settler was he, he meditated, but an explorer always.

Despair was sickening him, for he could not write, nor could Tansy give him wherewith to write.

The story of swamp and crouching negroes among the rotting cypresses which he had seen, definite as rock, when he had boasted of it to Myron, had crumbled day by day. He had nothing there, he realized, save one flaring chromo in his mind--no fable, no people, no truth.

Tansy gave him nothing new for his story. She knew no more about the voodoo or the slavery of the dark quarter of her ancestors than Ora knew about the history of Jonathan Edwards and Israel Putnam of Connecticut; she knew no more about swamps and poisonous moccasins and fevers and hidden cabins of refuge than he did about tobacco-curing in the Connecticut Valley. Both of them, the white hack writer and the part-white chambermaid, had about the same hash of American public-school knowledge; a little memory of Longfellow and Whittier and Poe; the opinion that Lee and Grant had, in vague forgotten ways, shown themselves to be excellent generals; the facts that the square root of four was two, that the chemical symbol of water was H_2O, that Beethoven was a widely esteemed musician, and that the United States was (1), the greatest nation in the world and (2), as a residence for sensitive souls like theirs, the most inferior nation in the world.

Out of this knowledge she picked items for the cultured chatter for which, all her life, while she had made beds and scrubbed out toilets and washed dishes, she had longed. She said excitedly, 'Boy dear, don't you think that Justice is the most important thing we all have to work for--even more than Beauty?' and 'Doesn't it just frighten you, how real Stephen Crane makes things when he writes?'

And he was bored. Her talk was just near enough to that of the more nearly literate of the Happy Hearts group to make him lonely for them. Had he been quite alone, he might have survived and been content, listening uninterrupted to the voices of his own self-praise, but she only tantalized him with memories.

He was so lonely for his fellow hack writers! And a familiar, dependable saloon around the corner! And a jolly burlekew show on the Bowery!

Here, in the evening, you could stay home, or go watch the Holy Rollers, shouting in their tabernacle roofed with palm-leaves, and that was all you could do.

He hated the view from his cabin door, though it had been utter enchantment at first: fishing-boats on the pewter surface of Pontevedra Inlet, poinsettias seen through the veil of Spanish moss, a log cabin set in arching cypresses.

It was so still--and the stillness was insulated by Tansy's loquacity as she stirred a hateful pot of beans.

He did not hear her. He was in despair. He could not write. The hundred dollars from Myron would be gone. He was in disgrace with that old devil Mousey Glebe--jumping his neck, that way, the jackass, for just doing what probably plenty of others did! He was marooned way off here, a million miles from New York. And he could not write. What the devil would he do?

'Boy dear, do you like Frank Norris's *The Octopus? Such* a time I had borrowing it. I was just dreadfully broke then--I was washing dishes at an orphanage! Did you like it?'

Ora drawled evenly, quite clearly, 'Like hell! I only like decent Northern beefsteak--and a little silence. Even you might occasionally note that I'm trying to plan a story, and keep your mouth shut!'

She stood so helplessly hurt, a hurt child, with idiotic quivering mouth and beseeching eyes, that he hated her. He stamped out and did not return for the lunch she had been cooking. She was gone, when he came back at five, after a wretched afternoon of planless crawling through the heat, and he was a little distressed. But that evening she crept back again, crawling to him like a bewildered dog which does not know why it has been beaten, and he hated her for her meekness. He was a man who merited tall proud women!

'Oh, for God's sake don't act like a slave--like your damn ancestors!' he snarled, assuring himself that he didn't really mean it, that he was much kinder than he sounded. 'Or if you have got to show up the nigger in you, why in hell don't you go out and get me some dope for my escaped slave in the swamp story, like I've asked you?'

He could scarcely hear her wail as she fled from the cabin. It was less a sound than a vibration in air.

He was ashamed--also hungry. He would apologize handsomely when she came back. Nobody could ever say that he failed to own up when he had been in the wrong, even just a little in the wrong!

She did not come back, all night, nor all the next day. Toward evening he was slightly anxious, and skulked about the log quarters where she lived with her uncle. He would have seen her if she had been there, easily enough; her uncle's dwelling had but two shallow rooms.

He was worried now, and bilious with his own cooking. He could not sleep, and he flung up from his pallet when, after midnight, he heard a long moaning outside.

He huddled in his doorway to watch a procession of negroes, lighted by pitch-pine torches and kerosene lanterns that threw maniac shadows on the writhing moss hanging from the live-oaks, on cypress trunks and the metallic leaves of scrub palmettos. They were bearing an old pine door, sticky with dry manure, on which, draped in the earthy jacket of a field-hand, was the body of a woman whose long black hair dripped water.

He burst out, to demand, 'My God, what is it?'

The foremost negro, powerful as Hercules and humble as a slave, his moulded black muscles shining greasily in the torch light, muttered, 'It's dat culled gal, Tansy, dat cook for you, boss. She's done got drowned. Reckon she must of caught her ankle in a cypress root and fell in de swamp. Get you another cook, boss? Ah got a smart sister.'

It was dreadful that none of them blamed him, none of them were interested enough in him to consider that he might be to blame. He must go unshriven, ignored or despised by these primitive people whom he had made his brothers.

He tramped the floor in horror. He stopped. His eyes bulged. 'Saints above!' he whispered, in awe at the wings of inspiration. He charged on his typewriter, and banged it from one in the morning till dawn, when he arose, staggering, to make coffee.

Thus he began his novel, *Black Slumber*.

He finished it in two and a half weeks, in first draft. He was so absorbed that no life existed beyond the edge of his vision. He wrote all afternoon, all night, living on coffee, bread on a smeary plate, cigarettes, and white mule; unbathed, unshaven, his shirt collar grey-black. He roused from his frenzy only to telegraph Myron, in New York, 'For heaven's sake send me hundred fifty dollars at once really writing nearly finished novel been lazy before but now come across gloriously bless you old brother.'

He got the money. He finished the tale.

It was the story of Tansy Quill--told from the side of Tansy, and relentlessly punishing her swine of a white lover. Ora gave her the grandeur of an ocean wave. He wept, real tears, the while his ceaseless clattering fingers brought to life her sitting amid hog-slop, longing for the simple culture that was the birthright of any white girl, the cowardly sneering of her lover, and the torchlight among the live oaks as they bore her home dead.

'How wonderfully impersonal a real genius can be!' he breathed.

He shaved, got very drunk, and took the manuscript to New York, revising it all the way up in a day-coach.

It was published, and had enormous critical success and no sale. He became a hack writer again, and never again did he write anything so honest, or financially so unnecessary, as *Black Slumber*.

Within six months he had almost forgotten there was such a place as Tippecanoe, such a person as Tansy, and he was more or less contentedly ghostwriting the memoirs of a rich dowager, and mocking at Myron for his simple-hearted glee in being on the staff of that gaudy New York hotel, the Westward Ho! Only when he was drunk, and Wilson Ketch had gone home and left him to himself, did he again rise to such impersonality as to mutter something about dogs and their vomit.

15

The Westward Ho! to the eyes of Myron Weagle, was a palace. The Westward, as its habitués called it, had 650 bedrooms, and in 1905 was one of the largest six hotels in the world. It was new, built in 1900, and had the benefit not only of Byzantine, Moorish, and Gothic architecture, but also of the room-telephones, elevators and telautographs of America.

Before Myron reported to Mark Elphinstone--the offices of the whole Elphinstone chain were in the Westward--he stopped to adore the façade of the new cathedral in which he was to serve altar. There were fifteen stories of brown sandstone, pleasingly diversified with balconies, grey marble plaques, and small pink marble pillars, all rising to minarets of corroded green copper and huge Moorish brick turrets shaped like hexagonal pears. The building's glory was its main entrance: the golden archway above authentic red porphyry pilasters from Syria, shadowed by the carriage-awning of glass and gilded iron. The lobby, inside, was two stories high, floored with pink marble, wainscoted with yellow marble, supported with pillars of marble pink and yellow and green and black. Above the wainscoting was a frieze (painted by one of the best firms of commercial painters in New York) showing the development of New York from the Dutch, through the English, Irish, and Jews, to the Italians: a fine and lively incitement to American patriotism. The elevator doors were of bronze--rather like the doors of St. Peter's in miniature. The café and bar-room at one side of the lobby was lined with green marble, and full of tapestries, silver medallions, carved oak cabinets, carved ivory chessmen under glass, a carved oak ceiling, onyx-topped tables, teak tables, Flemish oak tables, English oak tables, French iron tables from the boulevards, sporting prints, a gilded harp draped with a silken scarf, a portrait of Mark Elphinstone draped with a Shriner's sash, a photograph of Oscar of the Waldorf inscribed 'To my friend M.E.', tufted leather chairs, curved oak chairs, gilded bamboo chairs, and lights--a glory and miracle of lights--ceiling-clusters of lights, lights peeping out of mauve glass lilies, lights in a large horseshoe formation on the wall, lights and lights and lights behind the glassware that upreared like fairy stalagmites behind the bar.

'Good gracious what a room! Why, it's like--it's like King Edward's own palace!' said Myron.

But Myron had seen, as yet, only what a guest might see. The inner shrine was the world behind the green baize doors at the ends of corridors; the world of the real hotel-makers--the engine-room, large enough to heat and light a city, the shops of upholsterers and carpenters and plumbers, thousands of sheets, table-cloths, and sets of silver and glass and china, mounds of stationery and report blanks, detectives, paymasters, tailors, printers, musicians, florists, cooks, girls who did nothing all day save prepare salads, men who did nothing but open oysters and clams, *gardes manger* who did nothing but prepare cold meat and find use for scraps, assistant storekeepers who received (and save on written order would not issue to the clamorous cooks) everything from five hundredweight of sugar to a single vial of rosewater; and all the office-world: book-keepers, auditors, telephone-girls, telautograph-operators and all the other workers rarely seen by the guest, to whom the personnel of an hotel is composed only of clerks, bell-boys, elevator-operators, waiters, and the affable cigar-stand clerk.

The whole great hotel was to be torn down, as antiquated, by 1929.

And long before that, by 1911, Myron was to be an assistant manager, one of the princes royal of the Westward, and to regard it with affectionate contempt as merely a hovel in comparison with the new Plaza and the Ritz-Carlton which, now beginning construction, was *really* to be the Last Word in Modern Hotels!

Mark Elphinstone had, in a case in his tulipwood-panelled private office, one of the least spurious of the guaranteed authentic swords of Napoleon Bonaparte.

Elphinstone looked across the top of his desk at Myron and piped, 'Do you still want to be a king-pin hotel-man?'

'Yes.'

'Want to learn the whole thing?'

'Yes.'

'Well, I think I'll start you all over again--as 'bus boy, then maybe porter, then maybe ice-cream maker or even pot-washer in the kitchen, and then you can shovel coal a while in the engine-room . . .'

'No.'

'What?'

'No. I've pretty much done all that. I'm an executive now. I'm twenty-five and no use wasting time.'

'Oh, there isn't, eh? What do you propose to do this summer? What'll you do if you don't follow my advice, Weagle?'

'Don't know, till I've had a real talk with you! That's a pleasure you promised me six months ago, Mr. Elphinstone.'

Napoleon in spats chuckled. 'You're growing up. Growing up. Maybe you will be of some use to me! All right. Start in as day-clerk.'

Day-clerk. Assistant cashier. Cashier. A sudden switch to another department, and chief storekeeper, then assistant restaurant and banquet manager, then restaurant and banquet manager--a sort of industrialized *maître d'hôtel,* with the rank of assistant manager. During this time, after hours, two years of evening school in the New York University School of Commerce, really learning accountancy. A journey to inspect all the Elphinstone hotels and restaurants, and the devising, then, and installation of their first scientific food-cost-system.

It increased food-profits in various units of the chain from five to thirty per cent. Napoleon was pleased, and called in Myron one March day in 1911, when Myron was thirty-one.

The office was unchanged, and the two men seemed to each other, since they had been together almost daily, unchanged in the six years since Myron had first faced the old boar at the Westward. But Elphinstone was grey-faced, and puffed whenever he moved, while Myron's thinner hair had a sleekness, his clothes had an ease, his forehead had lines of worry, that had been unknown in the rustic and earnest young man who had come to New York from Tippecanoe and Florida.

'You've done pretty well, Myron,' said Elphinstone. 'Other hotels are copying our food-costs dope. Well. So it goes. You are now in a new job.'

'Yes. 'Bus-boy again?'

'It wouldn't hurt you a bit! Not a bit! Like all my young men, you feel you could run the whole shebang now. Run the whole show. Well, maybe you could. Wish to God you would! I'm tired! I'm sixty-two. Forty-five years I've been in the hotel business. I suppose I've helped to make beds and furnish chow for maybe three hundred thousand different folks. And all I've got out of it is confirmation of my suspicion that all my waiters drink the heeltaps of cocktails when they remove 'em, and all my accountants think I'm an old fogey who can't add a column of figures-- which is perfectly correct. But that isn't what I called you in to talk about, my boy. Your new job is chief purchasing-agent for the whole chain. I'll expect you to put in new systems. Fire any steward or housekeeper or chief engineer that doesn't toe the line about buying. Cut the costs, my boy, cut the costs, cut the horrid costs. Good morning. I'll dictate a memo about your duties, and authorization for you to disturb everybody that is singing at his work and just raise hell with him, raise hell, yes, lots of hell, *good morning?'*

Myron's chief worry, just now, aside from feeling more fagged than was normal, was that the better his food-cost-systems were, the more he made an enemy of Carlos Jaynes.

Carlos Jaynes had been the restaurant and banquet manager of the Westward, and was now the head of the Pan Dandy chain of Elphinstone restaurants. He was a cold, driving, handsome, disagreeable, uncomfortably competent man of thirty-five; one of the few college graduates, as yet, in the Elphinstone organization, and as ambitious as Queen Elizabeth, whom he resembled in everything save red hair and sex. He had criticized Myron's systems sharply and usefully. At first, Myron, the friendly, had been dismayed by the evident hatred of Carlos Jaynes; then it gave lively drama to his work to be not merely a serenely grinding machine but a human being in the midst of a feud, as the Elphinstone employees gathered behind Myron or Jaynes, and all of them looked to Mark Elphinstone and his royal power of life or death.

Myron was tired.

He was none the less tired in that, during this week when he was struggling to co-ordinate all his notions for the re-organization of purchasing, he had to get Ora out of trouble again.

Ora had, after the literary success but financial failure of *Black Slumber* and after a little ghostwriting and a little fiction-writing and the production of a Guide to Canada, which had cost him two whole weeks of travel, two more of research in the library, and three weeks of actual writing, been made editor of a fiction magazine named *Cherry Pie,* and had recently been discharged from the same for buying stories from himself under six other names. He went on a bender which was the talk of all Sixth Avenue, and Myron bought him out of jail, got him sobered and bathed and re-shaved, lent him another hundred, listened to his jeers--Ora aptly mentioned Horatio M. Alger--and found him a job with a theatrical press agent.

But dealing with Ora was picturesque compared with going on working. Myron believed that he was ripening for the 'flu, and in that irritable, feeble state, he recalled, rather surprised, that not in all his life since he was seven--over twenty-four years now--had he had a leisurely vacation.

Oh yes, he did like his profession; he did take pride in mastering it, in being one of the few hotel-men who were by new methods actually transforming it. But there had been so many details, so many years. Every new guest who arrived at any of the Elphinstone hotels on any new day was a new problem and there were so many hotels, so many guests, so many days, so many years, so many details . . .

He was cheered when Elphinstone's secretary whispered that he had a notion that the Old Man was, in his secretive mind, contemplating the raising of Myron to the position of vice-president of the whole chain, with a gambling chance that in another ten or twelve years he might actually be Elphinstone's successor, if Carlos Jaynes did not get in ahead of him.

That did excite him. And he told himself firmly that he was going on being excited. But it was not easy as he struggled with 'Standard of Towelling Specifications: test of weight per square yard, percentage of sizing, breaking strength, warp and filling, threads per inch, fibre', or 'Key Tag Specifications: size, weight, composition, mailability, legibility, remarks'.

So many details, so many years, in the warmed-over air of stale hotel offices and lobbies and halls and kitchens.

Mr. Jewett, this lady has left a pocket-book in the Palm Court and I want you . . .

I'm very sorry, sir; I would like to cash your cheque, but we have a rule that we must have identification before . . .

I want you to try out both sweet butter and salt butter on the same group of tables, and give me a detailed report on how . . .

If the room-service tables tend to rip the carpet seams, it would be economy to mount them on wheels not less than six inches in diameter . .

.

(This *must* be the 'flu. His head ached so.)

Experience has not shown that cafeterias require fewer employees than lunch-rooms and the wasted space behind the bar-room would make . . .

Mr. Exington, I have been very patient, but if you don't have that woman out of your room in ten minutes, I'll come up with the house officer myself and . . .

Dear Madame, in reply to your much valued communication of the sixteenth inst., would say that we shall be very glad to reserve accommodations with bath--without bath--at our lowest rate--at a special rate--with bath--with southern exposure--near fire-escape--away from elevators--with private bath--at our lowest rate--glad to reserve, delighted to reserve, enchanted to reserve, beatified to reserve--you are the only customer who has ever wanted lower rates--we love to make lower rates-- we prize your custom--with bath--without bath--at lowest rates . . .

Why no, Mr. Bobbable, I don't think I've ever heard that one before; it certainly is a mighty clever story; why no, indeed--our theatre-ticket office is closed for the night, but I'd be delighted to telephone myself and make reservations for seats--two in the orchestra?--with bath?--without bath?-- all the seats have baths, six hundred and fifty seats, six hundred and fifty baths, unexampled cuisine, a bath and a half for a dollar and a half . . .

Yes, indeed, Mrs. Javelain, I'll speak to the engineer about your radiator clanking; I'm terribly sorry you were disturbed, and I do hope it won't occur . . .

At our very best rates. With bath, oh yes indeed, Mr. Smith, Mrs. Smith, Mr. Smith, Jun., the very best we can do . . .

In contrast with entrees, oysters should gross at least two hundred and fifty on raw cost not taking in labour costs, overhead or . . .

If you furnished it in Chippendale you would get away from that heavy hotel-effect . . .

Even if you stretch your budget, you've got to include pointing up the stonework, and the operating valves have to be relined . . .

Yes, indeed, I thought the Flushing Ladies' League's St. Patrick's Day Bridge Tournament was one of the most recherché affairs we've ever had in the Carcassonne Room, and those score-pads covered with green cardboard cut like four-leaf clovers were about the most original and . . .

Gentlemen of the Staff, the thought I want you to take away from this Conference to-day is that an hotel is like a three-legged stool . . .

Yes, Miss Heatherington, at seven dollars a head we can serve each of your guests a pint of Rauenthaler Auslese with or without bath at our lowest rates with southern exposure near fire-escape away from elevators at a very special rate by the month with or without bath . . .

'Oh my Lord!' wailed Myron, as his head cracked.

'Influenza' or "flu' is one of those back-attic words into which is thrown everything for which no use can be found. It is to doctors what the back-attic words 'idealism', and 'patriotism' are to politicians, 'virtue' to the moralists, 'realism' and 'satire' to the critics, 'hysteria' to husbands.

Myron presumably did have the 'flu, and for years he had worked too steadily, with too little sunshine and exercise, eaten too irregularly, and never, in fifteen years, spent more than seven consecutive hours in sleep. When he let go, the hotel doctor made him stay abed for two weeks. His nose ran, his temples ached, his eyes were hot, and he was shamefully weak, yet all the while he rather enjoyed his first experience of being nursed and not having to be responsible.

He had time to think--even to think of something beyond the comparative costs of bed-linen with and without the hotel name woven into it.

Just why have I worked so hard and so long and with so little variety?

Just why have I, who am youngish and strong and without dependents, failed to see foreign lands, make love to more women, read more books that did not deal with oil *v.* washed coal for heating, ride horseback, go fishing, learn to paint?

He meant to be very profound about it. Possibly if his furlough had occurred not in 1911 but after the Great War, when it became the fashion to be disillusionized and revolutionary, he would have decided that his work, along with Faith, Hope, Charity, machinery, contemporary art, and the Government had been futile. But he could feel none of the puritanical guilt which afflicts young socialists and anarchists so much more than it ever does Presbyterian elders. He had enjoyed keeping hotel! He had enjoyed making better bedrooms at lower prices. He had enjoyed competing with other driving young men. He did not, he admitted, see that his career had contributed notably to making the world perfect. But then he did not see that anybody's career had done so, except possibly, just possibly, Shakespeare's and Goethe's and Edison's and Rembrandt's and Paul Ehrlich's.

He gave up his effort to make a frugal use of this time-off by fretting about his soul. If he fretted at all, it was because he could not seem to fret. He envied Ora, who could, on the slightest amount of alcohol, begin to fret like anything.

'I'm a smug, complacent, mechanical, ordinary food-merchant. But I enjoy it!' he lamented, touched at the spectacle of a man who couldn't be modern and melancholy.

He actually had time, that fortnight abed and another week achair after it, to see his friends, especially Alec Monlux, sometime manager of the Pierre Ronsard. Alec was manager now of the St. Casimir, a huge, dull, residential hotel near Riverside Drive. What small distinction had ever been made between them as chief and subordinate had vanished now; Alex was pleased to consider Myron an innovator in hotel-keeping, while he himself, he said, was 'simply a glorified boarding-house landlord for a lot of old women with more money and fox terriers than good sense'. Alec was more tender than any woman in his attentions to the sick hero, and he brought in the damndest gifts--a nice book of dirty limericks, a bottle of Piper Heidsieck, a puzzle in which (for no reason that the impatient Myron could ever discover) you were supposed to wiggle a steel ball through an asinine labyrinth of tiny nails, a box of Chinese candy one-quarter of which would have been enough to kill Myron in his present condition, and a most interesting pamphlet by John T. Semmelwack, of the Prince's Own Hotel, Wabasa, Oklahoma, entitled, 'A Study of Modern Flying Machines or Aeroplanes, with an Authoritative Account of the Achievements of Wright Brothers, Curtiss, Bleriot, & Deperdussin, and a Prophetic Suggestion of the Future Effect of Universal Flying on the Installation of Resort Hotels in Locations Now Inaccessible'.

'That's certainly a real idea,' said Myron, turning over his hot pillow.

'Yes, it certainly is--it gives you some real ideas,' said Alec.

Before Alec left, they had planned to open a magnificent tavern on top of Mt. Ranier, served by aeroplanes. They outlined the size, number of rooms, tariff, method of procuring milk, eggs, and oysters, decoration of the lobby, and whether to use bamboo or wicker chairs on the great porch. And that was the beginning and the end of the Mt. Ranier House.

More often, Myron saw Luciano Mora.

It was rumoured that Mora, the young, tall, curly-headed Italian, was the son of an important hotel proprietor in Naples, but whether or no, he had worked his way up from baggage-porter to reservation-clerk at the Westward. He was a student of hotel-keeping such as would not often be found among native Americans for another ten or fifteen years. He had worked in Paris and Baden-Baden and Madrid, and at the Adelphi in Liverpool; he had come to New York to learn Americanese and American mechanical methods, and he had gone so far that he now really liked corn on cob. He admitted that he knew more about omelettes, cognac, and room-waiters than most people at the Westward, but with all the fervour of any recent convert he worshipped, and incessantly talked about, the American hotel's superiority in mattresses, vacuum-cleaners, express elevators, automatically controlled central heating, and coffee.

The Myron who had had for pious dogma the belief that the worst American hotel had better 'service' and 'accommodations' than the greatest palace hotel in all Europe had been shocked to find that Luciano was swifter and suaver in conciliating guests than Mark Elphinstone himself, and from Luciano he had received confirmation of his own mystical belief in the pride and value and honour of hotel-keeping.

'Six generations my mouldy old ancestors have kept tavern in Napoli, and now I am going to show the old buffers a really *good* hotel,' laughed Luciano.

Not even with Mr. Coram of Torrington, or Alec Monlux or Elphinstone had Myron been able to discuss innkeeping as though it were anything more than an interesting way of earning a living. But Luciano was as fanatic as himself. He was the first hotel-man Myron had known who would not have been vaguely ashamed, after the hard-boiled Anglo-American non-emotional tradition, to hear innkeeping glorified as veritably an art. Now, Myron had time, and Luciano Mora took it, and for hours they raved in an agreeable, childish manner not so unlike that of bearded painters at a Montparnasse café.

'I've been considering,' said Luciano, whose English was, of course, better than Myron's, 'the necessary languages for the front office of a real international hotel. No one person there need speak all of them, but naturally, there must be someone who speaks any given one. Well. For a while I was content with English, Italian, French, German, Spanish, Russian, Dutch, Greek, Swedish, Dano-Norwegian, and Hungarian. An hotel could get along if it could provide those. But still, I've been feeling lately that if you're going to have a really efficient hotel, there ought to be people available who speak--here's my list that I wrote--who also speak Japanese, Portuguese, which would handle Brazilians also, Czech, Arabic, Croatian, Slovene, Chinese--the Pekin dialect--Hindustani, Finnish, Roumanian, and Turkish. But honestly, with these, too, I tell to you I simply cannot see any need of others at all, can you?'

Luciano was beaming with that naive, defenceless excitement which is to be found only in the well-lettered and well-bred young European, and he was gratified when Myron drawled, 'No, I guess with those, any hotel could get along fairly well, though I don't believe you should put your ideals too low!'

'Oh yes, that is so very so!'

'Say, Luciano, remember we were talking about central-station power versus the hotel's own plant? Now I've got some really reliable figures on the standard of steam costs per kilowatt. . . .'

'Splendid!'

Mark Elphinstone dropped in to inquire.

Something had happened to the Old Man; he did not chatter now, and he seemed, except for occasional glorious flashes of bad temper, not to care what happened to his hotels. He would come strutting in, bark 'How's the lad, how's the lad--how much longer you going to take a free vacation on me, heh, heh?' and subside in an armchair by the window, looking out up the zigzag of Broadway, and for half an hour the two men would keep each other company in silence. Then he would grunt, 'Wasting time--wasting time--thought you brats were going to teach me this new stunt you call "efficiency". Huh!' And stump out.

Myron believed that, in this dark valley between bright crags of industry, he had found his brother.

He did not expect much of Ora now--though he did keep reminding himself that Ora really had paid back one of the dozen or so loans. When he had his secretary telephone to the press agent's office where Ora worked that 'Mr. Weagle was kind of under the weather' and would be glad if 'your Mr. Weagle could find a moment to drop in', Myron did not expect a response. But Ora came that evening, and when for the first time in his life he saw his older brother inferior to him in energy and determination, he was all friendliness.

'Don't see why *you* should get run down! Nothing to do but hand out room-keys and collect from the goats!' he jeered, but it was a kindly jeer, and he actually drew up the covers--which Myron had just pushed down because he was too hot. 'Say, old man, why didn't you put me on to this theatrical press-game before? It's the best sport of anything I've ever tackled. Oh God, what we put over! Did you see this morning's papers about Lizette Lilydale's engagement to the Grand Duke of Eisbeintafelberg?'

'Yes, I noticed it.'

'I'll bet you did. Some story! Of course she's never seen His Blooming Highness, but why let little . . .'

'You mean it's a fake? Why, I don't know that I entirely like that, Ora.'

'Now what the hell! Don't be silly! You advertise single rooms with bath in the hotel here for three dollars. Have you got one?'

'Well . . . Yes we have!'

'Who's occupying it?'

'Oh . . . a fellow.'

'By the year?'

'Well, sort of.'

'And haven't you ever served fresh peas out of a can?'

'Not exactly--we call 'em "green peas" then, not "fresh".'

'Oh, how very scrupulous, Mr. Pickwick.'

'Well, I guess maybe you win, Ora.'

'Look here, when the doc lets you out of this, why don't you get away for a while?'

'Oh, I couldn't. I'll have to get right back to work. . . .'

'Why? Do you think the "hotel-world", as you always call it, won't be able to get on without you? Guests just be sleeping in the street?'

'No, but . . .' Proudly: 'They depend on me. I'm going to organize a whole new system of chain purchasing.'

'Isn't that nice! I certainly do love to watch you kid yourself, Myron! You really like to work, and so you do nothing else. You take refuge in it. You're afraid of adventure, you're afraid of facing anything unfamiliar, and so you wall yourself in with a lot of audit-forms and inspection-reports. And yet you get a kick out of feeling superior to us lazy dogs, because you think you're more industrious, when you're simply more timid. Why don't you, for once, let go of the hotel desk and try to swim? Jump on a ship and go to Africa?'

'Oh, that's all nonsense!' Myron said feebly.

He wondered if it was all nonsense.

'Well, it's none of my business. Heaven knows why I should horn in, old man. I'm certainly sorry to see you knocked out. What can I do to cheer you up? Shall I bring in a couple of pretty actresses from our shop? Like me to come and read to you?'

'Oh, thanks, no. Just want to rest.' Myron was so touched that he hinted, 'By the way, kid, how are you off for money?'

'Well, I didn't like to speak of it, but . . . You've been so darn decent to me, and I've been wretchedly slow about paying you back, but . . .'

Jump on a ship and go to Africa? No, that would be too much. But the kid was right. He had stuck too closely to his knitting. He might take a little more time off and go . . . But where? And it wasn't so much fun to travel alone. Now if he were only married. Well. But somehow he never seemed to meet women who were not hotel employees or guests, nor to think of them otherwise than as employees or guests. What had ever become of that lovely Tansy Quill? Ora had told him that when he had left Florida, six years ago, Tansy had been blooming and, Ora understood, engaged to a man with whom she was immediately going out West. Myron hoped she was well. But . . .

Where did he want to go? Why should he go anywhere? What he wanted to do, this minute, was to get back to planning the systematized purchase of knife-cleaning machines, pilot valves, butter-cutters . . .

Butter-cutter, cutter-butter, butter-cutter, with a bath, at lowest rates . .

Oh, lord, his head! No, he wasn't well yet, not by a long shot. He had to go away. But *where?*

He knew, suddenly. To Black Thread Centre, to the familiar shops and friendly citizens, to the little American House where he had made his start, to the fields that would be kindly with late May when he came out of the imprisonment of sickness, and most of all to his mother, whom he had not seen since the trip to New York he had given her two years ago. He had seen neither his father nor Black Thread in seven years. It would be, he admitted shyly, sort of fun to show off to the men he had known as kids-- to let them know, if they pressed him, that he was making six thousand dollars a year and apartment free!

Oh, that was childish.

Showing off, like a circus ring-master.

But it *would* be fun!

And so, for that least dignified and best of reasons, he prepared to go to Black Thread for a fortnight's vacation.

On the day he left, Mark Elphinstone called him in to bark that he was to take not a fortnight but two or three months, on pay.

'That's the only way you can get well. If you're here where I can get my hands on you and shove work on you, I'll do it. So you damn well stay away for at least two months!' yelped Elphinstone.

And that, Myron admitted to himself, was perfectly true.

Myron looked over his wardrobe. It was extensive; it had to be, in the hotel business. It was almost too extensive, for he would never dare to appear on the streets of a jeering Yankee village in the voluptuous morning coat and striped wedding-trousers he had worn as a desk-clerk at the Westward. Yet he bought seven new and expensive ties, white flannels and white buckskin shoes, a bathing-suit, very expensive, and a vaguely useful sweater, and it cannot be said that the researcher into Scientific Purchasing According to Standards showed himself any more scientific when he got into the hands of an uppish haberdashery clerk than any other oaf. He stood meekly and held up the tie which the clerk had so deftly twisted and cheeped, 'Yes, I guess that would look nice.'

Also he bought, unscientifically, a new pigskin bag.

And for his mother so many stockings, blouses, inlaid Italian boxes, fur tippets, satin dressing-gowns, and canisters of imported Russian caravan tea that he had to get still another bag to hold them. But for his father and Jock McCreedy, the bartender, who alone was left of the American House staff that Myron had known, he needed no great storage space: he wisely took each of them nothing but a bottle of forty-year-old Bourbon whisky.

The Myron who entrained at the Grand Central was thirteen years older than the boy who had left Black Thread for Torrington, at eighteen. His face was far older, thinner, more lined, yet his quick step was really younger than that of the lurching rustic who had gone doubtfully out to conquer the world. He had seemed a biggish club of a lout, then; now he was a thin sure blade.

He was excited as they came into Bridgeport, as he changed cars for Black Thread, as they crept up a valley filled with May. He was grateful to Ora. He felt that he was entering upon an adventure, perfectly concealed from him yet greater than any he had known. Perhaps it was that, after learning book-keeping and fish-frying and plumbing and buying pillow-cases, he was going to learn Myron Weagle.

16

He had not let his family know that he was coming. Not expecting him, the 'busman at the Black Thread station, who had sat beside him for years in school, looked at this City Feller and muttered "Bus, sir? Take your baggage?' with a show of respect which he certainly would not have yielded to ole Myron Wiggles.

His baggage he did send to the hotel, but he walked, greeting each small building--the paint-shop that had once been a chapel, the farm-machinery warehouse, Lambkin's Drug Store, old Mr. Doane's noble Greek residence. 'There's where I socked Herbert Lambkin with a snowball!' he rejoiced, 'and there's--yes sir, by golly, it's the same old sign--there's the grocery sign we stole on Hallowe'en and hung on Prof. White's privy!'

He had always heard that when you returned to your native village, everything seemed ludicrously smaller and shabbier than you remembered. He did not find it so; everything seemed extremely important and excellent. What city drug store had such a handsome display of soaps, tennis shoes, hot-water bags, collyriums and bottled pickles as Lambkin's? And that was a most interesting improvement: the ratty old junk-shop had been torn down and replaced with a handsome new galvanized-iron potato warehouse! He rounded the corner and saw the American House. It certainly was as tall as the Westward, so built upon with memories was it above the visible bricks. He had swept that upper balcony, he had washed that plate-glass window, he had tacked up the netting on that screen-door, he had hauled trunks out of that slanted basement entrance. And there was another Myron Weagle, a gangling broad- chested youth, sprinkling the sidewalk with, surely, the same battered green watering-can!

Instantly he was no longer Mr. Weagle of the Westward, but the unfledged Myron of thirteen years ago. He had to work at it, to play his city-feller joke on the boy.

'Hello, Cap'n!' (But did he really sound like J. Hector Warlock?) 'How's chances for a room here to-night?'

'Sure, boss, come in and we'll fix you right up. What you travelling for?'

'Trail and discovery.'

'Don't know the company. Is it a new one?'

'Yes, and probably already bankrupt.'

'That a fact? Well, that's hard luck. Come on in and register.'

Meek behind this self-confident young hotel man, Myron entered the office and beamed upon worn leather rockers, tall brass spittoons (not polished as he's polished them!). Behind the desk, in his shirt sleeves, sucking a toothpick and trying to play tunes on the strings of his suspenders, was his father.

'Gent wants a room,' said the boy.

'Right here, brother. Put down your John Hancock,' said old Tom, as he had been wont to say it fifty times a week, thirteen years ago. Tom whirled the register round with the familiar click. The only very modern improvement was that the clotted pen reposed in a jar of shot, instead of in a potato.

'This is something *like* an inn,' Myron gloated to himself. 'No signing of an elegant little card, while the clerk aims his gardenia at you!'

The old smell of tomato soup and soap and straw matting and roast pork crept round him, instead of the Westward's scent of marble and face-powder and fur coats. He sighed contentedly as he signed the register.

The old man had not looked at Myron's face. He did not care. He had seen too many guests, and he was sixty years old now, and very grey, and the apple-jack wa'n't what 'twas when he was a youngster, not by a long shot! He was uninterestedly reading Myron's signature, upside-down. Then he gazed, he gaped, and whooped, 'Well, I'll be everlastingly, teetotally doggoned! Myron! Why, boy, I never had such a fine surprise in my life! Come right out and see your Ma. Why, say, you're dressed as fine as a Jew pants-salesman! Well, I guess maybe it's true what they say--that you're making good, and pulling down your sixty dollars a week.'

His mother was basting a roast, wearing what might have been, and possibly was, the same spattered apron she had worn thirteen years ago. She straightened up, peered through crooked gold-rimmed spectacles as though she was frightened, and cried, 'Why, my boy, has anything gone wrong?'

'No! No! Mother! I've just come back for a little vacation!'

'Oh!' She kissed him, held him off to look at him, but with all her undiminished fondness there was a rustic awe of this man who was not so much her son as a Great Success from the Big City.

He felt that he had lost her, along with his home village; lost all of her save her unquestioning love. He felt the tragedy of the surrendering generation, in especial the tragedy of a woman like his mother who, just because she had dedicated herself to managing her men-folk, old Tom and Ora and himself, so that they would not go too wrong, and had never expected anything more than halfway decency in them, was humble before them when one of them did turn out normally competent and self-reliant. Had he been a leering failure, he might have kept her mothering intimacy!

The women who serve without knowing that they serve, or ever whining about it!

So, while he was being chatty and affectionate, he was reflecting, 'I've never done a thing for her. Ora was right! I've been so absorbed in making myself a swell clerk that I've forgotten to be a human being. But I will do something for her, something fine!'

Old Tom did not suffer from obsequiousness to his son. 'Well, boy, now you're here, you better strip your coat off and help us a little. You ought to have some pretty good hotel experience by this time. I want to figure out a way of perking up the office a little. Guests getting so doggone choosy these days. Maybe you might paint it for me.'

'Why, the very idea!' Myron's mother turned on Tom with moist, gravy-smeared wrath. 'He's not going to do anything of the kind! Painting! Him all tired out after all his hard work in that great, big, huge New York hotel and coming home for a rest, and then you expect him to work like a nigger! I'm ashamed of you! Don't you want to go up and lie down awhile, Myron?'

'No, I want to see the old place. Had lots of good times here!' said Myron. 'Let's have a look at the old bar!'

Tom found this an admirable excuse to go in for a drink.

As they went through the wash-room to the bar-room, Myron noticed that above the cast-iron stationary bowl still hung, on thin chains, a public comb, and a brush worn soft as old linen.

Behind the bar they found Jock McCreedy, who shouted, 'Well, I'm a son of a gun! Here's Charley Delmonico come back to the old shanty! Shake, boy! Mighty proud!'

'Well, he ain't done so much. He's done elegant, but why shouldn't he? I taught him all he knows,' observed Tom.

'That's right,' said Myron. 'Say, wait just a minute. I've got something for you boys out in my bag.'

He brought in the two bottles of ripe Bourbon.

Jock McCreedy, tasting, rolled up his eyes, held up his hand, and murmured, 'Say, Myron, that certainly makes it up to a man for all the woes and tribulations of a sinful world, like the fellow says!'

But Tom grumbled, 'Well, I suppose it's good licker, but it ain't got much kick. I like to have my stomach telegraph up that it's had something stronger than diluted well-water!'

Jock looked at him in pious horror.

Myron was considering that, though his mother was more beautiful than ever to him in her tragic timidity, yet Mark Elphinstone or Jock McCreedy was spiritually more his father than Tom Weagle, Alec Monlux or Luciano more his brother than Ora, and his tight sunless office at the Westward more his home, now, than Black Thread Centre.

While Tom was droning on about his expert opinions on 'store whisky', apple-jack, and white mule, Myron was thinking that he had paid a good deal for the privilege of helping to make a clear, efficient, merciful system out of the tangle of commerce and industry. His easy-going employees resented him as supercilious and fussy. His old friends--even, he now saw, perhaps his father--felt that he was a hard money-grubber and climber, who had lost the pleasant sentimentality of boyhood. The 'intellectuals', like Ora, were certain that he was a vulgar Philistine, because he provided excellent bathrooms and ice cream (which people wanted) instead of providing atrocious paintings or novels (which they didn't want). To the old friends, he was too top-lofty an intellectual. To the intellectuals, he was too low a pedlar. To the pedlars, he was too scrupulous a fanatic about exact financial reports and honest advertising.

'Well, let 'em all roast me. I seem to go on living through it,' he thought, and delighted Jock McCreedy by asking for a golden fizz--a drink in whose mixing, Jock believed, he was superior to any barman in Paris, Kokomo, Shanghai, or North Braintree.

During his two months in Black Thread, while he was roaming the hills and lying in the sun and swimming in clear streams, while he was renewing acquaintance with old friends--or really, while he first had the leisure to become acquainted with them at all--he was busy.

'Mother--Dad--I've got an idea,' he said abruptly at the family supper-table, 'I've got an idea.'

'Don't let it bite you,' said Tom.

'Hush! . . . What is it, dearie?' said his mother.

'If I'm to carry it out, I've got to have a free hand and no discussions. I haven't got much time here. Now listen. The new thing in travel, and in hotel-patronage, is going to be automobile touring. Within another five or ten years, automobile tourists will be more important than travelling-men to an hotel like this, on one of the through routes from New York to the Berkshires and Canada. But to cater to them, you've got to have a garage, more flexible meal-hours, European plan instead of American, and a better decorated house all through.'

'Rats!' said his father, authoritatively. 'Never amount to nothing, this auto-touring. I was reading here just the other day where folks are getting so sick of breakdowns and gasoline stink that they're going back to hosses. By 1916 or so, you won't hardly see an auto.'

'Yes? Well, you're wrong. I'll give you my plan, dad. Take it or sink it, but don't argue! You ought to own this place, not just lease it. I'll buy it for you, and put it in shape, and build a garage, financing the whole thing through the Hotel Enterprise Bureau, of New York, and we'll lease it to a good small-town hotel-man. Even with the interest on the mortgage, I think you can count, if my figures are correct, on fourteen or fifteen hundred dollars a year clear profit to live on, and then you two can rent a bungalow here, and you won't have to do anything but loaf. I think you deserve it, ma, after all the years you've worked!'

'Oh, it would be lovely to lie abed till seven o'clock every morning!' sighed Mrs. Weagle.

His father did argue, of course, and insist that he needed a few days (which meant a few drinks) to do a mysterious something to which he airily referred as 'thinking it over'. But his mother's nod and smile had been enough for Myron. With an hour or two a day of restful business between rather tiring spasms of devoting himself to loafing, Myron in two months carried on more activity than had gone on in the American House in twenty-four years.

He hired as stenographer the smart little daughter of Reverend Snibbs, just graduated from business school in Bridgeport. That by itself, said Tom, showed Myron had got his head full of nonsensical ideas; all his life, running this whole hotel, he'd been able to get along by writing all the necessary letters by hand. Why! In one single letter, he'd ordered as much as four new bureaus!

Myron dictated some fifty letters to people, all over the country, who were advertising for the lease of country hotels. While Daisy Snibbs was writing these, and for the first time the American House was echoing to the sound of any faster typing than that of a drummer picking out reports with two fingers on a portable, Myron dashed down to New York, saw the Hotel Enterprise people, and apparently came back with assurance of finances, on a contract signed by Myron and by Mark Elphinstone.

Mark had observed, 'You back? Why, damn you, Myron, I told you to get out and loaf in the sun even if it roasts your damn hide off! Sign what? All right, all right, don't bother me with the details. I got hired men like you to look into those things!'

It appeared, then, that a quiet, rather shabby little lawyer from Torrington, whom Myron had known as a guest at the Eagle Hotel, had already taken an option on the American House building and plot; and that of the old livery stable behind it--and that he had taken it on behalf of Myron, who, with a swiftness that made his mother's head ache and made his father almost civil for a day or two, took up the option, bought the two 'parcels'. Instantly, workmen were busy remodelling the stable into a garage; tearing out stalls, putting in a cement floor, work bench, air pump. Other men were building behind the American House a twenty-room addition, with five baths, out over the alley and back yard, and providing for deliveries and the disposal of garbage through a truck-entrance into the basement. Others were installing five new bathrooms in what had been single rooms, so that eventually the American House would have forty-nine bedrooms and fourteen baths. A brisk little lady from a Hartford department-store was looking with dislike upon the spittoons and honest old scruffy leather chairs in the lobby, the equally honest iron beds and straight chairs in the bedrooms, and practically, Tom mourned, throwing them away. She then, according to Tom, turned the office crazy; in place of the straight, respectable lines of chairs along the walls, she put in a nasty mixture of wicker chairs with cretonne cushions, and leather chairs that weren't rockers, all of them in different groups, so that there was no geometrical arrangement to the room. She reduced the lordly desk to a mere nook in a corner, and hid the key-rack. And in the bedrooms she installed still other despicable wicker chairs, and painted pine bedsteads without one ornamental iron curleycue. But it was the dining-room that she most disfigured. She got rid of the long, solid, satisfactory tables and put in small separate tables with red tops on which, she directed, not luxurious thick cotton table-cloths but dinky little d'oyleys were to be used; and the wall she painted a shrieking canary yellow!

When Ora ran up to Black Thread, as the work was being finished, he groaned, 'Well, Myron, you've certainly brought some elegant urban improvements to our hick town! The hotel used to be just an honest country inn, that didn't pretend to be anything else, and now you've made it into a very handsome fourth-rate imitation of a city tea-room, as kept by our best cultured spinsters! If there are any J. Hector Warlocks left, they'll be just tickled pink to sit in a painted wicker chair and satisfy their appetites with a cream cheese and jelly sandwich!'

'It's what motorists like. And it's comfortable and cheerful. It doesn't look like the inside of a rubber boot, now!' snapped Myron.

He was so vexed that this time he would lend Ora only fifty dollars. For days--well, for hours--he wondered if his new delight really was pretentious and bogus. Well, damn it, if the place didn't suit such original intellects as Ora, they needn't look at it!

And J. Hector Warlock? Where was he? A grand old boy!

No one had seen J. Hector for years. Jock McCreedy had vaguely heard that he had gone West and made money in mining.

'I wonder,' Myron thought uncomfortably, 'if J. Hector *would* like stripping for poker and sitting in one of Miss Bombazine's chairs? Well, anyway, Mrs. J. Hector would like 'em, and it's the Mrs. J. Hectors who are going to be considered in planning the automobile trip and the stopping-places and everything else, in the motor age, and . . . Oh, damn Ora and his damn superiority! I've got to hand it to his ability. He's managed to take all the fun out of my doing this!'

The remodelling of the hotel was finished and it was rented (though not for a couple of months after Myron had finished his vacation) for a sum sufficient to pay taxes, interest, and depreciation, and still give Myron's father and mother thirteen hundred dollars a year on which to lead a life of cultured leisure. Mrs. Weagle read clear through a book by E. P. Roe!

And for all his hotel-building, Myron was devoting himself to the task of being lazy.

17

He saw coming toward him, on his second afternoon in Black Thread, when he was wandering through the village and being edified by the information, 'Well, you been away quite a while', a tall man who looked as though he were vigorously going somewhere but was not quite sure where it was; a tall man with a high forehead, thin hair, large spectacles, and high black shoes. The man looked rather like Herbert Lambkin, but surely could not be, for Herbert was not older now than thirty-two or -three, and the man approaching looked forty.

It was Herbert Lambkin, right enough.

He manhandled Myron in greeting, and spouted, 'It certainly is fine to see you in the old town, Myron! I hear everything's gone fine with you.'

'Oh, so so.'

'Staying a while?'

'Yes, a few weeks, I guess.'

'Well, we must see a lot of each other. There's nothing sadder in life than the way old friends of boyhood, comrades at arms, you might say, permit the currents of life to part them. We must have some good walks and talks, and try to break bread together.'

'Yuh--yuh, sure!'

'I'm sorry, Myron, we didn't see more of each other in New Haven, but of course we were both so busy trying our fledgling wings and . . . I presume you are staying with your father and mother?'

'Yes.'

'A splendid couple! Such sterling characters!'

'But what are you doing here in town, Bert? Aren't you teaching in some university? Commencement time already?'

'No, not exactly, though I'm seriously considering one or two very flattering offers. But after I took my M.A. at Yale University, in English Literature, you know, I had an irreconcilable feeling that one ought, you might say, to enter education through the foundation, if you don't mind the metaphor, instead of just flitting in through the attic window--in other words, a really well-rounded educator ought first to familiarize himself thoroughly with the instruction of the child-mind, so for some years now I have been superintendent of schools here--a position, I trust, not without some credit and responsibility, and . . . We were pretty wild lads in college days, eh? beer and who knows what, but now I'm afraid my salad days are over, and I'm settled down, with a wife and a couple of bonny children!

We're planning to build an up-to-date bungalow, but just for the present, my little family and I are staying with my father--that big, roomy house, and father so pitifully lonely since the death of my mother, and you must certainly come and break bread with us there, Myron, and very soon, and I'm sure Julia will be particularly glad to see you. I seem to remember that you were a bit sweet on her, as a young lad.'

'Oh, Julia. That's right. Your sister. Yes--yes, sure--I was quite in love with her. Ha, ha, ha!'

'Ha, ha, ha!'

'Quite struck on her! Ha, ha, ha! Well, I've got to be . . .'

'Ha, ha, ha! That's so. Well . . .'

'What's become of Julia? She still in town?'

'Yes, uh, just, uh, temporarily. She married a fine fellow from Sharon, Willis Wood, the electrician. He isn't exactly a college man, but even so, he's got one of the finest minds you ever encountered. He can make the mysteries of electricity so plain that anybody who runs may read; he even makes them clear to me, though, to tell the truth, and this despite the fact that it is one of my less amusing tasks, among many others, to teach physics in high school, but what I mean to say is, I never did have a natural talent for the sciences--my natural bent is more artistic and literary and perhaps psychological, but Willis has a natural insight into electricity that's simply astonishing--just like the grasp of commercial problems that I'm sure you must have, old man.'

'I see. Well, I've got to be hiking on. See you later. I suppose Julia lives in Sharon, then?'

'Well, not just at the moment. The electrical profession has been a little overdone lately, and Willis is waiting for a new opening, and meantime he's here in Black Thread, helping father in the store, and he and Julia are also living with me and father at the old home, and she has two lovely children, too--just lovely! So you must come and dine with us all!'

'Yes, be glad to. Well, I've got to be skipping along. Fine to seen you. See you soon!'

Myron was too relieved at escaping from Herbert to get any particular joy out of seeing the humility of the retired Brahmin who had once considered him an Untouchable. After Herbert, it was sheer ecstasy to sit on the stone bridge and just gently, lyrically, spit in the creek.

That evening, while he was defenceless in the American House lobby, Herbert descended upon him again.

'Well, sir, it's mighty nice to see your face around the old town again, Myron! We certainly have missed you. This town needs enterprising men like you. Why, do you know, I haven't been able to get the business men of this town interested in either the Boy Scout movement or Rotarianism, although I have ventured to give them my opinion as an educator, as a University man and a Master of Arts, that there are no movements that tend more to develop patriotism, good citizenship, and the social point of view than these; so much so that it might be novel but quite sound to say that, despite the different origins of these two great spiritual awakenings, a Boy Scout is a young Rotarian, and every Rotarian is a Boy Scout in long trousers! I've thought of presenting this, perhaps, somewhat original point of view in a piece for the *Educational Review,* but I have been so engrossed in the cares of the poor driven educator that I have not had the time to . . . But that's not really what I dropped in to see you about. When I told the family of my good fortune in encountering you on our village street this afternoon, they all hailed my suggestion that you must somehow be coerced into coming and breaking bread with us and how about Friday evening, have you a date?'

'Well . . . no . . . I . . .'

'Then we won't take "no" for an answer! Friday evening then, six-thirty. You must pardon us if we merely have our customary village supper instead of the evening dinner to which I suppose you are accustomed in the great caravanserais of the Metropolis, and of course, you need not dress-- we practically never do.'

'That's good. I didn't bring any dinner clothes.'

'No need of them here at all, my dear fellow; no need at all. There are only one or two residences in the vicinity at which it is at all customary for the household to dress, except on the most formal occasions.'

('My God! Bert should tell me about Black Thread Centre!')

'So, then, we'll expect you at six-thirty on Friday, and I need not assure you that it will be a most grateful re-union and commemoration of our happy childhood. Now there is one other thing. Uh--say, Myron . . . The fact is: though I prize greatly the civic opportunities that lie open to the village educator, touching the minds of the Little Ones, who will later be our stalwart citizens and the pillars of the Republic, when they are still dewy and fresh, yet this great *métier* is not what you might call really well paid. Just between us, and I don't want you to tell this to any of our good old friends as you encounter them in New York, but my stipend for all the toil and responsibility which I must shoulder is only sixteen hundred dollars a year! And I must begin to consider my wife and the little ones and . . . Now you have a great and influential position in the hotel-world. . .'

'I have not! I hope I may have, some day, in eight or ten years, but I've merely made a good beginning.'

'Nonsense, nonsense, my dear fellow. I know you better than you do yourself! I can see, just talking to you, Myron, that you have great capacity and influence, if you care to use it. I could discern that way back when we were boys. Whatever else I may know, I have a curious natural gift for being able to judge people's characters on sight. I suppose that's the key to what humble success I may have had as an educator. But what I mean to say is . . . Now with all your influence in the hotel-world, I wonder if you couldn't put me on to a good opening where I could make better, or certainly much better-paid, use of my capabilities.'

'Why . . . well . . . uh . . . Just what training have you?'

'My dear fellow, a man who has cared for every detail of the lives of hundreds of children . . . Think of what I do here, daily, entirely aside from teaching and formulating curricula. I have to choose teachers. I have to be able to tell instantly whether some poor grubby little urchin is lying to me. I have to be a really skilled technician--you know the natural bent I have always had for architecture, and possibly it was a mistake not to have followed that up, but I mean: I have to be no mean expert on such sordid details as heating, lighting, ventilation, an adequate supply of clean, pure drinking-water and, uh, if you will pardon my being so realistic, the arrangement and conduct of toilets. And there is perhaps a yet more important factor. As I understand it, the making of entertaining yet informative after-dinner addresses is no mean part of the modern Boniface's equipment and if I may say so without boasting, it just happens, through no virtue of my own, that I seem to have the gift of oratory and, I am told, of rather witty eloquence . . .'

Myron did not get rid of him till after eleven, and he was not at all sure that he had made it clear he was not going to find Herbert a job at the Westward. Jock McCreedy, who had twice come in from the bar to try to rescue him, was very comforting. 'You've been sitting under Prof. Lambkin for two hours, kid. What I prescribe is a whisky sling.'

'Jock, did you know I'm an Eminent Boniface?'

'Well, if you are, they're certainly making the Bonifaces a lot skinnier than when I was a young fellow. Here's how!'

Like the streets of Black Thread Centre, the Trumbull Lambkin mansion had for Myron, at first, most of its ancient awe. The side porch no longer seemed unique, but the heavy cherrywood stairs from the hall, the heavy black walnut chairs and marble fireplace and glassed-in bookcases in the parlour still spelled for him unassailable respectability.

But the Lambkins themselves, in the mere flesh, had no particular sanctity.

Before he had returned to Black Thread, he had absolutely forgotten Julia, the queen of Gibson Girls. In the two days before the party supper, he had managed to work up considerable sentimental excitement about her, but it dropped dead the second he stumbled up to her in the parlour, breathed 'Julia!' and looked at her. She was a rather tall, long-faced woman, with sunken cheeks and wrinkles of anger about her eyes, and she seemed a generation older than himself. He was made nervous by the overpowering cordiality with which she shrieked, 'So you thought you were going to give your old friends the go-by and not come see us, now you're such a great success and all! I've certainly got a bone to pick with you for that! 'Well, Myron, it's grand to see you--it certainly is just dandy! I want you to meet my husband, and see my kiddies . . . . They were bound and determined they'd stay up to see their Uncle Myron!'

And so she stood, a thin woman worn with housework, surrounded by her jewels: Mr. Willis Wood, a youngish male with eyeglasses and hair parted in the middle, and two small children who looked extraordinarily like all other children; and she beamed, and Myron wiggled his face with grimaces and felt melancholy and a little embarrassed.

He had so often seen this same family group, with no magic for him, not even the elegance of Gibson-girlism, creeping awkwardly toward a hotel desk, wondering how much a double room would cost, and whether they could get the whole family into one room.

He was painfully cordial to Willis Wood, and bubbled, 'Well, I certainly congratulate you, Mr. Wood, getting this lovely bride.' ('Grrrr! The way she used to high-hat me, damn her!') 'If you'll keep it to yourself, I'll admit I fell pretty average hard for her as a youngster, Mr. Wood!'

'Call me Willis,' croaked Willis.

It was his brightest remark all evening.

Nor had the lordly Mr. Trumbull Lambkin preserved any grandeur. He had lost the selectness of grey side-whiskers; he was simply a meagre, stooped old man who mumbled that in his opinion, hotel-rooms in New York cost a lot of money.

Herbert's wife was a plump little woman, a nice little woman, a cheery little woman--in fact she was a Black Thread Centre little woman. It seemed that her two sprigs also invariably called the guest 'Uncle Myron', but they had not learned that they did so well as had Julia's kitty-witties-- on sight of their Uncle Myron they merely giggled and fled, for which he liked them better than anyone in the room, till Effie May came in.

She came from the kitchen, Effie May, Julia's younger sister, dimpling, laughing, her softly fuzzy cheeks a little damp from cooking, and she was a Scandinavian goddess, all gold and blue and ivory, plump but light-footed, looking on Myron as ever so good a joke, looking on all life as a joke and an adventure--young Freya, with skin like a silver birch.

'I guess you don't remember me,' she giggled.

'Why, it's . . . it's . . .'

'Effie May. Isn't it just the *silliest* name!'

'Well, now, Effie May, it was your grandmother's,' began Mr. Lambkin, clearing his throat as one who would a tale unfold, but he never unfolded it, for, to Myron's entire approbation, Effie May cut him short with, 'I guess I was just a brat when you first went away.'

'You still are!' snarled Herbert.

'How long you been gone, Mr. Weagle?' said Effie May.

'Thirteen years.'

'Oh, then I was only seven when you left. Was I pretty terrible?'

'Well, no, I wouldn't say that, but I remember your putting flour paste in my hat one time when I was courting Julia.'

'Were you courting me?' Julia was very coy about it. 'I declare, I wish you'd let me know. I'd of waited for you, instead of marrying a sawed-off trouble-shooter like Willis!'

'Oh, is that so!' said Willis.

'I think we can all sit down to supper now,' said Effie May.

In fact she was not only the comeliest but the most sensible of the Lambkins, to Myron's way of thinking.

Between them, Julia and Effie May had produced all the features with which their mother, in her lifetime, had adorned company suppers, and of which Myron had, as a boy, enviously heard from outside. There were not only the traditional Lambkin fried chicken, corn fritters, crab-apple jelly, and ice-cream, but the candied orange-peel and brandied peaches, the last a favourite viand among teetotallers in Black Thread.

But they had not arranged for much conversation.

Mr. Lambkin chewed and gulped, and grumbled that the chicken was tough and that it must be pretty fine for Myron to get back home after living 'round in strange hotels. Herbert champed and belched and talked without stopping, but as no one particularly noticed what he was talking about, that could not be called conversation either. The four children, who were supposed to be fashionably tucked away up-stairs, out of hearing, hung about the landing on the stairs and yapped, 'Maaaa-ma!' And all the rest of the company, including Myron, chewed and said nothing profounder than 'May trouble you pass salt?'

Yet Myron and Effie May were talking incessantly.

When Herbert slammed the table to emphasize a point--it was to the effect that education for children was, or possibly was not, a good idea--Effie winked at Myron. When Mr. Lambkin muttered to Julia something ending '. . . where did you *put* the toothpicks, then?' Effie giggled softly, and her glance and Myron's crossed.

Herbert had to go down to school-board meeting for half an hour after supper, Julia had a chance then, and Myron understood why he had been invited.

It seemed, according to Julia, that Herbert had a muted affection for Myron; that he regarded him as the best innkeeper since Noah; that the brightest moment in his life was Myron's return to Black Thread; that he had always longed to be a hotel-keeper; and that Myron would do a favour not only to Herbert, to herself, and the entire village and township of Black Thread, but to the travelling public, if he found Herbert a tidy little job in hotel-keeping at three or four thousand a year--for a start.

'I'm sure any hotel-owner would be awfully glad to get a man like him, with his fine education and social position and all his training in caring for children. They must have a terrible time, having to depend on ex-waiters and like that,' gurgled Julia.

Myron took to himself a good deal of credit for not saying 'I am an ex-waiter'. He felt helpless. But as his eye roved desperately round the parlour with its forbidding wall-paper of dark red, it rested on Effie, and she dimpled sympathetically at him, and gave him strength to say brazenly, 'I'll certainly look into opportunities for him the minute I get back to New York, though the business is dreadfully crowded just this *minute*. If I were he, I wouldn't give up my teaching job for a few months yet.'

Effie May giggled faintly. Julia looked at her savagely, and began to talk about 'our old gang'. They were, it seemed, severally and collectively, a 'bunch of cabbage heads'. This was married to a cat, this other was a cat herself, and the third was a vile housekeeper.

Now the persons of whom Julia thus disposed were precisely the lords and ladies of Black Thread who as princelings had most clung about her on the archducal side porch, and whose grandeur Myron had most envied. Yet he could get no satisfaction out of hearing their former sovereign offering them up to him as sacrifices. He would not have liked it, but he would have felt that life was more integral and logical if she had snapped, 'I love all my old friends implicitly, and you, you pot-walloper, you may have more money than we now, but we consider you as fortunate even to be allowed to sit there in mother's old chair'. He listened miserably, and wanted to smoke--apparently, even at this apex of modernity, 1911, one still did not smoke in a Lambkin parlour--and he escaped before the return of Herbert, although it appeared that Herbert would be agonized at missing his old chum.

Effie May walked to the gate with him.

'I'm glad you haven't turned out a crab, like ole Julia and Bert,' said Effie May. 'Don't they love to knock!'

'You think I'm not so bad?'

'You--I think you're just won'erful!' giggled Effie May.

Won'erful, he was to learn, was her favourite word.

He was delighted to find one person in Black Thread who considered life won'erful.

'Look!' he said urgently. 'I'll be just loafing around, for a few weeks. Can't you and I--we're the young, unmarried generation, apparently--can't we get off into the country?'

'I think that would be won'erful. Some of us kids are going to have a picnic on Lake Nekobee, next Sunday afternoon. Could you come along?'

'I'd love to,' said Myron.

And so he again walked from the Lambkin mansion to the American House, falling into love with a Lambkin daughter.

'She's twenty. Of course I'm pretty mature. Still, at that, I'm only eleven years older. Just right. Trained housekeeper. She certainly would be useful in checking up the housekeeping department in . . . No! I won't have *my* wife working!' reflected that mature New Yorker, Mr. Myron Weagle.

18

There was peace and healing in the hillside meadow, but no languor, so brisk were the small breezes; and the late spring flowers among stately grasses were bits of scattered enamel--white and purple daisies, buttercups, red clover, and the Pompeian red of devil's paint brush. Myron contentedly brushed the side of his hand against the tickling grasses, as he lay on his back, more relaxed than for years, then clasped the hand of Effie May, sitting up beside him.

This was good, to have a companion in the adventure of leisure. Her presence completed him. He had, in offices, in long talks with Alec Monlux and Mark Elphinstone and Luciano Mora, been so incomplete, the male without the female. And what freshness and goodness there was in the hand of this untainted girl!

He had, he meditated, been reasonably free of viciousness, and most of the guests had been good and decent, yet there had inevitably been so many others--the little hotel thieves, their very pettiness making it the nastier to have to deal with them, the 'skippers' and passers of 'rubber cheques', irritating in their angry roars of innocence, the suicides who so very bloodily brought shame to hotel-rooms, the sneaking immoralists, and the equally unpleasant prudes who objected, publicly, to other people's private immoralities. After the incessant tedium of bickering with such pests, Effie May's gaiety was the water of life.

It would be fun, Myron exulted, to see new great things with an unjaded girl like this--cities and tall towers and mountains. Not much fun to have these by himself, to be unable to share them. Of course her family *was* a good deal of a pain in the neck, but . . . All the more reason for saving her from them! . . . If he did get an hotel job for Herby, little Herby, the bounding Bert, it would be off in Alaska, with no return ticket! . . . Effie May, the poor kid! To do things for her, to show her the world--yes, and to have her show it to him, with her fresher and less weary eyes, that would give some purpose to life!

'Do you ever want to travel, Effie?'

'Oh, I'd just love to. It would be won'erful!'

'How much have you travelled?'

'Oh, not hardly at all. I drove with Julia and Willis up to Lake Bomoseen. That was before they had to sell the car. And Papa took me to New York once for two days, he had to go on business, my! I wish we'd known where you were, then, that was two years ago, we'd of gone and called on you, would you have been glad to see us?'

'*Would* I! You bet I would! I'd of shown you the whole shop, and given you a good bottle of wine.'

She giggled. 'That would be won'erful. But I guess wine would of been too strong for my poor little head. I never did taste it--except maybe some elderberry wine and dandelion wine and so on, and I just *hate* beer, it's so bitter. But oh, I would of loved to of seen a really big hotel; we stayed at a horrid pokey little place, hardly any bigger than that American House . . . Oh! How dreadful of me! I forgot the American House was . . .'

'But I agree with you. The American House is a fierce little dump. But you just wait till I finish remodelling it! It won't be any Inside Inn for size, but it will be as comfy and cheerful as any city hotel. But how would you like to travel way beyond that?--say to Europe, and see cathedrals and castles and a lot of art galleries and so on?'

'Oh, I'd love it! It would be just won'erful! I'm just as ignorant as a rabbit, Myron. I don't know a blessed thing about art or music or any of those things.'

'Well if you want to know, kid, neither do I! I certainly have picked up a fine junk-heap of information about electric dish-washers and combustion recorders and steel furniture, but the penalty I've paid is that I don't know much else. And God how I want to! I want to *know!* Everything.'

'But I bet you do, Myron. My! I always feel you know so much . . .'

'I don't. I'm an illiterate hash-hustler. And I like to learn. I wish I knew all about painting. I wish I could spiel French and German and Italian like Luciano Mora--he's a fellow at the Westward; you'll meet him some day and fall so hard for him I'll be jealous! And I wish I'd read all the poets, as Ora has.'

'Well, I'll bet he hasn't--of course I've only seen a little of Ora since I was a kid, but I'll bet he's a fourflusher, like my own darling brother . . . Gee, Bert never stops talking!'

'Now you look here, Effie May, that's the first time I ever knew you to be dumb. Ora is a very intellectual fellow, with the most extraordinary imagination and originality and insight into character and so on and so forth, and he's certainly read all the poets and authors--you can tell from the way he keeps referring to them. Of course to an old stick-in-the-mud like me, sometimes he seems pretty impractical and careless about financial details--I guess he'll always be hard-up and need a little help--but you can't expect a sensitive, sympathetic mind like his to stand the grind the way a hard-boiled old drudge like me does.'

'I won't have you calling yourself names! You aren't a stick-in-the-mud! You get ever so much fun out of trying new stunts--like putting that lovely new cretonne in the American House office. I won't have you calling yourself names! And let me catch Ora or Bert or anybody else doing it, and I'll scratch their eyes out!'

He looked up at her, her golden hair of a Norse goddess glistening as she bent a little over him. 'Would you, honestly?' he whispered.

She whispered back, 'I certainly would!'

He drew her down to him. So soft! She stooped, kissed his cheek with reckless heartiness, and sprang up, crying, 'Come on, silly! We'd better keep walking!'

They tramped over the hilltop, through the scarlet patches of devil's paint brush, their clasped hands swinging as though they were sixteen. In her free hand Effie May carried her old-fashioned flowery sunbonnet. Her sister Julia laughed at her for affecting anything so out of date and rustic, and Herbert scolded that if she was willing to disgrace *herself* socially by such *childishness,* at *least,* she might *try* to think a *little* of *his* official position, but she persisted in it, every summer--her only marked rebellion against the security of Black Thread Presbyterian circles. Now, when she appealed to that urban social arbiter, Myron Weagle, he assured her that there was nothing smarter than sunbonnets, as regularly worn by Van Rensselaers at Newport, and she panted with gratitude--and the unaccustomed walking--as they swung down the hillside to the Black Thread highway.

19

He admitted that he was probably sentimental in seeking, on this tramp by himself, the spot where he had stretched out beside Effie May, but it had a gay sanctity for him, and there he squatted, hands about knees, brooding while he looked unseeing across the valley of pastures, elm groves, and quiet old yellow houses with red barns.

'She's young yet. She doesn't know much. But how she will expand to the world outside! And me, what am I going to do? In ten or twelve years, I may be Mark's successor, if Carlos Jaynes doesn't cut my throat and convince the Old Man I'm a small-town book-keeper. But even that . . . It would be just a routine job. Old Mark created the chain, and his successor would just carry it on. I'd like to do something entirely new.'

And that hour he began--with notes on the backs of visiting cards, transferred later to a handsome pocket vademecum with seal binding and gilt edges, labelled, 'Hotel Project Notes'--what must, in exactness, be called 'The Note-Book of a Poet': the thoughts, story-plots, visions, observations, aspirations which he longed some day to write, only not in words but in steel and brick and composition flooring and best-quality bed-linen.

From the Note-Book of a Poet:

Most luxurious sanitorium in world, within hundred miles New York, freedom of a hotel but fine docs, elec equipment, baths, etc. but absolutely quiet, tennis and golf but far enough fr hotel no noise, no dances or music after 10 p.m., but movies nightly? large private balconies where can rest all day, extra big and up-to-date library, especially fine food bu simple like squab on toast and fresh veg & special milk, charge like hell but worth it. Note: have manicures etc.--God what a word, 'beautician'!--old dames have time for hair treatments, massage, etc., while getting in shape. Make it snotty & exclusive. I'd probably hate every guest in place, but fun building it.

Myron's note-book was a quarter filled before he had thrashed through the problem of what he really wanted to do--aside from immediately marrying Effie May Lambkin. In a sacred excitement he came full upon it.

He was an hotel-man, a professional innkeeper. Good. Well then, he wanted to build, to own, and without interference to conduct, the one Perfect Inn!

He wanted to create it as Ora (he supposed) wanted to create the Perfect Poem. And since in cities the modern hotel must be a combination of inn, restaurants, whole alleys of shops, rooms that were not so much bedchambers as offices for out-of-town business men, and gathering-place for conventions and public dinners and weddings, therefore he wanted his Perfect Inn to be in the country, by itself, altogether devoted to those blessings which no electricity or gasoline motor had made antiquated-- perfect food and perfect wine and perfect bedrooms.

Assemble the best notions of all the best innkeepers, American or European. Conceive it not as a quick and certain way of making money, nor as a happy-go-lucky fulfilment of somebody's notion that 'I guess we need another hotel around here', but as a planned, perceived, exuberantly rich yet severely chastened idea, noble as an epic and lively as a swimming-race.

'I'll do it!' Myron vowed.

He sat in his rickety room at the American House till dawn, and by dawn he had filled eight pages of his handsome new Poet's Note-Book (only it never occurred to Myron himself to call it that) with plans for the Perfect Inn (and he never called his vision that, either, but only 'The best resort hotel that can be built'). From his experience, his reading, his talk, he put down all the things to be avoided, such as the equal horrors of indolent 'service' and of service that was presumptuously chummy; and all the things to be desired, such as, since Luciano Mora was always scolding that American inns do not use the good out-of-doors, a tea and luncheon terrace, vine-sheltered and looking on sea or lake or mountain-valley.

Being a trained cuisinier, Myron was struck by the excellence and originality of the picnic lunch provided by Effie May. It consisted of ham and cheese sandwiches, hard-boiled eggs wrapped in waxed paper, coco-nut layer-cake, rather squashed, and coffee in a thermos bottle.

They had tramped three miles out of town, to Elm Hill, on the shore of Lake Nekobee. The hillside was thick with spruce and birch groves and a few elms, broken by pasture and meadow, and the lake, some two miles wide, was very clear, with sandy bottom, no marshy shores, and wooded hills or rolling farms all round it. There were a few flimsy summer cottages at one end, near the hamlet of East Black Rock, with its general store and two churches, but for the most part Lake Nekobee had not, in this day before the flood of motor cars, been popularly discovered.

'Say, this is *it!*' Myron cried suddenly when, full of hard-boiled egg and contentment, they lolled on a hot boulder above the lake, and Effie May smoked a cigarette with (it was A.D. 1911) extensive coughing and a gleeful feeling of sin.

'What is what?' demanded Effie May.

'This is just the place for my resort hotel. Nice hills, lovely clean lake, quiet, only three miles from the depot in town, and a hundred and twenty from New York.'

'Are you thinking about a resort hotel?'

'Well, sort of.' Humbly Myron spoke of his epic. 'Some day I'd like to build the best country inn in America--real out-door place, kind of simple, and yet as good grub and service and beds as the Plaza. You see--oh, really take some pains, put some thought into it, profit by all the other fellows' mistakes, and make it a corker. Do you think that would be fun?'

'Oh yes, I think it would be lots of fun. That would be--it would be won'erful!' said Effie May.

And so, the lady having approved his armour, his lance, and the general sensibleness of the whole expedition, the knight was ready to ride out with no more misgivings about his ability to bring back the Holy Grail.

The building of even a few shore cottages along Lake Nekobee had raised land-prices and when, six months later, after thinking it all over a few hundred times, Myron bought the Elm Hill property bordering on the lake, it cost him ten thousand dollars for one hundred acres--two thousand down, and two thousand a year. Before he had finished paying for it the land was worth two hundred an acre.

From the Note-Book of a Poet:

Arcade rite thru 6-8 blocks midtown NY, like the one you read of in Milan, Italy, (galleria or whatever it is?) just foot traffic, no vehicles, cafe tables, theatres, expens shops, gt gathering place noon and cocktail hr, heated in winter, pavement marble, 3-4 stories high, very handsome. Run N & S, middle of long blocks. Flowers. Also fountains?

T. J. Dingle was in his early thirties, but he was the president of the Black Thread National Bank. His grandfather, a farmer, a tobacco-grower from the Connecticut Valley, had started the first large dairy near Black Thread, and been founder of the public library. His father, also president of the First National but dead now a year, had been an upstanding, grey-moustached old gentleman, and he had been the first man whom Myron had ever seen riding a horse just for pleasure--the picture of a general on his tall bay. No Dingle in known history had worn a chin whisker or an icy eye, or foreclosed a mortgage if he could help it, or been suspected of exceeding the legal rate of interest by tacking on 'inspection fees', or shown any of the other interesting traits common to country bankers in fiction, and sometimes in real life.

T. J. Dingle himself was slim, eager but restrained, with a face out of which all the slackness and fat had been carved. He was the squire of Black Thread, and Myron remembered that the young Julia had been flattered when Ted Dingle had occasionally joined her side-porch court.

And if the Lambkins (aside from Effie May) had been inclined to believe Myron's assertion that he was only a small valve in the Elphinstone engine--as doubtless they would have, as soon as they got used to the sight of him--they would have been kept respectful by viewing the new friendship of Myron and T. J. Dingle.

When Myron went into the bank to cash a cheque, the third day of his visit, Dingle insisted on his coming into the private office, struggled a little with remarks about the weather, and abruptly invited him to dinner--his the only house in Black Thread that had the affectation of evening dinner.

Myron found that the dolorous old green and brown Dingle Mansion, with its high cupola, had been made almost tolerable with white paint and the removal of the scrollwork above the porch; the gloomy rooms had been brightened, and filled with books and flowers. Dingle's young wife, from New Haven, was given to gay sprigged house-dresses, playing the piano, and making Lobster Newburgh, all excellent habits. Sitting with them, in the first easy household he had found in Black Thread, Myron realized that T. J. Dingle was at once shrewder and more cultivated than anyone he had met since he had left home--except perhaps the supercilious Carlos Jaynes of the Elphinstone organization, who managed to combine Pan Dandy Lunch Rooms and dislike of Myron with devotion to Brahms and El Greco.

It seemed to Myron a little strange that his two intimates in his boyhood town should not have been his own family, nor Herbert Lambkin, nor any of the lively ruffians with whom he had once loafed at the livery-stable, but two familiar strangers whom, as the baby Effie May and the aloof Ted Dingle, he had seen without knowing them.

And it came to pass that at least one evening a week, while the Maison Lambkin fluttered more and more unctuously, Myron and Effie May spent with the Dingles, and had thus a social recognition and fixation without which their shy affection might not have crystallized into marriage.

He never did propose. It is, indeed, doubtful whether anybody in history, outside of novels, ever has really 'proposed'. They simply came to know that they liked each other and excited each other, and that, presumably, they were going to be married.

They were walking by the river in that last light of an early summer afternoon when the trees stand up like pyramids of green light and the world is content to slumber.

He held her hand to his breast, stroking it, and trembled, 'I guess--it kind of looks--it looks as if we'd be married. Let's be married in a fortnight, and run off to Canada or Maine or some place, before I have to get back to work. . . . We'll have a lovely suite in the Westward, and I'll make Mark redecorate the bathroom with marble floor and coloured tiles and a shower, besides the tub.'

'A suite? That would be awfully exciting. It would be--oh, in a big New York hotel like that--it would be perfectly won'erful!' said Effie May.

And so Myron did have to send hastily to New York for his morning coat and striped trousers and four-in-hand and have Luciano Mora take a chance on getting him a silk hat of the right size--his first silk hat, and he wore it to theatres four times the first year, twice the second year, never at all afterward.

They were married at the Presbyterian Church with (to Myron's mild astonishment) bridesmaids, flower-girls, Ora as best man, and T. J. Dingle, Luciano Mora, and Herbert Lambkin as ushers.

Julia had a perfectly won'erful time weeping, and informing the world that she had to be mother to 'poor little Effens', and Myron had never so loved Effie as when he overheard her snarling to Julia, 'Oh, for God's sake cut out the mothering and find my darn garters!'

And Myron had a perfectly horrible time. He ardently hated everyone at the wedding except Effie May, his mother, Luciano, Dingle, and Ora. He had started in hating Ora, also, for it was just the day after Ora had informed him that his remodelling of the American House had turned it from an honest inn into a gifte-shoppe. But this morning, at the church, when he was riding hard on Myron in the parlours till the bride should have come up the aisle, Ora re-established himself by producing a pint of rye, ordering Myron to have a sip, and grunting, 'Well, I never thought any Lambkin would ever crawl out from under the rocks--God, that Herby is a stiff!--but your Effie May is a peach; pretty as Lillian Russell, and a jolly kid. Congratulations. And I *have* got the damn ring all safe, right here! There they come! Hey, hey! Keep your nerve! One more quick swig!'

Myron thought that the parson, as Effie May and he stood before him, sniffed rather hoitily, but he lived through it, and ceased to be a young bachelor. He began, now, the second half of his life, as he squeezed her hand and muttered 'My wife!'

'Ouch!' she said, and giggled, and he glowed like a cat on the hearth.

Item in the *Hotel Era:*

BONIFACE A BENEDICT

Greeter Myron S. Weagle, long one of the right-hand men of Mine Host Mark Elphinstone of the Westward Ho, in the Big Town, and formerly Boniface of the Tippecanoe Lodge, Fla., than whom none among the younger hoteliers is better known for dispensing lavish hospitality and for postprandial eloquence, has let himself in for the chime of merry wedding-bells, the fortunate lady being Miss E. Laski of Thread Mill Centre, Massachusetts, and the lucky couple are now spending their honeymoon in the golden isle of Bermuda.

Blazing white reefs, white-edged breakers, deep waters that shaded from stainless green into pure blue, plaster houses white and pink and yellow among dark cedars, gardens of palm and banana, the creak of an old barouche with a darky driver proceeding with no haste, since it made no difference where they were going nor whether they ever went there--late-summer Bermuda, and Myron and Effie May honeymooning, and discovering, both of them, their first foreign land.

That the shops should sell coral and mother-of-pearl, and herring-bone heather just come from London; that the policemen should have an English accent and the postmen wear funny hats; that they should dine in a garden of oleanders and roses; it was all a fairy tale that made up for the tragic honeymoon discoveries that she was likely to giggle at his enthusiasms over non-dripping hotel teapots and folding baggage-stands, that she liked to eat chocolates in bed, with the results that she made nasty brown daubs on the pillows and afterward had the most indelicate fits of indigestion; that he made horrid noises in the bathroom and wore long thin cotton and wool underwear instead of this jaunty new 'athletic' sort, and that neither of them had had enough experience of love-making to do it gracefully.

But she did warm his heart by regarding him as an authority on everything in general. Since he had been in Florida and Missouri, she happily assumed that he knew everything about reefs, tides, deep-sea fishing, wistaria, planter's punch, the intimate biology of the coral anthozoa, the varieties of palms, the constitutions of the several British colonies, the social life of the Governor of Bermuda, and the productivity of banana plants.

And he told her everything, to their mutual satisfaction.

Few of the great hotels which were later to make Bermuda, next to Paris, the most agreeable suburb of New York had yet been erected, but they stayed at a shiny pink and blue inn between Harrington Sound and the open ocean, and so agreeable was it to sit out under the coconut palms after dinner, or at tea-time, with hot buttered English scones and marmalade in stone jars, that Myron's concept of the Perfect Inn grew and kicked and crowed--doubtless the more so because he had never dared expose it to the snicker of Ora.

It would take years for him to accumulate the necessary money and, plainly, to know enough, but he would create this right and beautiful thing and it would be his excuse for having lived. So they came back to New York and to work, looking a little regretfully from the boat deck of the steamer along the nickled wake to the bright reefs of Bermuda.

20

From 1911 to 1926, from his thirty-first year to his forty-sixth, Myron was busy about this hotel and that in New York City and Philadelphia and Long Island and Wilmington, except for eight months in 1917 and 1918, when he was a captain in the Quartermaster's Department, saving the world by sitting in a warehouse in New York and buying blankets and bacon and beans. He never lost his fantastic notion of the Perfect Inn, but each year he felt that he was not yet ready, and he had to content himself with filling new volumes of his little books of 'Hotel Project Notes'.

What is an art, what is a profession, what is a business, what is a job? Is a man who runs a great grocery store like Park & Tilford, Acker, Charles, or the gr dept of Macy's just a business man, while anybody who makes smart pictures of girls is artist, and doc or lawyer who thinks about nothing but making money a professional and cranky old prof who goes on handing out same lectures yr after yr a scholar and not just on a white collar job?

Myron did institute new methods as purchasing-agent for the whole Elphinstone chain. Till now, the stewards and other buyers even for great hotels had not been so very different from Tom Weagle, whose system of purchasing for the American House had been to stamp into the local butcher shop and drone, 'Whacha got to-day? That legga lamb any good?' But Myron and other pests of his kind made the whole process as delicate and complicated as determining the weight of Saturn.

After three and a half years he was made chief assistant to Mark Elphinstone, to help direct all the hotels and restaurants, with the title of third vice-president of the company. Mark himself never told him, but Myron knew that there had been a battle before he got the position, which was really that of heir-apparent to the throne of the little Napoleon. Carlos Jaynes, now resident manager of the Westward, had fought sharply for it. Though Elphinstone owned more than half the stock of the company, the millionaire brother-in-law of Jaynes and his friends controlled over forty per cent, and they had supported Jaynes.

Myron had won, though Mark's latest secretary, a young Y.M.C.A. man named Clark Cleaver, told him that the Old Man had been gambling on the market, and might have to sell some of his stock in the company. But Myron forgot his precariousness in working out life with Effie May, in accumulating plans for the Perfect Inn, and, after the comparative simplicity of being purchasing-agent only, in the whirlwind of dealing with every sort of detail of every sort of hotel and restaurant.

Every detail of hotel-keeping--and J. Hector Warlock had been right, years ago, when he had instructed the young Myron that an hotel-keeper had to be a combination of nursery-governess, financier, steam-fitter, detective, upholsterer, architect, dietitian, garbage-handler, ventilation-engineer, lawyer, orchestra-director, psychiatrist, florist, guide to the city, state, nation, and all hotels in Switzerland, the Argentine, and South Africa, garage-manager, after-dinner speaker, and supreme expert on insurance, taxes, depreciation, and amortization.

Insol prob of hotel-man matter of 'morals'. To what extent should he let all guests do exactly what they like so long as pay bills, not disturb other guests, & not get hotel bad reputation--couples probably unmarried, strange gents possibly fugitives from justice, even degenerates. Luciano Mora insists hotel-man no more right censor than physician refuse treat immoral or criminal patients; he says would you excuse Methodist hotel-man if refused take in Jewish, Catholic, Buddhist, or atheist guests. Alec says, yes, but immoral guests, so-called, sooner or later get joint bad name gradually even if at 1st no one kick. I don't know. Guess will be slack enough to do like Elphinstone and most canny mgrs.--not notice anything 'immoral' unless made to by kicks.

Every sort of detail of every sort of hotel--the details that the guest, interested only in his soft bed and his dinner, never knows.

Carlos Jaynes suggested that, though for their Buffalo, Worcester, Akron, Hartford and Scranton houses, English menus were all right, it would give what he called 'cachet' to the Westward to have the menus, at least in the Georgian Dining Room, in French. On the sample which Jaynes submitted, Myron found the item, 'Le ham and eggs'. Now that was perfectly sound, for had Jaynes not taken it from the menu of the Savoy Grill, in London?

Myron sent Jaynes's memorandum up to Mark Elphinstone, with one of his own: 'This seems an elegant idea, only I think the item I have checked should be in more idiomatic French and read "Le ham et eggs". It certainly would make a regular guest out of any Kansas buyer to know that he could get le oatmeal, gli scrambled eggs, y los wheat cakes avec der maplesirop instead of just plain grub in our shop.'

That was enough.

Myron's chief crusade, as Elphinstone's shadow and later as a manager on his own, made him unpopular among his successful colleagues, for it was against undue reverence for publicity and for what was called 'service'. He had a theory that however much the lonely guest, unused to hotels, delighted in being pumphandled by clerks and assistant manager, called by name by the doorman, and entertained by the meteorological discussions of the bell-boys and elevator-runners, there were just as many guests, veterans of travel and of hotel-living, who wanted to be let alone; who, safely away from the excessive attention and domestic discussion of Home, enjoyed being invisible. And such guests, he believed, resented such bids for publicity as the flourish with which a celebrated *maître d'hôtel,* boomed as 'official taster', tasted every dish to be served at a large banquet, though he might be so full of highballs that he could not tell well-done terrapin from over-roasted canvas back; and such guests were irritated by a wild hurrah about having the more expensive suites accurately decked out with 'period furniture'.

('Just the same, Ora was wrong about my putting too much tea-room agony into the American House when I remodelled it. Well, maybe he wasn't quite as wrong as I thought then, four years ago!')

Invariable courtesy, swift fulfilling of orders, honest conferences of department-heads as to what guests really wanted--Myron did not see why these obvious necessities of hotel-keeping should be trumpeted forth as extraordinary, nor why a tired and dusty guest, already jumpy over being made conspicuous by the room-clerk's caroling 'Boy! Take Mr. Jones up to 755', should be forced to admire placards reading approximately: 'Look at how tenderly we care for you, and notice us, please notice us, and don't forget that whether you use talcum powder or not, there is a nice free can of it in your bathroom'.

He did not see why a guest who had made a large night of it, and was doubtful whether he would last till breakfast, should be compelled to listen on the telephone to a birdie chirp of 'Good morning, this is roo-oom service, I shall be pleased to take your order' before he could snarl his needs. He did not see why a guest who had been perfectly contented with his room and breakfast should be compelled to think up a polite answer to repeated and patently mechanical inquiries as to whether everything was all right. If everything weren't all right, Myron suspected, the guest would let the management know! He wanted good food, a comfortable bed, a comfortable chair with a good light for reading, quick service on laundry and clothes-pressing and mail, accurate answers to his questions as to how to get about the city, but--or so Myron insisted to his colleagues--he rarely wanted to be mothered or brothered or wet-nursed, nor did he yearn to give information about the health of his Little Ones either to strange insurance-agents or to cooing hotel-clerks.

'The old-fashioned tavern-keeper, before 1860, used to enjoy being boss under his own roof, and bawling out anybody who didn't take a shine to dirty beds and greasy food. The new-fashioned one enjoys feeling what a gent he is, to be so kind to strangers for whom he obviously doesn't personally care a hang. Both are bad, and neither has anything to do with providing good beds and grub at a fair price', said Myron in a speech at a convention of the Hotel Greeters, and for such heresy, such red revolution, he was penalized all his life. . . . As well inform a convention of city specialists owning $3600 motor cars that they are not necessarily more clever than the country doctor in a second-hand flivver!

He was so much a crank as not to be much edified by such texts in elevators as 'Daily Message to Guests and Staff: If you have friends in every place, in every place you will find charm,' or 'To employees: Remember it is your duty to make every guest feel at home.' This, in a fifteen-hundred room hotel where nobody save a centipede could feel at home! And it occurred to Myron that a fair number of guests might be so earnestly sick of wives, yelping children, solicitous mothers-in-law, balky furnaces, household bills, trouble with cooks, and getting the lawn mowed that the one reason why they came to hotels at all was to get away from feeling at home.

Over this greeting-card philosophy Myron had his chief differences with Mark Elphinstone. He admired the Old Man, loved him like a son, but Elphinstone would scribble and gloat on and have printed a torrent of profound aphorisms that didn't mean anything. Among his deeper and more moving revelations were:

The heart of an hotel is its kitchen; the Front Office its nervous system.

Hotel success is a mathematical formula: co-operation plus pep.

Don't be stingy with towels. For every guest that asks for one more there is another that requires one less.

A modern hotel is like an automobile. It is made up of thousands of parts and not one can be neglected. If the boy in the washroom isn't on the job, the chief clerk in the come-to-Jesus collar can't function.

An hotel is the weary traveller's temporary home and his room is his castle.

As the fourth or fifth largest industry in the United States, hotels proudly take their rightful place in the nation's economic solidarity.

A smile of welcome from behind the desk is like a beacon to a mariner at sea.

Adam was the first hotel-keeper.

'Yes, and what of it?' snapped Myron, as the messages fluttered on his desk, on forms with 'Elphinstone Service Snappers' printed in red at the top. Well, Elphinstone was otherwise an excellent boss. There were hotel proprietors who used morphine or read paragraphs from Elbert Hubbard aloud or wanted their pictures in the papers or expected you to make engagements for them with pretty women guests.

'And maybe I'm all wrong, anyway. Maybe I'm too much opposed to hand-shaking and mottoes as a way of holding business. Probably my worst fault as an innkeeper.'

He was wrong. His worst fault as an innkeeper was his inability to be more than commonly civil and attentive, ever to be an unctuous foot-kisser, to overdemanding guests, even when they were Celebrities.

One of the dramas of his trade was the reception of Celebrities-- senators, generals, circumnavigatory aviators, prize fighters, diplomats, explorers, foreign lecturers. Some of them did not consider their visitations so great a favour that they expected to have accommodations free, and there were even rare souls who did not want publicity and did not expect the hotel press-agent to let the newspapers in on the secret of their presence. But there were others who expected not only Carlos Jaynes and Myron to be awaiting them in the lobby, with an entourage of clerks, porters, bell-boys, the press-agent, and a corps of reporters and photographers, but that Mark Elphinstone himself (they always had a card to him) should devote a day to the pleasure of giving them, free, the best suite in the hotel.

How warmly they strode from the taxi into the hotel! How surprised they were to be interviewed! How modestly they explained they knew nothing about politics--and then proved it! How reluctantly they sipped of what they believed to be Mark's private stock of Bourbon--it was a private stock, right enough, but not the sort he drank. How buoyantly they said, of a private suite priced at thirty dollars a day which they were getting for ten, 'Oh, this is quite all right. It will do very nicely--very nicely! The price is a little steep, but I am sure I shall be very comfortable.'

And you had to send them flowers, and a bushel of fruit.

Fortunately, you could sometimes get these from the leftovers of last night's banquet.

And just as hard to swallow as the Celebrities who expected you to telephone about them to city editors--who would growl, 'Who the hell is he? What's he got to say? My supply of dumb sob-squad reporters is pretty well exhausted to-day'--were the other, usually more authentic Celebs who really wanted to be let alone. When they crossed the Atlantic, they kept their names off the passenger-list, in the touching belief that no one would know they were coming, though the London or Paris correspondents had cabled of their coming before they sailed. Down on these unfortunates, the reporters came via the transom, the keyhole, the fire escape, the fireplace, or just generally through the air, and the Celebs blamed the hotel management; they always said, 'I did think that You People might be trusted to make at least some *slight* effort to respect my wish for privacy!'

After a Celebrity, Myron appreciated a sound and seasoned travelling-man.

Conventions--oh God, conventions!

As restaurant and banquet manager, Myron had had to make love to lodge secretaries and committee chairmen to persuade them to hold their dinners at the Westward. Now, as assistant to the president, he had to back up the several resident managers of the hotels in securing conventions.

To an hotel-man, a convention is a nightmare of being for ever caught in a subway rush.

There is an Elphinstone hotel, let us say, in the city of Golden Glow, which is distinguished for being the dirtiest and noisiest industrial huddle in the state of Winnemac. Now the state organization of shoe-dealers, autograph collectors, petunia-growers, Schnauzer-fanciers, pacifists, big navyists, wholesale and retail tripe-dressers, or alumni of Pettifoot Military and Agricultural Institute are going to hold a convention. The Golden Glow Chamber of Commerce, together with the hotel-keepers, theatre-owners, taxi-cab-owners and the like of the city, send letters, telegrams, and emissaries to the committee to proclaim the beauties of Golden Glow--the park system, the almost radioactive drinking-water, the extraordinary situation whereby Golden Glow can with equal ease be reached from Key West, Medicine Hat, or Constantinople, the number and vehement luxury and unparalleled cheapness of the hotels, the rural grandeur that the Golden River will have as soon as a couple of hundred factories and the stockyards are removed from its banks, the grim splendour of Mount Glow, which is only fourteen thousand feet lower than Mount Whitney, and the acoustics of Memorial Hall, in which twenty thousand people can hear the lowest whisper, provided listening to low whispers is their notion of fun.

The convention once secured, the hitherto chummy hotel-keepers separate and begin trying to get reservations away from one another.

Then the convention. The arrival of kings, field-marshals, and archbishops, each expecting suitable reverence: the president of the state organization, the secretary, the chairman of the committee on meetings, the chairman of the accommodations committee, the chairman of the banquet committee. Delegates flooding in, demanding the rooms they have forgotten to reserve. Lobbies jammed with men slowly circling and exchanging remarks, flasks, and chewing gum, and agreeing that a three-hundred-room hotel which cannot take care of two hundred extra guests at the last moment is not enterprising, and they certainly will never come *here* again! Secretaries of committees, sitting at small desks in large rooms off the lobby, with so many delegates surging about them that they become deaf and blind, and are sometimes found weeks afterward, hiding under the pile of unanswered messages.

And his incessant problem of employees.

Myron had been an underling himself; he had vowed then that if he ever became an executive, he would never be irritated, that he would tenderly instruct all the employees, and be delighted to advance money to them in the middle of the week. He still felt that he ought to feel so.

He didn't.

He still had an uneasy sense, probably derived from Ora, that he ought to be a socialist, a comrade to all the workers.

He wasn't.

There had been so many instances when the 'help' had failed him: the cook who showed up drunk for the preparation of Thanksgiving dinner; the bell-boy, supposed to be hustling an urgent message up to a guest, who was found smoking a cigarette and playing craps in the linen-room; the steward who was taking a percentage from the provision merchants; the clerk who gave his friend an eight-dollar room for four; the chambermaid who, ordered to wash the fly-specks from one electric globe did not wash the other dirty globes in the room; the elevator-runner who sneered at funny old women with purple hats . . . A hundred of them, daily.

Yet Myron was a reasonably just and kindly man, and he fretted over his workers. He had no pleasure in kicking out even the surliest of them. If day on day they worried lest they lose their jobs, so day on day he worried, 'Oh Lord, have I got to fire him?' as he watched a man growing slack, doing less work, and no employee had more sternly to nerve himself, to still his quaking stomach, before edging into the Boss's office to ask for a rise, than did Myron before sending for an employee to scold him.

It was hard on an employee, he admitted, to be dependent for the job that meant life for himself and his family upon the whims of a boss who could discharge him because he did not like the colour of his hair; to give all his laborious days for the profit of some absentee owner whom he had never even seen. 'Just the same, as long as it's my job to control them, I'm going to drive 'em as hard as--as hard as I've always driven myself,' he insisted.

After the Bolshevik Socialist revolution, and the installation of the Fascists in Italy, he was interested to learn that under these new systems, slackers and dullards and falsifiers of reports were worse driven--even to prison or the rebuke of an automatic--than under the Capitalistic Democracy which, with no particular will or thought in the matter, he himself represented.

The coming of Prohibition, which was annoying to most citizens, was a catastrophe to the hotels. They had depended upon the bar to pay, at least, rent and taxes, and it had enabled them to lose on the dining-room, to lavish game, terrapin, caviare on the guests and positively urge them to take from the heaped dish left on the table more butter than they needed, and if the meals brought a deficit, what of it? It was good advertising. With Prohibition, they were compelled to turn niggardly or close their doors in bankruptcy. Myron had for a while to return to his food-cost-finding and determine exactly what proportion of an ounce of butter could be given to each guest without loss; just how much, to the tenth fraction of a cent, they could spend on an egg.

And with the loss from Prohibition, taxes went up.

Hotels and theatres are always excellent institutions to tax, when in doubt. Rural legislators live decently at home, or in boarding-houses at the capital; they go neither to hotels nor to theatres and see no reason why other people should; and in framing taxation bills always agree that these lairs of luxury will stand another raid. Income taxes have always been an especial delirium to hotels. A factory can strike a reasonable average for depreciation of machines and plant; but so varied is the custom of a hotel that a minor prophet is required to estimate the annual damage. Such an agreeable fad as stealing souvenir spoons, springing up mysteriously and ragingly, will suddenly cost an hotel thousands a year, to be more or less allowed for on the income tax, provided the inspectors of tax-reports condescend to permit it.

It was particularly pleasant for hotels to pay extra taxes to support extra prohibition agents for the purpose of keeping them from earning the extra taxes, and just as pleasant to realize that, privately, the guests were drinking as much as ever, with the difference that the hotels received none of the profit, while the merry men, communally guzzling in their bedrooms instead of the bar, were ruining varnished tables and bureaus with spilled alcohol and cigarettes left burning, were setting beds and chairs and curtains afire, were throwing empty bottles out of windows upon the heads of litigious passers-by, were keeping other guests awake, for which only the hotel was blamed . . . It scarcely seemed worth while to pay much extra income tax to get these results.

If the details of conventions or taxation seem to have nothing to do with the soul of Myron Weagle, poet, then is the seeming wrong, for it was with such details that he had to harass himself, it was for them that he had to give up leisure and love and play, all the years after 1917.

Ora, engaged in ghosting the memoirs of a charming lady blackmailer who had driven half a dozen men to suicide, complained that for all of marriage and Bermuda, Myron was less adventurous and picturesque than ever, unfit for the reverence of a novelist like himself, who would have liked an explorer or a soldier for brother. Effie May, left alone for a good part of the time, and now less entertained by the luxury of hotel suites, complained that Myron was neglecting her.

Carlos Jaynes complained that the crank Myron, with his dirty little insistences on economy, kept him from making the public rooms of the Westward as smart as those of the Ritz or Plaza or St. Regis. Even Mark Elphinstone complained that Myron criticized his ideas for new restaurants.

But while they complained of his coldness to Romance, Myron warmed in his heart the desire to create the Perfect Inn.

He was the inventor, or one of the inventors, of the 'emergency overnight kit' for people held too late at the office to get back to the suburbs. It contained cotton pyjamas, cheap comb and tooth-brush, a small tube of tooth-paste; it was given free to sober-looking guests who were benighted, and led several hundred business-men to making a habit of staying at the Westward. Also, as they were supposed to leave the pyjamas behind, to be laundered and used over again, it did not cost so much as it seemed.

Ora laughed enormously when he heard of Myron's invention. It was, he pointed out, a perfect example of what a modern American businessman considered an advance in civilization, and he had the funniest suggestions (Effie May giggled at them) for other items to be included in the kit: a paper-bound copy of the Gospel According to St. John, a celluloid sardine sandwich which could be used over and over again, a collection of the poems of Edgar Guest, pink wool bed-socks, and an eighteen-foot telescope so that the guest could study astronomy from the lofty altitudes of the Westward.

Myron argued with Carlos Jaynes and the other resident managers about extra attention to travelling-men and sample-rooms.

Jaynes had figures--like all statistics very impressive but rather vague as to origin--to prove that in 1922 there were, thanks to catalogues and larger wholesalers, only fifty per cent as many drummers on the road as in 1902, and he hinted that Myron could not get away from the psychology of Black Thread Centre of 1895.

Perhaps that was all true, said Myron, but travelling-men were the most important of all critics of hotels. It was they who remarked, in the smoking compartments of trains, 'Going to Golden Glow for the first time? Try the Smith Hotel. They treat you right. All new mattresses, and the clerks make sure you get your mail, and the coffee--ummmm!' Or: 'Don't let anybody tell you the Grand Hotel Royal Magnificent is any good. You take my tip and give it a miss. They got enough gilt in the lobby to sink a ship, but if you take a room for anything under six bucks a day, they treat you like a poor relation, and they stick you fifty cents for orange juice. Out!'

So Myron outraged Carlos Jaynes, bewildered Effie May, and shocked Ora by insisting that every employee give more attention to the veteran travelling-men than to Neapolitan dukes who came in brushing off reporters, and in particular he did so after a day in 1923--though then he was no longer at the Westward.

He was behind the desk, checking over the credit-card rack, the telautographs, the transfer-racks, the mail-stamping machine, the three fire-alarm systems, the time-clock, and the other complicated contrivances of that nerve-centre of the hotel. Up to the desk to register came a man foggily familiar to Myron; a tall, stooped man, neat of linen but with a suit at once flashy and badly worn, his grey hair bushy at the edge of his cocky grey hat. He was, Myron guessed, a Failure, but a Failure who would never give up his flamboyant hopes.

A man of sixty or sixty-two?

Now who the devil was he? Myron seemed to associate agreeable, even exciting memories with him. Elbowing the room-clerk aside, he read the signature upside down. That signature was 'J. Hector Warlock, Chi. Benjamin Belt Buckles the Best'.

Myron was within an inch of saying 'Number Four, as usual, Mr. Warlock? Mr. Dummy Dumbolton is in the house.'

But Dummy Dumbolton, meek and bewildered and admiring to the end, was dead now. And the J. Hector Warlock who, at thirty-four, could stay up all night drinking and gambling, and still laugh in the morning, was just as dead.

Myron was silent.

J. Hector looked straight at him, unrecognizing, his kind eyes a little bleary. He was rumbling, and his rotund voice had not shrivelled with the rest of him, 'Brother, do you happen to have a nice room for about three-fifty?'

'We certainly have, Mr. Uh . . .' Myron pretended to look at the registry card. J. Hector's script was as bold as ever, but shaky on the down strokes. '. . . Mr. Warlock. Three-fifty exactly, and I think you'll like it. Uh-- Benjamin Belt Buckles, eh? How are they going?'

'Oh, pretty good'. Then J. Hector laughed, threw back his head with his old gesture of a matinée idol. 'That means pretty damn bad!' He looked away from Myron, awaiting a bell-boy, and Myron could not think of another question. He longed to bring back 1895, and credulity, and delight at the strangeness and variousness of life, and the round cheeks and mighty laugh and black locks of J. Hector. He nodded to the boy. 'Take Mr. Warlock up to 539.' He watched J. Hector bob wearily across to the elevator, his shoulders sinking as soon as he believed that he was no longer under observation. He vanished behind the elevator grill, bearing with him Myron's youthful certainty that somewhere in the beautiful world was to be found a blessed state called 'success'.

To the room-clerk Myron murmured, 'Just charge Mr. Warlock three-fifty for 539, and put the rest on my bill, and make a memo of this: Whenever he comes, he's to have any six- or seven-dollar room, the best that's vacant, for three-fifty. Charge the excess to me, and don't let him know, *understand?*

He was called to the telephone at once with, 'The gentleman in 539 wants to speak to you, Chief.'

'Is this the clerk that assigned me to 539?' J. Hector's voice was quavering, a little frightened.

'Yes.'

'Well, look, old man, sorry to bother you, but are you sure this is a three-fifty room?'

'Yes, absolutely; that's right.'

'It's such a swell room I was afraid . . . Hate to be a tight-wad, but you know how it is; firm won't just stand for more than that on the expense account.'

'Sure, I know how it is, Mr. Warlock. We like to cater to travelling-men here.'

'Well, I'm glad to hear that. I've been a drummer for more'n forty years and nowadays, it seems like most of these young glad-handers would rather have a bootlegger or a beautiful young movie actor guy than to have an old-time salesman that has to watch the nickels. Used to be a time I could blow myself to a six-dollar room, but somehow, nowadays. . . . Oh, excuse me; you don't want to hear my troubles! Much obliged, Cap'n; sorry to bothered you; sure am much obliged.'

Myron felt old, that night, and Effie May, prattling about the play to which they were going, seemed embarrassingly young. He wanted to get hold of J. Hector for a poker game. But--oh, Effie May would be so disappointed at missing the theatre, after being alone all day.

He liked novelties in food well enough, but when the manager of the Westward lunch-room innocently proposed a sandwich made of pineapple between halves of a doughnut, he forbade the crime without right of appeal. . . . And the question of the commercial value of a free basket of fruit in bedrooms; or could they sell such baskets, for fifty cents; or was the whole thing just an unprofitable extra bother? . . . And the comedy of the expansive gentleman who, after having a suite and vast meals for a week, so that the cash-drawer rattled with anticipation, paid for it with due-bills given for advertising. . . . And the growing importance of cafeterias and coffee-shops, as against the fact that the hasty gobbling of fodder in such places killed the tradition of leisurely dining. . . . And the question of how to provide amusement for lonely guests in the evening; how many liked a gramophone--later, a radio. . . . Lobby-sitters--well-dressed outsiders who all day long occupied chairs needed for guests. . . . The press-agent of the Westward, who pestered the officers by turning the whole hotel over to wedding-parties, so that Myron, however much that sentimentalist loved young love, was sick of dying flowers, dribbling champagne glasses, and weeping relations, who savagely stopped weeping when they had to pay the bills. . . . The newspapermen who blamed a thousand-room hotel because it served more stereotyped food and had more standardized bedroom-furnishings and less quaint, jolly, rubicund, Dickens-cum-Chesterton 'characters' than an 'old-world' inn of fifteen rooms and twenty seatings at table, as conducted by a famous retired chef who managed every detail. . . . The unhappy fact that, devoted to efficiency just as an impersonal ideal, Myron was as irritated by sloppiness and ignorance in rival hotels as in his own. To see on a table an ash-tray filled with cigarette-butts, unnoticed by the waiter, was to him what it was to a Black Thread deacon to catch the preacher kissing a choir-singer. There was no blacker shame--except, perhaps, a guest's marking on a linen tablecloth with a pencil. If he had no formal religion, nor gave any particular thought to his chances of Heaven, he did believe in Hell almost literally when he saw such a guest; and an otherwise perfect journey could, for a quarter hour, be ruined by a crooked tablecloth. He could see more things wrong with an apparently well-conducted restaurant in two minutes than the crankiest guest in as many hours.

He did not approve of himself for being so irritated by incompetence that it clouded the glory of life. He knew that he was 'fussy'.

He could scarcely avoid knowing it, with Ora and Effie May about.

All these details were so unimportant, they told him.

Yet to Effie May the health of her brother and sister and father, an extraordinarily indifferent matter to the world at large, appeared to be important, and equally so, the scent of her perfume, a pebble in her dancing-slipper, or runs in her stockings. And to Ora the horror of using the word 'delectable', the good harsh sound of words like 'grackle' and 'grunt' and 'starve', the crime of depending in stories upon roses, sunsets, and mother-love, and the not uninteresting question as to which magazines paid better, seemed weighty matters.

Sappy little truisms on red and green placards--the demands of Celebrities--emergency overnight kits--doughnut and pineapple sandwiches--unemptied ash-trays--Myron admitted that none of these atrocities singly much affected history, yet all together, he still insisted, they made the difference between doing his job excellently and doing it badly, and that to him was urgent.

The unfortunate thing is that though men have general resemblances in love, hunger, patriotism, and noses, they differ utterly in the technicalities of their work, and each grieves that all the others are idiots not to understand his particular language. Hotel-man or sculptor or sailor or manufacturer of tacks, each has a separate and self-conscious world, with a certainty of its significance to the universe, of the towering dignity of its every detail, and of the fascinating differences between colleagues who, to outsiders, seem indistinguishable 'types'.

To most guests at the Westward, every waiter looked like every other waiter, and a bell-boy was merely a bell-boy, but to one another, and to Myron Weagle, they were as different as Albert Einstein and John L. Sullivan, and all of them more reasonable and comprehensible than either Mr. Einstein or Mr. Sullivan.

Each world has not only its technicalities but its own heroes. To Myron, real history had nothing to do with Charlemagne, Moses, Garibaldi, Goethe, Thomas Edison, or Abraham Lincoln--except as Edison invented the lights that were so useful to hotels, and Lincoln took out an innkeeper's licence in Sangamon County in 1833. For him, the rulers of history were the greater American hotel-keepers: David Reynolds, the Boydens, Barnum (not P. T., but David, of the Indian Queen Tavern in Baltimore), Nathaniel Rogers, Cornelius Vanderbilt--until he gave up conducting the Bellona Hotel in New Brunswick for the outlandish occupation of captaining a steamship--Daniel Drew, who also abandoned innkeeping at the Bull's Head Tavern, on the Boston Post Road, for the vanities of railroad-financing, Rathbun, the Leylands, Paran Stevens, Potter Palmer, Oscar, Boldt, the two generations of Drakes, Statler, Muschenheim, Fred Harvey, Bowman, Boomer, Simeon Ford, Ralph Hitz, Willard, Flagler, Eppley, Ernie Byfield. To him, these names were as familiar and significant as the names of Dickens and Walter Scott to Ora. And to none of these masters, insisted Myron, when he defended himself against the scoffing of Ora or the incomprehension of Effie May, would an unemptied ash-tray be unimportant!

There had appeared in the *New York Messenger* and been copied all through the country a bit of free-verse doggerel in which, to Myron's fury, a wandering motorist made complaint against the hotel world:

    Landlords!
They advertise a roomandabath for a dollarnhalf
On great big bellowing billboards all over the landscape
But
When you get there they say that
Just toNIGHT
(The hotel being almost 27% full)
The best they can do is
Three bucks.

Clerks!
They don't know where any movie theatre, panteria, road to Hickville, or
fender-bander is,
They don't know anything!
Except manicuring their nails while they yawn at you.
Not a thing!

The hotel garage
Which they advertise as 'uptodate, quick service, low rates'.
They darn well ought to be low
(Although they ain't)
BeCAUSE the place is an old barn and so overcrowded THAT
Somebody smashes into you and dents your fender
AND
When you kick, the garridge attendant,
A lowbrow who likes bathing--in grease,
Says you done it before you came in and
Demands halfadollar,
May he have hives on the scaffold!

Bell-boys!
They whistle as they carry your bag and look at how shabby it is and
snicker and point it out to their fellow imps
AND
Hit your shins with it in the elevator
AND
When they have opened your window, on winter days, and slammed it shut
in August, and put their dirty paws on your towels, they just stand there
and

IF
You give them less than a quarter they sniff and bang the door.

Waiters
They either give you warm drinking-water or a CHUNK
Of ice so big in the glass your lips can never,
Can never, never, never get around it.
They bring you also warm butter BUT
You can count on them for cold coffee.
If they bring you eggs they forget the salt,
If they bring you flapjacks they forget the syrup,
If they bring you ginger-ale they forget to open it,
If they bring you meat they forget the knife
    And the fork
        And the gravy
           And the salt
              And the pepper
                  And sometimes the meat!

Hotel beds!
They either slope down to the sides,
So that you roll out all night long,
Or down to the middle so that all night,
You dream
You are an ant,
A little ant,
An unhappy little, little whimpering ant,
Who's trying,
All night long, to climb
Out of a pit of sand, and
The mattresses are stuffed with bricks,
Cement,
Old iron,
And rocks,
And smell, they smell of rags, old ancient rags
Lying a long time in a dark, damp place.

And all the hotel chow tastes all alike,
Clam chowder tastes like beef, and beef like pie,

The while the pie tastes--if you will excuse--
It tastes--it tastes like H-E-Double L.

And then next morning:
The elevator-runner says, 'I hope
You slept well,' and the bell-boys, with their hands
Outstretched in loving greeting, say, 'We hope,
Each miserable urchin of us hopes,
You slept like billy-oh.'

The beaming clerk he hopes you slept; he hopes,
'You have enjoyed your stay with us, old top,'
The while he murders slumber with the bill,
The monstrous inconceivably big bill.

Hotels!
Henceforward I shall sleep in ditches soft,
In barns, in owl-nests, or in piggies' pens,
Dine on the dew and sup the evening star,
Anything to avoid these blank hotels!

When he had recovered from what he conceived to be justified fury, Myron composed his first and last poem. He sent it to the *Hotel Era,* and during the next five years it was reprinted in seventeen hotel journals from New York to Cape Town:

Guests!
As an hotel-keeper I like guests pretty well--
I've got to.
I like them the way a prize-fighter likes getting socked in the jaw--
He gets paid for it.

Guests!
They steal the towels, the ash-trays, the blankets, the electric light bulbs,
the small rugs, the stationery, the pens, the pin-cushions, the table-ware,
the Hotel Red Book.
They never leave their keys, and rarely send them back.
They tell the hotel dick the girl is their cousin.
They want you to cash big cheques without identification,
AND

They say they'll never come back if you don't.
Thank the Lord for that, anyway!

Guests!
They burn cigarette holes in the bedspread, the carpets, the chair-arms.
They leave the water, the costly hot water, running in the bowl
For hours.
They sit on edges of beds and ruin the mattresses.
They cut the towels with safety-razor blades.
They use the towels to clean mud off their shoes.
They use same to wipe off mascaro when they are females of the species.

Guests!
The timid ones are scared of fire, burglars, earthquakes.
The gally ones try to borrow the manager's Tuxedo for banquets.
All of them complain that the clerks, the bell-hops, the porters, the
chambermaids, the telephone-girls, and practically everybody except the
Governor of the State,
Was rude.
Maybe so.
And maybe the guest was rude first.

Guests!
They want strawberries out of season
(And free, on the club breakfast) but
They sniff at strawberries in season,
Great, big, beautiful strawberries in season, and then
They want,
They whine that they 'just can't understand why they can't get',
Imported Norwegian herrings
And Mount Hybla honey
And plovers' eggs
And squab on toast
And all
On the eighty-cent club breakfast.
They want a special steak broiled in five minutes.
And then they kick
Because the steak is rare.
And then they kick

Because the coffee they left standing there
Ten minutes has got cold.

Guests!
The guest is always right.
I like guests.
I've got to.
I'm going on liking them until
That lovely day when I quit and take a claim
In North Saskatchewan, six hundred miles
From stations, taxis, telephones and GUESTS.

'Well, maybe some of the lines aren't quite smooth. My first poem. Maybe Ora wouldn't think it was equal to Longfellow or Ezra Pound or any of those old, classic bards. But the ideas are perfectly fine,' said Myron.

21

To Effie May, after a life of dusting and bed-making, with sodas at the drug-store and dances at Fireman's Wigwam as her maddest dissipations, their suite at the Westward was Paradise.

For himself Myron would have preferred to keep his suite as it was, with grey walls, few pictures, sparse furniture of waxed oak, and plenty of space; but he knew that Effie was all for brightness, and from Bermuda he had written to Luciano Mora asking him to have the suite properly littered. Effie May, when she first saw it, after blushing prettily at the manly greetings of Elphinstone, Mora, and Carlos Jaynes, down in the lobby, squealed, 'Oh, it's just too simply adorably ducky!' Myron beamed--and groaned. Luciano had jammed into bedroom and sitting-room, each twenty by twenty, nearly all the unnecessary furnishings they could hold. There were small applewood tables, large mahogany tables, and nests of Chinese Chippendale tables. There were side-lights in imitation of candles, and floor lamps of writhing gilded iron. There were a couch, and a chaise-longue piled with saffron cushions of leather, pink and gold cushions of satin, tan cushions of broadcloth embroidered with emerald blossoms, and a long, skinny, floppy, milk-faced, degenerate Columbine doll, which Effie May picked up with a scream of delight, and which Myron hated on sight. There were grey and blue lithographs of Paris, chromos of cats that were up to no good, and very funny and rather dirty French caricatures of *cocottes* and *chalets de necéssité,* over which Effie blushed again. There was a small piano, which she touched affectionately, proving that music was not one of her sounder accomplishments, and there were even books--Myron's books, consisting of a set of Dickens, two novels by Rex Beach and one by Conan Doyle, and sixty-seven volumes dealing with hotel-keeping and accounting.

And the bath-room was in glossy black tiles, with lavender tub and bowl, and two dozen assorted towels.

'My, they must expect us to get dirty!' giggled Effie May. 'But, oh, Myron, it's all just too won'erful for words!'

After rising at seven, in Black Thread, and preparing breakfast before she could sit down to it, in a room that still reeked of last night's creamed chipped beef, Effie May stretched her paws like an Angora at being able to have breakfast brought to her bedroom--and such a variety: a choice of three kinds of melons and thirteen kinds of cereal and four kinds of fish (fish for breakfast!) and French toast with honey or syrup, and English strawberry jam in 'ducky' little pots, and shirred eggs with little sausages, and kidneys with mushrooms! 'I'm so excited Myron, but I'm such a pig! I want to order everything! I'll get fat as butter! You better watch me!'

'I will, old lady! Trust me! Watching is my speciality. Kiss me!'

She loved the importance of having the floor-waiter--not a hired girl but a real man waiter, and in a dress suit at nine-thirty in the morning!-- bring in a table all for herself, and humbly murmur, 'Madame is served'. She loved the silver, the amethyst-coloured water-glass, the coffee in a thermos jug, the English muffins tucked under a clean napkin, and the single rose in a slim vase. She loved loafing for an hour and nibbling and gravely daubing herself with jam like a baby while Myron was already downstairs at work.

She could have a hair-wash, a wave, a manicure, or massage, at any time Her Ladyship chose, in her room or down in the 'beautician's', and the attendants were delighted to chatter about hotel feuds and scandal with the wife of the probable future president of the company.

Effie May was indeed an Angora; she loved strong, soft fingers at the roots of her electric hair, upon her flushed cheeks, across the nerves of her shoulder.

The chambermaids were equally obsequious. They crooned, 'Oh, no, ma'am, no hurry at *all!'* when she had kept them out of the suite till eleven. She was delighted with the luxury of fresh bed-linen daily, and she suspected now that, though the Lambkin household had regarded itself as Puritanically neat, she had never learned anything about dusting and sweeping. . . . To have them brush beneath the bed and the couch, and every day--that, she bubbled to herself, was 'class'. And the whole housekeeping department was complaisant about carrying out her notions of further decorating. In the sour and faded rooms of the Lambkin house she had longed for broad ribbons and laces and velvet. She rejoiced in having as much of them now as she wanted. To the welter on the chaise-longue she added fluffy sofa-pillows of apricot silk trimmed with lace; she put flounces on the apparently unflounceable maple twin beds; and the telephone in each of the rooms she hid under a doll with wide skirts of gold lace and tiny glass jewels, which caused Myron to curse wildly, though secretly, every time he had to telephone.

She hung photographs, of her father quail-hunting, of Julia in tulle, of Herbert undergoing the mystic process of being turned from flesh into a Master of Arts, and of the whole family on the ancestral lawn in 1902, a brown and faded print with Effie May herself a chunk of a child in a short, hiked-up skirt, a sailor hat, and a simper.

Myron never complained about her bills. She believed him to be a rich man and wondered--though she was good-natured enough not to nag him--why, with all his wealth, he went on working so anxiously.

There was so excitingly much to do, at first; rituals of the toilet, new to her who, for all the stuffy dignity of the Lambkin residence and the stores of cosmetics in her father's handsome establishment, had known nothing beyond a quick bath in a tin-lined tub, and hasty rubbing with a skinny towel. Now she revelled in a long, languid soaking in warm water scented each day with a new kind of bath salts, in fringed towels vast as a sheet, in eau-de-Cologne and powder and lip-stick, in nail-cream and orange-stick, and the gentle hands of a maid to do her hair--she who all her life had done it herself, or been subjected to the jerky impatience of Julia's harsh fingers. She bought 'lotions' with French names, and was surprised to discover from a saleswoman, after she had been using them as toilet waters, that they were intended for the hair. She initiated herself into the mysteries of creams which were to rub on and rub off, and creams which were to be rubbed in and to stay in. She even tried having purple and green eyelids, but at this Myron protested.

So much to do! After toilet and breakfast, and rearranging the flowers and cushions, and deciding whether the sandalwood cigarette box or the Chinese enamel box would look better on the teakwood stool, there was always window-shopping, with surprises unheard of in Black Thread: English shooting-sticks which turned into one-legged stools, aquamarine necklaces, Parisian hats, cut-glass dishes for hors d'œuvres, onyx-topped evening sticks, Benedictine in unnatural-looking squat bottles, silver evening-slippers. She had engagements at the dressmaker's, at the shoemaker's, and in between there were always these won'erful motion pictures, which had not yet reached Black Thread. When she saw 'Queen Elizabeth', with Sarah Bernhardt, and Zukor's imperial settings, Effie May gasped with ecstasy over her brilliant new life.

If there was nothing else, she could always stretch herself on the chaise-longue, looking down at her new slippers and silk stockings while she curled her toes and waved her small feet, rejoicing at being secure from Julia's demands from the kitchen, and slowly, luxuriously gulping down candy--real dollar-a-pound store-candy! Back home, they had had home-made fudge, or thirty-cent candy from the drug-store, the best their father sold. Dollar-a-pound candy, in gold and scarlet boxes with silver ribbons, was something a beau brought you in awe from Bridgeport, once in a year. Here, in the Westward, she could have all she wanted, and she wanted a good deal, so that she began to worry about becoming too plump, as she nibbled sweets, cakes, fruit preserved in syrup, all afternoon long.

Myron was always attentive--at first. However busy, he telephoned up to her every hour; he sent flowers daily; he took her to lunch and dinner either in the brocade-panelled Georgian Room of the Westward, or in outside restaurants, where she was gratified to have head waiters bow and croak, 'Good *evening,* Mr. Weagle--good evening, *ma'am,'*

They went often to the theatre.

'We've got to see a lot of shows. We both of us need to broaden our minds, and lead a more you-might-say social life,' said Myron.

The social life consisted largely of Luciano Mora, Alec Monlux, and Ora; and to Effie May that seemed a very fine social life indeed, after the Lambkin parlour and Herbert whining about the school-board and Julia quarrelling with Willis. It was both mind-broadening and lovely fun to listen to Myron and Alec and Luciano discussing Colonial Reproductions and the presidential chances of Governor Woodrow Wilson and the objections to the gear-drive in mechanical potato-peelers, while beautifully they drank whisky not straight but with soda-water out of little bottles! Then Luciano returned to Naples, to manage one of his father's smaller hotels, and Myron and Effie missed him, daily. Without his laughter, their cocktail-hours seemed a little dull. Myron was ever busier and, however fond when he did telephone, less likely to telephone at all. Suddenly, when neither Genuine Lotus Bath Salts from an Old Eyptian Recipe, nor looking at tortoise-shell mirrors in shop windows, nor rustling through the box for chocolates with nigger-toe centres, was so novel, Effie May discovered that she had nothing to do, and that she was bored.

It had never occurred to Myron or to Effie that in an hotel suite, without even dish-wiping or feeding the chickens, and with no particular longing to study Imagism or Assyriology or the History of Endocrinology, she would not have enough to do. Being bored, she began to feel neglected-- as she probably was, though the driven Myron could not think what to do about it. She felt the more neglected when Ora helpfully told her that she was. She took up French classes, dancing classes, daily exercise at a gymnasium where ex-pugilists anxiously tempered the labour to the fat lambs, and she had dress-fittings till Myron did begin to be alarmed about the bills. But she discovered in herself no talent for any of these arts save dressing. The jolly Effie May of Black Thread, with her three good frocks made by the village seamstress, became smart now, in tweed suits and Paris models, and just when she was falling into real discontent and whimpering at Myron that she could not endure the emptiness of her days, she met Mrs. Bertha Spinney.

Mrs. Spinney had red hair and alimony; she devoted half her life to preserving these treasures, and the rest to elderly young bachelors with exploratory fingers and imported Chartreuse. She was forty-five in the afternoon sunlight, twenty-five in the dark, her cheeks were powdered as with cake-flour, she laughed frequently, she told very good stories, and she clanked with heavy oxidized silver chains. Her suite was just down the hall from the Weagles' and Effie May had met her often in the elevator. She apparently knew all about Effie, and one day introduced herself and invited Effie in for a cocktail.

Immediately they were chums.

Myron did not like Bertha Spinney.

The blind, doting, efficient kindly Myron had never considered that in all of New York Effie had no woman friend, and indeed no friend of any kind save himself and Alec and perhaps Ora.

Effie May was happily occupied now. With Bertha Spinney she went window-shopping, and it was far more interesting, with Bertha to explain about diamonds that were blue and sapphires that were white, and how 'Couronne d'Amour' perfume, in a small black bottle shaped like a fig, cost ten dollars because it was so enticing that men were maddened by it. Effie secretly longed for a bottle, and saved up the ten dollars for it, but whenever she went back to the shop and looked into the window, she shamefacedly did not quite dare to go in and ask for it.

With Bertha she went to lunch, went to matinées, drove in the Park, ferreted out 'little dressmakers who make you real Paris models for just *nothing,* my dear!' and, at last, went to cocktail parties.

The era of penthouses and multiple cocktails and public kissing and universally saying 'Hello, darling', of gigolos posing as bond-salesmen and bond-salesmen posing as gigolos, and the other happy concomitants of Prohibition and the Great Peace had not yet come, but the Men About Town in 1911 did not do so badly on single cocktails. If they did not call the girls by their first names or manhandle them quite so quickly, when they got to it they meant it, and Effie May found herself the habituée of masculine flats that were floors of large old houses near Washington Square or Gramercy Park; found herself--giggling--the adored friend, suddenly, of a dozen Wall-Street men, or at least a-block-from-Wall-Street men, and occasionally even of genuine imported noblemen who, after five o'clock, when they had removed their alpaca office-coats, became great gentlemen, yet so simple of heart that they were willing to go to tea with any lovely Norse Goddess, provided she paid the bill.

Effie May discovered that she was charged and tingling with sex. She trembled, and felt as though fireworks had gone off inside her, when one of those public conveniences, the bachelors about town, stropped her damp arm or drew lingering finger-tips beneath her chin. She did respect Myron enough to remain what is technically known as a 'good woman', but she scampered back to him with such panting desire that he was overwhelmed with her ardour, her hot hands, her uncreased ivory skin, and while he seemed most strait-jacketed with filing-cards and kitchen-reports, he was most longing for her.

Probably he was too rigid of spirit ever to have aroused her vastly by himself; probably he owed a good deal to Bertha Spinney and the electrifying minor nobilities, but he never appreciated them.

Effie met a whole society of detached women dwelling in hotels, idle women, mostly living on alimony and displaying energy only when they dragged their former husbands into court. Many of them talked incessantly about their devoted care to their children, whom they got rid of by sending them away to school in winter and to camps in summer. Many of them were handsome, many of them were supporting lovers on the alimony from their curiously unwilling ex-husbands, and most of them were devoted to cocktails. In the Westward and other hotels within a dozen blocks, there were hundreds of these leeches, and Effie May was inducted into their splendidly blood-gorged society by Bertha Spinney.

One Mrs. Koreball, officially known as No. 772, The Westward, gave a 'party' for Effie May.

Effie May found it charming.

Mrs. Koreball, Effie perceived, was so sweet! Such a *little* lady, with black hair so sleek and shiny, exactly parted in the middle, and with demure lips and the small chin of a child, but such gay and knowing eyes! Her suite was ever so much bigger than Effie's, and had the most won'erful real genuine Spanish antiques: a great, big, thick oak table--a refectory table, it was called--with the *oldest* wooden chairs, hundreds of years old, from a Spanish monastery! And on the walls Mrs. Koreball didn't have ordinary pictures, but so different--images of the saints, very antique, and what she said were copes, all deep red with gold borders, hung right on the wall. And there was a candlestick of gilded oak with a candle four feet tall!

Mrs. Koreball did not serve cocktails, but a simply won'erful punch made, she said, of champagne and brandy and Mosel (that was a German wine) and vodka (that was a kind of Russian white-mule) and a lot of other things, but all with fruit juice, so it didn't seem strong, but Mrs. Koreball warned her--she must be careful, Mrs. Koreball told her, not to drink too much, because it was *awfully* strong and she couldn't have her new friend Effie get cockeyed at this first party, she said, and she laughed like anything, and kissed Effie, and her eyes were naughty but so nice.

'What do you think I had the nerve to do, Mrs. Weagle? I called up your handsome husband, and he says maybe he'll drop in, too.'

'Oh, I hope he does!'

'You still like him?'

'Oh, I think he's marvellous--so strong and you can depend on him and everything. But it is so hard to get him to go to a party before seven. They keep him so busy in the Front Office.'

'He's the handsomest thing!'

'Oh, do you *think* so, Mrs. Koreball? I suppose he is, but what I always think of first is how he's so strong, and so sort of dependable. Of course he does look kind of clean and all, like he did wash behind the ears, but handsome . . . now a *handsome* man is like that Duke of Essex or Earl of something or whatever he was in "Queen Elizabeth". That was a picture that . . .'

'Yes, I know. I saw it.' Mrs. Koreball seemed a little abrupt. 'Well, come, you must meet the Bunch.'

Round the punch-bowl was simply the nicest group of people Effie May had ever met--oh, of course, except Myron and Luciano and Alec. The men has such lovely diagonally barred ties, and two of them wore spats, though quite a few of them, unfortunately, were bald. The funniest one was a short little man with a red face that he screwed up like a monkey, but you just had to like him, he was so funny.

'My Lord, it's Helen of Troy herself!' he screamed, when Effie was introduced, and everybody laughed, so pleasantly.

Fortunately Effie knew that Helen of Tory was a very beautiful woman, who was named Helen and who lived in Troy, which was in ancient Greece, so she did not feel embarrassed.

'Come on, Helen, time for another glass,' said the monkey-man.

'Oh, I've just had one, and I'm afraid it's *awfully* strong--I wouldn't want to get cockeyed!'

'Nonsense! It's just orange juice with just a wee, tiny touch of dynamite and maybe a trace of carbolic acid! Come hither, lovely one, and let us converse!' He took her arm, guided her to a couch covered with purple brocade, and chattered, 'My name is Harry Burphy, and what, my rose of Sharon, is your monicker? I didn't catch it when our fair hostess threw you to us lions.'

'My name is Effie May Weagle. Isn't it just the *silliest* name!' She giggled.

'Well, Effie May, when are you going to have lunch with me? I've got the slickest imported Italian auto in town and even if it is winter now, I think it would be fun to run up the Hudson to Ye Bunche of Grapes some noon. What say? Good Lord, what lovely fingers you have! Why, I've never seen such lovely fingers as you have!' He seized them; he recited, with ample illustration, 'This little pig went to market'.

It certainly was not Black Thread, but Effice May liked it, while assuring herself that she didn't. His wiry little hands were strong, and he knew how to do such unusual and interesting things with fingers. She meant to refuse his luncheon invitation, but he hadn't yet given her a chance, and just when she was thinking out a good formula for it, he leaped up, dashed at the punch-bowl, and brought back an enormous glass--her third. She sipped it slowly, determining with each sip to stop sipping, and she felt odd and very happy, and presently she seemed to be arguing about going to Ye Bunche of Grapes, but a little uncertain as to just which side of the argument she was taking. And then, curiously, Myron was standing by the couch, looking down at them, enormously tall and, while his lips smiled, terrifyingly stern about the eyes.

Myron had never been in Mrs. Koreball's apartment, but he knew the lady and disliked her with simple fervour. She was a neat little trick, with baby lips and chin, and with the more decorative hotel clerks, she was plush-genteel and syrup-sweet. But she was always sending chambermaids out weeping, and bell-boys out cursing. Every month she made the deuce of a row with the cashier about her bill; she always insisted that the waiters were thieves and that she simply *couldn't* have had that much mineral water. When they begged her to add up her own initialed cheques, she said they were insulting, and stamped her dainty little foot, and her girlish eyes showed an active desire to boil the cashier in oil. She was one of the few guests who had furnished their own suites, and over that, too, there had been a gorgeous row. She had, Myron recalled, tried to jew them down to half the rent, though it meant only that they would have to store the furniture already installed.

He devoutly did not wish to attend the punch-bowl party, but when she insisted that it was in Effie May's honour, he had to go--merely cynically wondering in how many other people's 'honour' it might be also.

As he came in, he looked sharply at the gang: just the sort of well-pressed, well-spoken bill-dodgers who were an hotel's worst pest. The room-decorations, he saw, were atrocious: a big slab of a table, dining-chairs with backs that were too-straight and provided with knobs for the gouging of your shoulder blades, and priestly vestments desecrated by being hung as wall ornaments. Spanish, eh? Antique, eh? Oh yes? Well, he knew the venerable Iberian Händler from whom they came--none other than Señor Don Milton Pincus of the Bronx.

Mrs. Koreball was buzzing, 'So sweet of you to come, Mr. Weagle--though I almost feel like calling you "Myron", like your girl friend! She's the loveliest thing I ever saw! Now you two have found your way, you must drop in for a drink often--the latch-string is always out.'

('Gawd, it's certainly fine for Effie to get away from Black Thread hicks like Mrs. Ted Dingle, and meet cultivated women of the world like this female!')

'But it always seems so hard to get hold of busy executives like you, Myron, and I suppose you handsome men are just chased to death by silly women like me! Well, of course, ever since my Ex put me in my place and let me see what a mean, difficult wench I am, I've learned to sit and fold my hands and just wait to be noticed. Now you come and have some punch. It's quite good, even if I did make it--it's nice orange juice, with maybe a tiny touch of dynamite and just a trace of carbolic acid. Oh! Before I forget! I know it's shocking to talk business in society, but you're *so* hard to get hold of, and *do* you suppose you could persuade that dumb beast of a housekeeper to give me just *a few* towels, now and then? Won't you speak to her? But now come and have a nice glass of punch.'

(He did speak to the housekeeper, to have the pleasure of justified wrath, and he discovered, as he had guessed, that Mrs. Koreball never used the biggest hand towel more than once, and that she was, on her best days, able to get through sixteen of them.)

Even before he had noticed the Bronx-Spanish furniture, he had spied and waved to Effie May, sitting over on a couch with a fellow named Harry Burphy, whom Myron knew as a clever, competent, sometimes amusing importer, whose only fault was over-conscientiousness: he would never be content until he had seduced all the wives of all his friends. He watched them while he drank half a glass of punch. He was disturbed. Effie May was giggling helplessly, as though she were a little tipsy, and letting Burphy rub her hand against his lips . . . Myron had never thought so much of the New York husbands who made the glad cause of Freedom synonymous with Gin, and who let their wives crawl around the laps of other men. He stalked over, only the more annoyed at the innocent-eyed haste with which Burphy dropped her hand.

'Hello, Burphy. Effie! I'm afraid it's about time we were beating it. You know we're going out to dinner.'

'Oh . . . ur . . . we?' she said.

They weren't.

She was certainly not drunk, but she was voluble almost to hysteria. When they were back in their own suite, he coaxed her to lie down for a nap.

'Oh, I couldn't sleep! I feel like going somewhere and dancing! Oh, I feel won'erful!' she cried.

But she passed out as soon as she touched the pillow, and she slept heavily, hour on hour, moaning a little. He sat rigid in a straight chair by her bed, staring at her miserably. She was so desirable and young! It was vileness for her to be touched by slimy people like Burphy and the Koreball, and, he decided, it was his fault, not hers. What could she know of hotel life and hotel loafers? And he had planned nothing for her, he snarled at himself, except the beatitude of being with him when he had the time! He longed to touch her cheek with a cautious finger; there would be delight in just that frail contact. No, she must sleep. And afterwards there would be no more Burphys!

So he very sensibly went in and shaved.

When she awoke, toward eleven, he had hot coffee and cold clam juice waiting for her, and he droned, quite placidly:

'Effie, I've just been thinking that . . .'

'Oh, did I get cockeyed at Mrs. Koreball's party?'

'Oh, no, of course not, though I guess that punch had more kick than I realized.'

'She's a great sweetie, isn't she--so pretty and such fun!'

'Yes, yes, a fine woman. Look, Effie, I was just thinking: I guess you've enjoyed living in an hotel--I certainly hope so, anyway. But I wonder if there's quite enough for you to do, to keep you busy. How would it be if we took a flat, or maybe a house in the suburbs?'

'Oh, I . . .'

'Of course we'd have a first-rate maid to do all the dirty work, but still, what with ordering and maybe making up our room and visiting with the neighbours and so on, you'd have something to keep you busy.'

'Oh, but I've had so much of housework, all my life! Even times when dad could afford a hired girl, I had to help with the dishes and so on and so forth, and oh, Myron, you aren't going to send poor lil Effums back to the kitchen are you? She just loves to go to theatres and dances and restaurants and parties and all!'

'Oh, no, no, certainly not! Go to 'em just as much--evenings, the second I can get away from my office. But I mean . . . Daytimes.'

'Oh, I know, but let's wait a while yet. It's sort of fun here. But listen, honest, I didn't fall for that lil chimpanzee--Murphy or Burphy or Brophy or whatever his name was--Mrs. Koreball called him Harry--but I *mean:* I thought he was just *silly!'*

He awoke at dawn, thinking coldly.

'No. She's good and honest and kind. She has a real happy nature. But she has nothing in herself, in her mind, to keep her occupied. And she could never, possibly, hold down a job, the way Miss Absolom and the Wild Widow and Tansy Quill could . . . That's darn curious, that the three women that have impressed me should have been a Jewish school-teacher, prob'ly from one of these international Jewish families that are interested in music and painting the way I am in stew-pans, and a grocery-demonstrator old enough to be my aunt, and a quadroon chambermaid! Oh, and then Effie for the fourth--four in all, of course, not three.

'And it was my fault. Effie never for a second pretended to be anything she wasn't. And I am crazy about her! Apparently just wanting to kiss a woman is a bigger bond in marriage than brains or virtue or beauty or any other darn thing! And she is so kind and good. I've got to coax her into a real home, away from these alimony-leeches. I wonder if it will keep me from making my resort inn? Well, if it does. . . .'

The candy and cakes and fruit in syrup, the chocolate with whipped cream and coffee with four lumps of sugar, the hot rolls and fat mutton chops and heaps of hashed brown potatoes, which the healthy Black Thread appetite of Effie relished and for which idleness gave her time, were all in competition with massage, with massage a bad second. Daily Effie May weighed herself in the bathroom and wailed, 'Oh, I'm getting terribly plump! I *must* diet!' And didn't.

She still saw enough of Bertha Spinney and of Mrs. Koreball, though she was less naive and more suspicious about the innumerable Harry Burphys. And if she was still bored, now and then, she was rewarded for having to be that popular martyr of the era, a Bird in a Gilded Cage, by the admiration of her family when they descended from Black Thread.

Julia, with Willis and young, came, not very much invited, to spend a fortnight with her before Christmas, and Julia, an authority, said that the Weagle suite was 'simply elegant--so much taste'. She treated Effie May almost with respect. Herbert, with wife and young, offered themselves as guests for the following Easter vacation. Herbert insisted that Myron stop shilly-shallying now, and produce that large and well-paid hotel job right away, as he had promised. (Myron did not remember promising it.) He let it be known that he had been ever so generous; he had given Myron his own sister, he had forgiven Myron for not being a Yale Man, and he had made a point of cutting out every reference to hotel affairs in the newspapers and mailing them to Myron.

Myron reflected that there are so many people in the world who are eager to do for you things that you do not wish done, provided only that you will do for them things you don't wish to do. He made a plot, with the not-too-unwilling Alec Monlux, now manager of a large residential hotel in Yonkers. Alec came calling, affected to be awed by Herbert's training and vocabulary, and offered him the position of assistant manager of the hotel. It was, he said unenthusiastically, a hard job. The last three occupants had died of overwork or had committed suicide, and for that reason they needed a man with Herbert's powers of philosophy. Herbert looked anxious but flattered until, after several acts of comedy, Alec led up to the climax, which was that Herbert's salary would be thirty dollars a week.

Herbert did not come to New York again for a year, and when Effie 'ran up' to Black Thread next summer, Myron went with her for only forty-eight hours, of which he spent thirty-two with his mother.

Most of that summer, a year after their marriage, Effie May loafed through at Frigate Haven Manor, a vast wooden pile of an hotel on the South Shore of Long Island. Myron came out only for week-ends, but Bertha Spinney had joined her, and all summer they munched candy, napped on the beach, yawned on the porch, giggled at flattery, and read novels about sheikhs and civil engineers.

All through one week, a man of whom she later remembered only that his white flannels were beautiful made whispered love to Effie May by moonlight. She did go to sleep on his shoulder one evening, but after that she was snappish. But when Myron came out on Saturday, she was waiting for him so impatiently that he was gratified and rather bewildered; she was at the station when he came in, and when he chuckled, 'What do you say to a little tennis before dinner?' she panted, 'Oh, no, I want to kiss you, first!' and, her hand in his, she dragged him to their room and seized him with so desperate a clutch that his whole being rose to delight in her.

He had intended to spend most of that week-end in making plans for interesting Mark Elphinstone in the Perfect Inn. But he swam with her, he loafed close beside her in hot little pine woods, and about building the Inn he never thought.

Eyeing the men who were moved by Effie May's pink and gold and by her ardent dancing, and who said that she was not one of your doggone, modern, intellectual women that bothered you with deep questions, Bertha Spinney had hopes for Effie's social career. As they rocked together on the Frigate Haven Manor terrace, knitting bright scarfs which no one would ever wear, Bertha hinted, 'If you ever got divorced from Myron, how much alimony do you think you could get?'

'Get divorced? Get divorced from Myron? Why! I'd never dream of such a thing! I love him like anything! Ummmm! I could just hug him to death!'

'Oh yes, of course, my dear! I didn't mean . . . Don't be silly! I just meant, I was thinking about alimony in general. Women have to stand together. I never went out for the vote and women's rights and all that silly rot, but I do remember--I was so interested, I heard Dr. Malvina Wormser, this lady doctor, lecturing, and it's just as she said, women must stick together and not let these men try to put it over on them, and what I meant was . . . of course Myron and you will get away with it, but I do think every lady ought to know about these things, so that--so she can advise others! Just like a lady friend of mine that was the first to put me wise that you always got to keep men waiting and guessing, or else they'll take advantage of you. And what I was thinking of: if you ever have a friend that's going to get divorced, you just keep right after her, and what is most important, make sure she doesn't sign any contract so her alimony ceases if she gets remarried. That's where these dirty dogs of Ex's get you! You have to watch 'em like a hawk! Of course the second or third time you might marry somebody that's richer than the first one was, but on the other hand, you might want to marry some nice boy that wasn't just mean and penny-pinching and commercial like the Old Man was, and that couldn't hardly support himself, let alone you, but was so kind and loving you didn't mind, and *then,* of course, you'd want to go on getting your income and not give your Ex a chance to cut it off, the dirty hog! And serve him right, too! I tell you, a girl that's been married to a man, any man, and given herself to him, and stood for his nasty tempers and his disgusting habits and his behaving the way he does, so he prevents you from going on and taking your rightful place in social circles, I tell you you've *earned* your share of his cash, and it's your right and *duty* to go on *compelling* him to give you your just rights, and if he's been fool enough to go and make new marital arrangements in the meantime, why, that's just *his* hard luck--he certainly never consulted *you* about it! So that's how I mean. If anything *should* ever happen between Myron and you . . . But nothing ever will, of course, or I'll be the most surprised girl that ever lived!'

'Oh, no-o! I hope and pray that Myron and I will always stick to each other!'

She did not like Bertha Spinney, just then. She was inexplicably afraid. She wished that Myron were there, to protect her, to explain away the hints of danger she felt in the Spinney's toothily smiling confidences. She had a won'erful idea! She would run into New York to-morrow, to surprise him, and stay with him till the next Saturday.

But the day after was so hot, and Bertha had planned a swimming party.

When she returned to the Westward, in the fall, Myron had worked out a plan of saving her from sloth. ('Another of my darn plans! Oh, Lord, I do hope this one is intelligent!')

Many wives of hotel-men took part in running the shop, and seemed to enjoy it. Myron had had an uncomfortable feeling that he must save Effie from such toil, but pondering through lonely evenings all this summer-- sitting on hot nights in a large chair by a window that looked up hectic Broadway, stripped to his undershirt, a cold drink in his tired hand--he had convinced himself that this was a prejudice springing from the memory of his overworked mother in an hotel kitchen.

Effie May might become a great executive of the Back of the House, and have activity, triumphs, an income of her own. Wasn't she a trained cook, housekeeper, buyer--for you couldn't tell *him* that it had been the horse-faced Julia, and not his shining Effie May, who had controlled the Lambkin mansion!

Effie May was scarcely back from Frigate Haven when Myron cried that he had an Idea!

That was nice, said Effie.

Why didn't she look over the Westward kitchens and see if she could think of any useful changes? Here was her commission to do so, signed by Elphinstone and Carlos Jaynes, and they had promised that if she had any valuable notions, they would pay her.

She was delighted, and next morning, early--for her--she was exploring the kitchen, alone. Myron would not go with her. No, he would only be in the way.

She had had a tour of them a year ago, but she had noticed little beyond the obsequiousness (or so she had considered it) of everyone to her big, handsome, clever Myron. Now venturing through a swinging door into the vast main kitchen, she was bewildered and intimidated.

The second cook waddled up with, 'Good morning, Mrs. Weagle. Anything I can do for you?'

'No--no--I just thought I'd like to look around.'

She dared not flourish her pretentious 'commission'.

She bravely poked ahead, and at every step was more confused by the complex of coal ranges, charcoal broilers, steam tables, steam bake-ovens, soup-boilers large as three wash-tubs, electric ice-cream freezers, electric egg-boilers, machines for grinding bread crumbs and peeling vegetables and polishing silver, the butcher-shop, refrigerator-rooms with various temperatures for fish, game, joints, and milk, storerooms like whole groceries, and skilfully operating all these mysteries, a hundred brisk men and girls.

Their uniforms were so neat, their hands moved so surely. They looked at her as an outsider.

She fled.

When Myron came up to the suite for lunch, expectant, Effie May howled. 'I went down and looked at the kitchen, and I was absolutely scared! I got all confused! I don't know a thing! I just know about frying chicken and scrambling eggs and like that, and sitting down and peeling potatoes with a little knife and not with a great, big, huge machine! Oh, dear!'

'But you could learn . . .'

'Oh, no, no, no! I'm too stupid! And the noise scared me--it was so noisy, and the cooks--oh, they were nice as pie, but they were all laughing up their sleeve at me, they were, and I was scared!'

To comfort her, he took her shopping.

He had always worried because he had never felt able to buy jewellery for her. He had heard that pretty women have a strange liking for jewellery.

That was not very comprehensible to him. He had always disliked diamond cuff-links and pearl stick-pins on desk clerks. Why didn't they buy New York Central stock, or real estate equity, or something solid, whose value couldn't ever decrease? But still, authorities like Luciano Mora, who understood women, assured him that they really did care for these shiny stones, and he bravely led Effie May to one of the gaudiest shops on Fifth Avenue. There, he was appalled to find that what he believed to be such a pretty amethyst, for which he would be willing to pay three or four hundred dollars, was an alexandrite priced at five thousand.

He was glad to be allowed to sneak off with a hundred-dollar opal.

Effie May said she liked opals better than anything; there was so much fire in them. Just like they were alive!

True, Mrs. Koreball convinced her, next day, that opals were unlucky, so she never wore the ring again.

Every day Myron wished that they had a baby. They both asserted that they wanted one, Effie May most fervently, but the gods in charge of that department, so gratifyingly prompt with couples who did not want more children and could not afford them, had not seen fit to be generous to the Weagles. And, he fretted, a baby would save Effie May from slipping down into fat uselessness.

After three years of marriage, and four, and five, Effie May accepted him as a necessary part of her good-natured, candy-nibbling existence, except that now and then she tried to be witty about his laboriousness and his preference for sleep after midnight.

He suspected that she had caught this from the witty, the never-sleeping Ora.

22

Luxury yacht round-world cruise, on selling basis many esp new rich pay almost anything to be known as exclusive, like special motors for $20,000. Seven or 8 month cruise cost $100,000 p. person (anyway 60,000). Adv point, you get all luxury (and they really will) of billionaire's yacht that had initial cost fifteen million & fifty to 100,000 yr upkeep for a fraction and meet same kind of society. Social host, a count or earl (real stuff), hostess, princess. All fine suites; family of four with maid, valet, secretary get seven bedrms, 7 baths, huge salon, small sit room servants, private dining rm, balcony desk, own steward and stewardess. Price includes wines & booze, all vintage. Shore excursion not in busses etc. but Rolls-Royces and guides not the usual talking machines you read about but smart natives, young docs, lawyers, college profs, etc. who speak English & introduce passengers into native homes both rich and slum, wh ordinary tourists nev see. Carry big launches for fishing, going up rivers too small for yacht, etc. Yacht at least 12,000 ton or whatever make it biggest in world--social credit just to been on it. Limit to 100--80?--pass. Best chef and grub in world, plus take on native chefs with own supplies-- example Hindu chef w curries, Bombay to Bangkok, then in turn Siamese, Chink, Jap, etc. Carry private theat co., dancing instructors, language teachers. Special mail service by aeroplanes. Be fun to plan--spend other people's money--but maybe hell to travel on, with all the fat rich cranks that want their money worth and want the purser to know how much they made.

Now and then, in café confidences, Myron and Ora Weagle had given to their friends curiously similar opinions about the effect of childhood environment upon their characters.

'My father,' said Ora, 'was a sloppy, lazy, booze-hoisting old bum, and my mother didn't know much besides cooking, and she was too busy to give me much attention, and the kids I knew were a bunch of foul-mouthed loafers that used to hang around the hoboes up near the water-tank, and I never had a chance to get any formal schooling, and I got thrown on my own as just a brat. So naturally I've become a sort of vagabond that can't be bored by thinking about his "debts" to a lot of little shop-keeping lice, and I suppose I'm inclined to be lazy, and not too scrupulous about the dames and the liquor. But my early rearing did have one swell result. Brought up so unconventionally, I'll always be an Anti-Puritan. I'll never deny the joys of the flesh and the sanctity of Beauty.'

And, 'My father,' said Myron, 'was pretty easy-going and always did like drinking and swopping stories with the boys, and my mother was hard-driven taking care of us, and I heard a lot of filth from the hoboes up near the water-tank. Maybe just sort of as a reaction I've become almost too much of a crank about paying debts, and fussing over my work, and being scared of liquor and women. But my rearing did have one swell result. Just by way of contrast, it made me a good, sound, old-fashioned New England Puritan.

In 1920, when Myron was forty, and Ora thirty-eight, they had almost exchanged appearances, except that Myron was five inches the taller. He, who had been round-faced and slow, was fine-drawn now, and nervously quick, and his stiffly rearing flaxen hair, as it grew thinner, had become more brown, and lain humbly down under decades of severe brushing. The slim, Shelleyan Ora had grown fat. His face was an orb of complacency, about the dapper moustache of an English police sergeant, and sulky, thickening lips. He was, as ever, darker of tint than Myron, but not in every light evidently so, for after dinner his cheeks were likely to shine greasily.

Myron often looked at you but did not seem to see you. Ora usually saw you but did not seem to look at you.

Myron was incorrigibly and perpetually bewildered by Ora's zig-zag of fortune, and occasionally, for a year at a time, he could not make out at all what Ora was doing and why he should not be even more bankrupt than he was. After *Black Slumber;* between 1905 and 1920 Ora had five other books published: three novels, one very daring, dealing with a prostitute who was a good girl, one still more daring, dealing with a prostitute who actually was a bad girl, and one comic, with involuntary assistance from Mr. Dooley, Irvin Cobb, George Ade, and P. G. Wodehouse. Then there was his guide to Canada--favourably reviewed by all newspapers not published in Canada--and 'The Scientific Meaning of Dreams: A Handbook that Shows You to Yourself', in which Dr. Freud had been an unconscious collaborator.

Myron was proud at the appearance of each of these, and he earnestly tried to find out what the book-reviews meant. He was excited when he found a publishers' publicity note to the effect that Ora Weagle ('Marcel Lenoir'), author of *Slippers, Be Still,* reported as one of the twenty-seven best sellers in Augusta, Tallahassee, San José, and Mankato, this past month, was planning a trip around the world on a whaling-vessel. Or had taken a cottage in sight of Bailey's Beach for the summer. Or was learning to fly. He never ceased feeling a little puzzled and unhappy when he learned from Ora that he had no plans whatever for whaling, flying, or viewing Newport.

What Ora did between novels, Myron could not comprehend, and though he admitted that he was not one who could ever understand the ardours and stress of creation, he did timidly wonder if five books in fifteen years was so very much. And the guide-book and dream-book such little thin books, just trickles of mint-flavoured text around large raw hunks of illustration.

Authors generally were inexplicable, felt Myron. He knew that there were differences between individual hotel-keepers, travelling-men, and pot-washers, but it did not occur to him that authors were ever anything save authors. All his life he was to picture Bernard Shaw as Ora Weagle with a beard, and Thoreau as an Ora who drank his whisky and sang 'Frankie and Johnny' in a log cabin instead of in a Fiftieth Street speakeasy.

Whether or no his ponderous and hypocritical brother understood him, Ora was always busy. A fellow had to be, to make a living in a world that rewarded such mutton-heads as hotel-keepers and stockbrokers, but too much feared the mad power of beauty to give decent support to its creative artists. It wouldn't even provide a tiny pension, so that he might be secure, with bare provision for his modest wants--a cot-bed, a chair or two, a little porridge and lobster salad, a quite infrequent jaunt to Europe or China, a few cigarettes and bottles of whisky and champagne, some girls, a refreshing summer in the mountains, a humble little motor car for the gathering of material, just enough of a wardrobe so that the Maestro would not be shamed in the presence of supercilious millionaires, a cocktail now and then, a flat no larger than might be necessary for the entertainment of the combined editors of America, a couple of Monets for inspiration, just a shelf or so of hand-tooled books, with a mere emergency-stock of liqueur brandy, absinthe, Swedish punch, arrack, Burgundy, Chateau Yquem, and perhaps rum--and he was even willing to give up the rum. Yet no one, even among those who pretended to be patrons of genius, was willing to give him such an insignificant pension. And Ora knew. He knew! For he had made it his business to approach every foundation for the cultivation of the arts, every committee in charge of awarding prizes or fellowships, and every publisher rumoured to have gone insane and to have given advances on unwritten books.

Myron did not merely bore him but furiously irritated him by incessant, clumsy, pawing hints about leading what he comically called a 'more regular life'. Yet he had to see Myron often. He had to live! And he really liked Myron's new wife--a kid from their own home town, Effie May Lambkin. She was good fun, for she thought Ora was the wittiest man she had known, and worshipped him instead of trying to get cute, like so many of these women. She was always glad to order up a late supper for him or, when Myron got stuffy, to lend him enough to get through till Monday.

Ora was proud of the fact that, though Effie May was a beauty, in a coarse, hoydenish sort of way, he was so loyal to the family that he had made practically no effort to seduce her. And then Myron thought he was a rounder!

Oh yes, he was busier than his brother could possibly know, and he had to do everything by himself, without any help from a crew of clerks and stenographers such as Myron had, so that Myron could sit on his bottom and never do any real work at all. Say what they liked, Ora knew that he was systematic. He had compiled a list of fifty fellow American authors who were sufficiently well rewarded, i.e., commercial, so that they were worth soliciting, and he spent days in composing a letter confiding to these colleagues his difficulties, which were, it appeared, as follows: he was engaged in the last fatiguing months of finishing a long novel, his wife was ill, his two children were hungry and without enough clothing to go to school, his rent was unpaid, and unless the benefactor could send him three hundred dollars at once, the whole bunch of them would have to commit suicide. This form letter he changed only in the first paragraph, in which he mentioned several books by the author--which was easy, because they were all listed in *Who's Who*--and the last, where in the simple, grave-eyed manner of a genius willing to face starvation and bend his pride to begging, he explained that though they had not met him personally, through the master's books (give titles) he knew his kindness, justice, and astounding knowledge of human nature.

On the first letter, from fifty prospects he had sixteen answers, with seven refusals, and nine cheques ranging from ten dollars to one hundred and fifty, in total, six hundred and five dollars. None of them sent the full three hundred, but they crawled with apology for not doing so, which was precisely his reason for having put it so high.

On a second letter to the thirty-four hounds who had not answered, he collected eleven more replies, with another hundred and thirty dollars, netting seven hundred and thirty-five dollars for six days' work--two days composing the form and four in typing the letters, and if the swell-head Myron could ever do as well as that, Ora would just like to know! Beaming upon his honestly and arduously earned pile, Ora went on a splendid drunk with Colonel Falkenstein, Wilson Ketch and, from time to time, various girls, most of whom he did not remember having met before. They did, though.

Sober again, and very sick, with only sixteen dollars left of the seven hundred and thirty-five, and three months' rent due for his attic, Ora devoted himself to the twenty-three megalomaniacs who even yet had not been courteous enough to answer. Regarding these snobs, he had an airy wine-born plan. He wrote them a third time, not tenderly but insultingly. They were, he eloquently put it, boors, ingrates, cowards, and reactionaries. While they were making fools of themselves by trying to ape the rich with their Palm Beach villas, Vermont stock farms, and royal suites on liners, he was forced to support himself by stoking furnaces twelve hours a night, that he might devote himself to creating a Real American Art.

This drew, from the twenty-three, twelve more blanks, three cheques, and eight letters of furious reply. It was for the last that he had really been hoping. Here he had eight original and unpublished manuscripts, three of them holograph, in which eight of the most competent writers in America ungrudgingly devoted themselves and their noblest blasphemy to making it clear that they regarded him as a liar, a crook, and a damned nuisance. He read them with shouts of happiness, and bustled out to sell them to an autograph dealer, at from three to sixty dollars apiece.

He made second and third and fourth lists of fifty philanthropists each, extending his sales-appeal from the innocent composers of books to newspaper editorial writers, colyumists, cartoonists, playwrights, and rich women reported as having attended public poetry-readings, and he widened his selling area to take in Canada, Great Britain, Ireland, France, and Germany. Each three months he made a spirited campaign of high-pressure-salesmanship, and cannily did not return to any list oftener than once a year.

So on the whole, the Ora who with shy boyishness, with wistfully quivering thick lips, showed to Myron and Effie May the gin-scented attic in which he had to live, had a slightly larger income than Myron's, which thought made him laugh secretly but very much.

Though he gallantly continued with his books and infrequent magazine fiction, and though his four lists demanded so much painful typing, Ora was most occupied by ghosting--the writing of books to be signed by other and more famous persons. He came to have rather a sound reputation for the work, and various publishers sent for him, though they disgusted him by sourly refusing to pay one penny till the work was done--the dirty money-grubbers! Thus, at various times, Ora was an ex-senator who had destroyed the Wall Street millionaires, another ex-senator who had wiped out the Reds, a Russo-Polish-Spanish-Iowa actress who had three kings as lovers, a forger who had done twenty years in the pen, a chess champion, and a Hollywood dog.

Ghosting paid better than the composition of begging letters, but he never gave them up, for no sacrifice was too great for his art. And it was as an artist, as a seer, that he was able, he crowed, to put it all over Myron.

Ora had been thinking about a new realistic novel in which he would crucify a horrible parent named Tim Wiggins, who kept a foul restaurant and was beastly to his sensitive son, and possibly in connection with this enterprise he had run up to Black Thread Centre for a week.

Returned, he charged in on Myron.

'Well, the great innkeeper and psychologist, that can tell a crook before he's signed the register, has certainly pulled one swell boner!' said Ora, winking at Myron's pretty typist.

Myron hastily sent her out, and stormed, 'What the devil do you mean now?'

'I've been up to the Centre, and I saw Dad and Mom, and since you were so kind as to rescue them from working and give them a nice easy old age, in their lovely little bungalow among the roses--well, they're simply going nuts with nothing to do, that's all!'

'Nonsense!'

Myron went to Black Thread next day.

His mother was sitting in a filthy kitchen, before a sink of dirty dishes, crying. She had, she sobbed, so got out of the habit of activity that now she could not stir at all, and old Tom, no longer needing to make an appearance as host, was drinking worse than ever.

'I've tried reading, and I've tried church-work and I've tried knitting and talking to the neighbours, but I guess folks like us, that have worked real hard all our lives, just don't know how to loaf,' she said. 'I'm kind of scared, dear. I've been noticing how many business folks seem to suddenly pop off and die, when they retire and say they're so glad they're out of the harness and now they're going to have a good time.'

He was bewildered. He assured himself that he really had meant well. He told himself that he would not afford to buy off the present lessee of the American House, and that if he did, his parents would let it go dirty and slack. He thought about a farm for them--he tried to consult them, but his mother only wept and looked forlorn. He might have rented a farm, except that at the Lambkins', when he hinted of his problem, Herbert blatted, 'Now you're married into Our Family, you can't go on being selfish and just thinking of yourself, the way you always have! . . . That fellow Monlux, offering a man with my degrees fifteen hundred a year, and you never even called him down! . . . And I want to tell you that I'm not going to have *my sister's* father-in-law running a miserable little tavern right here in our own town! Why don't you put 'em on a farm?'

That did it. Myron gave his father and mother a wild week in New York--Tom said that the Westward wasted a lot of good coin, dressing up the bell-hops in fool monkey jackets, and as a seasoned executive he disapproved of such incompetence--and he settled them again at the American House, where Edna Weagle, as she toiled twelve hours a day, began again to whistle.

And Ora commented on it all, 'Just as I've always told you, Myron, you lack the artist's sense of people. You're probably more generous than I am, in some ways, but I see inside people and let 'em alone.'

The young woman whom Ora brought up to the suite to meet Effie May and Myron, late in the evening, was a very friendly young woman. Within ten minutes she was calling them 'Teeny the Swede' and 'Snookums', and she was demanding, 'Well, where's the hooch? What's the idea of holding out on the girl friend like this?' And after the whisky, a good deal of it, she offered to take off her clothes and do imitations of Isadora Duncan.

Myron saw that the perplexed Effie May was wondering whether she ought to take her brother-in-law's lady-friend as a model. He lured Ora to the bedroom, and remarked, 'Take that girl away. Chase her out of here.'

'What the devil do you mean?'

'I don't like her, though probably she's merely silly. Out!'

'Then I'll go, too! And I'll stay away!'

'All right. Sorry not to see you again, but this is my house. . .'

'Oh no, it isn't, darling! It's anybody's house that's got the money, no matter what a stinker he may be, and you're just a hired man in it--you and your hick wife!'

Myron raised his fist, dropped it to his side, and muttered, 'Get out.'

He did not see Ora for a year after that.

He felt guilty and considerably relieved. He pictured his poor little brother in that poor little attic of his, and doubtless he would have suffered if it had not been for the fact that, as Ora was unanimously agreed, he lacked imagination.

23

It was in the early autumn of 1916, when they had been married for five years, that Myron became prouder than ever he had been in his life, prouder and taller and more excited. Effie May announced that she was going to have a baby!

Healthy wench as she was, though too well fed, she had no unusual trial, and in the spring in 1917, they had an eight-pound son, very fine and exceptionally handsome--which meant that even in the first month he was recognizably human. Now, along with every thought about his Perfect Inn, Myron gave another thought to the future when he would go hunting and fishing and travelling with His Son.

He was named Luke, more or less after Luciano Mora.

Before the baby's birth, Myron did what he called 'putting his foot down', and insisted that they must have more of a home than an hotel suite . . . How he reconciled it with his advertisements that 'A Suite at the Luxurious Westward Ho! Will Solve All Your Housekeeping Problems-- We're Glad to do Your Hiring and Firing!' he never explained to himself nor ever tried to.

Effie May said that she 'wasn't--quite--sure--it's kind of convenient living in the city'. Myron was sure for her. 'I'm certainly not going to have our baby grow up one of these horrible, ringleted hotel-children, yelling in the corridors and bossing the servants and showing off to strangers,' he said, and was beautifully unconscious of any heresy to his faith as a sealed hotel-keeper.

They found and rented a seven-room house with a small garden in Mount Vernon, not too far from the station. Once it was veritably his, his own house, at least for a year, Myron found it magic with privacy. Its white wooden pillars and roofing of green imitation slates, its short sidewalk of parti-coloured slabs of stone, its yellow brick fireplace, its piano and glassed-in unit-bookcases and ash-tray stands were different, obviously, from those of any other house in Westchester County, and possibly in America.

The doubtful Effie, as the neighbours came in to see whether she was correct in the matters of piety and bridge, found the place at least won'erful. 'Why, now we got all the nice things in both New York and Black Thread!' she would explain, with awe. 'I can go in for the theatre or to see Bertha, and still have a garden and quiet for Junior, and such dandy neighbours to run in on--high-class--lots of them have tea almost every afternoon, and they play real bridge, for money!'

Myron loved the peace of it--what time he had it. Often he could not get home till midnight; often he had to be away by seven in the morning. But he rejoiced in seeing Effie May and Luke in the diminutive garden. He was only a little angry, so used was he to this attitude, when certain of his neighbours hinted that as an hotel-man, he would be able to direct them to gay but economical ladies and to powerful but inexpensive booze.

In the solitude of the many, on trains, he had the leisure now to make plans in his latest note-book for the Perfect Inn. During the war, when he served in the Quartermaster's Corps, he enjoyed that dangerous position, because he could be home every evening and all day Sunday. When the conflict was over, at least theoretically, he went back to his regular work as Mark Elphinstone's first assistant and to his irregular hours at home with Effie and the miraculous Luke, who was no dullard as he himself had been but, at eighteen months, could say 'Da!' He was saving money constantly, investing it, after a good deal of inquiry, mostly in hotel shares. Its accumulation was in his mind related with Effie, Luke, and the Perfect Inn.

He never missed a train into the city, but he was never seen to hurry . . . A tall man, inexpressive of face, a typical dull captain of business, making little business notes in a little pocket-book, in the smug smokiness of a commuters' train that clattered through dun fog streaked with factory fumes, while in his attic Ora still lay dreaming of damsels in Poictesme.

24

Or again just opp of Luxury Yacht and personally wd prefer: for people who like sailing yachts etc. & cant afford boat big enough open ocean: reg old-fash full-rigged sailing ship to Europe; advant.: quiet, rest, really feel at sea, get away fr jazz, motors. But good beds, wireless for safety, & elec. for lights, refrig., gas engines used only to charge batteries daily and as auxiliary in dead calm. Also appeal youngsters just out college.

Through all of 1918, Mark Elphinstone was weakened by attacks of angina pectoris, and the instant he was out of the army, Myron became unofficial president of the Elphinstone chain. Now he first really knew Mark as a human being.

For years Mark had lived in a large and very pseudo baronial apartment on the top floor of the Westward, with imitation beams, a heraldic fireplace, and a mute musicians'-gallery in the salon. Myron had rarely been in it, but now Mark lay abed and Myron went daily to see him. He was present through two of Mark's dreadful attacks, brought on by anger, or by an effort to get up and dress. Then, in an agony that lasted a minute and seemed to last an hour, Mark felt as though he were dying, as though a great hand were squeezing his heart, while the pain cut a gash up to his neck and down his left arm. He panted, his eyes bulging with terror. Myron and the nurse stood by the bed, in the embarrassment of futility. The horror gone, he would try to laugh, and mutter, 'Tell Carlos Jaynes to stop grabbing my heart--tell him to stop it--want it stopped right away.'

He talked now, wanderingly, of his private life. He was a widower; his one child, a daughter, was married to a lawyer of elegance, living in Brookline. Myron guessed, when he saw her, that she was gallantly trying to forgive her father for still living. She wore satin with chastely dangling chains, and was very crisp and literate, and her father was humble and conciliatory in her presence. For hours, when she had gone, Mark boasted to Myron about his daughter's music, her Italian, her friendship with bishops.

The doctor warned Mark that he must 'avoid all muscular excess and all emotion', and Mark's latest secretary, the clean, swift, amiable, rather dull young Mr. Clark Cleaver (he was rumoured to be a wizard at the parallel bars and flying rings in the Y.M.C.A. gymnasium) kept stirring Mark into furious emotion by coaxing him to avoid all emotion. Myron had sense enough to let him rave and get it over.

It was the Carlos Jaynes faction who brought on the catastrophe.

Jaynes' brother-in-law, large stockholder in the Elphinstone Company, called on Mark. Myron was not present, but he learned from Clark Cleaver that the brother-in-law pussy-catted about, patted Mark's hand, assured him that he would instantly be out and playing eighteen holes of golf, and then, with just the playful tactfulness which the bluff brigand most detested, hinted that Mark ought to resign and make Jaynes his successor.

The brother-in-law gone, Myron was sent for, and arrived by Mark's bed along with the hotel doctor. Mark was raving, 'That damned Jaynes and his damned relatives! I'll fire him! He's fired right now! Cleaver, you get on the 'phone and tell Jaynes he's fired, right now.' Cleaver dared not move. 'Get him, I tell you, get him, get him, get him on the 'phone, I tell you! They think they've got me down! They think they can jam Jaynes down my throat! I'll show 'em! I'm not afraid of any man living. I'm not afraid of anything!'

He choked. He clenched his fists in agony. His face was grey as March snow, and was greased over with cold sweat.

'But I am afraid of death!' he whimpered.

His old kneaded face fell into the blankness of childhood; defiance and courage dropped from it, and he muttered, 'Afraid of death! Myron! Cleaver! Stick by me! Stay there. Don't go away. I feel lonely. I'm afraid!' Veteran wisdom and courage came back into it, as the spasm lifted, and he snarled, 'I won't let 'em make me afraid, with their damn sympathy! Eighteen holes of golf! There's no man living can make me play golf! My game is Men, and they can't beat me! I've licked 'em!'

And he gasped and died.

The directors of the Elphinstone Company met two hours after the funeral, and learned that Mark Elphinstone's daughter, his sole heir, had contracted to sell all her holdings in the company to Carlos Jaynes and his brother-in-law. They elected Jaynes president of the company.

An hour after that, Jaynes sent for Myron and merrily offered to him the assistant managership of the Elphinstone Akron hotel.

Carlos Jaynes was not vastly popular with his fellow hotel-men throughout the country. It did not at all hurt the reputation of Myron to have been kicked out. After a week--though that week, with its agonizing enforced idleness, was long enough--he was offered the managership of an hotel in Wilmington, and took it, leaving Effie May and Luke in Mount Vernon.

He left Wilmington for the not-too-important but instructive job of chief assistant manager at the Hotel Crillon of New York, which had only five hundred rooms but was the newest and smartest hotel in the country, with a clientele altogether different from the run of amiable and prosperous social nobodies at the old Westward. The Crillon was patronized by ambassadors, princes, international crooks, and Americans so wealthy that they could afford to live on Long Island and again be farmers like their grandparents. He learned not to blink at hundred-dollar-a-day suites and small sleek dinners in private dining-room at fifty dollars a plate; he learned that one-half, at least, of the excessively rich are as annoyed as one-half, at least, of the excessively poor when they are insulted by receiving bills; and learned an Alice in Wonderland arithmetic whereof the chief problem was: 'Which pays better, ten dollars a day that you get or a hundred dollars a day that you don't get?'

He did not vastly care for the Crillon, its deftly obsequious staff, or its deftly supercilious guests. Not even yet was he fond of foot-kissing.

For one summer he was manager of the Frigate Haven, with Effie and Luke near him in an hotel cottage; for nearly a year and a half he was managing director of a large hotel in Philadelphia; and by then, in 1922, when he was forty-two years old, he had enough reputation and enough advantage from the hotel-world's continued enmity to Carlos Jaynes, to be able to stop roving, and settle down in a position that was by far the most important and best paid he had yet held: general director of all the Pye-Charian Hotels of New York, and managing director of their largest house, the Victor Hugo.

The Pye-Charian Company consisted of four men: Richard Montgomery Pye, the president; Adolph Charian, a fat, thoroughly vulgar, and thoroughly shrewd contractor; Colonel Ormond L. Westwind, the celebrated criminal lawyer, after-dinner speaker, and vestryman of St. Thomas's, and Nick Schirovsky, who called himself a manufacturer of mineral waters and whom Myron more than suspected of being a wholesale bootlegger. Myron himself and 'Jimmy' Shanks, manager of one of the Pye hotels, also had each a few shares in the company.

The holdings consisted of the Victor Hugo, a new eleven-hundred-bedroom, each-with-bath, transient hotel in upper Broadway, and six residential hotels on the West Side of New York between Seventieth and One-Hundred-and-Twenty-Fifth Streets. The largest of the residential hotels was The Dickens, on Riverside Drive, managed by Shanks. Jimmy was big and jovial and grinning and practical-joking, with his crisp rolls of the blackest hair; a shrewder and modernized version of J. Hector Warlock.

He had played football for two years at the University of Kentucky, and been expelled for inattention to his books and general hell-raising.

An old friend of Myron, Clark Cleaver, Elphinstone's last secretary, was also with Pye-Charian, as chief clerk of the Walter Scott Hotel.

Of all these men, it was Richard Montgomery Pye whom Myron saw most often. His job, as president, was to control the somewhat mysterious finances of the chain, and to demand improvements which Myron had to carry out.

Dick Pye was slender and suave as a greyhound on a silver chain. He was chief among the new sort of hotel-men, detested by Mark Elphinstone, who were as likely to arrange their affairs on the golf links, in country-club bars, or in fast motor cars as in offices or the kitchen. He was a smiling man, not very tall and not over forty; he was apparently accepted as one of their own by the most pretentious country-club-and-estate circles on Long Island, and he played polo with the second team of the Old Chapel Club.

Pye's origin was in dispute. One faction asserted that he was the son of a doubtful minor Tammany official and had begun his career by selling newspapers and continued it as bell-boy in a scabby hotel in the old Tenderloin, but his friends contended that he came from what is known as a 'fine old family'. Virginians said he came from a fine old family in Massachusetts, and Massachusettsans said he came from a fine old family in Virginia. Harvard men said he was a graduate of Yale, Yale men said he was a graduate of Princeton, and Princeton men were divided between Harvard, Yale, the University of Oklahoma, and Maine Agricultural College. And Dick Pye smiled and never explained and played polo and arranged for mortgages and persuaded smart but liquorous young men to take costly suites at the Victor Hugo or The Dickens for the whole winter season, and seemed to know what Myron and Jimmy Shanks and Clark Cleaver were doing, every moment, and what unknown clerks, in some second-rate houses a thousand miles away, could be trained to take their places.

All very old and very rich women said that 'Dicky' was the sweetest boy they had ever seen, and all professional gamblers said that his poker was worthy of the most eminent practitioners.

Myron liked Dick Pye and the Victor Hugo enormously, for a few months, then dreaded them as poisonous, after the honest piracy of Mark Elphinstone.

His job was to control every department of the Victor Hugo, as resident manager, and to glance over the conduct of the six residential hotels. To these he was to give not so much time as experience and dependability. He looked into their kitchens or linen-rooms or garbage-trucks or the pile of chambermaids' O.K.'s on made-up rooms, and sometimes there was fatherly advice to department-heads and sometimes there was quick guillotining.

Most of his hours were devoted to the Victor Hugo.

The changes in hotels, in New York, and in all America, between 1905, when Myron had gone from Tippecanoe Lodge to the Westward, and the 1920's, were illustrated by the differences between the Westward and the Victor Hugo. The Hugo was intended to appeal to the same sort of solid, upper-middle-class, prosperous patrons, and it was on the same Broadway, though twenty blocks farther north. But it was nearly twice as large, eleven hundred rooms against six hundred and fifty, and it had none of the spurious grandeur which had gladdened the guests of the Westward in 1905; none of the velvet or tortured ironwork or carved teak or copper minarets or bread-pudding marble. It had, indeed, the 'good taste', or what to the 1920's and 1930's, seemed the good taste, of massive simplicity. The main entrance was a severe doorway of Indiana limestone, with no awning of glass and gilded iron; the lobby, lined with uncarved cedar panels, was half the size of the Westward's, and considerably less inviting to lobby-loungers; the elevators bore no sunbursts of brass, but they were thrice as swift and silent, and the elevator-runners discoursed on the current weather only with clients who desired it. The Victor Hugo bedrooms were free of imitation-brocade and lace table-covers, armchairs with frayed fringes, and ornamental brass beds which, even after many renovations, were still to be found in the Westward. There was less of tax-breeding space and fewer dust-collecting ornaments.

Mechanization had increased hugely, with air-conditioning, radios in all rooms, central vacuum-cleaning plant, electric refrigeration, stainless metal alloys instead of damp and seamy surfaces throughout the kitchens. There was a 'coffee-shop', approximately as large as the Grand Central and as busy. There were graduates of the Cornell and other hotel-schools in every corner.

But if the Victor Hugo was more expeditious and sophisticated and in better taste than the Westward, the trim bedrooms were far smaller, with less room for nervous patrons to poke about; if the washed and filtered air was purer, there seemed to be less of it for placid breathing; if the restaurants were better lighted, they were less leisurely; if there were more tropical fruits, there was less generous cooking; if the whole thing had become a better machine, it had become a less comfortable home.

America and the hotel of 1905 were not far from the America and the inn of Martin Chuzzlewit; America of the late 1920's had lost for all time that large, loquacious, gallant, often comic, rusticity. It had driven from Saratoga Springs to Nice, in a sixteen-cylinder car. It had gone from cotton stockings to silk; from the small beer of Weber and Fields to the champagne in 'Of Thee I Sing'; and sometimes Myron was bewildered and a little uneasy.

The guests of the Victor Hugo had familiar faces--more regularly shaved than at the Westward--yet their hearts seemed to Myron different, and he did not altogether like the change.

He still had the old dependables: the up-state banker and his family who came to New York for a month, for shopping and the opera, the Detroit purchasing agent and the Phoenix department-store buyer and the branch-manager from Spokane, all of them trained travellers who appreciated service. But among them, as was natural to an hotel which had Nick Schirovsky as one of its owners, had crept a new race of mild and solid-looking and well-behaved men, quietly dressed and most generous with tips, whom he guessed to be gamblers, racketeers, sellers of dubious stock and real estate. They did nothing of which you could complain; indeed they were ever so much quieter about sending for mineral water to accompany illicit whisky than were the innocent buyers, and they were less likely to sing 'Mandy, Mandy, Sweet as the Sugar Cane' after it. Yet Myron hated them, and felt insecure when he observed their intimacy with the aristocratic Mr. Richard Montgomery Pye.

He knew that the bell-boys were procuring liquor for the guests, from the lofty superintendent of service, but he could do nothing about it. They were under licence of Dick Pye, and they shared the profit with Pye, Charian, Schirovsky, and the pious Colonel Westwind.

But they shared, neither profits nor confidences with Myron. That was the one detail of the hotel-management that he neglected.

He had some comfort out of investing in Frigate Haven Manor, and a larger, more ambitious summer resort, Laurel Farms, and in improving his investments by giving advice as an expert.

But after three and a quarter years as general director of the Pye-Charian Hotels, he felt that he was in a blind alley. He might be a good innkeeper. He believed that he was. But just as he had never been particularly obsequious to the German barons and French vicomtes and

Long Island squires at the Hotel Crillon, so he could make no especial effort to impress the slick friends of Nick Schirovsky as their natural provider and protector.

He said so to Gritzmeier the chef, and was shocked into doing something about it, instead of merely sitting around and enjoying his noble discontent.

Otto Gritzmeier was managing chef of the Hotel Victor Hugo, and for him Myron had more respect and liking than for any other officer in the Pye-Charian chain. He was a Swiss, trained in Lausanne, Biarritz, Hamburg, Milan, and Bournemouth. At fifty he had come to America as chef of the distinguished Restaurant Sylvère, but that shrine of gourmets had closed with Prohibition, and Gritzmeier had reluctantly turned from Homard Sauté à la Dumas to the Standard Cost per Ounce of Hamburg Steak.

Myron was merely supposed to confer with him several times a week, in the director's office, about menus and special dinners and the equipment and personnel of the kitchen, but almost every day found Myron sitting at Gritzmeier's desk, in his tiny glass-walled office in the good reek of the enormous kitchen, happily recovering from Schirovskism. Just Gritzmeier's appearance, the floury yet healthy cheeks, the grey huzzar moustache and imperial, the tall cap and apron and overalls (for Gritzmeier was one of the few managing chefs who refused to dress in a lounge suit) was refreshing after the pink-cheeked, ebon-haired, glossily brown-suited guests in the more expensive suites of the Victor Hugo. He became almost as intimate with Gritzmeier as he once had been with Luciano Mora--the cautious ultra-Yankee released by his admiration for an ultra-Continental.

This day in September, 1925, he growled to Gritzmeier, 'We've got to get together next week and plan the supper-dance menus for the season for the Laurentian Grill. Damn the grill! I hate planning anything for a bunch of drugstore cowboys with pocket flasks--trying to compete with the speakeasies! I've always wanted to have a really good country inn--good as any resort hotel in Europe.'

'Then vy don't you, Chief?'

'Well, it's difficult getting started . . .'

'T'ree years you've been talking about your fine inn. Talking! Vy don't you *do* it?'

'Oh, I . . .'

'You got some money saved, aind't you? You can get the rest, cand't you? Vy don't you do something? You aind't going to get a whole lot younger, Chief!'

'You're right. I'm forty-five and . . . I'll do it! I *guess* I will!'

And, rather scared, he knew he would.

It was easier to undertake the labour of financing and building his Perfect Inn than it was to loiter and face the cynical old eyes of Otto Gritzmeier.

25

'I just don't know where all my time goes to,' was Effie May's favourite observation. She said it oftener, these days, than 'won'erful'.

They had a larger house in Mount Vernon now, but in the same neighbourhood. Playing after school-hours with Luke, a tall boy of eight, finding out what orders the maid had decided to receive and then giving them, playing Russian Bank with Myron on evenings when he did not feel like reading, discussing garden seeds and the wearing-quality of boys' trouserings with the neighbours, trimming the church with flowers and rather irregularly going to a women's musical and literary club, she lived the same busy and unplanned life that she would have lived in Black Thread, save that once a fortnight she went into the city for the theatre or a placid, domestic afternoon in a speakeasy with Bertha Spinney.

She was well content, and gnawed candy as delicately and as much as ever. She was extremely fat, and at thirty-four looked a cheerful forty, and now that she rarely heard Ora's sneers, she regarded Myron as a sage, and knew that he depended on her as on cool water.

Myron had telephoned that he would be home at seven, and Luke had been permitted to sit up for him. Luke was riding his tricycle back and forth on the cement walk from street to house, occasionally falling off it into the bug-eaten rose-bushes. The tall, nervous shape of his father swung around the street corner.

'Hello, daddy!'

'Hello!'

'Hel-LO!

'Hello, son.'

'Whaja bring me?'

'Not a thing!'

'Not *any*thing?'

'Not one darn thing!'

'Not anything at *all?'*

'No, sir! Expect me to bring you a present every night?'

'Sure-pop!'

'Who ever taught you to say that?'

'In school and then, of course, you always say it to ma.'

'Oh, I do, eh?'

'Uh-huh, sure, every day!'

'Well, then, I guess I'll have to see if anybody's stuck any chocolate in my pocket. Though, mind you, Luke, I disapprove of bribery as a means of enforcing discipline in large, efficient, modern institutions like this.'

'Uh-huh. Oh, that's swell--peanut brittle!'

'Luke! How would you like to live right out in the country, but near a lovely inn with grand food--fishing and swimming and meadows and hiking and squirrels and--oh, and flowers--you know, everything! Real country! How'd you like that?'

'Punk.'

'No, really! Wouldn't you love the country?'

'Naw. I like it here. It's all hicks in the country--like at Uncle Herbert's. Let's stay here. Or maybe move into New York. That would be dandy! Then I could go to the movies twice a day!'

Myron meditated, 'That helps! I can see that everybody is going to approve enthusiastically of my going off to run a country inn. Splendid! Oh hell. . . . But Luke will like it! I'll make the kind of place he'll like!'

'I've told you lots of times about building a really first-class inn,' said Myron. 'You know--my farm near the Centre. Lake Nekobee.'

'Yes, sure, ten thousand times,' said Effie. She yawned, then smiled in apology.

'Well, at last, after chewing the rag about it so many years and being scared of undertaking it all the time, I'm really going to do it!'

'Honestly?' She was affectionate, and entirely unimpressed.

'Yes. I mean it. Now I want you to pay some attention, Effie. If I put this through, or rather, when I do, it will affect you. We'll have to live there--I aim to have a place I can keep open all the year round--winter sports, too--and we'll have to live there.'

'Oh, but darling!' She squeaked like a cornered mouse. 'I can't leave the nice neighbours here, and Junior used to the school and all, and the Centre--oh, of course, it would be lovely to be near the Family, I suppose, but to not ever be able to get to New York and see some shows. . . . Oh, I don't think that would be any fun at all!'

'We'll try to get down to New York for a month every winter, or say late fall, between seasons, and not do a blessed thing then but raise Cain and enjoy ourselves, and that's something we've never had time to do, never.'

'Well . . .'

She looked about her well-loved sitting-room, the huge cabinet gramophone, the automatic heat-regulator, the silver cocktail shaker that would be taboo within reach of Brother Herbert. He knew that she was trying to nerve herself, and for her confused gallantry he loved her.

'Well, if you think it's best, Myron.'

'Look! I'll build us a grand cottage near the Inn--lots more room for Luke to play than here, and I don't know that the school in the Centre will be so much worse for him. These kids around New York are so frightfully fresh and knowing and impertinent. "Sure-pop"!'

'Well, I guess there'd be some nice folks at the Inn, too.'

He knew that she felt insecure. Oughtn't he to give up this unnecessary plan and go on with Pye-Charian? No! Be valet to Nick Schirovsky and his friends or, at best, give his life to wholesale cafeteria-keeping? There was peace and quiet skill in the tradition of every ancient Cat and Fiddle, or White Hart, or Old Bell, in which immemorially tired and drenched and hungry men had taken their ease. And he would make a greater masterpiece than any of them.

'But I wish Effie could see it like that,' he pondered.

He talked frankly about it to Ora, for Ora, he told himself, was the one person who would understand his doing something a little unconventional.

A year after he had kicked Ora and his girl out of the Westward--almost ten years ago, now--they had run into each other on the street, sheepishly shaken hands, and gone to lunch. He had seen Ora occasionally ever since. Hugely approving, he discovered that Ora had an almost regular job writing two-reelers for the movies, and articles for the new magazines devoted to the movie world, and he said profoundly, 'If he does get drunk pretty often, still there's quite a few fellows with good minds that have that unfortunate habit!'

He outlined the Perfect Inn and his determination to leave Pye-Charian. He waited for the first approval since Otto Gritzmeier's.

'Huh!' said Ora. 'I think you're a damn fool. Here you've got a good chance to go ahead with these high-class bootleggers and be a member of the firm some day, and then you can transfer to some other big outfit that isn't crooked, or only just average crooked. And you want to chase off and start another fancy arty tea-room, the kind you made out of the American House! My dear Myron, a man who doesn't have originality for his long suit oughtn't to strut around trying to show off his originality!'

'I'll do it, just the same!' growled Myron, and talked of baseball.

Richard Montgomery Pye, giving audience in his office, which resembled a Louis XVI boudoir reproduced by a steel-manufacturer, remarked formally, 'I won't say that the firm, or at least Adolph Charian and I, might not come in on financing your inn. But I think the project is pretty small for a man of your executive ability. At best, it would only pay a fair profit on a few hundred thousand. You see, I'm laying my cards on the table, Weagle. We're more than satisfied with you. I think sometimes you're too cautious, and worry too much about penny-pinching, but then, we're all four too much inclined to gamble, and you check us, and you have the patience to fuss with which firm will sell crackers at a sixteenth of a cent less a pound, and you don't customarily steal the handles off the office safe. Why don't you stick with us, and get in on the big money? We might take you in as a partner in a few years, and make it easy for you to acquire a share, and I can see us swinging an hotel twice as big as this.'

'And twice as noisy!' Myron thought silently.

'So give up this idea of yours for a year or so, anyway, and stick around.'

'No, I'm sorry, Pye, but I'm all set on it. Will you talk to Charian, or shall I? Or shall I arrange for the financing outside? I figure I'll need about two hundred thousand over and above what I have. Shall I see Charian?'

'No, I will. I'll let you know. But I hope you'll change your mind.'

Within two days, Dick Pye informed him that Charian and he would come in, but would leave their other partners, Westwind and Schirovsky, out of it, since their fine talents were better suited to criminal law--to the breaking and the avoidance of the same--than to country inn-keeping and the exploitation of daisies. Pye and Charian had a hundred and fifty thousand or so in hand; the other fifty thousand could be provided on mortgage.

'But we still think you're foolish to start anything so half-faced as a little resort hotel like that, and we're willing to invest in it only because we believe you're competent and dependable. We still want you to think this whole business over again,' said Pye, unapprovingly.

And almost as unapproving was Alec Monlux, who quivered, 'If it should flop, you'd be right out of things here; hotel game moves so fast it changes overnight. And I'd of thought you'd had enough of associating with the golden rod and gophers. I certainly did, in Iowa. I agree with what Effie May was arguing: New York is the only place where you can rub up against all the big, rich, important guys, and keep polished.'

In fact, no one approved, beside Gritzmeier and, unexpectedly, Jimmy Shanks, the beefily affable manager of that Pye-Charian house, The Dickens.

'Sure, it's a swell idea, Myron, and don't let these crêpe-hangers tell you anything different,' crowed Jimmy. 'You'll put it over, and then you'll go on and build others, till you have a whole Lake Placid of your own--that is, if you want to take the trouble, and I'll bet you won't. You'll have too much fun just running a good small place with a high-grade clientele and swell grub, and be able to call your soul your own and get out and breathe a little fresh air and catchum a fish whenever you feel like it. Swell idea! Like to do it myself, by golly, instead of holding the fevered hands of four hundred stock-brokers twenty-four hours a day!'

It did not occur to Myron that Jimmy Shank's enthusiasm might be connected with a certain willingness to inherit Myron' position, when he should be gone.

26

Chain of garages, to be as well known as chains of groceries and restaurants. All auto tourists wd use them, because know dependable. And adv in wholesale purchasing.

He would call it the 'Black Thread Inn'.

He would be so wise as not to expect any gratitude from Black Thread Centre for bringing them this new industry which might employ some scores of natives. He was even willing, or so he told himself, to have his old schoolmates, who now remembered him so well and whom he had so blankly forgotten, scold at him as one who was trying to 'high-hat' them.

Just the same, it would be doing something for his boyhood home to create there this mould of fashion and glass of form.

But he would be careful not to take any credit, or to become boastful if he should succeed in making a Grand-Trianon. He'd be the same blunt, unassuming business man he'd always been, with no nonsense about trying to be imaginative, idealistic, original.

The Frigate Haven Manor had, in cottages and main building, three hundred and ten bedrooms. That was too large. He planned for the Black Thread Inn a hundred and twenty bedrooms, and a cottage for himself, at first, with situations plotted for a future annex and cottages to provide a hundred bedrooms more.

He hastened up to Black Thread to look over his site. It was better than he thought. He talked it over with T. J. Dingle, the youngish banker of the Centre, who willingly said that he would invest $10,000, and with Mrs. Dingle, who more than willingly said that when the inn was built, Myron could count on Ted and her coming for supper every Sunday, 'Get some decent food in this wilderness at last!'

'Tut!' said Dingle. 'It's notorious that New England home food is the best in the world.'

'I know, my darling. Notorious is right. It's so good that they hide it away from you,' said his wife.

All winter, while he was conferring with the architects about plans for the Inn, Myron was trying to give Pye and Charian a notion of what he was up to, a task rather complicated by the fact that he did not entirely know. They could not in the least comprehend the idea of a Rose and Crown adapted to America of the late 1920's; they pictured a bawdy road-house which would be in the country only to be safely away from prying federal officers and divorce-seeking wives, and possibly for the sake of a little golf and swimming to whet the appetite between drinks.

But, 'Oh, I can handle 'em. They'll get the idea when they see the place all furnished. And, of course, I do want it to be cheery--only, not dissipated,' insisted Myron.

He worked out the details of financing the Inn. Pye and Charian were generous enough in this gamble, as they would have been generous in sending flowers to a bootlegger's funeral. They did not object to accepting Myron's Lake Nekobee property as the desired site for the Inn, at a valuation of $25,000, though it had cost him only $10,000 when lake sites were cheaper, to granting him 400 extra shares in the company for his services in building the Inn and assembling the staff, a salary of $12,000 a year and living-quarters in an hotel cottage when the Inn should be opened.

He cautiously sold his securities and his small interests in the Pye-Charian Company, Frigate Haven Manor, and Laurel Farms for slightly over $65,000 which, with the Lake Nekobee inn-site appraised at $25,000, gave him $90,000 to invest in the project.

The new company was capitalized at $300,000, with 3000 one-hundred-dollar shares, of which Myron had 1,300, Pye and Charian each 800, and T. J. Dingle 100. . . . It was true, admitted Myron, that with their 1600 shares together, Pye and Charian could outvote Dingle and himself, but what did that matter? They'd be so delighted with the way he'd build and run the place that they would never interfere, and in five or six years, he'd buy them out, and if they made a nice piece of change in profit, why, he'd be tickled to death--they'd deserve it for being so generous at the beginning. Everything rosy!

The actual assets, then, were $250,000 of the $300,000, and if the stock could be called 'watered' at all, since they were allowing for the experience and influence of Myron alone, it was only to the extent of $50,000. Myron calculated that it would cost $220,000 to build a hundred-and-twenty room hotel and lay out the grounds and lake shore, and $80,000 for furnishing and equipment and losses until they should begin to make a profit. It was agreed that they would obtain a $50,000 mortgage, but not until the building should be finished. Myron was against shoestring methods, and Dick Pye more or less agreed.

(Actually, of course, the building, furnishings and reserve against loss took $40,000 more than had been expected, and the mortgage had to be increased, but their friend and adviser, Colonel Ormond L. Westwind, took care of all that.)

Myron had to train as his successor in the management of the Pye-Charian Hotels a newcomer from Chicago. Jimmy Shanks, who had hoped for the place and who suspected that Myron had advised against him--'which I did, but the damn fool has no right to go around *saying* I did!' Myron confided to Alex--was not pleased. But Jimmy was no cultured and childish Carlos Jaynes. He was friendlier and jollier and more uproarious with Myron than ever, and much more dangerous.

He had to see the European inns and restaurants before he approved the architects' plans or let them build one cement-form for the Inn. He had to. He was going to combine with American tradition everything in European hotel-practice that could be acclimated here. Pye and Charian agreed to his taking three months in Europe, in the spring of 1926, but at his own expense.

Europe!

He was going to Europe! Going to see all its renowned historical sights and beauties, such as the Savoy, the Embassy Club, the Smithson & Batty Hotel Furnishings Co., the Café Royal, Simpson's, the Cheshire Cheese, Foyot's, Voisin's, the Paris Ritz and Crillon and Meurice, a bottle of Vouvray, Ciro's, the International Wall Tapestry Cie., the Chambertin vineyard, the Tour d'Argent, the Adlon, the Stephanie, the Frankfort-a-M., Wurst Gesellschaft, the Beau Rivage of Lausanne, the Villa D'Este, the Albergo Russia of Rome, the Royal Augustan Antipasto Exportation Company, the Grand of Stockholm--everything in Europe that mattered. He might even have time for Westminster Abbey, Napoleon's Tomb, Pompeii, and an art gallery.

The passionate pilgrimage!

He had his plans quite ready before he told Effie May, on a February evening at home in Mt. Vernon. He was jubilant about it, and he wound up, 'We'll simply have one whale of a good time, to say nothing of learning a whole lot, and if you don't want to chase around to all the hotels and so on that I'll have to see, you can stay in Paris and Rome.'

But she looked doubtful. She did not say 'Won'erful.' She hesitated, 'Could we take Luke?'

'Not awfully well, and I don't think he'd enjoy it, moving so fast--get pretty tired, a kid of nine.'

'I couldn't leave him for three whole months--more than three, with the steamer.'

'Well, I'll try to work it out so we can take him, if you feel we ought to. He could stay in Paris with you, I guess. There's a lot of things he'd enjoy seeing.'

'But . . .'

'Don't you want to go, pie?'

'I guess I do. Europe! But . . .'

He saw, beyond escape, that she was agitated by the fear of losing her familiar security, the fear of the unknown and probably hostile. He was wretched. He did not want to draw away from her; he had no liking whatever for the matrimonial experiments of the day. Experimentation in business was enough for him, in which he was not notably inferior to the biologists or explorers who flirted with every new concept in biology or jungle-piercing but were conservative as boiled codfish in religion and politics and love. He wanted Europe less for himself than for the egotistic utter unselfishness of seizing it in his two hands and showing it to her.

'But you had a great time out of going to Bermuda!' he said.

'Yes, I know. But I was young then. And I didn't have any responsibilities--a house and a child and all. And . . . Oh, probably I'd have a fine time, once I got there and got used to it. But your planning to go in just three weeks--three weeks--oh, I couldn't possibly get ready as quick as that--a trunk and dresses and underclothes and reading it up and all--I couldn't do it!'

'But, honey, they still sell dresses in the Old Country!'

'Oh, no, no, no! I couldn't do it!' He saw that she was becoming actively terrified. 'You run over by yourself, and Luke and I will go with you some time when you can make a longer stay, and when he's older.'

'Sure, sure, lamb, whatever you'd like! Play game of pinochle to-night?'

He wouldn't go at all then. Rats! He could get all he needed out of books and magazine articles. Just for once, he scolded himself, why not do something for Effie--the poor kid, buried here with nothing to amuse her!

He did not listen to himself. He had to go. He could do no other.

He was on the promenade deck of the S.S. *Duilio,* to sail for Naples.

At a cry of 'All ashore that's going ashore!' he said tremulously to Effie May and Alec Monlux, 'I guess you'll have to be getting off. I wish you were going. It won't be any fun without you two to cuss and discuss with. Be good, you two, and don't take any wooden money. Oh, Lord, I do wish you were going! Why don't you just get carried off accidentally on purpose? Well, guess you better start!' He kissed Effie, not as a husband, as he had done of late years, but with a real kiss, overwhelmingly conscious of her lips, and fretfully he led her toward the gang-plank.

He wondered afterward if he hadn't hurried her a bit. Still, it was just as well; it was only another half-hour before the gang-plank slid across to the pier, cutting off America for ever.

The great steamer incredibly began to move--only it seemed on that steel immensity, that it was the pier that was moving. He waved tirelessly to Effie and Alec, standing out in the crowd as though they were each of them twice as big as the others. He loved them! Who had so understanding a wife, so loyal a friend? And it pleased him that good old Jimmy Shanks, though he could not stay, had dashed down to say good-bye and bring a box of cigars.

Now the end of the pier was moving backward from the steamer. He could not make out Effie and Alec. He was suddenly desolated with loneliness, with a fear that he would never see them again, with a speculation as to whether he was not a fool to leave his familiar work and to go thus pretentiously spying into foreign ways that he would never understand.

He was so lonely that he went to bed early--and slept beautifully, for nine hours; his longest sleep, he remembered, for he did accurately remember such things, since he had been down with the 'flu, before his marriage.

Next morning he sent his business card to the chief steward.

All the rest of the crossing, he was viewing refrigerator-rooms, electric grills, the decoration of the suites, the preparation of menus by the chef and chief steward, the stewards' quarters, the choice and making of the sandwiches for the ten-o'clock evening trays, the storage of linen. He was busy and happy, and only occasionally did he remind himself that he must be lonely. He took time to look at Gibraltar, but he really did not have time to look, as he had planned, at the bridge, the captain, or the Atlantic Ocean.

He had written to Luciano Mora with a good deal of reserve. After all, Luciano wasn't just a Westward room-clerk any more, but manager of the lordly Hotel Pastorale in Naples, and probably he was nibbled to death by guests whom he had known in New York, just as Myron had been pestered by clients who, because they had once seen him at Connecticut Inn or Tippecanoe Lodge, expected to get a couple of floors free.

He was pleased when Luciano radioed, on the last day out: 'Keys of Napoli yours shall be at pier.'

So the Passionate Pilgrim entered one of the most beautiful harbours of the world and, gaping at the revelation of Vesuvius and the amphitheatre of Naples, he meditated, 'Golly, I knew Europe would be quaint and old and all that, but I didn't expect such grand scenery, except maybe in the Alps. I wonder if those big white blobs are hotels? Dandy situation!'

Luciano Mora was not on the pier--he was suddenly and mysteriously on the ship, while they were docking, and yelping as youthfully as when he had been a baggage-porter at the Westward, 'Myron, this is splen-did! I present to you Italy! How are Effie and the boy and Alec? It was so too bad about old Mark! . . . Luigi! Mr. Weagle's luggage! . . . He will see it through the customs and take it to your rooms. Come!'

(Luciano was the only person in Italy who could master Myron Weagle's amusing foreign name. To every one else it was 'Mee-ron Vee-ag-ley'.)

Myron had expected quantities of quaintness, good food and complete inefficiency in the Pastorale. He was a little astonished by the English and by the swiftness of the porter, who had the baggage in Myron's suite fifteen minutes after his arrival; he was astonished by the magnificence of Luciano's Isotta-Fraschini car and its uniformed chauffeur, by their speed through the streets, and later, by their exceeding great speed when Luciano took him down to Amalfi and Sorrento. He had always understood that only the free and dashing Americanos drove fast; he was to learn that any crippled centenarian in Italy, Paris, or Germany would feel disgraced if he drove a car at an average of less than a hundred kilometres an hour or if he regarded a skid as worth noticing.

He found the lobby of the Pastorale too small and, with its chairs of yellow satin, too like a drawing-room; he found the elevators creaky and much too small. But he was again astonished, even a little embarrassed, as though he had been caught lying, by the leather-and-marble splendour of his suite, the flowers on the occasional tables, and a bath-room with a mosaic of nymphs in blue and green and pink on a golden ground, and conveniences new even to a plumbing-expert like himself. He was astonished at the speed with which a floor-waiter appeared when Luciano rang for him, astonished at his bowing and murmuring, 'Si, Commendatore.'

He decided that Commendatore must be some kind of a title. Luciano with a title! Was he a Sir? And do you suppose he had the title all the while he was in America, and him so chummy and all? And here he was, the director of an hotel in which the smallest bedroom was the size of a

Waldorf ballroom. Pretty nearly. Seemed so, anyway. And yet Luciano--'Commendatore'!--he was chattering just like in the old days! 'Myron, did you remember the time we sent Carlos Jaynes a loffly bottle of Scotch that was filled with ginger ale?'

There were vain interludes during which Myron felt that he was not learning much, though he shamefully admitted that he did enjoy them. Luciano took him to Capri, but they spent only a couple of hours on the kitchens and offices of the Hotel Quisisana, for Luciano insisted on talking about views and on dragging Myron out for a monstrous two-hour walk, all up and down hill, to the entirely disorderly and useless ruins of a villa or castle or something that had belonged to a Roman emperor whom Luciano called 'Timberio'. It was kind of interesting to see a floor of tiles which, Luciano claimed, was almost two thousand years old, and yet scarcely worn. But still! Myron had only three months in Europe. And no matter what Luciano said, he didn't remember learning in school about an emperor named Timberio. There had been Julius Caesar and Augustus Caesar and Mark Antony and Marcus, or something like that, Aurelius. And Nero, of course, who had fiddled while Rome was burning. But no Timberio, never. But then, probably it was just a Wop translation of some regular name.

It was the longest walk that Myron took in Europe--or in America either, all that decade--unless you counted ten miles or so a day through hotel corridors and kitchens.

Luciano gave for him a dinner to all the hotel dignitaries in Naples and the neighbourhood--managers and owners and chief clerks from the Grand, the Excelsior, Bertolini's, the Bristol, Parker's, the Britannique, the Eden, the Victoria, the Santa Lucia, the Quisisana. Half of them seemed, to Myron's romantic delight, to be Commendatores or Cavilieres, and he wondered if a Garden Party at Buckingham Palace wouldn't be very much like this--only not so many black beards and rotund white waistcoats.

So, sitting between Commendatore Luciano Mora and the owner of a pension (which meant a high-class boarding-house) who was apparently a Conte (which seemed to be an even higher title than Commendatore, though it didn't sound half as swell), Myron actually tasted the Animelle di Vitello alla Minuta con Tartuffi of which he had read when he was meat-cook of the Eagle Hotel, Torrington, Connecticut. The gilded plaster cupid on the ceiling of the private dining-room quivered to the vehemence with which the mayor, no less, shouted that the whole city was humbly honoured to greet Meeron Veeagley, who was not only the lifelong friend of Commendatore Mora, but the noblest example this season of American efficiency and hospitality, and a witness of the historic friendship between America and the entirely new and improved Italy.

Seven of them saw him off at the station, and Myron was sorry to leave Luciano, and impressed with the porters' linguistic skill as he handled the luggage. He spoke Italian so rapidly!

He saw, in Italy, Switzerland, France, and England, everything that he had longed for as being cultured and of good repute. And he saw distinguished small-city restaurants--invariably, it seemed, personally conducted by that ubiquitous superman, the former chef of the Kaiser--of which he had never heard. Having been reliably informed that Europe was very small, he was perplexed to find it so very large that, with only three months for travel, he was able to have only a week in Germany and Austria, and unable to see Scotland, Ireland, Scandinavia, Holland, Belgium, Spain, Hungary, Poland, or the Balkans at all, though with the accurate planning for which he was known in the hotel-world, he had designed to do them thoroughly, with three full days devoted to Spain alone.

'Whew!' he said, as his steamer left Southampton, 'I've got enough ideas to last a lifetime! But I won't be sorry to get back. I do believe I'm a little tired! . . . Funny how many top-notch European hotels have toothpicks right on the table!'

He spent hours in his cabin, filling up two new volumes of 'Hotel Project Notes'.

He concluded that the European system was better in room-service, in the guest's pressing a button instead of telephoning, and in having one garçon, who came to know his ways, instead of a horde of unfamiliar waiters and bellboys. He concluded that the food was as much better as had been fabled, because of more time taken in preparation, more patience with the processes of even a simple consommé, training of a lifetime among cooks and, as to the guests themselves, more knowing palates and freedom from the superstition that the world will fail if the office is not reopened promptly at 2.01 p.m.--though what anybody could do about it, in a large American city dining-room, where the guests expected to have lunch and dash away in twenty-five minutes, he did not see. He liked the Continental habit of eating outdoors, in an arbour or on the side-walk, whenever it was possible, and this custom he would have at the Black Thread Inn.

Yet he vehemently did not, like the professional expatriates, believe the worst European inn was better than the best American hotel. He had found plenty of bad hotels. He had known supercilious porters, managers who never left their stinking little offices but hid there always with their beards brushing the ledgers, waiters who believed that all Americans loved being chummily informed about the weather, cashiers who refused to charge a fifty-franc telegram on the bill, and bills on which the taxes were invariably overcharged, restaurants which had never heard of veal, and restaurants in other lands which had never heard of anything except veal, bar-keeps who believed that ice in a whisky-soda was against all the principles of the English Constitution--and also, that the only purpose of American visitors was to conform to the principles of the English Constitution, English reception-clerks who could scarcely endure speaking to a strange guest without an introduction by the vicar's aunt and who had to be wooed before they would admit that, in a completely untenanted inn, there were rooms for rent. French cashiers who went hysterical over ten centimes but remained admirably calm about a few millions of war-debt and, in no case, even when he was a guest, thought much of a son of Uncle Shylock, Italian stewards who could not respect anyone who did not care to fill up like a balloon on ravioli before beginning the real dinner, Swiss clerks who understood that all Americans understood that, after the outrageous charges in their own country, they were lucky to be able to get a room for twelve dollars a day, German and Austrian clerks who chuckled, 'In Dollars ist es nur ein Bagatelle', caravanserais with original Holbeins and no hot water except on Saturdays from 5.30 to 6.17 p.m., hotels with marble floors and total absence of heating--generously provided as ways of counteracting the tropical temperature of 38° Fahrenheit on a March morning, damp napkins, Italians who believed that cuttlefish are edible, Germans who regarded pig's knuckle as a vegetarian health-food, and Englishmen who had the same high opinions of wilted lettuce, tripe, and gooseberry tart drowned in custard, German guests who despised the French, French guests who despised the Italians, Italian guests who despised the English, English guests who despised everybody, and American guests who despised only all the other Americans, but so wholeheartedly as to make up for their narrowness. He had quaked in dancing elevators, and been smothered in the dust that lay like a model of the Sahara on brocade chairs, and been racked on beds stuffed with damp sea-weed. And once, though once only, he had found a French hotel with a filthy tablecloth, paper napkins, and chicken which could have been used for chips to kindle a fire.

Yet it had been the passionate pilgrimage he had prayed for.

He would not forget hotel terraces looking on the Alps and the Bay of Naples, nor the salmon at Macon, nor the boiled beef with Schnittlauch sauce at Madame Sacher's. But he privately jigged as he steamed toward his own native varieties of poetry--toward American elevators and circulating ice water and telephones that worked, all night service, and corn pudding, and adjustable heating and free daily papers that *were* newspapers, and Alpine views from thirtieth-story windows, the American belief that quick laundry-service did not require special permits from the police, and the even more surprising belief that coffee should be served hot and should, preferably, be made from coffee.

Only on the last day of the return crossing was he melancholy, as he groaned, 'Good Lord, I knew I forgot something! I forgot to see an art gallery!'

27

Resort for Protestant preachers & families on vacation, & important Meth Bapt etc. laymen & profs from denominat colleges. All housekeeping cottages but w restaurant (cafeteria?) and general store--much of profits from this. Daily lectures on economics, history, rhetoric, oratory, etc. Circularize preachers' congregations: 'the best gift yr pastor & family, vacation at Camp Luther (Beulah? Pilgrim? Moody?)' All denominations, not just one like Ocean Grove; gt talking point--here Meth, Bapt, Cong, Epis, Xian, Presbyt, Lutheran, etc. get together, get acquainted, imp part of move unite all Protest bodies. Not expect over 6% profit. Note! try woman manager--be good at it and less fuss about which denom she belongs to than if man. Genl store must stock groceries, some meat, respt bathing suits, tennis sneakers, Bibles, patent medicines.

Excavations for the Black Thread Inn and its outbuildings were begun late in June, 1926. Myron's cottage was ready in May, and the Inn formally opened on June 10, 1927. Myron gave half his time, during this year, to the Pye-Charian Hotel in New York; the other half he divided between nagging the builders, and selecting and training his staff, which seemed to him rather more important than the building.

From the Pye-Charian organization he took only two officers: Clark Cleaver, chief clerk of the Walter Scott, for assistant manager and chief clerk of the Inn, and Otto Gritzmeier as chef. In so small a place, Otto was an extravagance, even though he was willing to come for three hundred a year less than he had in the steamy bedlam of the Victor Hugo.

Myron was happily able to hire his brother, Ora, to write publicity during most of the building. He had always felt guilty at doing so little for Ora, who just now happened to be rather hard up, having lost his job as editor and advertising manager of the Hidden Sex Truths Book Publishing Company for having offered to teach hidden sex truths to the stenographers. Before the Inn opened, Ora sold a series of very interesting 'Confessions of a Press-Agent' to a muckraking magazine, and was able to take a richly deserved rest and trip to Europe, to the satisfaction of Myron, who had always regretted that while a mere business man like himself had had that opportunity, it had hitherto been denied to Ora, with his splendid knowledge of history and literature.

As permanent press-agent and 'host' of the Inn, Myron hired Benny Rumble, hotel-news correspondent of *Smart Mart*. He did not like Benny, a dapper little young man with a smirk and clothes too well-fitted around the hips, given to dancing, bridge, poetic quotations, and rose-tipped cigarettes, but Dick Pye insisted that Benny would be just the lad to entertain the old ladies at the Inn, and absolutely safe with the young ladies.

The head waiter was to be Frank Rabatel of the Restaurant Cocarde, Philadelphia; the hotel detective--always known as 'hotel dick'--was Dutch Linderbeck from the Fishkill House of Albany, who was said to know more politicians more gloomily than even the Capitol janitor. For a hundred-and-twenty-room hotel, a detective was not necessary, but Myron wanted to protect the wealthy guests he was presumably going to have against every manner of confidence-man and fake Russian prince.

A yet greater extravagance was the veteran floor-waiters. His whole scheme of superior service would fail if guests, when they rang the bell, were answered by the amiable but untrained college students on vacation who were the bellboys and waiters in most summer hotels. The experienced guest wanted the bell answered by an initiate, to whom the procuring of coffee, stamps, aspirin or wrapping paper and cord, was a passionate duty.

For a month before the opening, Myron and his lieutenants drilled the kitchen staff, the waiters and bus-boys, the desk-clerks and bell-boys and telephone-girls and porters, and even the cigar-and-candy-stand girl, and when the last was offended at the suggestion that there was anything she could learn, Myron was pleased at having it happen so early, and hired another young lady. The chambermaids had blue-prints of what ought to be done in every room every day; precisely what must daily be swept, dusted. They were dragooned as thoroughly as chorus-girls--though they were expected to be more charming than chorus-girls during working-hours and considerably less so after hours. The whole Inn would open as smoothly as though it had been running for five years. Myron did not remember it, but he was carrying out vows he had made amid the deliriums of Tippacanoe Lodge, twenty years before.

His chief trouble in organizing the staff was in refusing the offers of Black Threaders whom he had known as boys. He would have hated himself had he been supercilious to men with whom he had once smoked cornsilk cigarettes in the livery stable; he was uncomfortably and almost too noisily cordial when they came poking about the rising walls of the Inn; but he tried to persuade them that their training in the railroad section gang or the clothes-pin factory or the shoe store hadn't really qualified them as to clerk in an expensive hotel, an occupation which they pictured as doing nothing all day long but wearing lovely new tail-coats and shaking hands and swapping dirty stories with fashionable guests. Myron heard, seven times a day, 'Sure, I know: you've gotten too good for your old friends. Your hat has got too small for you, since you went off to the City.'

He explained to himself, 'Anybody with the intelligence of a rabbit would have known that I was a fool to start this thing too near the old home town. You aren't very bright, Myron. You work hard, but you haven't got much intuition or inspiration. That's what Ora's told me, all along. Oh, damn Ora! Now, the old bunch here in the Centre will want me to fail. Oh well, damn them, too! Nobody can stop me, nothing can stop me, from making this the greatest success in the world! I'll have Vanderbilts begging for a reservation a year ahead!'

It was in such a mood of boastful depression that he determined to get even with the Fates by raising the minimum rate-per-day, room and meals, from twelve to fifteen dollars.

His old acquaintances, who remembered him so much more lovingly than seemed probable after twenty-eight years, continued to come around and, when he was most trying to be affectionate and very jokey, they drawled, 'Now don't try to pull any high-hat stuff on *me!* I knew you when you was emptying slops at the American House!'

He had some thirty local workmen employed in building, and when the Inn opened, he would use as many people from Black Thread as showed themselves willing to keep their shoes blacked and endure strict training. But he saw that to one faction he must forever continue to be an ingrate who 'pulled high-hat stuff'.

'Cheer up', said T. J. Dingle; 'consider what they think of *me,* the blood-sucking banker!'

His father was a trial. He was a case of hives. Not that old Tom ever bothered him by presenting his qualifications for working at the Inn. Tom was entirely satisfied with his present two hours a day of supervising the American House clerk. But he did come over to Lake Nekobee to tell the workers that he was Myron's dad and had taught Myron all he knew, and to direct them in their building. All that, Myron could settle easily enough. He set his mother on Tom and thereafter his father stayed home, grumbling to all guests whom he could persuade to listen that a serpent's tooth is nothing at all compared with a thankless child, and that throughout Myron's youth, half a century or so, he had risen at five daily to instruct his ungrateful son in every art of inn-keeping.

But Myron's mother was beatific. Now, as the Black Thread Inn advanced, she knew absolutely, where formerly she had only suspected, that her son was the greatest hotel-man the world had ever known, and late afternoons, guiltily leaving the supervision of supper at the American House to the second cook, she walked arm in arm with Myron about the scaffolding-covered walls, while he triumphantly showed the future terrace, sun-porch, cabañas, squash court.

Naturally, Professor Herbert Lambkin, B.A., M.A., was the worst pest of all. The moment Myron began to build, Herbert charged in with suggestions.

Myron must come stay with them at the Old Home.

Thanks no. Myron was perfectly comfortable at the American House. Besides. He had to be in New York so much--only spent a few nights at the Centre.

Well, look here, then. Did Myron remember that conceited fool, Monlux, who had offered Herbert a miserable thirty a week in New York? Herbert had always been pretty sore about that, and he didn't entirely absolve Myron from blame, and now was Myron's chance to make up for the insult. He, Herbert, as superintendent of schools, was free in the summer time, just when Myron would most need him in the Inn, and he would be willing to sink his social prestige and serve as assistant manager for seventy-five or eighty a week, and then he thought he might bring himself to forgive Monlux, Myron, Effie, and Heaven.

No . . . Myron was so sorry . . . But he had already chosen his whole staff.

That was only the beginning of happy talks between the brothers-in-law.

Myron reported it to Effie May, in Mt. Vernon, but for once she did not back him. 'Why, I think that's real mean of you! It would mean so much to Berty to have the job; it would please him like anything, and I think it's horrid giving all these dandy jobs to complete strangers when our own family need them!'

'He isn't trained--he hasn't the temperament--he'd make lots of trouble', Myron said feebly. But he was considerably less feeble when he returned to Black Thread and Herbert again pounced.

Then Herbert granted that if Myron would build a summer cottage for him and let him have it for the cost of electricity and telephone only, he would forgive Myron to a considerable extent and try to forget his origin.

Back in Mt. Vernon again, Myron suffered with a pity for her that was purest love when Effie May cried, 'Listen, duckie! If you'll give Herbert the job, like he wants, I'll turn in and help you, with ideas! I've been thinking them up all this week you've been gone. Listen! This would be just won'erful! Why not have a great big picnic ground, with big rustic tables, and get all the Sunday Schools for miles around to have their basket picnics there every summer! Of course you couldn't charge them, but it would make the Inn grounds so lively, and advertise the place like anything!'

And the question of liquor, that to any hotel project in 1926 was a sick headache.

Myron had planned space for a bar in the basement billiard-room of the Inn, and he intended, if Prohibition should be repealed, to have the best cellar in the State. He did not expect to interfere with guests who brought their own flasks, and were not too noisy. But on the other hand he would not sell any illicit liquor, nor permit any employee to sell it.

Then Mr. Everett Beasy came to him, and Mr. Everett Beasy was the sheriff of the county. He did not resemble the sheriffs of fiction; he had neither chin-whiskers combined with shrewdness in finding which tramp had fired the barn, nor a leather vest and a notched six-gun. He had been a respectable grocer, and he still looked like a respectable grocer: a small man in a well-pressed pepper-and-salt suit and a new derby.

'Well, Weagle, fine thing for the whole country round here, your putting up this big hotel. Give work to lots of needy folks, and set an example of nice living for all our young people.'

'Glad you like it.'

'You bet we like it. You're a real public benefactor. And now listen. I know how it is. You're going to have a lot of city folks that will want a little drink. Mostly, of course, that's against the law, but we don't feel disposed to be too hard on folks that will bring good money here, as long as they behave themselves and don't kick up any rows. If they mind their business, we'll mind ours. But of course you want to be able to give 'em first-class stuff that you can guarantee. Now myself, I'm against booze, and I never touch a drop, hardly, you might say, but I know a fellow that's a really honest bootlegger . . .'

'Shan't need one.'

'Look here. I don't know as we can allow anybody supplying you that we can't depend on. We officers of the law have got a responsibility to the public, let me tell you!'

'But I shan't sell any liquor at all. Really. I mean it. Not a drop'.

'Oh yes, you will! You don't think you will, but you will! And if you deal with the right people, it'll save you a lot of trouble in taxes and building-inspection and any fights that drunk guests might get into and traffic charges and all sorts of things. I just want to help you out. Think it over, and when you get ready, I'll have this fellow I know come see you.'

It took Myron a time to believe that Sheriff Beasy's honest friend was also Sheriff Beasy, and that a country political gang could be as intimidating as any city gang in compelling him to handle illicit booze whether he wanted to or not. He thought of Beasy's hard little eyes. He thought of the Inn being raided on a gay and prosperous evening. He shivered.

By contrast he almost had relief in the details of insurance. He had, it appeared, to insure against injury to employees, injury to the public, fire, lightning, burglary, floods, earthquakes, cyclones, termites, elephantiasis, insurrection, and the Acts of God.

In seeking the righteousness of creation he had not, he saw, altogether freed himself from the body of sin and doubt. Yet irritated or apprehensive or dreary with details, he was, all this tiring and glorious time, uplifted by the sight of the rising Inn, the actual coming into existence of his masterpiece.

28

Cruise: Long Island Sound steamer, two weeks up to Bar Harbour or beyond, exploring shores of Conn. Mass, L. I., Nantucket, etc. Anchor in quiet harbour every night, with dance on deck, movies, etc. and boats going ashore, and fishing & swimming in morning. Cd do very cheap, for summer vacation for clerks, stenogs etc. Daily lecture on history of coast. Specialize sea food--'catch your own mackerel & we'll cook it for you.' How about campfire on big iron plate, asbestos lined, on deck one evening of each cruise?

To make an inn that should be not merely good but near perfection, Myron asserted, he had to be fussy as an old-time housewife at spring-cleaning. He had to make himself an expert equally on the plan of the building in regard to convenience, quiet, light, and view, on the furnishing of bedrooms and public rooms, on food, linen, silver, china, glass, on amusements outdoors and inside. In any one of these departments, the Black Thread Inn might be surpassed; it was his job, as creative builder, to make sure that no other inn should surpass his in the combination of all the details.

All day, when he was not at Black Thread, he was consulting interior decorators, salesmen for hotel china and glass, books on furniture and, always, the realistic and experienced Mr. Otto Gritzmeier.

As to decoration, he was for awhile tempted by the heathen ritual of Modernism, particularly after he had lunched at the Tall Town Club, the best speakeasy in New York, which had been bedizened by Josef Lazaraki with a circular bar of black glass edged with a silver band, bright aluminium bar- stools with red leather seats, pictures made with outlines of silver wire against a powdery blue background, walls splashed with sunbursts and torch-flames of aluminium, and sunflowers whose petals were mirrors, Myron was impressed. Prohibition, he realized, had been an excellent thing for America: it had not only taught the traditionally unalcoholic American woman to drink and smoke with her men, but had, in its freedom from old standards, encouraged the arousing orgies of modernistic decoration, and all citizens, especially the surprised and delighted women, ought to be grateful to the Methodist and Baptist shepherds who had brought on Prohibition. But for his inn among New England hills, this jazz splendour would be false, and Myron was equally uninterested in the other extreme: an Olde Inne that should be a Colonial museum, with huge and dirty brick fireplaces bristling with sooty cranes, straight-backed oak chairs, and walls so prickly with warming-pans, candle-moulds, revolutionary muskets, grandfather clocks, wedgwood platters, grimy iron pots, and Currier & Ives prints that any honest guest would dash out shrieking. He decided on a key-note of Duncan Phyfe mahogany in accurate reproductions, graceful for summer, warm-hued for winter fire-light, and he was able to have all of it made together by one manufacturer, at a comfortingly reasonable price. He was able to get standard yet not too familiar patterns of glassware, china, and silver which harmonized with the mahogany. They were all marked with the BTI embroidered on the linen.

Not even the lounge, centre of the Inn, was planned so carefully as the kitchens, and these were planned to the last centimeter, as though he were devising a new motor engine. In everlasting headachy conferences with Gritzmeier, after reading everything he could find in the hotel magazines, he arranged exactly what and how long should be the path from refrigerator to work-table to condiment cupboard to stove to serving-bar to dining-room; what materials were best for sinks, for table-tops, floors and the weary swollen feet of cooks.

Food he studied as Duke Godfrey studied the imaginative maps to the Holy Land. Gritzmeier was one of the not-too-many Continental chefs who had added a study of native American foods to his knowledge of French and German and British cookery. As piously as Myron he revered the American dishes which would be the staples of this good provincial inn: clam chowder, planked shad with roe, crab-flakes, canvas-back with wild rice and black currant jelly, raisin pie, corn pones, pepper pot, and the breakfast doughnuts and waffles and buckwheat cakes which can be so delicate or so leaden, in accordance as the cook is a worthy man or a scoundrel.

To 'amusements' he gave scientific research. He had noticed that the chief horror of summer hotels in the evening, when it is too dark for golf and swimming, is that there is nothing to do. He would have either dancing or a movie, or both, every evening, along with radio, backgammon, dice racing, masquerades, a larger library, moonlight picnic-suppers, billiards, and a chief job of Benny Rumble would be to introduce poker-players and bridge-maniacs to one another.

The first building to be finished, in May, was Myron's cottage, which was to be the start of a whole crescent of hotel cottages on the hillside above the Inn. He had planned it himself, more precisely than any known housewife, with everything built in that could be built in, with composition floors that could be cleaned with a look, and enough sleeping-porch space for his family and for a guest . . . only he hoped that the guest would not too constantly be Professor Herbert Lambkin, M.A.

It was May 27th, 1927, just two weeks before the day set for the opening, and the Black Thread Inn was finished--at least as nearly finished as it would be, this season--and Myron could look upon his Works, bound in grey shingle.

The Inn fitted into the hillside. It was rather long and low, with wide dormers in the third story. The sides were finished in fire-proofed shingles, stained the soft grey of the sunless lake, with the shingled roof a little darker, and under the eaves was one violent band of scarlet. A terrace of red tiles was cut in under the building, on the ground floor, and extended outside along the whole length of the front, with French windows opening on it, with white wicker chairs and white-painted steel tables. Here lunch and tea were to be served on bright days. At one end was an untouched grove of elms and maples; at the other end was planted a garden of roses, peonies, and autumnal lilies, where tea would also be served when the garden should have grown.

The tennis-courts, the squash-courts, the stables of riding-horses, the garage, with titanic buses to meet the trains, were tucked among the woods behind the Inn, and here, next winter, would be a ski-slide and possibly a toboggan course. Golf was available at the Olde Mill Country Club, four miles away, and at three other clubs within eight miles. Some day, the Inn would have a nine-hole course of its own. Myron had insisted on laying out, on one of the lawns, croquet-grounds, though every one in the world, practically, rushed up to assure him that croquet was dead. There was to be a swimming-pool, warmed, for early spring and late autumn, when the lake would be too cold, but as yet there was only the excavation for the pool. It would be finished in the fall. The sandy lake shore was kaleidoscopic as the Riviera, with a huge T-shaped dock, four diving-boards, yellow and crimson canoes, row-boats with blue and crimson awnings, and cabañas with awnings grey and crimson. Only the beach was garish, however; the Inn itself was tranquil.

'Well,' grumbled Tom Weagle, 'it's all right, but strikes me it's a pretty simple shack to be making such a fuss over! Why didn't you make one of these French chateaux, or a Japanese garden, or something with class?'

'I planned it to be simple. I want it to fit in between the lake and the hill as if it had grown here, and still have as much luxury as the Ritz,' protested Myron.

'It's simple, all right! It just growed, all right! It certainly don't look like any good 220,000 bucks to me. What I could have done with that money, with *my* experience! Built you an hotel that'd bat you in the eye ten miles off. Just growed here on the hill is right! Like a doggone ole grey stump! After all the pains I've spent on you, I've never been able to learn you it pays to advertise!'

June tenth, then, and the publication of the Perfect Inn.

It was opening with every bedroom full save one, and that empty only because it was held for Adolph Charian, Pye's partner, who might or might not be able to come from New York for the ceremonies. Dick Pye would be there all week. Myron had had to reject more than sixty applications for rooms. He had captured for the first five days of the opening the convention of that extremely wealthy organization, the New England Brass Industries Institute. Benny Rumble, the natty press-agent, had lavishly invited the press to the opening of what he asserted to be the finest inn on the Atlantic Coast, and fifteen rooms were reserved for reporters from New York, Philadelphia, Boston, New Haven, Hartford, Bridgeport, and Greenwich, who did not mind submitting a few sticks to the society editors so long as the food and Benny's private stock were good. The other rooms were taken by a miscellany of regular guests, who drove up in expensive cars, well stocked with gin.

The opening evening!

The lobby and corridors at last whooped with voices besides those of the workmen and hotel staff, and Myron beamed owlishly as he heard, 'It's a charming place.' Everything began joyfully, with two big dinners--that of the Brass Institute, served in the Ballroom and entertained by the Jolly Rovers Jazz Orchestra, and the dinner for the press, in one end of the dining-room, which could be completely shut off by an electrically controlled screen of steel and rubber.

Even Myron took three cocktails, that evening: one in his cottage, with Effie May and Ora, who was their guest for the week; one with Benny Rumble and the press; one in the suite of the secretary of the Brass Institute. He was slightly hysterical with the success of his masterpiece. The Institute insisted on his joining them for a toast, and when its president stated (but not so briefly) that Mr. Weagle was another of those enterprising Yankees who was restoring New England to her former supremacy in industry and the resort business, and to hell with California, Myron bowed and flushed and felt very happy--and was suddenly a little homesick for a hotel in

Naples and a black-bearded man toasting Signor Veeagley, while Luciano clapped his hands.

He himself dined, when he was not darting away to do most energetically nothing in particular, with a group composed of the press, the county and town dignitaries, his father and mother, Effie and Ora, the Dingles, and the entire Lambkin clan. It was a lovely dinner, with Moselle, bombe surprise, and brook-trout. It was addressed. It was a good deal addressed, though the press seemed not to mind, since 1909 brandy was served during the addressing. Myron told them, in a speech lasting exactly seventy seconds, that he was glad to see them. Dick Pye told them that Myron was a second George Boldt. T. J. Dingle told them that Black Thread had quantities of history and fishing. The mayor of Black Thread made a comic speech, Sheriff Everett Beasy made a witty speech, and then the real work was turned over to Pye's partner, Colonel Ormond L. Westwood, who was historic, comic, witty, impressively reverent regarding the church, the state, the press, and hotel-keeping, and wound up with one of his celebrated after-dinner stories which managed to be so delicate that it did not shock the ladies and yet so smutty that even the reporters laughed.

They did not break up till midnight, when the guests swayed up to their rooms.

Altogether, the opening evening was as nearly perfect as the Inn itself.

He was too happily excited to go back to his cottage and sleep. At half-past one he made the round of the Inn, just for the pleasure of seeing it. He looked upon his work and saw that it was good . . . The passionate pilgrim come to his shrine. The poet reading the first typescript of his epic, astonished by his own eloquence.

There was no one about save a watchman somewhere in the building, and the night-clerk in the office, working on accounts.

These glories he noted again:

The office, near the main door, though it was complete in every trick of telautograph and pneumatic chute, was not large, and it did not intrude on the lounges.

The main lounge was furnished in old maple, with a moulded plaster fireplace, and pine panelling and authentic old pine, for which Myron had sent a man searching Connecticut, studiously examining old barns, even fence-rails.

Whatever any guest might think of the excellence of Myron's Inn, he would have to admit that the main lounge did not have a single rustic rocker of unpeeled boughs, or a single cart-wheel candelabrum.

The second room was the radio lounge, sound-proofed, so that radio-fans might have as loud a speaker as they wanted, yet no one outside the room need listen. The third was the writing-room and library, with all known varieties of magazines, and three thousand books, chosen by a librarian and not by Ora, since Myron suspected that nothing would so much please Ora as to include every bawdy novel calculated to shock respectable guests. The dining-room was in moulded plaster, slightly tinted, with heavy mulberry-coloured curtains. The ballroom, on one side of the hotel, became by day a huge sun-room. In the basement was a clubroom for billiards, pool, cards, with another and more feminine card-room on the second floor.

'Well, if there's any prettier public rooms anywhere, in America *or* Europe, than those seven, I'd just like to know!' said Myron now, content.

As Charian had not been able to come, there was one bedroom which he could inspect, and he entered it, snapped on the light, happily. As pleasant to him as the Sheraton furniture were the candlewick spread on the four-poster, and the thick, faintly peach-coloured Bridgewater blankets. To him, a fine wool blanket had always been lovely as a sunset. The fireplace was of mahogany, painted white, with a deep chair before it. The curtains were cretonne, and the two, only two, pictures were German colour-prints. The whole room was gay.

'Why should it be supposed in a country inn that there will never be any wet, gloomy days when the guests will keep to their rooms, and so any old dark furniture and brindle walls will do?' inquired Myron, not without self-approval.

The bathroom was in white tiles with canary-yellow floor and ceiling border. It was bright yet not too orchidaceous, though it had been decorated at a period when America had been roused to a mania for wildly coloured bathrooms, stoves, stew-pans, typewriters, even toilet paper. They had all to be in pink or lavender, and a citizen who had to endure any article in white or brown was ashamed, and staggered away from the scorn of friends, a broken man.

Though at hotel-association meetings Myron had attacked a superfluity of accessories in rooms, and in particular the profusion of little cards advertising the meals, the courtesy, and other desirabilities of the hotel, in this bedroom there were many dodges--conceivably too many: bedside lights, of course, a box opening into both the room and the corridor, so that shoes and suits might be taken off for cleaning without disturbing the guest, extra folding chairs and baggage-stands ready in the closet, stacks of towels and washrags, shoe-cloths and cloths for wiping razor blades, a full-length mirror, an electric light in the closet, a desk that was not a rickety table but a real and solid desk, with ample stationery and a supply of free picture post-cards, which would presumably advertise the inn. The chambermaids were ordered to make sure that there was a low table beside each easy chair, and in each room, always, at least three ash-trays--and more if it proved that the guest was a conscientious smoker.

But there were other gadgets less common: A scale with the dial flush with the bathroom floor, for guests anxious about daily increase of weight. An electric door-bolt, controlled by tiny levers beside the bed. A package of cigarettes free in the morning, and fruit brought in every evening when the bed was turned down. A device which Myron had discovered in Switzerland and in which he poetically rejoiced: an automatic electrical arm-clock for morning calls. When he went to bed, the guest plugged in at the desired rising hour, and in the morning the alarm rang until he turned it off. There was thus no argument with the desk as to the time at which the guest had asked to be called, nor did the telephone girls go mad from trying to call forty rooms simultaneously at seven-thirty and eight and eight-thirty.

And by each bed were three buttons, for chambermaid, bell-boy, and room-waiter--though if the guest considered it a patriotic principle to telephone to room-service, he could do so. There was a breakfast kitchen on each floor, and no charge for meals in rooms.

He would have been glad, had he thought about it, that Ora was not with him on his tour. Ora would have remarked that the colours of blankets and of bathroom tiles, the number of ash-trays in a bedroom, and the convenience of Swiss automatic clocks were, judiciously considered, perhaps the most ludicrously unimportant details in the world, at least to one who gave earnest attention to such really important matters as whether, in a Western, it is sweeter to begin with a murder, a rodeo, or the arrival of the grouchy old ranchman's niece at Helenhighwater Forks.

There were yet other rare delights for Myron to gloat upon, and in particular the kitchen, with its stainless steel and surfaces of copper and nickel alloy, its cork floor, its charcoal and electric grills. He was, to his wonder, hungry, and realized that he had been too excited at dinner-time to eat even fresh brook trout. With a visage of solemn beatitude, a look of happy childishness uncommon in so plodding an adult, he sat at the end of a work table, admiring a steam cooker and sucking up soda crackers and milk.

He descended by the back stairs to the basement, stopping to admire the particularly large and numerous fire-extinguishers which he had planted all over the Inn. Huh! How many ghastly times it had happened that hotels had burned down on the very night of their opening! Nothing could happen to *his* inn! For he had taken pains--he had trained the staff before opening, he had provided all these fire extinguishers, he had proven that, by thoughtfulness and care, a man could make his handiwork perfect!

In the basement he gazed reverently on the oil furnaces, the laundry machinery, the store-rooms, the tile-and-marble barber-shop, the club room with its billiard tables, and then slowly, wearily, most triumphantly happy, he clumped up the front stairs from the basement to the office.

He heard a clamour. He hastened his step and in the entrance-hall he found the night-clerk, and Dutch Linderbeck, the hotel detective, listening to the night watchman, who was shouting, waving his arms. Alarmed guests were coming down the stairs, led by the president of the Brass Institute, in dressing-gown, and a sharp young Bridgeport reporter in top-coat over his pyjamas.

'What is it? What is it?' raged Myron.

'They're not married!' said Linderbeck. 'They're not Mr. and Mrs. Wood of Springfield, as they registered. The fellow is the son of U.S. Senator Colquhoun, and apparently she's Mardie Paxton, that professional alimony hound.'

'But my God, what of it? Why all this damn fool row?'

'Because they're dead! Looks like he shot her, and then killed himself. Anyway, they're dead as Moses. Shall I 'phone the sheriff, Boss, or will you? My managers have always said I did a good job on 'phoning the cops when a couple mess up an hotel room with blood.'

29

Myron fled up the stairs to Room 97, followed by Dutch Linderbeck, a growing push of frightened guests--and fifteen newspaper reporters, charmed that they had been invited to stay the night.

Mardie Paxton, a celebrated habituée of roadhouses, lay on the bed in 97, blood on the breast of her scant silk nightgown. The son of Senator Colquhoun was lurched down in a flowery new armchair by the clean, white, new fireplace, and his right temple was torn away, and blood had slavered on chair and hearth.

'What proof you got they're who you say?' the oldest New York reporter demanded of Dutch Linderbeck.

'Here's letters to both of 'em, from their baggage, and the young fellow's address-book. Look here!'

'God, it's a lulu of a story! Senator Colquhoun is the old gink that was always protecting the domestic hearth against naughty films and books!' exulted the reporter.

Said Myron, impersonally, not very loud, 'Yes, it's a good story for the reporters. A front-page story. And it's the end of my Inn! On the opening night!'

'Say, Weagle, can I use that statement?' shrieked the youngest of the reporters, who a fortnight ago had been covering nothing more journalistic than piles of gents' suitings at closing-hour.

'Oh *God!*' said the other reporters.

Myron ordered, 'Will all of you except the staff and the newspaper-men kindly return to your rooms? There is nothing you can do.'

The blanket-shawled guests glared at him, but he pushed them back, closed the door.

'You stand here at the door and keep everybody out,' he ordered Dutch Linderbeck.

'Yes, but . . .'

'Yes but *hell!* Do what I tell you! I always did hate yes-butters!' stormed Myron. 'Everybody out of this corridor, right now! And you reporters, I'll have the two 'phone girls out of bed immediately, and you can all put in your calls to your papers from your own rooms.'

'I want to see the letters these two bozos had in their stuff,' said the oldest reporter.

'When the sheriff gets here, he'll decide whether you can or not. I certainly won't let you.'

'You look here, Weagle! If you want us to give you a break . . .'

'The only break you boys could give me would be to revoke this Act of God, and I don't believe even the press could do that! Beat it, everybody! Out of this hall! Beat it!'

He stood at the end of the corridor, looking toward the stairs down to the office. He ought, he felt, to be doing something. All his life, whenever he had been in distress, he had been able to bounce to his stove or silver-closet or desk and importantly do things. And now he could see nothing to do, save look from the stairs to Dutch Linderbeck, on guard, and back again.

Dick Pye was marching up stairs, leisurely, completely dressed--except that he had forgotten his trousers. He yawned, 'Well, Weagle, I hear we've had bad luck. Glad you were around, to stop any panic.'

'I don't know. I don't think I was so good!'

'What the devil! Don't sound so guilty! You didn't kill 'em--or did you?--not that I care much!'

'No, but I wish I had, before they got here and registered. Why is it that almost every swine who wants to commit suicide gets so much pleasure out of ruining the business of some innocent hotel-man? Swine!' Then Myron laughed. 'I thought I'd open this place right. I'm a good deal of a fool, Pye. Ever notice it?'

'Oh yes. I notice it about most people. That's an hotel-man's first job. I think the Lord God must in His omnipotent way be a little like the head of a big hotel-chain. Well, if our guests are good and safely dead, I think I'll go back to sleep. Good night, son--you're all right--don't worry one second--you've got Dolph Charian and me behind you.'

'Yes? And doing what?' muttered Myron, as Pye swaggered away.

In five minutes Sheriff Everett Beasy was running upstairs, followed by a deputy, in private life a garageman, and by a Black Thread doctor. Myron turned them over to Dutch Linderbeck and staggered down to the office.

Gritzmeier, the chef, stopped him there. 'Heard about it, Chief. Doesn't matter. Everybody'll forget it in two weeks. Look. I knew you'd be worried, and I've made you a cup of coffee, myself. Come out to the kitchen and drink it. Do you good.'

'Thanks. Terribly good of you, but I couldn't touch a thing.'

'Oh yes, you can, Chief!' Gritzmeier chuckled. 'Here!' From under the shelter of the office desk he whisked a highball. Myron drained it and, 'Yes! That does feel better. Good night, and thanks!'

He wavered, in a trance, across the gardens to his own cottage. He could do no more. Suddenly all strength and patience and desire had gone clean out of him, and he was more dead than that smashed boy sunk in the armchair.

It was a quarter of three, but there were lights in his cottage.

'Effie, poor kid! I wonder what blazing fool woke her up to tell her? She'll be all busted up.'

He heard music. When he swayed into the cottage living-room, Effie May was at the mechanical player-piano, producing the popular ballad, 'Don't you worry, little pet. Hey you kid, I'll get you yet. Life is all a bed of roses, when wise guys like us rub noses.' Leaning against the player-piano, waving a gin fizz, was Ora, grinning laxly while he sang the pretty thing.

'For God's sake stop that abomination!' snapped Myron.

Ora protested, 'What the hell's the matter with you? Have you always got to be glum, even on the opening night of your ole Inn?'

'Opening--and closing. Son of a U.S. Senator killed himself and his mistress.'

'Shot himself?'

'Yes.'

'Good Lord! Good *Lord!* Why didn't you send over and let me know? Oh, I could murder you for being so thoughtless! Why didn't you let me know, early? I've never seen a man that's just been killed. I could've made a swell short story out of it!'

It was Effie May who was turning on Ora: 'Shut up, will you! Oh, Myron, my poor lamb, with the Inn that you loved so!'

She held him, and his head rested on her bosom. He felt safe again. But in his daze he did not know that it was on Effie May's breast that he had found refuge. He thought that it was the breast of his mother.

He was just nerving himself to go up to bed when a ring sent him weaving to the door.

Benny Rumble, the little press-agent, was on the step, panting, 'They just told me about the tragedy! It's awful! Why, it'll just ruin my reputation to be mixed up with a place where things like that happen! Couldn't you tell everybody that I quit yesterday, before it happened? Oh! What Mrs. Van Gittels will say I can't conceive!'

Myron slept till ten in the morning.

That was late enough for him to learn, when he went across to the Inn, that the Brass Institute had already voted to cut its convention short, that the president of the Institute had fled, and that most of the other guests were going that afternoon.

30

Cdn't you grow oysters, clams, crabs, saltwater fish etc., nr Chi, Detroit, Cleveland, etc. to have fresh for hotels & restaurants in artificial s.w. pools? Possible 3 methods get s.w., (1) have it analyzed, and synthesize on spot, (2) bring actual s.w. out in tank cars or (3) evap s.w. of ocean and add resultant salts to fresh water before it flows into pool? Remem. ask chemist.

The account in the weekly news-magazine, *Time,* began: *'Sin in Inn.'*

'Boniface Myron Weagle strode the floor of the Royal Suite, whisky & soda in hand. "Let's drink a toast to my new hotel, the Black Thread (Conn.) Inn, the best lil ole inn in the world," he indicated. Tycoon B. F. Vince, president & founder of the Brass Institute, price-fixing and high-talk-slinging organization of Yankee pot-manufacturers, answered, "Brother, I'm with you". The six magnates present, and Mine Host Weagle, drank jovially. It was four o'clock on the morning of June 11th, after a successful opening of the Inn. As they swung into "For He's a Jolly Good Fellow," they heard a pistol shot & another. They stopped, aghast. It was merely an incident of conducting a successful roadhouse, however. Nothing had happened save that the motor-boat-racing only son of Former United States Senator Burnside Farragut Colquhoun (pron. Cahoon), celebrated advocate of the Christian virtues, had murdered self & lady, Cinemactress Paxton.

'Denizens of Black Thread Centre, small agricultural centre on the Housatonic River, do not know the name of their own town. They assume that its present designation refers to some imaginary textile mill once producing black mourning stuffs for unfortunate widows of Mexican & Civil Wars. The name should be Black Threat. It was historically a black threat to early Connecticut settlers, when it was an Indian encampment, and apparently it is now a more serious black threat to young motor-racers seeking a refuge for self & lady.'

The tabloid newspapers had little text but many pictures, showing the actual site of the tragedy, with the corpses--as obligingly posed by a male and a female cinema extra, in a room at the Gaiety Hotel on Broadway. They also were able, through the process of combining two pictures, to show the terrace of the Black Thread Inn crowded with chorus-girls in negligible bathing-suits; and they had dozens of views of Myron, Effie May, and Luke together. For days Myron was driving photographers out of the shrubs about his cottage. And it was one of the tabloid papers which gave to the Inn the name of 'Murder Tavern'.

On the noon after the murder, when the bodies had been taken away and Myron had already sent scrubwomen and painters to redecorate Number 97, Sheriff Beasy amiably called upon Myron in his office, and brought Dutch Linderbeck in with him.

'Well, my boy, this whole affair has certainly been tough! Little did we think, when we were having a good lively time with the newspaper boys just last evening, that anything like this would happen! I tell you, my boy, it certainly is a lesson about how little we know what Fate has in store for us! Yessir, it certainly makes a fellow stop and think! But don't you worry one bit, my boy. I'm going to do everything I possibly can, with the reporters and at the inquest and everything, to cover you up, and keep folks from thinking this is a tough joint. Now I never was one to say "I told you so", but don't it beat the dickens how just the other day I was telling you how necessary it is for you to stand in with the authorities? Now this bootlegger I was telling you about, Purvis, his name is, he's a fellow . . .'

'I get your idea, Sheriff! I don't worry about breaking the law in selling booze. It's just that bathtub gin and fine food and good service don't mix.'

'Well, do murder and suicide mix any better?'

'None of that!'

'Oh, I didn't mean to be fresh. But you'll see reason--just *can't* run a backwoods joint like this without sufficient likker on hand, convenient. I've talked this all over with your hotel dick here, and he agreed with me. How about it, Dutch?'

'Sure. You bet your life. Fellow's got to be *reasonable,* see how I mean, Chief?'

Myron murmured, 'It would give me the greatest pleasure if both you gentlemen went straight to hell. Good-day!'

Three deputies--though not, of course, led by the friendly Mr. Everett Beasy--raided the Inn a week later, and found a pint of whisky behind the bar. They were just arresting Clark Cleaver, chief clerk (an assonance which Ora found very funny indeed) when Myron telephoned to T. J. Dingle.

That ended the process of law and justice.

Two weeks later, when Myron was driving back from the Centre by moonlight, some one shot at him from the bushes. The shot bored his windshield. In his office at the Inn, he immediately telephoned to Beasy.

'Hello. The sheriff? Good evening. This is Myron Weagle.'

'Well, well, I was terribly sorry to hear about that outrage!'

'What outrage?'

'Uh, uh--I mean the murder and suicide.'

'The murder two weeks ago, Sheriff?'

'Yes, sure. What the hell did you think I meant?'

'Better than that, Beasy. I know what you meant! Listen. You remember the older New York reporter that was here at the opening? Denmack? The tall thin fellow, a little bald?'

'I guess so. What about him?'

'Didn't he strike you as a pretty competent man--rather too good to just do an hotel opening--probably got the assignment just to give him a little vacation?'

'What of it?'

'Didn't Denmack strike you as a fellow that would be very enterprising, and yet very judicious and accurate, and not easily scared?'

'I don't know as he struck me at all! I didn't pay any attention to him in any way, shape, or manner! Darned fresh, that's how he struck me!'

'Exactly! Well, you'll be interested to know that I'm typing out a complete account of everything I know about the officers of the peace around here; names and everything, from the time of your first call on me, through the phony raid here, to this evening--original and two carbons. I'll finish it before I get to bed to-night, and to-morrow one copy will be in T. J. Dingle's hands, and another in Denmack's, but sealed, with instructions that he is to open it only in case anything happens to me. It might make a nice piece for the household page of his newspaper. So if I were you, I'd tell your man to stop shooting so recklessly--or else shoot to kill, next time!'

'Weagle, I do believe you've gone plumb crazy! I just haven't got the slightest idea what you're talking about!'

'Well, I'm glad to hear that, old man. Certainly glad. And look now, as an expert, do you feel that Dutch Linderbeck, my dick here, is a competent loyal fellow?'

'He certainly is, Weagle. I don't understand one bit what you were kidding me about before, but when it comes to Dutch, he's O.K., a swell reliable guard.'

'Thanks a lot! I'll fire him first thing in the morning.'

It occurred to Myron that he had invited Beasy to shoot him that night, and the window-door of his office, opening into a grove, was perfect for convenient assassination. Yet he could not face being so melodramatic as to set out a guard or to borrow a revolver--provided, indeed, there was any revolver at the Inn, outside of Dutch Linderbeck's hip-pocket. He pulled down the curtain. His shadow fell on it, and he was uncomfortable as he sat typing not only his own experiences with the good Sheriff Beasy, but T. J. Dingle's information about Beasy's relationship to the Pinetop Dancing Pavilion.

He stopped, paralyzed. There was a distinct sound on the brick walk outside his window. He could not endure the inaction. He flung the window open, his back cold and shivering. He found the origin of the sound.

It was a porcupine, waddling away, terrified, looking back at him with the bleary, timid little eyes of a bear-cub, and skidding on the smooth brick as it tried to hurry.

In mid-August, two months after the opening, a time which should have been the best season, the Black Thread Inn was half empty. There had been other hotels aplenty in which there had been suicides, but the chance of one occurring on the opening night had tickled the imagination of that considerable part of the public which leads cautious lives and takes it out in gloating over the delights of suicides, torch-murders, sash-weight-murders, hangings, poison, and warfare. Myron knew that Sheriff Beasy and his intimates were scuttling about saying, 'I'd see my son or daughter dead before I'd let 'em so much as step foot in that den of iniquity!' And the tabloid newspaper had done much for Myron by its headline about 'Murder Tavern', run between an editorial on the necessity of church-going and a special article on Honour as one of the best-thought-of virtues.

There was a brisk scattering of sensation-lickers motoring for lunch, sometimes staying overnight. They vastly furthered the Inn's reputation as a sanctuary for illicit lovers. Some of them got more noisily drunk and burned more cigarette holes in the carpet than even a veteran hotel-man expects, and all of them hinted that they would just love to have a glimpse of the Murder Chamber. Occasionally the clerks satisfied them, by showing them any convenient room which happened to be empty; sometimes Myron indulged himself in the pleasure--his only one, just now--of refusing to do so, and thus losing for life their scabrous patronage.

Of the respectable couples who were neither rude nor greasy nor drunk, there was a proportion that had as much virtuous and smirking curiosity in peeping at the Inn as a haunt of vice as do respectable couples who go to slimy cafés in Paris or Berlin and are irritably disappointed when they see no degenerates to disgust them, but only other rabbit-nosed tourists like themselves.

Yet Myron was patient as he had never been in his zealous life. Daily he told himself to be patient--Effie May told him to be patient--Gritzmeier told him to be patient--Clark Cleaver begged him to be patient--Tom Weagle whined at him to be patient--and despite all this, he actually was patient. But he hated the loose-jawed gapers who believed that his clean place was a den of rottenness, and whose shambling curiosity polluted the Inn more than any swift and honest murder.

This too would pass away. People would forget. It was impossible that they should go on thinking of his Inn as merely a cheap bawdy house and not see the kindly rooms, the gay beach, the beautiful food that every day was lovingly prepared and at night had to be thrown away, untasted.

And people did forget. Other events claimed them. Labour Day, and the beginning of a new year in the office. The World's Series. New feature films. It was the year of Lindbergh and Clarence Chamberlin, and of Byrd and Maitland, and after their ocean flights, they were never out of the papers. Princess Lowenstein-Wertheim, Philip Payne, Mrs. Frances Grayson and half a dozen others winged out to sea and were never heard from again. Young Mr. Hickman, a prominent Sunday School scholar, kidnapped and murdered a child named Marion Parker, which entertained up-to-the-minute readers even more than an hotel-suicide. The Case of the Murder Tavern began to slide back into the indifference with which any democracy views any incident, noble or vile, that is more than four months old; and by October 1927, it was only history, as inconceivably ancient as the events of a whole year before--the positively medieval happenings of 1926, such as the coming over of Queen Marie and Ivar Kreuger to bear messages of Europe's love and its desire to do America good, or the re-opening of the Hall-Mills case, with its altogether elegant murder of a rector and his choir-singer.

The only son of Senator Colquhoun was one now with Hector.

Even in September, when the oaks and maples hung out the banners of a gallant and dying host, guests who did not snoop and giggle began to appear at the Inn, from nowhere in particular, and a few of them stayed a week, riding, tramping, playing golf, and shyly informing Myron that they had never known such food or such beds. For the first time, there was honest young laughter from the cabañas and diving-boards, and youth discovered as dizzily modern the croquet of its grandmothers. There were reservations scattered through October.

After all, Myron complimented himself, if the Inn wasn't really perfect, at least he had chosen the site prophetically. There was no rival within fifty miles.

Then, four miles away, the luxurious Olde Mill Country Club had financial trouble, and bid for transient strangers. On all the roads about Black Thread were placards reading: 'Hotel Prices but Club Exclusiveness--Rooms & Restaurant Open to Transients--Live *At* the Golf Course Not *Near* it.' The lettering was in black, except that the 'at' and 'near' were tastefully done in red.

The club had had no murder scandal. Customers who would have gone to the Black Thread Inn went there, and were delighted at being able to step from the golf course directly into the dining-room.

So Myron was apprehensive again, after a week of autumn-coloured tranquillity.

Pondering it all, he began to see vaguely now, in 1927, what he would see sharply in the early 1930's: that the entire 'resort-hotel business' was changing, and much of it would be lost; that with all love and devotion he had built his 'perfect inn', at exactly the worst possible time, as if one should triumphantly set up shop as epic poet just when the prose novel was ousting the hexameter, perhaps for ever.

The former summer resort, frequently centred about just one hotel, had been self-contained, with a social life that was exciting, however naive it might be, in the manner of William Dean Howells and the Golden Nineties. The chief travelling of the families who so joyously came for a fortnight or a month to Bar Harbour, Saratoga Springs, Bretton Woods, was the long, dusty, creaking journey by train that ended so gloriously in the sight of grey breakers or glistening hills, and the familiar, funny little station which signified that they were here again for a glorious recreation, and then the sad return home to New York or Boston. In between, the only locomotion was joyous sails and picnic-rides in haywagons or parades in smart red-wheeled buggies. Travel was the least of their vacationing. They needed no delicate coaxing by hotel-keepers to amuse themselves; no talkies nor golf-courses nor $20,000 a year leaders of jazz-bands to tickle jaded spirits. So long as they had a croquet ground, a big room and a piano for dancing, plenty of boats, and the hills and sea which, in those careless and uncharted days were provided by the Lord God and not by a hotel-keeper, they were content . . . as nearly content as any group of people ever are anywhere. Even among the Idle Rich, the elegants of the '90's who had actually been in Europe and married off a sister to the cousin of a baron, there were summer dramatic societies, yachting parties, men who needed no snarl of an outboard-motor to stomach them for fishing--who, indeed, for fishing chiefly demanded fish.

And they stayed put. Even the transients who remained but two weeks (which would correspond to-day to the lunchers who stay for but thirty minutes) were as eager as the passengers on a slow steamer to establish a social life.

The motor car changed the whole affair, as it changed the whole plan of cities and suburbs. It is not determined, but one may guess, that Benz, Haines, and Henry Ford have altered the world as much as Napoleon, Alexander, and Caesar.

The new motor tourists spent most of their time in travel, for its own sake, and hotels became to them not centres of amusement, to which they were eager to contribute their own efforts at conviviality, but merely stations for food and beds and gasoline.

There was an increase, also, in the number of families who had once been content to stay at hotels, but built now their own cottages, near their own friends, with a social life from which the strangers of the hotels were excluded.

The golfing mania finally finished the concentration of resort life. Swimmers and tennis-players and those content with the tepid thrills of croquet had been well-enough satisfied to go on swimming and playing tennis and clicking croquet balls on the same grounds. But the golfers were for ever leaping into automobiles and going on to new, distant hazards.

Though the motor brought more people out of the cities, the hotels did not profit. The motorists were neither willing to pay for nor so much interested in the excellences of hotel food and service which had once been the chief zest of citizens gossiping and rocking all day long on hotel porches. And many who were sufficiently prosperous to stay in decent hotels stopped at the farmhouses all over the land which began to hang out the sign 'Tourists Accommodated'. The food there was good enough, they said, and the bedchambers, and it was more convenient to make an Early Getaway from a farmhouse than from an elaborate hotel.

A little later to come--unknown as yet in the east, just beginning in the west, but by the early 1930's to be the final menace to resort hotels--were the professional Tourist Camps which grew out of the farmhouses: overnight cottages with restaurants and supply shops which were frankly and entirely devoted to the flying motorist and, with no corps of professional attendants, no effort to provide great lounging-rooms and varied meals and parking grounds, could so lower prices that the resort hotel, and the small-city hotel on main routes, were both to be bankrupted.

And, Myron saw, worrying, it was just at the beginning of this period of prose that he had brought forth his epic.

He tried every device of growing desperation. He cut the minimum rate, 'American plan', from fifteen dollars a day to ten. He gushed selling-letters like a fountain. To save money, he did not complete the swimming-pool, in the autumn. He pleaded with Dingle, who wanted to sell out his share for what he could get. He spent hours with Gritzmeier devising ways of saving money on food without lessening quality. After working all day, he swayed home to dress, and brought Effie May to dance all evening. He tried to act as 'social host', vice the departed Benny Rumble, to unite the suspicious guests in some sort of authentic gaiety.

Effie May liked dancing with him, but she was a bit shy of what seemed to her the grander guests and she, once so avid of crystal-lighted evenings, murmured to him, 'You seem so tired. Hadn't we better go home?' If ever he had fancied her provincial and inelastic and a little stupid, he forgot it all in clinging to her kindness . . . He had sometimes thought that he would, before it was too late, have an 'affair' with some woman brilliant and imaginative. He reflected now that this was one of the luxuries he would have to give up to reserve enough strength to make the Perfect Inn which, he now perceived, was not finished at all, but simply begun.

While he dealt with major misfortunes, he had the annoyances that he would have had in any resort hotel, however well established and patronized. The staff, being in the country yet barred from most country rollicking, were bored. They hadn't much fun in off hours in swimming under the eyes of those nobles, the aristocracy-by-grace-of-fifteen-dollars-a-day. They quit, just to have something amusing to do, and there were no hotel employment agencies round the corner. There was always a waiter or two on his way to New York, and a substitute supposedly, but not certainly, on his way to the Inn. And they took it out in feuds. Colleagues whom in June they had regarded as playmates they discovered in August to be anarchists who were plotting to give them poison in their coffee.

Clark Cleaver, the spotless chief clerk, came in to wail to Myron that another clerk was 'shystering on the job', and very perky about it, and that 'one or the other of us will have to leave'. The once benign Myron glared, and astounded his disciple by shouting, 'Then I've got a damn good mind to fire both of you! I'm not an ambulance surgeon! Go back and take care of your own troubles!'

'Oh yes, Mr. Weagle!' trembled the faithful Cleaver.

And the pretty young chambermaids would always be out in the woods by moonlight with the pretty young waiters, and the old and less pretty chambermaids would find this rural bliss very low and nasty, and *they* would threaten to quit, and Myron would try to keep from thinking of his clean sweep once at Tippecanoe Lodge, and how nice it would be to discharge every one of his trained staff, chase out every guest with a shot-gun, and sit happily alone amid the ruins.

As in every summer hotel, the hardest guests to manage were not the crooks, the blackmailers who pretended to have lost a case of jewels, and threatened to sue, nor the noisy boozers, but the respectables who were just plain nuisances: the run-of-the-mill pests, the bores, the imaginative old gentlemen who wanted the moon, and wanted it fried, and wanted it quick.

The resolute young lady who played the piano all afternoon in the ballroom-sunroom, and played it badly, so that her fellow customers went pale and thought about moving away. The resolute old lady who, happily spying, saw evil where none existed and--what made a great deal more trouble--where it did exist. The other old ladies who just rocked and watched and rocked and watched until less locomotive people went crazy. The man who wanted the desk to get impossible long-distance telephone-calls for him, and wanted his mail before it had ever reached Black Thread; and his cousin the man who was extremely important in Bellows Falls or Augusta or Tacoma, and who expected to be known here and treated with reverence--and flattering room-rates. The middle-aged ladies who all day long, with firm, quiet, steady, never-ceasing voices, told agonized strangers about their relatives--in particular about what Professor Pibkik-- of course you know his name and what an *authority* he is, and he told me himself, he said, Mrs. Snodbody, in *my* opinion, after my thirty years of teaching, your son has one of the most remarkable intellects I have ever encountered, and I predict for him an extraordinary . . . Firm, quiet, steady, relentless voice, and Myron, hearing it through his open office window, longed for a decent drunken quartet singing 'Down Mobile Bay'.

But these were just the normal pleasures of his business. With them, he was beginning to have distresses out of the ordinary.

31

For weeks they had been holding acrimonious conferences, but it was in December, 1927, some six months after the opening of the Inn, that Pye and Charian told their partners, Myron and T. J. Dingle, what changes they were going to make in the management, to 'save' the place . . . and they had an excess of stock, to give them control. It was so peaceful-sounding a conference: the four men sitting in tilted chairs about Myron's desk, Pye's voice light and cheerful, Dingle polite and wary, Myron and Charian speaking slowly, as though nothing in particular was afoot--as, indeed, there was nothing, save perhaps as regarded Myron, and for him only the ruin of everything he had planned in his forty-seven years of life.

They would, announced Dick Pye, lower rates to six-to-eight dollars a day. To make it possible, they would consciously cheapen food and service; discharging Gritzmeier, with Clark Cleaver, and a certain number of chambermaids, waiters, bell-boys. The skilled floor-waiters would be replaced by ordinary tray-toters. The number of rooms served by each chambermaid would be increased from ten to fourteen, with a proportionate lessening in the dusting, sweeping, check of furnishings.

And they would sell liquor.

That is, they wouldn't exactly *sell* it, Pye explained. That would be illegal, and might subject the hotel to being closed. But they would make peace with Sheriff Beasy--and what could be more legal than that?--and the staff would be permitted to oblige guests with the name of the sheriff's friend, the bootlegger, and it was none of the hotel's business if the bootlegger sold his wares here; the hotel would have nothing to do with it, except taking a percentage from him. And if he used a loft of the stable to store his wares, and the hotel didn't know it, how was that their fault?

Myron, trying to sound no more serious than the chatty Dick Pye, fought him point to point, particularly in regard to discharging Gritzmeier and selling liquor, and was beaten point by point, and at the last Pye prattled, 'Now one final suggestion. At first you won't care for the idea, Weagle, but when you think it over you'll see that it will make things easier for you. Charian and I appreciate the way you've tried to make this the highest-class joint possible, and we understand thoroughly that it isn't your fault that things haven't broken right. We're sure they will later, and then you can go back to all your original arrangements, and nobody'll be gladder about it than we. We've decided that since a lot of the changes will be distasteful to you, we'll bring Jimmy Shanks out here from the Dickens to take charge. No! Wait! We'll promote you to the title of General Director--though at the same salary, I'm afraid--and you can devote yourself to direct-mail advertising, and to getting acquainted with the guests. Or, if you would rather try something else, we'll try to buy out your interests at a fair price--perhaps Mr. Dingle, here, can help us in arbitrating . . .'

'In other words, Pye, since I have a contract with you, you can't fire me, so you're going to run me out on it.'

Dick Pye looked seraphic as he warbled, 'Oh, I wouldn't say that! Come now! Title of "General Director"? Think how much better that sounds than just "Manager"!'

The system technically called 'running a man out on his contract' is one of the most admirable devices known to the modern business-world of doing illegal things legally. It exterminates any executive, any employee important enough to have a contract whereby he cannot be discharged except for proven fault.

First, he is humiliated. His private office and secretary are taken from him. He is treated with mocking courtesy, while he is being crucified, but he is stationed at a contemptible little desk, in the main office among his former subordinates. Then, if he is lazy, if he would merely read newspapers all day if he were given nothing more important to do, he is set at such petty tasks that every one begins to laugh at him. On the other hand, if he is industrious and ambitious, he is left idle and ignored day after day after day, till his pride explodes, and he quits. In neither case is he likely to endure it, for the term of his contract.

Since Myron was industrious and ambitious, Pye and Charian through Jimmy Shanks, used the second method. He was relieved from all duties save sitting in his office, frenzied with the first enforced idleness since he had lain abed with that less tormenting illness, the 'flu--nothing at all to do, except watch Jimmy Shanks, the new manager, briskly and amiably defiling the shrine.

Gritzmeier and Clark Cleaver were discharged.

The new chef was a fancy fellow from New York, with experience in night clubs, large cheap hotels, chain cafeterias, and the summer roof-garden of an hotel. He could prepare splendid desserts for special dinners, with glistening ropes of spun sugar, but he cared not at all for the patient processes of making bouillon with a real taste, nor for the freshness of vegetables. Jimmy Shanks and the new chef between them did a great deal of what was known as 'effecting economies.' They mixed evaporated milk with the cream. They made butterless and eggless cakes. They introduced at the Inn all the women's-club and women's-page desserts that Myron hated: horrible drug-store things with raspberry syrup and nuts and slices of pineapple and marshmallows and canned cherries. They advertised and were successful with the 'Old-time New England Dinner, every Friday evening'--with clam-chowder, beans, corned beef and cabbage, and pumpkin pie made with cornstarch instead of eggs--and made every motoring New Yorker, exclaim over its delicious quaintness.

And if Shanks provided less edible food, he put more items on the menu, and printed it on cardboard edged with gold, and most customers liked the change, and the chagrined Myron wondered whether he knew anything about hotel-keeping.

And if Shanks changed the excellent orchestra for a cheaper one, the new players were much noisier, and he introduced in this ballroom just the changing coloured lights and confetti and paper-hats and streamers beloved in the worst night clubs, and again every one was happy, and Myron thought about going back to sweeping floors till he learned his profession.

The arrangements with Beasy's bootlegger ran quietly and well; the guests were not much more noisily drunken than when they had brought their own liquor, and the hotel had profit on it. The new chief clerk was much less inquisitive about the relationships of ladies and gentlemen than Clark Cleaver had been. And for all the lower rates, the general profits of the Inn increased. That winter of 1927-8, there was a fairly large crowd for the Winter Sports, and if most of them found dancing and drinking more reasonable than going out into the cold for skiing and luging and skating why, that merely lessened all worry as to whether there was enough snow. Under Shanks, the Inn was settling into a sensible, realistic position as one of the most comfortable houses of assignation and refuges for prosperous drunks within an afternoon motor-run of New York, and every one was happy, except Myron Weagle.

'I suppose they really are what is called "sensible". They accept sporting gentlemen for just what they are, and give them just what they want. Only I can't be satisfied with anything except what I think is a fine hotel,' thought the fanatic.

He sought to make clear to his few confidants, to Effie May, Ora, Alec Monlux, and perhaps to himself, just what he had been trying to do. 'I would have made a solid success here, that would have gone on for fifty years, if they had given me time,' he insisted.

Alec, for all his affection, was not much interested. He was no creator of hotels nor of anything else; he was a man on a job, who did as well as he could just what he was told to do. Ora scoffed. Even Effie May could not see anything to grieve about, if Myron would just get rid of Shanks. 'What's the difference between your letting your guests bring their own hootch, and selling it to them, except that this way the hotel gets some of the profit?' she demanded, and Myron was foundered; he had no logical answer.

He gave up trying to explain--except to himself, and himself he found no very good audience.

He felt lonely and shamed as he watched Shanks ruin the Inn. He tried often enough to seize control again, but Pye and Charian could have forced him out by court action. He wanted to run away from the spectacle of sacrilege, but perhaps if he stayed, he could get back into power. He was always making suggestions to Shanks, who agreed with him heartily, and never took them. For the rest, Myron sat in his office, idle, for as many minutes at a time as he could endure it. He was certainly not going to invite his private list of faithful guests to the sort of place this had become!

He did not sleep well. He got into a wretched habit of awakening at five, with nothing to do till seven. He would lie still, not to disturb Effie May, in the bed by his, till his muscles were racked with staying in one position, and he crept out into the cold, shawled himself in a grotesque costume of overcoat over dressing-gown over pyjamas, and padded down to sit by the cold fire-place and smoke cigarettes and, with scarlet aching eyes, try to read magazines. On the first mornings of this insomnia, he made coffee for himself, but it became too much trouble, and he just sat, trembling with sleepiness--till he lay down, when the enemy leaped on him again. All the while, he was coldly hungry, yet when the waiter came from the inn with breakfast, at eight, he could only sip coffee.

Effie May hardly suspected this tortured prowling. She was a healthy young sleeper, that one!

In all his life, Myron had never thought much about himself, as an individual, detached from his work. He had been old-fashioned in having, even now, after the war, no fascinating Troubles, Complexities, Maladjustments or what not. He became aware of himself as Myron, a person naked, no longer sheltered by the walls of work, and he got very tired of that ever-present person. Once he awoke to see the familiar hand of Myron Weagle lying on the counterpane, visible in moonlight through the window and in the divided personality that sometimes persists for seconds after awakening, he quaked, 'That's that man, still here! Oh my God! How he bores me! Have I got to be with him all day?'

He brooded, as he had not before, on every one who had ill-used him--on Pye, Ora, Herbert and Julia Lambkin, Carlos Jaynes, Sheriff Beasy, his father. Hitherto he had had his quarrel and done something about it and forgotten it; now, a sick man, he sat in the empty hours of early morning going over and over his grievances.

He tried to rouse himself to healing activity, but the habit of sloth was breaking him, and when he decided to find a new job, he could not get down to writing letters, could not even plan what to do, whom to see. In such hours he longed to get wholesomely and thoroughly drunk, but he was afraid of that anodyne; he had seen its too successful drugging, not only in a thousand unhappy guests, hiding out in hotels, but in his own father and brother. Afraid--definitely he was afraid; and never before had he been afraid.

Effie May was sleepily sympathetic, but she did not know. It was to his mother, still in the kitchen at the American House--though a chef emeritus now--that he fled. And to her who would have understood fast enough, he could not confess, for what sustained her life was the belief that her son was a conqueror. With her he actually boasted a little of how completely he was controlling Pye and Shanks, while his father fussed about them and waggled his little beard and piped, 'You want to stand in with those fellows--you want to stand in with those fellows--they're on to this high-class city trade and after all, you're just a small-town boy! What you need is to come ask my advice oftener!'

But Ora was helpful. Ora stayed away! He came once, saw the lay of the land, tried to become chummy with Jimmy Shanks, was snubbed, and did not come back.

Through it all, Myron's one consolation, and surprise, was that he became acquainted with his own son.

Even after years of seeing hotel children snatch things from waiters, Myron liked to picture the little things as all clinging sweetness, like warm cotton. But when he faced it, he admitted that, at ten and a half, Luke was as hard and sharp as a steel blade. He was independent, demanding, logical, secret. He was less blundering than either of his parents, and if he was less softly playful than either of them, and seemingly less sympathetic, he was more resolute. He knew what he wanted--apparently, for just what it was, Myron could never quite find out. Luke felt himself a representative of the great and dazzling city of Mount Vernon and, condescending to Black

Thread Centre, amused himself by leading the sixth grade in the Centre public school. He was as civil as he was secret; only two things made him scowl--Effie May's fussing about such private matters as his nails, and the habit, seemingly inborn in all hotel-guests, of trying to be showily friendly, and screaming, 'Well, old man, I suppose you think you'll run a hotel too, when you grow up.'

He just did not answer.

Here, then, was a new thing for Myron to be afraid of, just as parents in general had been afraid of their children's hidden opinions, ever since the war. He cultivated Luke as he had never cultivated Mark Elphinstone or any gilded guest of the Hotel Crillon. Almost timidly he invited Luke to go tramping up the snowy hill above the lake. He panted beside him, longing for some magic by which he could enter the mind of this citizen of a new world that was more distant from his America of the 1890's than was Italy or Tibet. He guessed that the only passport to his son's heart, territory, uncontrollable by any Versailles Treaty of domesticity, was silence. He had noted how irritated Luke was by his mother's questions, that is (for he was just, as children often are) when they were foolish: 'Did you eat the sandwiches that mother gave you for lunch all up?' and 'Why don't you get better marks in Reading when you do so good in Arithmetic?'

So, mostly, Myron said nothing, except when he inquired about the names of shrubs and winterbound birds, which Luke knew better than he did, and if he had any talent at all for fatherhood, he showed it in not resenting Luke's quicker knowledge.

One day in February he was rewarded. They were squatting on a rock at the top of Elm Hill, looking down on the snowy roofs of the hotel and its outbuildings, and the glare of the lake where, on cleared ice, guests in red and yellow mackinaws were skating. Myron was smoking a pipe, which he had taken up as a sound, outdoor equipment, and which he disliked extremely. Luke was jabbing imaginary whales with a stick. He spoke suddenly:

'Dad, I guess I'll be a sailor.'

'Um-huh?'

'We been reading about whaling. I guess that would be pretty exciting.'

'Yes, I imagine it would.'

'Or in the army, and get sent to Alaska and China and places!'

'I'd like that.'

'But still . . . Maybe I'd like to keep a hotel, like granddad and you. Because I guess I could do that better 'n anybody! Because you can do it better 'n anybody! Gee, I think Mr. Shanks is a lousy hotel keeper! Why don't you fire him? He's--he pats me on the head! I hate him!'

That moment broke the patience with which Myron had waited for the Lord to cause something to happen.

32

Four days later, Richard Pye and Nick Schirovsky decided that their labours in distributing booze to the solidest citizens of New York, the worthies who kept every law except inconvenient ones, merited a vacation. There were few guests at the Inn, and all of them of a reasonable, dripping sort, so Pye and Schirovsky took it over for a week-end, with a company of a dozen sympathetic ladies and gentlemen not of Pye's polo set. They had a splendid time. Everyone was drunk daily by noon, and slept it off, and was drunk before evening again, and danced till dawn. There was a pyjama parade, and much laughter about gentlemen who were found in wrong rooms at breakfast time, and the time when Nick Schirovsky, wearing only his drawers, went out and rolled in the snow.

Myron was on hand nineteen hours a day, protecting the decorations of the Inn so far as he could, for Jimmy Shanks, normally no fool, had gone native and become one of the most lush of the gay Bacchantes. Several times, not without roughness, Myron put to bed guests who wanted to play billiards with bottles for balls, or to toy with the firehose, and Dick Pye became irritated. After three days, he began gently, then much less gently, to tease Myron about his undignified exile-at-home. Whenever Myron made suggestions--such as that one of the joyous party really ought to stop setting his bed afire--Pye said mockingly, 'Anything you say goes with me, Boss, I'll certainly attend to it.'

Late one night, he swaggered and staggered into Myron's office, much drunker than Myron had ever seen him, and crowed, 'Everybody's insisting you come on join us. We're going to have an impromptu masquerade ball, right now! And chase your wife over here, too. Need more gals.'

'Nothing doing! And you better go to bed. You've got no right to raise such Cain. There are a few guests besides your party, Pye.'

'Oh, damn the guests! There wouldn't be even a few, if I hadn't taken hold! You always did want to run this place like a Methodist prayer-meeting.'

'We won't go into that now.'

'The hell we won't! You think you're a partner, but you're just a plain clerk, and you come when I ring the bell for you! You're a plain pen-pusher!'

Myron found himself in front of the desk, shaking Mr. Richard Pye like a school-boy. He shook him with all the fury of six months of brooding. Pye tried to hit back, but Myron rocked him till he was dizzy. He slapped

Pye, then, and was frightened by discovering how homicidally he wanted to give him one sweet, ringing, murderous clip on the jaw and, lest he do it, he shoved Pye into the closet in his office, locked it, put the key with absurdly sober-looking methodicalness into the top drawer of his desk, and went quietly crazy.

Now that he had begun, he burned to go on and wipe out Schirovsky, Shanks, all their guests, and anybody else who came handy. He fled down into the quiet basement, to get hold of himself. He found himself in the furnace-room, staring at a heap of wrapping paper, excelsior, fragments of boxes. What suddenly made him really insane was this litter. When he had been in charge, the basement had been tidy as a parlour.

It would make a lovely fire! By God, he would burn up the whole place! With fire and fury he would destroy the abomination! He was a pen-pusher again, was he? He had to answer the bell to Dick Pye's fancy, did he?--yes, and to the whim of that murdering bootlegger, Schirovsky! He'd destroy them, along with their stinking den! He touched a match to the excelsior, and a flame ran up the wall, tasted a dry beam.

He gaped, surprised. Then he leaped. For forty years he had been trained to be ready for hotel-fires. Not thinking, not having to think, he snatched a fire-extinguisher from its bracket and, quite coolly, directed the chemical stream at the base of the writhing flare of paper and kindling.

It was a good fire-extinguisher, for it had been chosen, long before this building had been finished, by none other than Manager Weagle. If it had not been so good, so chosen, the Black Thread Inn, with Mr. Richard Pye locked in a closet, would have burned complete.

Myron stood trembling. He was too shocked to tamper with blaming himself. So quivery and weak of knee that he could scarcely walk, he got himself up the stairs, into his office, and unlocked the closet door.

Dick Pye was placidly asleep, and from the ballroom came the cheerfullest sound of jazz as the masquerade ball began. Then Myron laughed, gently shook Pye awake, and still more gently crooned, 'Sorry to disturb you, Dick, but I thought you ought to know that I have resigned, and my lawyer will be glad to arrange with you about the sale of my stock in this place--what's it called?--Black Thread Inn? Any time it's convenient. Good night.'

And walked across to his cottage, feeling exalted, while Dick Pye sat up stupidly, among brooms, dust-cloths, and letter-files, clumsily brushing a cob-web out of his hair.

33

Like Deacon Wheelwright of the Connecticut Inn, Mr. Henry Fiesel was a vestigial remnant of the rustic tradition in hotel-keeping. He was as crafty and secretive as Wheelwright, but more boldly speculative, and considerably meaner. For years he had kept hotel in New York, but he remained a suspicious, penny-pinching, country innkeeper. He still wore rubbers and long woollen underwear. Though he was actually smooth-shaven, you remembered him as wearing sandy side-whiskers. Spiritually, he did wear sandy side-whiskers. They had merely grown inside.

He had risen from working in a lodging-house in New York to the sole proprietorship, now that he was sixty-eight, of the nine-hundred-and-fifty-room Fiesel Hotel, a respectable, cheap, yet lavishly gilded pile which made much of its income from the cut-rate drug store and the 'beauty-shop' off its large lobby, and from its bustling Gothic Coffee Shop, where business men saved time (it was never explained for what they saved it) by lunching on stuffed eggs, toast Melba, and coffee, and their stenographers in a more leisurely and elegant way trifled with a bacon-and-tomato sandwich and an ice cream soda.

The Fiesel Hotel was a railway station minus anything so romantic as trains destined for Key West or Seattle. And of this camp under a roof, Myron was made manager-in-chief in the autumn of 1928, eight months after quitting the Black Thread Inn.

He had, for his share in the Black Thread Inn, theoretically worth $130,000, been able to get only $60,000, and he had been glad enough to have that. He had diligently lost $15,000 in his only stock-market gamble and, back at real work, awakened from nightmare, he was relieved to have so much as $45,000 left, invested in bonds.

In the eight months, a little sick of a career of hotel-keeping that could wind up in Dick Pye's drunken party at the Inn, he had wandered, he had peeped into other dodges, such as starting a chain of garages and, not altogether content yet no longer feeling futile and ridiculous, no longer awakening at five to crouch and brood, he had gone back to his last, at the Fiesel Hotel.

Old Fiesel was snuffling and sniffling about his need of a vacation after years of unrelenting work, and a month after Myron took charge, he went off with his wife to Los Angeles and rented a bungalow for the winter. He had stayed in New York just long enough to give Myron an appreciation of his quality, which was that of decaying ragweed.

Myron's systems of food-cost-finding were as naught beside Fiesel's natural genius for getting raw materials at a seventh of a cent per ounce cheaper. He loved to save pennies even if it cost him pounds. When canned vegetables were cheaper than fresh, Fiesel convinced himself that he preferred the taste of the canned ones. He had the lights cut off in the servants' rooms at ten-thirty. He never permitted a new carpet to be purchased so long as the old one could be painfully stitched together. He spent hours of joyful energy in working out codes of fining dish-washers for broken dishes, chambermaids for missing towels, no matter whether they were stolen by guests or otherwise lost, cashiers for shortage of petty cash, bell-boys for being one minute late in the morning or for smoking cigarettes in corridors.

He was an enthusiast about 'the value of fraternal organizations,' which value, to him, was providing banquets and conventions for his beloved fraternity brothers. He was astounded to find that Myron was such a novice at inn-keeping as to belong only to the Masons and Elks, and pointed out that the manager of the rival Hotel Bonnie Claire (also a large and gilded stable for human cattle) was no less than Monarch of Ramadan Grotto, Occult and Brotherly Order of the Winged Warriors of the Cretan Caravan. He insisted that Myron become a Monarch, or a Perpetual Potentate, or at the very least a Princely Prophet.

Myron said he'd look into it right away and, for once, didn't. He grumbled to himself that he was an innkeeper, not a pedlar, and he was altogether unimpressed by Fiesel's long-winded tale about Myron's predecessor who, as Past Worshipful Master of Israel Putnam Lodge, 'had captured a lodge banquet for twelve hundred at seven dollars a plate, though a rival hotel had quoted $6.90 and had included squabs, whereas the Hotel Fiesel had given them only Long Island duckling, at a time when duckling was going begging at twelve and fourteen cents a pound'.

When Old Fiesel had gone off to California, nervously leaving Myron in charge, he wrote to Myron every day the treasures of his travel observation--which had nothing to do with mountains and sea. ('And serve me damn well right,' admitted Myron. 'Didn't I go to Europe, and see nothing but hotels, all for the purpose of making a private joint for Dick Pye? Next time I go, I'll look at nothing but art galleries and the damn scenery, I will!') Fiesel wrote to Myron, on a faded picture postcard, that hot tamales ought to be featured on the menu, because they cost approximately nothing to make, and could be played up as a Mexican Delicacy. Again he wrote that the east had not begun to appreciate the cafeteria. And Myron hated his busy meannesses more than he had the jolly scoundreldom of Jimmy Shanks.

He was confused, still, and he told himself, not quite accurately, that he was coming to dislike everything connected with hotel-keeping. Unreasonable and complaining guests. Dishonest and thievish guests. Oily guests who wanted favours. The incessant headachy effort to save tenth-pennies on food. The clever Jewish girl public stenographer with her desk on the mezzanine balcony, who asserted, 'I'm some little kidder--I certainly know how to handle the fresh guys,' and who, when she said 'Good *morning,* Mr. Weagle,' sang it, crooned it, coyly narrowing her eyes at him in invitation. He did not the more like her because he knew that she was the owner's private spy, and was reporting to Fiesel about him and the rest of the staff daily.

He particularly, now, disliked the whole cosmetic-beautyparlour-manicure-hairdressing-perfumestinking-powdersmeared business that was increasingly important in urban hotel-keeping. He was glad that Effie May was out of it--back in Mount Vernon, while Luke impressed his Mount Vernon schoolmates by possibly fanciful tales of hunting bear, wolves, and moose in the shrieking wilds of Connecticut. He detested the new fashion whereby women had their nails stained so scarlet that they looked like the harem. 'That's what hotels are getting to be--harems!'

Yet he was guiltily dreaming again of the Perfect Inn. . . .

He saw it now as a small and simple place, for small and simple people, but with pleasant rooms, and food that should be an event--the real descendant of such inns as the Cat and Fiddle, with no bastard union with the Riviera. He began to wonder if the Black Thread Inn had not been too ornate, and, still more, too dependent on the fickleness of that brazen-hearted tribe, the Rich--began to wonder if, in his first epic, there had not been too many Purple Passages.

And in particular he wanted an inn that he should really own by himself, and manage by himself, so that if it should fail, he would be honestly responsible, and not the victim of collaborators with too lush a style.

His life, in 1929, was complicated by Ora's falling into an immense success--call it success.

Working night and day for six days, with a well-known Hollywood actor, clever but now out of favour, Ora had written a play, the play of the hour, with all the right condiments of the moment: a dash of racketeers and murder, a spoonful of sarcasm about Washington politicians, a delicate suggestion of Lesbianism, but under it all a sturdy romance and a lovely ending which combined a passionate kiss with a funny slap at all passionate kissing.

It was accepted immediately. It was rewritten in collaboration with a standard playwright. It was tried out in a summer theatre, brought into New York in September, became the sensation of the autumn, and was sold to the movies for eighty thousand dollars. It is true that Ora had to drop both his collaborators because, as he explained to Myron, they were crooked and did not keep their promises, but he found a new one and, late in the autumn, was writing another play, with a two-thousand dollar advance. Ora's picture was in every paper, with accounts of his lonely boyhood, struggles in earning his way through Yale, his three years hidden away in a Florida swamp while he wrote and tore up sixteen plays.

None of these accounts mentioned the manager of the Fiesel Hotel.

Ora had a suite at the Victor Hugo, where he often entertained his friend Dick Pye, he had a Lincoln car, an autographed set of the works of S. S. Van Dine, and sixteen suits of clothes. He took a good deal of light exercise in the way of walking from the Victor Hugo to the Fiesel, to tell Myron why he had failed at the Black Thread Inn. He explained that Myron was right enough in his way, but he ought not to try to associate with the smart friends of Dick Pye.

He even paid back all he had ever borrowed from Myron, with interest at five per cent.

It is true that his figures did not agree with those kept through the years by Myron. Always, Myron had been willing to let 'the kid' have money when in need, but he had never been able to keep himself from setting down the exact sums in his private account book--along with every five cents he had ever spent for an apple. But Ora did not know this, and Myron did not tell him, even when Ora chuckled (in the presence of Myron's secretary), 'The joke of it is that you've always thought I was too much of a wild, dreamy poet to be accurate, and you've always hammered me for it, whereas, you can see, the fact is that I'm much more considerate and exact than you are.'

Indeed, as he said, Ora *was* considerate. For he waited till the secretary was gone before he added, 'You're an interesting case, Myron. Take this matter of your going haywire at the Inn, and getting sore at *others* because *you* failed! You spent half your life doing things for people out of weak good-nature, and now, apparently, you're going to spend the next half, out of weak resentment, kicking about their doing you!'

Myron did not answer. He did not, though he longed to, shake Ora as he had shaken Dick Pye. He was tired of quarrelling.

'Am I losing all my grip?' he whispered to himself. 'I'm cranky to guests. I can't get myself to care when some fool woman complains her chambermaid has been rude. I'm suspicious of Fiesel, who's a decent enough old codger, after all. I'm getting lazy, I guess.'

He was kept from too much fretting by his routine duties--and actually, he rarely was 'cranky to guests'. The routine duties were about all he could find, so frozen was the Fiesel Hotel in Fiesel's cold breath. The principal changes he could make were to add his old sergeants, Gritzmeier and Clark Cleaver, to the staff.

Even in these days of 1929, the height of prosperity (yet obviously only the beginning of a new and unexampled prosperity, now that America had secured the financial leadership of the world) Gritzmeier and Cleaver were going badly, and were glad to come to the Fiesel for no great salaries. They were of doubtful repute, for Mr. Richard Pye had let it be known that they had 'let him down' at the Black Thread Inn. Myron felt responsible for them and, in interminable nagging correspondence, made Fiesel pay them quite a percentage of what they were worth.

And Myron went on, day after day, with the details of middle-class hotel-keeping which he had thought to give up forever. Yet if by some miracle Fiesel should decide to stay in California permanently, he could make something a little different and interesting of the hotel.

He was just beginning a day's work with plans for a children's playroom, to tempt parents who come to New York for shopping, when he was conscious of someone standing by his desk, waiting, and looked up to see the goat-like smile of Henry Fiesel.

'Why, I thought you were . . .'

Myron got no farther. Fiesel tittered, 'Yeh, I been here since six this morning. I came in by the delivery entrance. They bought some new ash-cans when they could of repaired the old ones. I caught a chambermaid eating candy in a linen-room. That new clerk, Cleaver, was two minutes late. I checked up on some of the stock in the storeroom. They was two boxes of corn flakes shorter than their figures. There's too many floor-brushes in the broom-closet on the twelfth floor. There's six guests that--I know their financial standing--they're paying four dollars for rooms that you could get five dollars from 'em, and what I always say is, hotel-keeping ain't a charity.'

He giggled, laid his umbrella on Myron's desk, sat down, carefully pulling up his faded old blue serge trousers, fondly stroked a small wart on his chin, and rattled on: 'This high-toned new Dutch chef of yours, Gritzmeier, ain't so good. He's only had hash on the breakfast bill of fare twice in ten days, and what I always tell my boys is, Hash is what pays the taxes. You been advertising too much in charity programs. The hotel detective smokes Havana cigars--where'd he get the money, that's what I want to know. There's a busted soap-dish in the bathroom in 676. There's a cobweb in elevator seven. That Dutch chef of yours uses too many mushrooms in a mushroom omelet. The Do Not Disturb card in 892 has fly specks on it. Your tie ain't quite straight. Way I figger it, it's details that make good hotel-keeping. Probably you up-and-coming young swells never think of it that way, but it's attention to details that does it, and that means *work* and *hours* and not going out dancing or looking at theatre shows every night. Good morning. I'll be seeing you.'

He was gone, and Myron's chief concern was that he had not shown resentment of this snooping driveller, as he would have done in days when he was more sure of himself.

Never, from that morning, did he quite feel himself manager of the Fiesel. The old man--he lived now in an apartment in Jackson Heights-- came in anywhere from once a week to thrice a day, any time from four in the morning to one in the morning, and he never failed to find flaws, no difficult feat of scholarship in a hotel of nine hundred and fifty rooms which he deliberately kept a little understaffed. He used his criticisms as a water-dripping torture to keep Myron nervous and busy--only he, who always and most tediously boasted of possessing a 'kind of gift for seeing right through folks' did not see that this was not the best method of getting the most labour out of the particular sort of wage-slave that Myron was.

Myron did not want to resign again, not so soon. But he thought about it enough.

Then the catastrophe.

Fiesel dashed into Myron's office, shrieking, 'You hired this Gritzmeier!'

'Yes. Why?'

'Yes! *Why!* That's what I want to know--*why!* Max Sussman, of Sussman Brothers, the wholesale butchers, has been to see me. God! I've known Max for years. He's an honest man. If he gives a commission to a steward or a chef, it's only what's customary. And your Gritzmeier has been trying to hold him up for five per cent over the right amount of graft! I heard it this morning, and I've been looking around. Gritzmeier and your other man, Cleaver, have been stealing from me by juggling their food accounts. Cleaver worked the cheque in the front office. And them two have padded the kitchen pay-roll and drew down money for help that don't exist! Well, Mr. Smarty Manager, you and your pets, what do you propose to do about it?'

Myron knew that Fiesel was not the kind of fool to have his accusation wrong.

'What do their stealings come to?' he said heavily.

'I figure about thirty-seven hundred dollars, so far.'

'I'll fire them, of course. And I'll see the money is paid back.'

'Oh, ain't that sweet of you! But that ain't enough, Mr. Manager! I'll not rest till I see those two dirty crooks behind the bars! Stealing from *me!*'

'Then you'll never get the money back. I didn't know they were stealing. I don't know what they've done with the swag. But I do know they're both clean broke. It isn't worth all that money to you to see them in jail. Three--thousand--seven--hundred--dollars!'

'Well, yes, mebbe something to what you say. But no man ever put nothing over on Henry Fiesel! No, sir, I . . .'

'I understand just how you feel, sir, but three thousand, seven hundred dollars!'

'Well. All right. I'll be merciful. I'll be merciful if you guarantee the return of the money, personal.'

'I do.'

'All right. Have 'em in, and I'll give 'em such a talking to . . .' Fiesel rubbed his dry hands together so that they rasped.

'No, I've got to see them alone. Otherwise I can't be responsible. Who's got the exact dope, if I need it?'

'The hotel dick and that public stenographer on the mezzanine.'

'All right. Let me talk to them.' For the first time his tone said distinctly to Fiesel, 'Now get out.'

Myron sighed, as he waited for the traitors. He thought nothing. There was nothing to think.

Otto Gritzmeier shambled in trying to look jolly. It was a ghastly look of jolliness--like the face of a Santa Claus coated with thick flour. Clark Cleaver was trembling.

Myron sat still, waving them to chairs.

'Well, what about it?' he said.

Gritzmeier's great red hands fluttered about his chin. 'Vat about vat?' he demanded belligerently.

Myron merely looked unhappy. 'I thought you two were loyal! You alone.'

Gritzmeier's eyes were damp, with the rheumy, undignified grief of old age. He sobbed.

'What happened?' Myron said more sharply.

With endless winding excuses, his accent almost unintelligible in his emotion, Gritzmeier told the story. Out of work after he had been discharged from the Black Thread Inn, his widowed daughter-in-law and three beloved grandchildren on his hands, he had got into debt before Myron had taken him on at the Fiesel. Then his grandson had infantile paralysis. He had spent thousands on the boy--and he did not have the thousands. He hated Fiesel, hated the sneakiness and the smirk of the old devil. 'He iss chust like a stale doughnut in a lunch-room, dat fellow!' wailed Gritzmeier. It angered him to think of working to make money for that human tin bank; angered him the more that Fiesel wanted none of his fine cooking, but only glorified hash. And the 'leetle boy' was so broken. He had felt that he was taking it out of Fiesel. He had never thought of injuring Myron.

He could not work out his happy plans of stealing without someone in the Front Office to falsify the accounts, and that one he found in his colleague at the Inn, Clark Cleaver.

'Yes. I understand, more or less,' Myron interrupted, not ungently. On Cleaver he turned with a terrible blazing: 'But you, you sanctified young pup! You turner on parallel bars! What the hell excuse had *you*?'

'Well, I just--I figured I could double it on the market and put it back. And Otto persuaded me . . .'

'All you characters in the Bible are alike! "Somebody tempted me and I did eat"! You make me sick, both of you. Either of you got any money left?'

'No-uh,' groaned Gritzmeier.

'Then I'll pay it, God damn you--I'll take it from my family for your damned families. What makes me sickest isn't you two, with your dirty little small-boy stealing--it's the fact that I'm supposed to be an executive, and I let this obvious stealing go on--that apparently you two didn't respect me enough to be loyal!'

'Oh, no, Chief, we . . .'

'Chief! Chief! Get out of my sight! I don't blame you. I that let you be weak. Only I'm not a superman. I simply can't stand the sight of you, or of myself. Get out!'

And he watched some large part of his honesty as a craftsman melt away, and he sat there in his prim, efficient office lonelier than he had been in all his life.

He paid to Fiesel the amount of the defalcation--slightly over thirty-five hundred dollars it came to, when the books had been checked.

He knew that Fiesel suspected him of having been guilty along with Gritzmeier and Cleaver. Why else, reasoned the good weasel, would a man willingly pay out money? Fiesel had never liked him, anyway; he felt, with justice, that Myron was a flippant fellow who had none of his own reverence for pennies. From now on, he bedeviled Myron in every little way. Fiesel's genius for observation would have made him a great journalist. For every torn towel or loose stair-rod that he had found before, he found a dozen, now, and he chattered to Myron about all of them.

And this time, Myron had no contract! He had at the beginning agreed to wait for a contract till they should 'see how they got along together'. Yet now he was not restrained and unresentful. The loss of Gritzmeier and Cleaver had shaken him into recklessness. He would growl at Fiesel, 'Kindly take that up with the housekeeper. I'm busy.'

He wondered slightly at the old man's simper. He knew that it meant something nasty.

In the late summer, he rejoiced in being able to slip away for a three-weeks motor trip with Effie May and Luke. He avoided equally the Lambkins and all hotels. They stayed at farmhouses, and for ten days camped out in a lakeside cottage.

He came back feeling calmer, surprised that he had ever let Fiesel make him jumpy. He'd just have it out with the old devil; really talk frankly. After all, Fiesel was a good hotel-keeper, at least in ingenuity about details. Yes. They'd have it out.

On Myron's first morning back in his office, Henry Fiesel came squeaking in, accompanied by a square-faced, youngish man with grave eye-glasses.

'Weagle,' peeped the old man, 'I want you to meet Mr. John Eggthorne, formerly of the Blakeslee Hotel Chain.'

'I'm pleased to . . .'

'Yes, you'll be interested in him, Weagle. Because he's your successor! As of this morning, Weagle!'

Mr. Eggthorne smiled.

Fiesel was watching Myron with all the affection of a copperhead.

Then, as when he had seen Dick Pye among the cobwebs in a closet, Myron laughed. His worried face cleared. 'Welcome, Brother Eggthorne! I'll have my personal stuff out of this desk in fifteen minutes. Be sure and inspect Room 504. There's a blown-out bulb there. Good morning!'

34

The years of the Great Depression were not at all lean for the well-known author, Mr. Ora Weagle. In 1930, '31, and '32, he had two plays on Broadway, and half a dozen scenarios in Hollywood, to which he generously lent half his time now. He made twenty-five thousand a year, and as he did not spend more than twenty-seven, he was financially comfortable. Early in 1932, he happened on a device which made him more famous than all his plays. He created the character of Old Aunty Depression for the radio, and in a voice sometimes facetiously feminine, sometimes splendidly virile, he gave to several million fond listeners the message that no Depression could defeat the America which had endured grasshoppers, William Jennings Bryan, earthquakes, the Civil War, hurricanes, and Henry Ward Beecher.

He received a thousand fawning letters a day, and ten stenographers (paid by the studio) were kept busy answering. Sometimes Mr. Weagle drifted in and laughingly glanced at a letter and at the charming response he was sending, but he grew tired of it, and at parties he often complained whimsically of his wearing duty to his radio audience.

His brother, Myron, a hotel clerk, had been fired from the Fiesel Hotel in New York, and Ora had lost track of him. He heard of him, now and then, without much interest--he had always tried to be friendly with Myron, but the fellow was, and he hated to say this of his own brother, but he had to admit that Myron was a suspicious crank. He was told, he did not know how accurately, that Myron had also been discharged from a hotel in Milwaukee for rudeness to guests, and that he had drifted still farther west, with his sappy wife and fresh kid.

He would--he was almost sure--have written to Myron if he had known his address.

He wondered sometimes if he had been just to Myron. The fellow had his merits. He was industrious and even generous. But--hell! Curious! He, Ora, the delicate poet, was a realist, while his brother, the drudge, the steel and rubber robot, was essentially a sentimentalist. Ora saw that life was a battle. It was, he admitted, just too bad that people were killed in battle, but strangely enough, they were! It was too bad that an essential rustic like Myron offended well-bred people, but strangely enough, he did! And Ora could not change it. He sighed a little, and had another drink, and planned to do a novel about the tragedy of a clodhopper like his brother who, because he was for a while and by chance able to buy decent city clothes, thought he was civilized, and then was hurled back into his manure heap.

Most of 1933 Ora was to spend in Hollywood, continuing his radio labours with a new character wittily christened Prosper E. Tee, while he prepared scenarios based on his own experiences as an aviator on the Roumanian, Russian, and Italian fronts in the Great War. He was pretty tired. He had slaved all winter on a magnificent book, 'Christ, the First Playwright', which his publishers (a new firm, for Ora had had to reject his former publishers, as crooks who did not keep their promises) ardently expected to equal the sales of 'The Man Nobody Knows' or even of Culbertson's manual of bridge.

It seemed a sound notion to drive out to California, in May, with his newest girl, that altogether spiritual and entertaining young actress, Miss Dimity Dove, in his newest car, a Twelve. (But next year he would have a Sixteen). And Dimity, the darling, certainly had earned a rest, with her agonized labours of singing in 'Buckety-Buckety-Buck' for seven minutes daily and fourteen minutes on Wednesdays and Saturdays. What a journey! What a forth-faring into the magic of May! New book, new publishers, new talkie-contract, new girl, new car, new scented airs of spring!

'I certainly am a lucky guy! Though I have worked for it!' he confided to Dimity Dove. 'Nobody ever knows how an author toils! Fifteen hours a day, every day, and all the damn publishers and managers trying to do him all the time.'

Yet with all this promised vernal splendour, the journey was not completely successful.

Ah, Dimity Dove was not what he had thought! Fooled again! Poor, soft, fluttering tender heart, was it always to be the victim of the steely selfishness of women?

Dimity said that he was a rotten driver. Dimity said that he made her sick by singing 'Wee Rose o' the Rockies.' Dimity said that when by ill chance they came on a country hotel, he hogged the whole bed--she actually said the coarse word, 'hogged', she of the lissom little body and grey eyes, so truly, if illegally, named Dove!

She made him so furious that he could never think of any retort more brilliant than 'Oh, go to hell!'

He was glad now that he had planned, before starting, to chuck Dimity and take up again with Gloria Gurss, when he got to Hollywood.

He had intended to be very historic and romantic, for Dimity's benefit, about the trail of Daniel Boone that he knew so poignantly. But Dimity's most appreciative remark was 'Say, where do you think we are? Back in the Eighth Grade? Going historical--on *me!'*

He was silent for a hundred miles, save for the moment when he answered 'Oh shut *up!'* to Dimity's protest of 'For the love o' God, were you trying to *hit* that guy? Cancha drive on the righthan side?' All that hundred miles, a curiously smaller Ora Weagle, nervous behind the wheel, inwardly whimpered, 'A mess of pottage--a mess of pottage'.

In a moonless and unbroken darkness, Ora was blazing across the plains of Kansas. Through the smells of gasoline and of Dimity's powder and of candy and of new dogskin gloves, he caught the smell of corn bursting the dark earth.

His great headlights devoured and spewed out a village that was only a general store, a section house, a garage, and four cottages rimmed with cottonwoods. Ora was dreaming. He was homesick for a home he had never before seen.

'I'd like to be one of the fellows here. Sit and chin. Talk about corn.'

And, 'I don't think so much of being a smart literary guy in speakeasies,' he grieved.

He was sorry, that second, that he had in all his life nothing as strong and enduring as this Kansas night, that Dimity was nothing but a convenient companion whom he would abandon in Los Angeles. Myron wouldn't do that and--oh, curse Myron, that hypocritical old Puritan! He'd ruined Ora's entire life by his smug correctness!

But it was a shame about Dimity.

He took his right hand from the wheel for a second to stroke her knee, consolingly.

'Say, for the love o' Christ, will you keep your hands on the wheel, and quit pinching my knee?' said Miss Dimity Dove.

It was after nine, and Dodge City, with the first possible hotel, was two hours ahead of them when Ora shot, horn-shrieking, into the prairie town of Lemuel, Kansas.

'Say, we might be able to find a taverno where we can stay here,' said Ora. 'Think you could stand another hick hotel, Dim?'

'Hell with you!' snarled Miss Dove.

'Well, hell with you, too! But I'm sick of driving. Ay-up! Let's have a look,' he pleaded, as he saw the electric sign 'Commercial Hotel' hung out across the sidewalk.

He came up all standing, and stiffly crawled out, on the cement sidewalk. He was so tired! If he could just have fried steak and a bed that wasn't too buggy, it would be all right. Somehow, he couldn't go on, challenging that darkness of cornfield and derisive prairie road and the sullen scent of land.

He swayed from the pavement up on the wooden porch of the hotel, and looked through the plate glass window into the office.

Um. It wasn't so bad. Leather rocking-chairs in two long lines, with brass cuspidors between, and the pine desk and register that revolved on a brass standard at the end. Not so unlike the American House of his boyhood, except that it was cleaner. Yes, try it. The fellow grim-faced behind the desk, the night clerk, looked quite decent. . . .

Ora clenched his hands, bit his doubled knuckles choked down a shriek. The grim-faced fellow behind the desk, in the Commercial Hotel, Lemuel, Kansas, was his brother Myron.

He fled back to the car. He was starting it before he had settled on the seat. He babbled, 'No, no, no, no!'

'What's the matter with you now?' snapped Miss Dimity Dove.

He awoke. He drove more steadily than he had all these past eighty miles. He droned, 'Looks kind of sloppy. Guess we better stick on till Dodge City. We'll make it in a couple hours, and maybe we'll pick up a hot dog on the way . . . Oh, my darling!'

'Now don't get sentimental,' said Miss Dimity Dove, with virtuous smugness.

Ora felt old and tired. The one thing in the world he wanted to do was to hasten to Los Angeles, that he might get rid of Dimity. He was old and tired. He was fifty-one, he realized. But on the way to Dodge City he found some admirable beet-sugar whisky at a garage, and next morning, free of the accusing darkness of the cornfields, he nervously assured himself, 'Well, that's *his* fault! Certainly can't blame me!'

After a week he had ceased babbling to himself, 'Myron, General Director of the whole Pye-Charian chain, a night-clerk in a lodging-house in Lemuel, Kansas! Well, it certainly isn't my look-out!'

He never saw Myron again.

35

During his two years as manager of the Alfred Hotel, Milwaukee, Myron was not discontented. The Alfred, with its four hundred and fifty rooms, had been built in 1900. It was astoundingly ugly: a vast cracker box, broken only by lines of bow-windows from second floor to top. The dull lobby was on the second floor; the ground floor was taken up by shops--a cut-rate tailor shop, a 'book store' which sold Easter cards and Christmas cards and newspapers and magazines of Western stories and almost everything except books; a jewellery shop with a gilded clock that was a veritable antique for a sign.

The hotel lobby smelled, ineradicably, of soap.

No Milwaukee fashionable ever entered the Alfred, except on the unfortunate occasion of a country relative's coming to town. The guests were travelling-men, merchants from small towns in Wisconsin and Southern Minnesota, dolorous widows come to help bury cousins.

It was an American House magnified ten times--and Myron was happier there than he had been since his first days with the Pye-Charian Company.

For the Alfred was genuine. It was exactly what it purported to be: a city inn for ordinary people. It had no gilt, and the honest menu did not do agonizing things with pineapple. The old German brewing family who owned it did not expect extravagant profits; they trusted Myron utterly, and had him and Effie May and Luke in for enormous dinners with Rhine wine. Myron ran the place as efficiently and as simply as a veteran engineer runs a locomotive, and his self-respect came flooding back like a spring freshet. 'I *am* an hotel-man, after all, by God!' he crowed, sure that he knew the whole craft, from carpet tacks to *truite sauce bleu.* And in their pleasant midwestern flat, with its sun-porch where she could sit and embroider and listen to the radio from the living-room, Effie May felt only a little bewildered and lost, and the tall young Luke played basket-ball in school, and told his respectful new friends about the glories of New York.

And all the while Myron had a feeling like the strained waiting before a thunder-shower, and he knew that he was again going to do something exciting, and he began, for the first time since the Black Thread Inn had opened, to put down plots in his little note-books.

Large summer camp not for older kids but 2 to 8. Appeal to parents going Europe summer. 1st consid, safety. 'Less danger of kidnapping than at home.' Guards keep every visitor out. And safety re health: resident pediatrician & full trained nurses. Visiting oculist, dentist. Regular weekly health examination. Every provision fun--wading pool, ponies, fish pond, & regular toy town--miniature houses, stores, rr. station & train. Sleep in sep dormitories, not over ten kids to dorm, & nurse sleeping in each. All bldgs one story for fire safety? Encourage kids compose and act own play?

He was certain that he wanted to do something a little different, but what it was, he did not know. It came to him quite simply, on an evening at home when the radio was playing the lush sentimentality of the 'Tales of Hoffman'. He would buy, own altogether by himself, and build up a small hotel in a country town . . . without any 'beauty shop' by thunder! Then, if he was successful, he might go on, might some day own a whole Elphinstone chain of hotels urban and rural. But that wouldn't matter if he could, for once, make a Perfect Inn!

The instant the Barcarole was finished, he strode across, turned off the radio, and cried to Effie May and to Luke--doing his 'home work' at the centre table, as once a small Myron had done it at a dining-room table in a rustic hotel--'Listen, you two! How'd you like to go out to some town farther west, and own our own hotel, and run it to suit ourselves?'

'Grand!' exulted Luke. 'Then I'd ride a horse!'

Effie May looked frightened. She clutched her chair-arms, as if to save herself from being dragged away. 'Oh! To move again! And to have to make new friends!' she whimpered. But she folded her hands in her lap and thrust her head back and whispered, 'All right, of course, dear.'

He had no particular, fanatic, escapist desire to tuck himself away in a country town just for its own sake. He did not believe that all the denizens of small towns were necessarily friendlier and nobler than city people. As an hotel-keeper, he had found all people everywhere much alike. It was simply that, with the reduction in the value of securities during the present depression, his holdings now were not worth much over twenty-five thousand. If he had had ten millions, he would have taken a large city hotel. He hadn't. And if he was ever to have a place of his own, he could not wait much longer, for he was fifty-two now, in 1932.

Among the places advertised for sale in the *Hotel Era,* he was most tempted by the very banal notice of the Commercial Hotel in Lemuel, Kansas. Though he had so firmly stated to himself that he was not, like a movie fanatic, tempted by the alleged romance of the west--he was! He had never forgotten the exhilaration of going from Connecticut to St. Louis, as a youngster.

The Commercial Hotel had exactly the same number of rooms and baths as the American House in Black Thread Centre before Myron had enlarged it.

'But will you be satisfied in a little place like that? After New York and Philadelphia and Long Island? Will you be satisfied?' begged Effie May.

'Of course I will! I like small towns. Why, certainly, I . . . Hell, no, of course I won't be satisfied! I guess I never will be, you poor kid!' said Myron.

Luxury Chinese restaurant, N.Y., charge five bucks for dinner, make it a Chink garden, real birds in trees (but screens over table then because of little fault of birdies), river flowing thru garden, on which Chink musicians in boat singing Chink songs, not too often. Also: *for hot New York summers, a real 'winter garden': artificially chilled so have real snow for sliding, ice for skating & serve grub in a New England farm kitchen. But probly both these too phony--better for a Jimmy Shanks.*

They drove out to Lemuel in the summer. Effie May lost her fear of new environment as she saw the enormous sky benign above the living corn. (It was just as well, for her, that she did not see a cyclone or a dust-storm.) 'The folks at hotels and garages', she admitted, 'are awful friendly.'

'You'll be the most popular girl in Lemuel', said Myron, and not till he had driven for miles did his Rotarian enthusiasm strike him as a little comic.

Luke was bouncing with love of it. As his father once had done, he saw himself a real Cowpuncher on a Pinto (he wasn't quite sure whether a pinto was a hoss or an herb, but it certainly sounded swell) and when they got back to Mount Vernon (as of course they would, when his dad got over his funny ideas about going west) what stories he would have! . . . Catamounts. Yosemites. Rattlesnakes. Deppities. Gentlemen nicknamed 'Two Gun'. Oh, won'er-ful!

Lemuel, Kansas, when wearily and dustily they came into it toward evening, after driving four hundred and fifty miles since five that morning, was no great city. It looked exactly like a hundred other towns through which they had driven: the same Main Street, the same two-story, wooden, transitory-looking stores.

'It seems--kind of--kind of small!' squeaked Effie.

'Oh, no, ma, it's dandy country to ride in!' bubbled Luke.

'We-ull,' said Myron.

The Commercial Hotel had been solidly built, by leisurely country carpenters: a white wooden cube, with a long porch giving on the cement sidewalk. The giddiest thing about it was the pot of geraniums on the sill of the large office window. The hotel was badly kept. The porch was dusty, with loose boards. The office, as they reluctantly trailed into it, was dirty; the inevitable brass spittoons were smeared; the inevitable leather upholstery of the row of rocking chairs was scarred and torn; the proprietor, behind the pine desk, was in his shirt-sleeves, and that shirt had not had attention from a laundress.

Myron was in a panic.

He thought of telegraphing to Carlos Jaynes about a job in New York. Surely he could always get one, now that he could again endure it.

His name was not known to the proprietor, because he had dealt only with an hotel-broker's office, bidding them keep his interest secret. When he registered, the gentleman in shirt-sleeves yawned 'Kind of hot for driving to-day', with that listlessness that only a country hotel-keeper can show.

Their two bedrooms were fairly dreadful. The beds squeaked. The lights were unshaded globes in the centre of the ceiling. The pine bureaus were tilted. The rooms smelled.

'Oh, I can't *do* it!' wailed Effie May.

'I know. Pretty lousy. But think of the fun of making a first-class place out of this!' said Myron. 'Look. Take this room. Put on a sort of old-fashioned wall-paper with little springs of flowers. Paint all the furniture a glossy white, and use a screw-driver and a little elbow-grease on that bed to keep it from squeaking. Put in a floor-plug, and have a bedside lamp, on a bedside table, with side-lights by the bureau. Chintz curtains. One easy chair--it could be just cane, with a bright cushion. Chuck out that filthy cotton comforter on the bed and put on a decent silk one. Whole thing wouldn't cost much over twenty-five dollars a room--and some intelligence and industry, which are obviously what this fellow here lacks.'

'Ye-es. And throw out those long tables in the dining-room--did you look in there from the office?--and put in small ones, and make that waitress I saw in there wash her hair,' considered Effie May.

She had, for the first time, become an hotel-man's wife.

Candy of the Week Club. Picture of ideal customer: She's old lady in New Eng village. Loves candy, but no place there to buy it, except stale quarter a lb. stuff. Her son in NY well to do. Sends her subscription to C of W club. Each week she gets lb absolutely fresh--mailed from factory, not over week old--and different kind for ea wk of yr: not only standard brands but Chink candy from S.F., those famous chocolates, what do they call em, from Victoria, B.C., cactus candy fr Mexico, even foreign imports, those swell Swiss candies I had in Paris, on which be willing to lose $$ for that week, to advertise. Ad: 'Make yr prest last fifty-two weeks'

In redecorating the Commercial Hotel, when he had bought it, Myron deliberately kept it as heavily simple as it had been. 'I guess probably the greatest lesson I ever got in hotel-keeping was when Ora razzed me for making the American House into a tea room,' he meditated. The bedrooms he changed as he had planned. It was surprising what a coat of white paint and ten minutes tightening up joints and a new mattress and eiderdown did to a greasy pine bed. He added six bathrooms. The office he kept much as it was--except that he had the chairs re-upholstered and the floor and walls actually washed. It was in the matter of food that he went revolutionary.

He had always believed, the more so after peering at Europe, that American country food could be at least as good as French country food, provided that the proud ladies who earned their living by it took the trouble to learn to cook. No country in the world had better raw meats and fruits and vegetables than America. And a good many years ago he had learned the apparently occult fact that there are guides called 'cook books'.

He could not afford a Gritzmeier. (He would have forgiven old Otto completely, and have given him a partnership, if the red-faced scoundrel had suddenly appeared!) He would have to depend on the local talent.

He picked out for cook not the most experienced lady in Lemuel who offered herself, but the one who seemed least resentful at being told that there were things she could learn. She was the skinny widow of a farmer West of Town; she did sing hymns, but she took chervil seriously, once she had heard of it. While he was redecorating the hotel, Myron closed it for four weeks, and during that time, he stood beside his cook, evening after evening, showing her precisely what to do . . . She even got over the notions that it was very comic indeed for men-folks to think they could cook and that cook-books were all written by crazy Easterners.

When he had bullied her into shape, the Commercial Hotel began to serve steaks, chops, roast beef, roast pork, soups, coffee, pies, fresh-water fish that would have enchanted Brillat-Savarin.

Myron's chief woe had been in persuading the local butcher shop that he really wanted the cuts he wanted. He solved that. He bought the shop.

His one complete innovation was to persuade the considerable number of old Lemuel couples who were tired of housekeeping to board at the hotel, in a special private dining-room made out of the frowsy billiard-room, and to persuade the few comparatively rich people in town to give their parties at the hotel, with special supper-menus prepared by himself.

For motorists he had daily new information about every road out of town. When he could not get it from the drivers themselves, he or his clerk or Luke--suddenly a man, and not discontented that if he had not become a glamorous cowboy, he was known as the 'best doggone automobile driver for a kid of his age in town'--drove out to inspect road-repairing and detours for a hundred miles around.

He had the greatest praise that any country hotel-keeper could have: The travelling-men told him that his was he best hotel in their territory, and they planned their routes so that they could spend Sunday there.

Effie May was elected president of the Ladies' Aid of the Lemuel Presbyterian Church, and a committee of citizens waited upon Myron to ask him whether he would care to run for Alderman of the First Ward this year, and for Mayor in another couple of years. He overheard a heavy chair-sitter outside the office say, 'Best thing ever happened to this burg was when Weagle came here and put a lil pep into it. Say, in less 'n a year, that fellow has become the most prom'nen' citizen in town!'

It was, by chance, on this same evening that his brother Ora saw him and wept over him as night-clerk of a country hotel.

36

Young Luke Weagle, sixteen years old in 1933, had never, in the east or in Milwaukee, been allowed to drive a car. On the swooping straight section-line roads of Kansas, he became a demon driver, and he viewed thereon the Tourist Camps.

He spoke to his father.

'Say, dad, listen.'

'Uh-huh'.

'You know how you're always talking about these darn old English Inns, and how they were the real thing, without any fake?'

'Yes.'

'Well, why ain't these tourist camps the same way? They furnish dandy beds and pretty good grub and don't put on any side?'

'Well, I suppose they are sort of the same.'

'Why don't we run one? Listen, Dad, I bet you could run a better one than anybody!'

'I sort of thought we had a job *here!*'

'Aw, *this!* Aw, thunder! You got this licked! It's going like a prairie fire! You're making money on it, aren't you?'

'Well, yes.'

'Well then, I guess you won't be interested in it much more, and you'll want to start something new!'

'Maybe that's so, Luke, but what about my going back east and being manager of a big hotel in New York again?'

'Oh, them Easterners . . .'

'*Those* Easterners!'

'Those Easterners, they like everything so fancy! Gee, dad, I'd hate to think of going back to those swell-heads in Westchester County! I like it here, where you got room to move around! Look, dad, would you come out with me and look at Kit Carson Park? That's a tourist camp only a hundred miles west. Gee, it's a swell place!'

'*Only* a hundred miles? You must remember I'm an old-fashioned Easterner. Will you drive?'

'Sure, you bet!'

And indeed Kit Carson Park, to which that intrepid Wild Westerner driver Luke Weagle, took them in three hours, was to a professional hotelman a study of the newest thing in the world. It was honestly and completely devoted to the needs of the million tourists, from unemployed workmen in third-hand Fords with the bird-cage and the radio hung outside the body, to Santa Barbara villa-owners in Cadillacs, who had as a matter of course given up railroad travel and who motored, three hundred, four hundred, six hundred miles a day, from Minnesota and Illinois and Ohio and Pennsylvania to California or Oregon. Kit Carson Park had eighty cottages, each with shower-bath and roofed shelter for a car, a community store for groceries and automobile accessories, a community restaurant and dance-hall. The cottages were clean, the grass between them was crisp, and the paths were outlined with white-washed stones.

'Well, what d' you think of it?' demanded Luke, as they drove homeward.

'I don't know,' grumbled Myron . . . Fathers have to grumble every so often, for otherwise they would have no chance at all in the clear-eyed world of children.

'No, but *honestly,* dad, what do you think?'

'Well, I'll tell you. It's pretty well done. But it's too hard. Those white-washed stones. Too prim. It certainly does provide a fine night's lodging for motor tourists--probably better than I do at the Commercial. But it's forbidding. Not only would no tourist who was tired out want to stay on there for a day or two, but the whole place positively forbids him to stay. I know. It's the new thing. Fine. The auto tourist can start out at five a.m., and no twisty city streets to bother him. Yes. All right. But I'd like to have a place as efficient as that, for the fast driver--like you!--but that would also have a view or scenery or whatever you want to call it, and where a certain percentage of the tourists would like to stay for a couple days.'

His voice grew strong and confident. Luciano Mora was lost, and Alec, and Mark Elphinstone, but he had a loyal friend now, who took him seriously--his son.

'I don't see, Boy, why we couldn't have everything that Kit Carson Park has: Low prices. Neat, clean cabins. No damn beauty-parlours! Ease in parking late at night, when you're tired out, and ease in getting away next morning. But different: Much better food--not just Hamburger sandwiches and apple pie. Daily specialities in food. Something to do for folks you could persuade to stay over a couple days: tennis courts, a library, a big terrace with wicker chairs where they'd like to loaf, and some sort of view besides the level prairie. Well, I'll think about it.'

Ten miles from Lemuel, Myron cried, 'Hey! Whoa-up! I want to go up this next side-road to the left.'

'Sure, you bet, dad. Where's it go?'

'You'll see.'

Two hundred feet along the side-road, they climbed in sunset over the rolling billows of the prairie to an upland which, though it was only eighty feet above the general level of the plain, looked across twenty miles, with a creek bordered with cottonwood and willows just below them.

'Kind of a pretty place, don't you think?' said Myron.

'Gee, it certainly is, dad!' said Luke.

'Swimming pool down there. Golf course there to the right. Central building, stores and dancing and everything, with rooms for lone drivers that don't want cottages, right here. And the best mince pie in the State of Kansas. I can beat Kit Carson Park as a tourist camp--you and I can, if we work together.'

'I bet we can, dad! Why don't you buy the land?'

'I did. Yesterday,' said Myron.